C0-AYF-052

PAUL FABER, SURGEON

PAUL FABER.

PAUL FABER,
SURGEON

By
George MacDonald

Printed and published by
Johannesen
p.o. box 24
Whitethorn, California
95589
U.S.A.

VNYS PZ 8 .M1754
1992 c.1

eshen037

Originally Published in 1879 by
Hurst & Blackett,
London.

This Printing has been reproduced from
the 1900 Edition of
George Routledge & Sons, New York,
by Photo Lithography.
With appreciation to Simon Filbrun
for the master copy of this Edition.

1992 Edition

These Classic Editions
are all Hand-Bound by
the Johannesen family.

ISBN # 1-881084-08-6

TO

W. C. T.

TUUM EST.

Clear-windowed temple of the God of grace,
From the loud wind to me a hiding-place!
Thee gird broad lands with genial motions it;
But in thee dwells, high-throned, the Life of life
Thy test no stagnant moat half-filled with muc,
But living waters witnessing in flood!
Thy priestess, beauty-clad, and gospel-shod,
A fellow laborer in the earth with God!
Good will art thou, and goodness all thy arts—
Doves to their windows, and to thee fly hearts!
Take of the corn in thy dear shelter grown,
Which else the storm had all too rudely blown;
When to a higher temple thou shalt mount,
Thy earthly gifts in heavenly friends shall count;
Let these first-fruits enter thy lofty door,
And golden lie upon thy golden floor.

G. M. D.

PORTO FINO, *December*, 1878.

CONTENTS.

CONTENTS.

PAUL FABER.

CHAPTER I.

THE LANE.

THE rector sat on the box of his carriage, driving his horses toward his church, the grand old abbey-church of Glaston. His wife was inside, and an old woman—he had stopped on the road to take her up—sat with her basket on the foot-board behind. His coachman sat beside him ; he never took the reins when his master was there. Mr. Bevis drove like a gentleman, in an easy, informal, yet thoroughly business-like way. His horses were black—large, well-bred, and well-fed, but neither young nor showy, and the harness was just the least bit shabby. Indeed, the entire turnout, including his own hat and the coachman's, offered the beholder that aspect of indifference to show, which, by the suggestion of a nodding acquaintance with poverty, gave it the right clerical air of being not of this world. Mrs. Bevis had her basket on the seat before her, containing, beneath an upper stratum of flowers, some of the first rhubarb of the season and a pound or two of fresh butter for a poor relation in the town.

The rector was a man about sixty, with keen gray eyes, a good-humored mouth, a nose whose enlargement had not of late gone in the direction of its original design, and a face more than inclining to the rubicund, suggestive of good living as well as open air. Altogether he had the look of a man who knew what he was about, and was on tolerable terms with himself, and on still better with his neighbor. The heart under his ribs was larger even than indicated by the benevolence of his countenance and the humor hovering over his mouth. Upon the countenance of his wife rested a placidity sinking almost into fatuity. Its features were rather indications than completions, but there was a consciousness of comfort about the mouth, and the eyes were alive.

They were passing at a good speed through a varying country—now a thicket of hazel, now great patches of furze upon open common, and anon well-kept farm-hedges, and clumps of pine, the remnants of ancient forest, when, half-way through a lane so narrow that the rector felt every yard toward the other end a gain, his horses started, threw up their heads, and looked for a moment wild as youth. Just in front of them, in the air, over a high hedge, scarce touching the topmost twigs with his hoofs, appeared a great red horse. Down he came into the road, bringing with him a rather tall, certainly handsome, and even at first sight, attractive rider. A dark brown mustache upon a somewhat smooth sunburned face, and a stern settling of the strong yet delicately finished features gave him a military look ; but the sparkle of his blue eyes contradicted his otherwise cold expression. He drew up close to the hedge to make room for the carriage, but as he neared him Mr. Bevis slackened his speed, and during the following talk they were moving gently along with just room for the rider to keep clear of the off fore wheel.

"Heigh, Faber," said the clergyman, "you'll break your neck some day ! You should think of your patients, man. That wasn't a jump for any man in his senses to take."

"It is but fair to give my patients a chance now and then," returned the surgeon, who never met the rector but there was a merry passage between them.

"Upon my word," said Mr. Bevis, "when you came over the hedge there, I took you for Death in the Revelations, that had tired out his own and changed horses with t'other one."

As he spoke, he glanced back with a queer look, for he found himself guilty of a little irreverence, and his conscience sat behind him in the person of his wife. But that conscience was a very easy one, being almost as incapable of seeing a joke as of refusing a request.

"—How many have you bagged this week ? " concluded the rector.

"I haven't counted up yet," answered the surgeon. "—*You*'ve got one behind, I see," he added, signing with his whip over his shoulder.

"Poor old thing ! " said the rector, as if excusing himself, "she's got a heavy basket, and we all need a lift sometimes

—eh, doctor ?—into the world and out again, at all events."

There was more of the reflective in this utterance than the parson was in the habit of displaying; but he liked the doctor, and, although as well as every one else he knew him to be no friend to the church, or to Christianity, or even to religious belief of any sort, his liking, coupled with a vague sense of duty, had urged him to this most unassuming attempt to cast the friendly arm of faith around the unbeliever.

"I plead guilty to the former," answered Faber, "but somehow I have never practiced the euthanasia. The instincts of my profession, I suppose are against it. Besides, that ought to be your business."

"Not altogether," said the rector, with a kindly look from his box, which, however, only fell on the top of the doctor's hat.

Faber seemed to feel the influence of it notwithstanding, for he returned,

"If all clergymen were as liberal as you, Mr. Bevis, there would be more danger of some of us giving in."

The word *liberal* seemed to rouse the rector to the fact that his coachman sat on the box, yet another conscience, beside him. *Sub divo* one must not be *too* liberal. There was a freedom that came out better over a bottle of wine than over the backs of horses. With a word he quickened the pace of his cleric steeds, and the doctor was dropped parallel with the carriage window. There, catching sight of Mrs. Bevis, of whose possible presence he had not thought once, he paid his compliments, and made his apologies, then trotted his gaunt Ruber again beside the wheel, and resumed talk, but not the same talk, with the rector. For a few minutes it turned upon the state of this and that ailing parishioner; for, while the rector left all the duties of public service to his curate, he ministered to the ailing and poor upon and immediately around his own little property, which was in that corner of his parish furthest from the town; but ere long, as all talk was sure to do between the parson and any body who owned but a donkey, it veered round in a certain direction.

"You don't seem to feed that horse of yours upon beans, Faber," he said.

"I don't seem, I grant," returned the doctor; "but you should see him feed! He eats enough for two, but he *can't* make fat : all goes to muscle and pluck."

"Well, I must allow the less fat he has to carry the better, if you're in the way of heaving him over such hedges on to the hard road. In my best days I should never have faced a jump like that in cold blood," said the rector.

"I've got no little belongings of wife or child to make a prudent man of me, you see," returned the surgeon. "At worst it's but a knock on the head and a longish snooze."

The rector fancied he felt his wife's shudder shake the carriage, but the sensation was of his own producing. The careless defiant words wrought in him an unaccountable kind of terror: it seemed almost as if they had rushed of themselves from his own lips.

"Take care, my dear sir," he said solemnly. "There may be something to believe, though you don't believe it."

"I must take the chance," replied Faber. "I will do my best to make calamity of long life, by keeping the rheumatic and epileptic and phthisical alive, while I know how. Where nothing *can* be known, I prefer not to intrude."

A pause followed. At length said the rector,

"You are so good a fellow, Faber, I wish you were better. When will you come and dine with me?"

"Soon, I hope," answered the surgeon, "but I am too busy at present. For all her sweet ways and looks, the spring is not friendly to man, and my work is to wage war with nature."

A second pause followed. The rector would gladly have said something, but nothing would come.

"By the by," he said at length, "I thought I saw you pass the gate—let me see—on Monday: why did you not look in?"

"I hadn't a moment's time. I was sent for to a patient in the village."

"Yes, I know; I heard of that. I wish you would give me your impression of the lady. She is a stranger here.— John, that gate is swinging across the road. Get down and shut it.—Who and what is she?"

"That I should be glad to learn from you. All I know is that she is a lady. There can not be two opinions as to that."

"They tell me she is a beauty," said the parson.

The doctor nodded his head emphatically.

"Haven't you seen her?" he said.

"Scarcely—only her back. She walks well. Do you know nothing about her? Who has she with her?"

" Nobody."

" Then Mrs. Bevis shall call upon her."

" I think at present she had better not. Mrs. Puckridge is a good old soul, and pays her every attention."

" What is the matter with her ? Nothing infectious ? "

" Oh, no ! She has caught a chill. I was afraid of pneumonia yesterday."

" Then she is better ? "

" I confess I am a little anxious about her. But I ought not to be dawdling like this, with half my patients to see. I must bid you good morning.—Good morning, Mrs. Bevis."

As he spoke, Faber drew rein, and let the carriage pass ; then turned his horse's head to the other side of the way, scrambled up the steep bank to the field above, and galloped toward Glaston, whose great church rose high in sight. Over hedge and ditch he rode straight for its tower.

" The young fool ! " said the rector, looking after him admiringly, and pulling up his horses that he might more conveniently see him ride.

" Jolly old fellow ! " said the surgeon at his second jump. " I wonder how much he believes now of all the rot ! Enough to humbug himself with—not a hair more. He has no passion for humbugging other people. There's that curate of his now believes every thing, and would humbug the whole world if he could ! How any man can come to fool himself so thoroughly as that man does, is a mystery to me !—I wonder what the rector's driving into Glaston for on a Saturday."

Paul Faber was a man who had espoused the cause of science with all the energy of a suppressed poetic nature. He had such a horror of all kinds of intellectual deception or mistake, that he would rather run the risk of rejecting any number of truths than of accepting one error. In this spirit he had concluded that, as no immediate communication had ever reached his eye, or ear, or hand from any creator of men, he had no ground for believing in the exist-ence of such a creator ; while a thousand unfitnesses evident in the world, rendered the existence of one perfectly wise and good and powerful, absolutely impossible. If one said to him that he believed thousands of things he had never himself known, he answered he did so upon testimony. If one rejoined that here too we have testimony, he replied it was not credible testimony, but founded on such expe-riences as he was justified in considering imaginary, seeing they were like none he had ever had himself. When he was asked whether, while he yet believed there was such a being as his mother told him of, he had ever set himself to act upon that belief, he asserted himself fortunate in the omission of what might have riveted on him the fetters of a degrading faith. For years he had turned his face toward all speculation favoring the non-existence of a creating Will, his back toward all tending to show that such a one might be. Argument on the latter side he set down as born of prejudice, and appealing to weakness; on the other, as springing from courage, and appealing to honesty. He had never put it to himself which would be the worse deception —to believe there was a God when there was none ; or to believe there was no God when there was one.

He had, however, a large share of the lower but equally indispensable half of religion—that, namely, which has respect to one's fellows. Not a man in Glaston was readier, by day or by night, to run to the help of another, and that not merely in his professional capacity, but as a neighbor, whatever the sort of help was needed.

Thomas Wingfold, the curate, had a great respect for him. Having himself passed through many phases of serious, and therefore painful doubt, he was not as much shocked by the surgeon's unbelief as some whose real faith was even less than Faber's ; but he seldom laid himself out to answer his objections. He sought rather, but as yet apparently in vain, to cause the roots of those very objections to strike into, and thus disclose to the man himself, the deeper strata of his being. This might indeed at first only render him the more earnest in his denials, but at length it would probably rouse in him that spiritual nature to which alone such questions really belong, and which alone is capable of coping with them. The first notable result, however, of the surgeon's intercourse with the curate was, that, whereas he had till then kept his opinions to himself in the presence of those who did not sympathize with them, he now uttered his disbelief with such plainness as I have shown him using toward the rector. This did not come of aggravated antagonism, but of admiration of the curate's openness in the presentment of truths which must be unacceptable to the majority of his congregation.

There had arisen therefore betwixt the doctor and the curate a certain sort of intimacy, which had at length come to the rector's ears. He had. no doubt, before this heard many complaints against the latter, but he had laughed them aside. No theologian himself, he had found the questions hitherto raised in respect of Wingfold's teaching, altogether beyond the pale of his interest. He could not comprehend why people should not content themselves with being good Christians, minding their own affairs, going to church, and so feeling safe for the next world. What did opinion matter as long as they were good Christians? He did not exactly know what he believed himself, but he hoped he was none the less of a Christian for that! Was it not enough to hold fast whatever lay in the apostles', the Nicene, and the Athanasian creed, without splitting metaphysical hairs with your neighbor? But was it decent that his curate should be hand and glove with one who denied the existence of God? He did not for a moment doubt the faith of Wingfold; but a man must have some respect for appearances: appearances were facts as well as realities were facts. An honest man must not keep company with a thief, if he would escape the judgment of being of thievish kind. Something must be done; probably something said would be enough, and the rector was now on his way to say it.

CHAPTER II.

THE MINISTER'S DOOR.

EVERY body knew Mr. Faber, whether he rode Ruber or Niger—Rubber and Nigger, his groom called them—and many were the greetings that met him as he passed along Pine Street, for, despite the brand of his atheism, he was popular. The few ladies out shopping bowed graciously, for both his manners and person were pleasing, and his professional attentions were unexceptionable. When he dropped into a quick walk, to let Ruber cool a little ere he reached his stall, he was several times accosted and detained. The last who addressed him was Mr. Drew, the principal draper of the town. He had been standing for some time in his shop-door, but as Faber was about to turn the corner, he stepped out on the pavement, and the doctor checked his horse in the gutter.

" I wish you would look in upon Mr. Drake, sir," he said. " I am quite uneasy about him. Indeed I am sure he must be in a bad way, though he won't allow it. He's not an easy man to do any thing for, but just you let me know what *can* be done for him—and we'll contrive. *A nod*, you know, doctor, etc."

" I don't well see how I can," returned Faber. " To call now without being sent for, when I never called before !— No, Mr. Drew, I don't think I could."

It was a lovely spring noon. The rain that had fallen heavily during the night lay in flashing pools that filled the street with suns. Here and there were little gardens before the houses, and the bushes in them were hung with bright drops, so bright that the rain seemed to have fallen from the sun himself, not from the clouds.

" Why, goodness gracious !" cried the draper, " here's your excuse come direct ! "

Under the very nose of the doctor's great horse stood a little woman-child, staring straight up at the huge red head above her. Now Ruber was not quite gentle, and it was with some dismay that his master, although the animal showed no offense at the glowering little thing, pulled him back a step or two with the curb, the thought darting through him how easily with one pash of his mighty hoof the horse could annihilate a mirrored universe.

" Where from ? " he asked, by what he would himself have called a half-conscious cerebration.

" From somewhere they say you don't believe in, doctor," answered the draper. " It's little Amanda, the minister's own darling—Naughty little dear ! " he continued, his round good-humored face wrinkled all over with smiles, as he caught up the truant, " what ever do you mean by splashing through every gutter between home and here, making a little drab of yourself ? Why your frock is as wet as a dish-clout !—*and* your shoes ! My gracious ! "

The little one answered only by patting his cheeks, which in shape much resembled her own, with her little fat puds, as if she had been beating a drum, while Faber looked down amused and interested.

" Here, doctor ! " the draper went on, " you take the little mischief on the saddle before you, and carry her home : that will be your excuse."

As he spoke he held up the child to him. Faber took her, and sitting as far back in the saddle as he could, set her upon the pommel. She screwed up her eyes, and grinned with delight, spreading her mouth wide, and showing an incredible number of daintiest little teeth. When Ruber began to move she shrieked in her ecstasy.

Holding his horse to a walk, the doctor crossed the main street and went down a side one toward the river, whence again he entered a narrow lane. There with the handle of his whip he managed to ring the door-bell of a little old-fashioned house which rose immediately from the lane without even a footpath between. The door was opened by a lady-like young woman, with smooth soft brown hair, a white forehead, and serious, rather troubled eyes.

"Aunty! aunty!" cried the child, "Ducky 'iding!"

Miss Drake looked a little surprised. The doctor lifted his hat. She gravely returned his greeting and stretched up her arms to take the child. But she drew back, nestling against Faber.

"Amanda! come, dear," said Miss Drake. "How kind of Dr. Faber to bring you home! I'm afraid you've been a naughty child again—running out into the street."

"Such a g'eat 'ide!" cried Amanda, heedless of reproof. "A yeal 'ossy—big! big!"

She spread her arms wide, in indication of the vastness of the upbearing body whereon she sat. But still she leaned back against the doctor, and he awaited the result in amused silence. Again her aunt raised her hands to take her.

"Mo' 'yide!" cried the child, looking up backward, to find Faber's eyes.

But her aunt caught her by the feet, and amid struggling and laughter drew her down, and held her in her arms.

"I hope your father is pretty well, Miss Drake," said the doctor, wasting no time in needless explanation.

"Ducky," said the girl, setting down the child, "go and tell grandpapa how kind Dr. Faber has been to you. Tell him he is at the door." Then turning to Faber, "I am sorry to say he does not seem at all well," she answered him. "He has had a good deal of annoyance lately, and at his age that sort of thing tells."

As she spoke she looked up at the doctor, full in his face, but with a curious quaver in her eyes. Nor was it any wonder she should look at him strangely, for she felt toward him very strangely: to her he was as it were the apostle of a kakangel, the prophet of a doctrine that was evil, yet perhaps was a truth. Terrible doubts had for some time been assailing her—doubts which she could in part trace to him, and as he sat there on Ruber, he looked like a beautiful evil angel, who *knew* there was no God—an evil angel whom the curate, by his bold speech, had raised, and could not banish.

The surgeon had scarcely begun a reply, when the old minister made his appearance. He was a tall, well-built man, with strong features, rather handsome than otherwise ; but his hat hung on his occiput, gave his head a look of weakness and oddity that by nature did not belong to it, while baggy, ill-made clothes and big shoes manifested a re-action from the over-trimness of earlier years. He greeted the doctor with a severe smile.

"I am much obliged to you, Mr. Faber," he said, "for bringing me home my little runaway. Where did you find her?"

"Under my horse's head, like the temple between the paws of the Sphinx," answered Faber, speaking a parable without knowing it.

"She is a fearless little damsel," said the minister, in a husky voice that had once rung clear as a bell over crowded congregations—"too fearless at times. But the very ignorance of danger seems the panoply of childhood. And indeed who knows in the midst of what evils we all walk that never touch us!"

"A Solon of platitudes!" said the doctor to himself.

"She has been in the river once, and almost twice," Mr. Drake went on. "—I shall have to tie you with a string, pussie! Come away from the horse. What if he should take to stroking you? I am afraid you would find his hands both hard and heavy."

"How do you stand this trying spring weather, Mr. Drake? I don't hear the best accounts of you," said the surgeon, drawing Ruber a pace back from the door.

"I am as well as at my age I can perhaps expect to be," answered the minister. "I am getting old—and—and—we all have our troubles, and, I trust, our God also, to set them right for us," he added, with a suggesting look in the face of the doctor.

"By Jove!" said Faber to himself, "the spring weather has roused the worshiping instinct! The clergy are awake to-day! I had better look out, or it will soon be too hot for me."

"I can't look you in the face, doctor," resumed the old man after a pause, "and believe what people say of you. It can't be that you don't even believe there *is* a God?"

Faber would rather have said nothing; but his integrity he must keep fast hold of, or perish in his own esteem.

"If there be one," he replied, "I only state a fact when I say He has never given me ground sufficient to think so. You say yourselves He has favorites to whom He reveals Himself: I am not one of them, and must therefore of necessity be an unbeliever."

"But think, Mr. Faber—if there should be a God, what an insult it is to deny Him existence."

"I can't see it," returned the surgeon, suppressing a laugh. "If there be such a one, would He not have me speak the truth? Anyhow, what great matter can it be to Him that one should say he has never seen Him, and can't therefore believe He is to be seen? A god should be above that sort of pride."

The minister was too much shocked to find any answer beyond a sad reproving shake of the head. But he felt almost as if the hearing of such irreverence without withering retort, made him a party to the sin against the Holy Ghost. Was he not now conferring with one of the generals of the army of Antichrist? Ought he not to turn his back upon him, and walk into the house? But a surge of concern for the frank young fellow who sat so strong and alive upon the great horse, broke over his heart, and he looked up at him pitifully.

Faber mistook the cause and object of his evident emotion.

"Come now, Mr. Drake, be frank with me," he said. "You are out of health; let me know what is the matter. Though I'm not religious, I'm not a humbug, and only speak the truth when I say I should be glad to serve you. A man must be neighborly, or what is there left of him? Even you will allow that our duty to our neighbor is half the law, and there is some help in medicine, though I confess it is no science yet, and we are but dabblers."

"But," said Mr. Drake, "I don't choose to accept the help of one who looks upon all who think with me as a set of humbugs, and regards those who deny every thing as the only honest men."

"By Jove! sir, I take you for an honest man, or I should never trouble my head about you. What I say of such as you is, that, having inherited a lot of humbug, you don't know it for such, and do the best you can with it."

"If such is your opinion of me—and I have no right to complain of it in my own person—I should just like to ask you one question about another," said Mr. Drake : "Do you in your heart believe that Jesus Christ was an impostor ?"

"I believe, if the story about him be true, that he was a well-meaning man, enormously self-deceived."

"Your judgment seems to me enormously illogical. That any ordinarily good man should so deceive himself, appears to my mind altogether impossible and incredible."

"Ah ! but he was an extraordinarily good man."

"Therefore the more likely to think too much of himself ?"

"Why not ? I see the same thing in his followers all about me."

"Doubtless the servant shall be as his master," said the minister, and closed his mouth, resolved to speak no more. But his conscience woke, and goaded him with the truth that had come from the mouth of its enemy—the reproach his disciples brought upon their master, for, in the judgment of the world, the master is as his disciples.

"You Christians," the doctor went on, "seem to me to make yourselves, most unnecessarily, the slaves of a fancied ideal. I have no such ideal to contemplate ; yet I am not aware that you do better by each other than I am ready to do for any man. I can't pretend to love every body, but I do my best for those I can help. Mr. Drake, I would gladly serve you."

The old man said nothing. His mood was stormy. Would he accept life itself from the hand of him who denied his Master ?—seek to the powers of darkness for cure ?—kneel to Antichrist for favor, as if he and not Jesus were lord of life and death ? Would *he* pray a man to whom the Bible was no better than a book of ballads, to come betwixt him and the evils of growing age and disappointment, to lighten for him the grasshopper, and stay the mourners as they went about his streets ! He had half turned, and was on the point of walking silent into the house, when he bethought himself of the impression it would make on the unbeliever, if he were thus to meet the offer of his kindness. Half turned, he stood hesitating.

"I have a passion for therapeutics," persisted the doctor ; "and if I can do any thing to ease the yoke upon the shoulders of my fellows——"

Mr. Drake did not hear the end of the sentence : he heard instead, somewhere in his soul, a voice saying, "My yoke is easy, and my burden is light." He *could* not let Faber help him.

"Doctor, you have the great gift of a kind heart," he began, still half turned from him.

"My heart is like other people's," interrupted Faber. "If a man wants help, and I've got it, what more natural than that we should come together ?"

There was in the doctor an opposition to every thing that had if it were but the odor of religion about it, which might well have suggested doubt of his own doubt, and weakness buttressing itself with assertion But the case was not so. What untruth there was in him was of another and more subtle kind. Neither must it be supposed that he was a propagandist, a proselytizer. Say nothing, and the doctor said nothing. Fire but a saloon pistol, however, and off went a great gun in answer—with no bravado, for the doctor was a gentleman.

"Mr. Faber," said the minister, now turning toward him, and looking him full in the face, "if you had a friend whom you loved with all your heart, would you be under obligation to a man who counted your friendship a folly ?"

"The cases are not parallel. Say the man merely did not believe your friend was alive, and there could be no insult to either."

"If the denial of his being in life, opened the door to the greatest wrongs that could be done him—and if that denial seemed to me to have its source in some element of moral antagonism to him—*could* I accept—I put it to yourself, Mr. Faber—*could* I accept assistance from that man ? Do not take it ill. You prize honesty ; so do I : ten times rather would I cease to live than accept life at the hand of an enemy to my Lord and Master."

"I am very sorry, Mr. Drake," said the doctor ; "but from your point of view I suppose you are right. Good morning."

He turned Ruber from the minister's door, went off quickly, and entered his own stable-yard just as the rector's carriage appeared at the further end of the street.

CHAPTER III.

THE MANOR HOUSE.

MR. BEVIS drove up to the inn, threw the reins to his coachman, got down, and helped his wife out of the carriage. Then they parted, she to take her gift of flowers and butter to her poor relation, he to call upon Mrs. Ramshorn.

That lady, being, as every body knew, the widow of a dean, considered herself the chief ecclesiastical authority in Glaston. Her acknowledged friends would, if pressed, have found themselves compelled to admit that her theology was both scanty and confused, that her influence was not of the most elevating nature, and that those who doubted her personal piety might have something to say in excuse of their uncharitableness; but she spoke in the might of the matrimonial nimbus around her head, and her claims were undisputed in Glaston. There was a propriety, springing from quite another source, however, in the rector's turning his footsteps first toward the Manor House, where she resided. For his curate, whom his business in Glaston that Saturday concerned, had, some nine or ten months before, married Mrs. Ramshorn's niece, Helen Lingard by name, who for many years had lived with her aunt, adding, if not to the comforts of the housekeeping, for Mrs. Ramshorn was plentifully enough provided for the remnant of her abode in this world, yet considerably to the style of her menage. Therefore, when all of a sudden, as it seemed, the girl calmly insisted on marrying the curate, a man obnoxious to every fiber of her aunt's ecclesiastical nature, and transferring to him, with a most unrighteous scorn of marriage-settlements, the entire property inherited from her father and brother, the disappointment of Mrs. Ramshorn in her niece was equaled only by her disgust at the object of her choice.

With a firm, dignified step, as if he measured the distance, the rector paced the pavement between the inn and the Manor House. He knew of no cause for the veiling of an eyelash before human being. It was true he had closed his eyes to certain faults in the man of good estate and old name who had done him the honor of requesting the hand of his one child, and, leaving her to judge for herself, had not given her the knowledge which might have led her to another conclusion ; it had satisfied him that the man's wild oats were sown : after the crop he made no inquiry. It was also true that he had not mentioned a certain vice in the last horse he sold ; but then he hoped the severe measures taken had cured him. He was aware that at times he took a few glasses of port more than he would have judged it proper to carry to the pulpit or the communion table, for those he counted the presence of his Maker ; but there was a time for every thing. He was conscious to himself, I repeat, of nothing to cause him shame, and in the tramp of his boots there was certainly no self-abasement. It was true he performed next to none of the duties of the rectorship—but then neither did he turn any of its income to his own uses ; part he paid his curate, and the rest he laid out on the church, which might easily have consumed six times the amount in desirable, if not absolutely needful repairs. What further question could be made of the matter ? the church had her work done, and one of her most precious buildings preserved from ruin to the bargain. How indignant he would have been at the suggestion that he was after all only an idolator, worshiping what he called *The Church*, instead of the Lord Christ, the heart-inhabiting, world-ruling king of heaven ! But he was a very good sort of idolator, and some of the Christian graces had filtered through the roofs of the temple upon him—eminently those of hospitality and general humanity—even uprightness so far as his light extended ; so that he did less to obstruct the religion he thought he furthered, than some men who preach it as on the house-tops.

It was from policy, not from confidence in Mrs. Ramshorn, that he went to her first. He liked his curate, and every one knew she hated him. If, of any thing he did, two interpretations were possible—one good, and one bad, there was no room for a doubt as to which she would adopt and publish. Not even to herself, however, did she allow that one chief cause of her hatred was, that, having all her life been used to a pair of horses, she had now to put up with only a brougham.

To the brass knocker on her door, the rector applied himself, and sent a confident announcement of his presence through the house. Almost instantly the long-faced butler,

half undertaker, half parish-clerk, opened the door; and
seeing the rector, drew it wide to the wall, inviting him to
step into the library, as he had no doubt Mrs. Ramshorn
would be at home to *him*.   Nor was it long ere she
appeared, in rather youthful morning dress, and gave him a
hearty welcome; after which, by no very wide spirals of
descent, the talk swooped presently upon the curate.

"The fact is," at length said the memorial shadow of the
dean deceased, "Mr. Wingfold is not a gentleman.   It
grieves me to say so of the husband of my niece, who
has been to me as my own child, but the truth must
be spoken.   It may be difficult to keep such men out of
holy orders, but if ever the benefices of the church come to
be freely bestowed upon them, that moment the death-bell
of religion is rung in England.   My late husband said so.
While such men keep to barns and conventicles we can
despise them, but when they creep into the fold, then there
is just cause for alarm.   The longer I live, the better I see
my poor husband was right."

"I should scarcely have thought such a man as you describe could have captivated Helen," said the rector with a
smile.

"Depend upon it she perceives her mistake well enough
by this time," returned Mrs. Ramshorn.   "A lady born and
bred *must* make the discovery before a week is over.   But
poor Helen always was headstrong!   And in this out-of-
the-world place she saw so little of gentlemen!"

The rector could not help thinking birth and breeding
must go for little indeed, if nothing less than marriage could
reveal to a lady that a man was not a gentleman.

"Nobody knows," continued Mrs. Ramshorn, "who or
what his father—not to say his grandfather, was!   But
would you believe it! when I asked her *who* the man was,
having a right to information concerning the person she
was about to connect with the family, she told me she had
never thought of inquiring.   I pressed it upon her as a duty
she owed to society; she told me she was content with the
man himself, and was not going to ask him about his family.
She would wait till they were married!   Actually, on my
word as a lady, she said so, Mr. Bevis!   What could I do?
She was of age, and independent fortune.   And as to
gratitude, I know the ways of the world too well to look for
that."

"We old ones"—Mrs. Ramshorn bridled a little: she was

only fifty-seven !—" have had our turn, and theirs is come,"
said the rector rather inconsequently.

"And a pretty mess they are like to make of it !
—what with infidelity and blasphemy—I must say it—
blasphemy !—Really you must do something, Mr. Bevis.
Things have arrived at such a pass that, I give you my
word, reflections not a few are made upon the rector for
committing his flock to the care of such a wolf—a fox *I* call
him."

" To-morrow I shall hear him preach," said the parson.

" Then I sincerely trust no one will give him warning of
your intention : he is so clever, he would throw dust in any
body's eyes."

The rector laughed. He had no overweening estimate
of his own abilities, but he did pride himself a little on his
common sense.

"But," the lady went on, " in a place like this, where
every body talks, I fear the chance is small against his hearing of your arrival. Anyhow I would not have you trust
to one sermon. He will say just the opposite the next.
He contradicts himself incredibly. Even in the same sermon I have heard him say things diametrically opposite."

" He can not have gone so far as to advocate the real
presence : a rumor of that has reached me," said the rector.

" There it is !" cried Mrs. Ramshorn. " If you had
asked me, I should have said he insisted the holy eucharist
meant neither more nor less than any other meal to which
some said a grace. The man has not an atom of consist-
ency in his nature. He will say and unsay as fast as one
sentence can follow the other, and if you tax him with it,
he will support both sides : at least, that is my experience
with him. I speak as I find him."

" What then would you have me do ? " said the rector.
" The straightforward way would doubtless be to go to him."

" You would, I fear, gain nothing by that. He is so
specious ! The only safe way is to dismiss him without giving a reason. Otherwise, he will certainly prove you in the
wrong. Don't take my word. Get the opinion of your
church-wardens. Every body knows he has made an atheist
of poor Faber. It is sadder than I have words to say. He
was such a gentlemanly fellow ! "

The rector took his departure, and made a series of calls
upon those he judged the most influential of the congregation. He did not think to ask for what they were influen-

tial, or why he should go to them rather than the people of the alms-house. What he heard embarrassed him not a little. His friends spoke highly of Wingfold, his enemies otherwise : the character of his friends his judge did not attempt to weigh with that of his enemies, neither did he attempt to discover why these were his enemies and those his friends. No more did he make the observation, that, while his enemies differed in the things they said against him, his friends agreed in those they said for him ; the fact being, that those who did as he roused their conscience to see they ought, more or less understood the man and his aims ; while those who would not submit to the authority he brought to bear upon them, and yet tried to measure and explain him after the standards of their own being and er.deavors, failed ludicrously. The church-wardens told him that, ever since he came, the curate had done nothing but set the congregation by the ears ; and that he could not fail to receive as a weighty charge. But they told him also that some of the principal dissenters declared him to be a fountain of life in the place—and that seemed to him to involve the worst accusation of all. For, without going so far as to hold, or even say without meaning it, that dissenters ought to be burned, Mr. Bevis regarded it as one of the first of merits, that a man should be a *good churchman.*

CHAPTER IV.

THE RECTORY.

THE curate had been in the study all the morning. Three times had his wife softly turned the handle of his door, but finding it locked, had re-turned the handle yet more softly, and departed noiselessly. Next time she knocked—and he came to her pale-eyed, but his face almost luminous, and a smile hovering about his lips : she knew then that either a battle had been fought amongst the hills, and he had won, or a thought-storm had been raging, through which at length had descended the meek-eyed Peace. She looked in his face for a moment with silent reverence, then offered her lips, took him by the hand, and, without a word, led him down the stair to their mid-day meal. When that was over, she made him lie down, and taking a novel, read him asleep. She woke him to an early tea—not, however, after it, to return to his study : in the drawing-room, beside his wife, he always got the germ of his discourse—his germon, he called it—ready for its growth in the pulpit. Now he lay on the couch, now rose and stood, now walked about the room, now threw himself again on the couch ; while, all the time his wife played softly on her piano, extemporizing and interweaving, with an invention, taste, and expression, of which before her marriage she had been quite incapable.

The text in his mind was, " *Ye can not serve God and Mammon.*" But not once did he speak to his wife about it. He did not even tell her what his text was. Long ago he had given her to understand that he could not part with her as one of his congregation—could not therefore take her into his sermon before he met her in her hearing phase in church, with the rows of pews and faces betwixt him and her, making her once more one of his flock, the same into whose heart he had so often agonized to pour the words of rousing, of strength, of consolation.

On the Saturday, except his wife saw good reason, she would let no one trouble him, and almost the sole reason she counted good was trouble : if a person was troubled, then he might trouble. His friends knew this, and seldom came near him on a Saturday. But that evening, Mr. Drew, the draper, who, although a dissenter, was one of the curate's warmest friends, called late, when, he thought in his way of looking at sermons, that for the morrow must be now finished, and laid aside like a parcel for delivery the next morning. Helen went to him. He told her the rector was in the town, had called upon not a few of his parishioners, and doubtless was going to church in the morning.

" Thank you, Mr. Drew. I perfectly understand your kindness," said Mrs. Wingfold, "but I shall not tell my husband to-night."

" Excuse the liberty, ma'am, but—but—do you think it well for a wife to hide things from her husband ? "

Helen laughed merrily.

" Assuredly not, as a rule," she replied. " But suppose I knew he would be vexed with me if I told him some particular thing ? Suppose I know now that, when I do tell him on Monday, he will say to me, ' Thank you, wife. I am glad you kept that from me till I had done my work,'—what then?"

"All right *then*," answered the draper.

"You see, Mr. Drew, *we* think married people should be so sure of each other that each should not only be content, but should prefer not to know what the other thinks it better not to tell. If my husband overheard any one calling me names, I don't think he would tell me. He knows, as well as I do, that I am not yet good enough to behave better to any one for knowing she hates and reviles me. It would be but to propagate the evil, and for my part too, I would rather not be told."

"I quite understand you, ma'am," answered the draper.

"I know you do," returned Helen, with emphasis.

Mr. Drew blushed to the top of his white forehead, while the lower part of his face, which in its forms was insignificant, blossomed into a smile as radiant as that of an infant. He knew Mrs. Wingfold was aware of the fact, known only to two or three beside in the town, that the lady, who for the last few months had been lodging in his house, was his own wife, who had forsaken him twenty years before. The man who during that time had passed for her husband, had been otherwise dishonest as well, and had fled the country; she and her daughter, brought to absolute want, were received into his house by her forsaken husband; there they occupied the same chamber, the mother ordered every thing, and the daughter did not know that she paid for nothing. If the ways of transgressors are hard, those of a righteous man are not always easy. When Mr. Drew would now and then stop suddenly in the street, take off his hat and wipe his forehead, little people thought the round smiling face had such a secret behind it. Had they surmised a skeleton in his house, they would as little have suspected it masked in the handsome, well-dressed woman of little over forty, who, with her pretty daughter so tossy and airy, occupied his first floor, and was supposed to pay him handsomely for it.

The curate slept soundly, and woke in the morning eager to utter what he had.

CHAPTER V.

PAUL FABER fared otherwise. Hardly was he in bed before he was called out of it again. A messenger had come from Mrs. Puckridge to say that Miss Meredith was worse, and if the doctor did not start at once, she would be dead before he reached Owlkirk. He sent orders to his groom to saddle Niger and bring him round instantly, and hurried on his clothes, vexed that he had taken Ruber both in the morning and afternoon, and could not have him now. But Niger was a good horse also : if he was but two-thirds of Ruber's size, he was but one-third of his age, and saw better at night. On the other hand he was less easily seen, but the midnight there was so still and deserted, that that was of small consequence. In a few minutes they were out together in a lane as dark as pitch, compelled now to keep to the roads, for there was not light enough to see the pocket-compass by which the surgeon sometimes steered across country.

Could we learn what waking-dreams haunted the boyhood of a man, we should have a rare help toward understanding the character he has developed. Those of the young Faber were, almost exclusively, of playing the prince of help and deliverance among women and men. Like most boys that dream, he dreamed himself rich and powerful, but the wealth and power were for the good of his fellow-creatures. If it must be confessed that he lingered most over the thanks and admiration he set to haunt his dream-steps, and hover about his dream-person, it must be remembered that he was the only real person in the dreams, and that he regarded lovingly the mere shadows of his fellow-men. His dreams were not of strength and destruction, but of influence and life. Even his revenges never ·reached further than the making of his enemies ashamed.

It was the spirit of help, then, that had urged him into the profession he followed. He had found much dirt about the door of it, and had not been able to cross the threshold without some cleaving to his garments. He is a high-souled youth indeed, in whom the low regards and corrupt knowledge of his superiors will fail utterly of degrading influence ; he must be one stronger than Faber who can listen to scoffing materialism from the lips of authority and experience, and not come to look upon humanity and life with a less reverent regard.   What man can learn to look upon the dying as so much matter about to be rekneaded and remodeled into a fresh mass of feverous joys, futile aspirations, and stinging chagrins, without a self-contempt from which there is no shelter but the poor hope that we may be a little better than we appear to ourselves.   But Faber escaped the worst.   He did not learn to look on humanity without respect, or to meet the stare of appealing eyes from man or animal, without genuine response—without sympathy.   He never joined in any jest over suffering, not to say betted on the chance of the man who lay panting under the terrors of an impending operation.   Can one be capable of such things, and not have sunk deep indeed in the putrid pit of decomposing humanity?   It is true that before he began to practice, Faber had come to regard man as a body and not an embodiment, the highest in him as dependent on his physical organization—as indeed but the aroma, as it were, of its blossom the brain, therefore subject to *all* the vicissitudes of the human plant from which it rises ; but he had been touched to issues too fine to be absolutely interpenetrated and inslaved by the reaction of accepted theories.   His poetic nature, like the indwelling fire of the world, was ever ready to play havoc with induration and constriction, and the same moment when degrading influences ceased to operate, the delicacy of his feeling began to revive.   Even at its lowest, this delicacy preserved him from much into which vulgar natures plunge ; it kept alive the memory of a lovely mother ; and fed the flame of that wondering, worshiping reverence for women which is the saviour of men until the Truth Himself saves both.   A few years of worthy labor in his profession had done much to develop him, and his character for uprightness, benevolence, and skill, with the people of Glaston and its neighborhood, where he had been ministering only about a year, was already of the highest.   Even now, when, in a fever of honesty, he declared there *could* be no God in such an ill-ordered world, so full was his heart of the human half of religion, that he could not stand by the bedside of dying man or woman, without lamenting that there was no consolation—that stern truth would allow him to cast no feeblest glamour of hope upon the departing shadow. His was a nobler nature than theirs who, believing no more than he, are satisfied with the assurance that at the heart of the evils of the world lie laws unchangeable.

The main weak point in him was, that, while he was indeed tender-hearted, and did no kindnesses to be seen of men, he did them to be seen of himself : he saw him who did them all the time. The boy was in the man ; doing his deeds he sought, not the approbation merely, but the admiration of his own consciousness. I am afraid to say this was *wrong*, but it was poor and childish, crippled his walk, and obstructed his higher development. He liked to *know* himself a benefactor. Such a man may well be of noble nature, but he is a mere dabbler in nobility. Faber delighted in the thought that, having repudiated all motives of personal interest involved in religious belief, all that regard for the future, with its rewards and punishments, which, in his ignorance, genuine or willful, of essential Christianity, he took for its main potence, he ministered to his neighbor, doing to him as he would have him do to himself, hopeless of any divine recognition, of any betterness beyond the grave, in a fashion at least as noble as that of the most devoted of Christians. It did not occur to him to ask if he loved him as well—if his care about him was equal to his satisfaction in himself. Neither did he reflect that the devotion he admired in himself had been brought to the birth in him through others, in whom it was first generated by a fast belief in an unselfish, loving, self-devoting God. Had he inquired he might have discovered that this belief had carried some men immeasurably further in the help of their fellows, than he had yet gone. Indeed he might, I think, have found instances of men of faith spending their lives for their fellows, whose defective theology or diseased humility would not allow them to hope their own salvation. Inquiry might have given him ground for fearing that with the love of the *imagined* God, the love of the indubitable man would decay and vanish. But such as Faber was, he was both loved and honored by all whom he had ever attended ; and, with his fine tastes, his genial nature, his quiet conscience, his good health, his enjoyment of life, his knowledge and love of his profession, his activity, his tender heart—especially to women and children, his keen intellect, and his devising though not embodying imagination, if any man could get on without a God, Faber was that man. He was now trying it, and as yet the trial had cost him no effort : he seemed to himself to be doing very well indeed. And why should he not do as well as the thousands, who counting themselves religious people, get through the business of the hour, the day, the week, the year, without one reference in any thing they do or abstain from doing, to the will of God, or the words of Christ? If he was more helpful to his fellows than they, he fared better ; for actions in themselves good, however imperfect the motives that give rise to them, react blissfully upon character and nature. It is better to be an atheist who does the will of God, than a so-called Christian who does not. The atheist will not be dismissed because he said *Lord, Lord*, and did not obey. The thing that God loves is the only lovely thing, and he who does it, does well, and is upon the way to discover that he does it very badly. When he comes to do it as the will of the perfect Good, then is he on the road to do it perfectly—that is, from love of its own inherent self-constituted goodness, born in the heart of the Perfect. The doing of things from duty is but a stage on the road to the kingdom of truth and love. Not the less must the stage be journeyed ; every path diverging from it is "the flowery way that leads to the broad gate and the great fire."

It was with more than his usual zeal of helpfulness that Faber was now riding toward Owlkirk, to revisit his new patient. Could he have mistaken the symptoms of her attack?

CHAPTER VI.

THE COTTAGE.

MRS. PUCKRIDGE was anxiously awaiting the doctor's arrival. She stood by the bedside of her lodger, miserable in her ignorance and consequent helplessness. The lady tossed and moaned, but for very pain could neither toss nor moan much, and breathed—panted, rather—very quick. Her color was white more than pale, and now and then she shivered from head to foot, but her eyes burned. Mrs. Puckridge kept bringing her hot flannels, and stood talking between the changes.

"I wish the doctor would come!—Them doctors!—I hope to goodness Dr. Faber wasn't out when the boy got to Glaston. Every body in this mortal universe always is out when he's wanted : that's *my* experience. You ain't so old as me, miss. And Dr. Faber, you see, miss, he be such a favorite as *have* to go out to his dinner not unfrequent. They may have to send miles to fetch him."

She talked in the vain hope of distracting the poor lady's attention from her suffering.

It was a little up stairs cottage-room, the corners betwixt the ceiling and the walls cut off by the slope of the roof. So dark was the night, that, when Mrs. Puckridge carried the candle out of the room, the unshaded dormer window did not show itself even by a bluish glimmer. But light and dark were alike to her who lay in the little tent-bed, in the midst of whose white curtains, white coverlid, and white pillows, her large eyes, black as human eyes could ever be, were like wells of darkness throwing out flashes of strange light. Her hair too was dark, brown-black, of great plenty, and so fine that it seemed to go off in a mist on the whiteness. It had been her custom to throw it over the back of her bed, but in this old-fashioned one that was impossible, and it lay, in loveliest confusion, scattered here and there over pillow and coverlid, as if the wind had been tossing it all a long night at his will. Some of it had strayed more than half way to the foot of the bed. Her face, distorted almost though it was with distress, showed yet a regularity of feature rarely to be seen in combination with such evident power of expression. Suffering had not yet flattened the delicate roundness of her cheek, or sharpened the angles of her chin. In her whiteness, and her constrained, pang-thwarted motions from side to side, she looked like a form of marble in the agonies of coming to life at the prayer of some Pygmalion. In throwing out her arms, she had flung back the bedclothes, and her daintily embroidered night-gown revealed a rather large, grand throat, of the same rare whiteness. Her hands were perfect—every finger and every nail—

Those fine[1] nimble brethren small,
Armed with pearl-shell helmets all.

---

[1] *Joshua Sylvester.* I suspect the word ought to be *five*, not *fine*, as my copy (1613) has it.

When Mrs. Puckridge came into the room, she always set her candle on the sill of the storm-window : it was there, happily, when the doctor drew near the village, and it guided him to the cottage-gate.   He fastened Niger to the gate, crossed the little garden, gently lifted the door-latch, and ascended the stair.   He found the door of the chamber open, signed to Mrs. Puckridge to be still, softly approached the bed, and stood gazing in silence on the sufferer, who lay at the moment apparently unconscious.   But suddenly, as if she had become aware of a presence, she flashed wide her great eyes, and the pitiful entreaty that came into them when she saw him, went straight to his heart.   Faber felt more for the sufferings of some of the lower animals than for certain of his patients ; but children and women he would serve like a slave.   The dumb appeal of her eyes almost unmanned him.

"I am sorry to see you so ill," he said, as he took her wrist.   "You are in pain : where ? "

Her other hand moved toward her side in reply.   Every thing indicated pleurisy—such that there was no longer room for gentle measures.   She must be relieved at once : he must open a vein.   In the changed practice of later days, it had seldom fallen to the lot of Faber to perform the very simple operation of venesection, but that had little to do with the trembling of the hands which annoyed him with himself, when he proceeded to undo a sleeve of his patient's nightdress.   Finding no button, he took a pair of scissors from his pocket, cut ruthlessly through linen and lace, and rolled back the sleeve.   It disclosed an arm the sight of which would have made a sculptor rejoice as over some marbles of old Greece.   I can not describe it, and if I could, for very love and reverence I would rather let it alone. Faber felt his heart rise in his throat at the necessity of breaking that exquisite surface with even such an insignificant breach and blemish as the shining steel betwixt his forefinger and thumb must occasion.   But a slight tremble of the hand he held acknowledged the intruding sharpness, and then the red parabola rose from the golden bowl.   He stroked the lovely arm to help its flow, and soon the girl once more opened her eyes and looked at him.   Already her breathing was easier.   But presently her eyes began to glaze with approaching faintness, and he put his thumb on the wound.   She smiled and closed them.   He bound up her arm, laid it gently by her side, gave her something to drink, and sat down. He sat until he saw her sunk in a quiet, gentle sleep : ease had dethroned pain, and order had begun to dawn out of threatened chaos.

"Thank God !" he said, involuntarily, and stood up : what all that meant, God only knows.

After various directions to Mrs. Puckridge, to which she seemed to attend, but which, being as simple as necessary, I fear she forgot the moment they were uttered, the doctor mounted, and rode away. The darkness was gone, for the moon was rising, but when the road compelled him to face her, she blinded him nearly as much. Slowly she rose through a sky freckled with wavelets of cloud, and as she crept up amongst them she brought them all out, in bluish, pearly, and opaline gray. Then, suddenly almost, as it seemed, she left them, and walked up aloft, drawing a thin veil around her as she ascended. All was so soft, so sleepy, so vague, it seemed to Paul as he rode slowly along, him-self almost asleep, as if the Night had lost the blood he had caused to flow, and the sweet exhaustion that followed had from the lady's brain wandered out over Nature herself, as she sank, a lovelier Katadyomene, into the hushed sea of pain-won repose.

Was he in love with her ? I do not know. I could tell, if I knew what being in love is. I think no two loves were ever the same since the creation of the world. I know that something had passed from her eyes to his—but what ? He may have been in love with her already ; but ere long my reader may be more sure than I that he was not. The Maker of men alone understands His awful mystery between the man and the woman. But without it, frightful indeed as are some of its results, assuredly the world He has made would burst its binding rings and fly asunder in shards, leaving His spirit nothing to enter, no time to work His lovely will.

It must be to any man a terrible thing to find himself in wild pain, with no God of whom to entreat that his soul may not faint within him ; but to a man who can think as well as feel, it were a more terrible thing still, to find himself afloat on the tide of a lovely passion, with no God to whom to cry, accountable to Himself for that which He has made. Will any man who has ever cast more than a glance into the mysteries of his being, dare think himself sufficient to the ruling of his nature ? And if he rule it not, what shall he be but the sport of the demons that will ride its tempests, that will rouse and torment its ocean ? What help then is there ? What high-hearted man would consent to be possessed and sweetly ruled by the loveliest of angels ? Truly it were but a daintier madness. Come thou, holy Love, father of my spirit, nearer to the unknown deeper me than my consciousness is to its known self, possess me utterly, for thou art more me than I am myself. Rule thou. Then first I rule. Shadow me from the too radiant splendors of thy own creative thought. Folded in thy calm, I shall love, and not die. And ye, women, be the daughters of Him from whose heart came your mothers ; be the saviours of men, and neither their torment nor their prey !

CHAPTER VII.

THE PULPIT.

BEFORE morning it rained hard again ; but it cleared at sunrise, and the first day of the week found the world new-washed. Glaston slept longer than usual, however, for all the shine, and in the mounting sun looked dead and deserted. There were no gay shop-windows to reflect his beams, or fill them with rainbow colors. There were no carriages or carts, and only, for a few moments, one rider. That was Paul Faber again, on Ruber now, aglow in the morning. There were no children playing yet about the streets or lanes ; but the cries of some came at intervals from unseen chambers, as the Sunday soap stung their eyes, or the Sunday comb tore their matted locks.

As Faber rode out of his stable-yard, Wingfold took his hat from its peg, to walk through his churchyard. He lived almost in the churchyard, for, happily, since his marriage the rectory had lost its tenants, and Mr. Bevis had allowed him to occupy it, in lieu of part of his salary. It was not yet church-time by hours, but he had a custom of going every Sunday morning, in the fine weather, quite early, to sit for an hour or two alone in the pulpit, amidst the absolute solitude and silence of the great church. It was a door, he said, through which a man who could not go to Horeb, might enter and find the power that dwells on mountain-tops and in desert places.

He went slowly through the churchyard, breathing deep breaths of the delicious spring-morning air. Rain-drops were sparkling all over the grassy graves, and in the hollows of the stones they had gathered in pools. The eyes of the death-heads were full of water, as if weeping at the defeat of their master. Every now and then a soft little wind awoke, like a throb of the spirit of life, and shook together the scattered drops upon the trees, and then down came diamond showers on the grass and daisies of the mounds, and fed the green moss in the letters of the epitaphs. Over all the sun was shining, as if everywhere and forever spring was the order of things. And is it not so? Is not the idea of the creation an eternal spring ever trembling on the verge of summer? It seemed so to the curate, who was not given to sad, still less to sentimental moralizing over the graves. From such moods his heart recoiled. To him they were weak and mawkish, and in him they would have been treacherous. No grave was to him the place where a friend was lying; it was but a cenotaph—the place where the Lord had lain.

"Let those possessed with demons haunt the tombs," he said, as he sat down in the pulpit; "for me, I will turn my back upon them with the risen Christ. Yes, friend, I hear you! I know what you say! You have more affection than I? you can not forsake the last resting-place of the beloved? Well, you may have more feeling than I; there is no gauge by which I can tell, and if there were, it would be useless: we are as God made us.—No, I will not say that: I will say rather, I am as God is making me, and I shall one day be as He has made me. Meantime I know that He will have me love my enemy tenfold more than now I love my friend. Thou believest that the malefactor—ah, there was faith now! Of two men dying together in agony and shame, the one beseeches of the other the grace of a king! Thou believest, I say—at least thou professest to believe that the malefactor was that very day with Jesus in Paradise, and yet thou broodest over thy friend's grave, gathering thy thoughts about the pitiful garment he left behind him, and letting himself drift away into the unknown, forsaken of all but thy vaguest, most shapeless thinkings! Tell me not thou fearest to enter there whence has issued no revealing. It is God who gives thee thy mirror of imagination, and if thou keep it clean, it will give thee back no shadow but of the truth. Never a cry of love went forth from human heart but it found some heavenly chord to fold it in.   Be sure thy friend inhabits a day not out of harmony with this morning of earthly spring, with this sunlight, those rain-drops, that sweet wind that flows so softly over his grave."

It was the first sprouting of a *germon*.   He covered it up and left it : he had something else to talk to his people about this morning.

While he sat thus in the pulpit, his wife was praying for him ere she rose.   She had not learned to love him in the vestibule of society, that court of the Gentiles, but in the chamber of torture and the clouded adytum of her own spiritual temple.   For there a dark vapor had hid the deity enthroned, until the words of His servant melted the gloom. Then she saw that what she had taken for her own inner-most chamber of awful void, was the dwelling-place of the most high, most lovely, only One, and through its windows she beheld a cosmos dawning out of chaos.   Therefore the wife walked beside the husband in the strength of a common faith in absolute Good ; and not seldom did the fire which the torch of his prophecy had kindled upon her altar, kindle again that torch, when some bitter wind of evil words, or mephitis of human perversity, or thunder-rain of foiled charity, had extinguished it.   She loved every hair upon his head, but loved his well-being infinitely more than his mortal life.   A wrinkle on his forehead would cause her a pang, yet would she a thousand times rather have seen him dead than known him guilty of one of many things done openly by not a few of his profession.

And now, as one sometimes wonders what he shall dream to-night, she sat wondering what new thing, or what old thing fresher and more alive than the new, would this day flow from his heart into hers.   The following is the sub-stance of what, a few hours after, she did hear from him. His rector, sitting between Mrs. Bevis and Mrs. Ramshorn, heard it also.   The radiance of truth shone from Wing-fold's face as he spoke, and those of the congregation who turned away from his words were those whose lives ran counter to the spirit of them.   Whatever he uttered grew out of a whole world of thought, but it grew before them— that is, he always thought afresh in the presence of the people, and spoke extempore.

" ' *Ye can not serve God and mammon.*'

"Who said this ?   The Lord by whose name ye are called,

in whose name this house was built, and who will at last
judge every one of us. And yet how many of you are, and
have been for years, trying your very hardest to do the
thing your Master tells you is impossible! Thou man!
Thou woman! I appeal to thine own conscience whether
thou art not striving to serve God and mammon.

"But stay! am I right?—It can not be. For surely if a
man strove hard to serve God and mammon, he would presently discover the thing was impossible. It is not easy to
serve God, and it is easy to serve mammon; if one strove
to serve God, the hard thing, along with serving mammon,
the easy thing, the incompatibility of the two endeavors
must appear. The fact is there is no strife in you. With
ease you serve mammon every day and hour of your lives,
and for God, you do not even ask yourselves the question
whether you are serving Him or no. Yet some of you are
at this very moment indignant that I call you servers of
mammon. Those of you who know that God knows you
are His servants, know also that I do not mean you; therefore, those who are indignant at being called the servants of
mammon, are so because they are indeed such. As I say
these words I do not lift my eyes, not that I am afraid to
·look you in the face, as uttering an offensive thing, but that
I would have your own souls your accusers.

"Let us consider for a moment the God you do not serve,
and then for a moment the mammon you do serve. The
God you do not serve is the Father of Lights, the Source of
love, the Maker of man and woman, the Head of the great
family, the Father of fatherhood and motherhood; the Life-
giver who would die to preserve His children, but would
rather slay them than they should live the servants of evil;
the God who can neither think nor do nor endure any thing
mean or unfair; the God of poetry and music and every
marvel; the God of the mountain tops, and the rivers that
run from the snows of death, to make the earth joyous with
life; the God of the valley and the wheat-field, the God who
has set love betwixt youth and maiden; the God and Father
of our Lord Jesus Christ, the perfect; the God whom Christ
knew, with whom Christ was satisfied, of whom He declared
that to know Him was eternal life. The mammon you do
serve is not a mere negation, but a positive Death. His
temple is a darkness, a black hollow, ever hungry, in the
heart of man, who tumbles into it every thing that should
make life noble and lovely. To all who serve him he makes

it seem that his alone is the reasonable service. His wages are death, but he calls them life, and they believe him. I will tell you some of the marks of his service—a few of the badges of his household—for he has no visible temple ; no man bends the knee to him ; it is only his soul, his manhood, that the worshiper casts in the dust before him. If a man talks of the main chance, meaning thereby that of making money, or of number one, meaning thereby self, except indeed he honestly jest, he is a servant of mammon. If, when thou makest a bargain, thou thinkest *only* of thyself and thy gain, though art a servant of mammon. The eager looks of those that would get money, the troubled looks of those who have lost it, worst of all the gloating looks of them that have it,— these are sure signs of the service of mammon. If in the church thou sayest to the rich man, ' Sit here in a good place,' and to the poor man, ' Stand there,' thou art a mammon-server. If thou favorest the company of those whom men call well-to-do, when they are only well-to-eat, well-to-drink, or well-to-show, and declinest that of the simple and the meek, then in thy deepest consciousness know that thou servest mammon, not God. If thy hope of well-being in time to come, rests upon thy houses, or lands, or business, or money in store, and not upon the living God, be thou friendly and kind with the overflowings of thy possessions, or a churl whom no man loves, thou art equally a server of mammon. If the loss of thy goods would take from thee the joy of thy life ; if it would tear thy heart that the men thou hadst feasted should hold forth to thee the two fingers instead of the whole hand ; nay, if thy thought of to-morrow makes thee quail before the duty of to-day, if thou broodest over the evil that is not come, and turnest from the God who is with thee in the life of the hour, thou servest mammon ; he holds thee in his chain ; thou art his ape, whom he leads about the world for the mockery of his fellow-devils. If with thy word, yea, even with thy judgment, thou confessest that God is the only good, yet livest as if He had sent thee into the world to make thyself rich before thou die ; if it will add one feeblest pang to the pains of thy death, to think that thou must leave thy fair house, thy ancestral trees, thy horses, thy shop, thy books, behind thee, then art thou a servant of mammon, and far truer to thy master than he will prove to thee. Ah, slave ! the moment the breath is out of the body, lo, he has already deserted thee ! and of all in which thou didst rejoice, all that gave thee such power over thy fellows, there is not left so much as a spike of thistle-down for the wind to waft from thy sight. For all thou hast had, there is nothing to show. Where is the friend-ship in which thou mightst have invested thy money, in place of burying it in the maw of mammon? Troops of the dead might now be coming to greet thee with love and service, hadst thou made thee friends with thy money; but, alas! to thee it was not money, but mammon, for thou didst love it—not for the righteousness and salvation thou by its means mightst work in the earth, but for the honor it brought thee among men, for the pleasures and immunities it purchased. Some of you are saying in your hearts, ' Preach to thyself, and practice thine own preach-ing; '—and you say well. And so I mean to do, lest having preached to others I should be myself a cast-away —drowned with some of you in the same pond of filth. God has put money in my power through the gift of one whom you know. I shall endeavor to be a faithful steward of that which God through her has committed to me in trust. Hear me, friends—to none of you am I the less a friend that I tell you truths you would hide from your own souls: money is not mammon; it is God's inven-tion; it is good and the gift of God. But for money and the need of it, there would not be half the friendship in the world. It is powerful for good when divinely used. Give it plenty of air, and it is sweet as the hawthorn; shut it up, and it cankers and breeds worms. Like all the best gifts of God, like the air and the water, it must have motion and change and shakings asunder; like the earth itself, like the heart and mind of man, it must be broken and turned, not heaped together and neglected. It is an angel of mercy, whose wings are full of balm and dews and refreshings; but when you lay hold of him, pluck his pin-ions, pen him in a yard, and fall down and worship him— then, with the blessed vengeance of his master, he deals plague and confusion and terror, to stay the idolatry. If I misuse or waste or hoard the divine thing, I pray my Mas-ter to see to it—my God to punish me. Any fire rather than be given over to the mean idol! And now I will make an offer to my townsfolk in the face of this congregation— that, whoever will, at the end of three years, bring me his books, to him also will I lay open mine, that he will see how I have sought to make friends of the mammon of unrighteousness. Of the mammon-server I expect to be judged according to the light that is in him, and that light I know to be darkness.

"Friend, be not a slave. Be wary. Look not on the gold when it is yellow in thy purse. Hoard not. In God's name, spend—spend on. Take heed how thou spendest, but take heed that thou spend. Be thou as the sun in heaven ; let thy gold be thy rays, thy angels of love and life and deliverance. Be thou a candle of the Lord to spread His light through the world. If hitherto, in any fashion of faithlessness, thou hast radiated darkness into the universe, humble thyself, and arise and shine.

"But if thou art poor, then look not on thy purse when it is empty. He who desires more than God wills him to have, is also a servant of mammon, for he trusts in what God has made, and not in God Himself. He who laments what God has taken from him, he is a servant of mammon. He who for care can not pray, is a servant of mammon. There are men in this town who love and trust their horses more than the God that made them and their horses too. None the less confidently will they give judgment on the doctrine of God. But the opinion of no man who does not render back his soul to the living God and live in Him, is, in religion, worth the splinter of a straw. Friends, cast your idol into the furnace ; melt your mammon down, coin him up, make God's money of him, and send him coursing. Make of him cups to carry the gift of God, the water of life, through the world—in lovely justice to the oppressed, in healthful labor to them whom no man hath hired, in rest to the weary who have borne the burden and heat of the day, in joy to the heavy-hearted, in laughter to the dull-spirited. Let them all be glad with reason, and merry without revel. Ah ! what gifts in music, in drama, in the tale, in the picture, in the spectacle, in books and models, in flowers and friendly feasting, what true gifts might not the mammon of unrighteousness, changed back into the money of God, give to men and women, bone of our bone, and flesh of our flesh ! How would you not spend your money for the Lord, if He needed it at your hand ! He does need it ; for he that spends it upon the least of his fellows, spends it upon his Lord. To hold fast upon God with one hand, and open wide the other to your neighbor—that is religion ; that is the law and the prophets, and the true way to all better things that are yet to come.—Lord, defend us from

Mammon. Hold Thy temple against his foul invasion. Purify our money with Thy air, and Thy sun, that it may be our slave, and Thou our Master. Amen."

The moment his sermon was ended, the curate always set himself to forget it. This for three reasons : first, he was so dissatisfied with it, that to think of it was painful—and the more, that many things he might have said, and many better ways of saying what he had said, would constantly present themselves. Second, it was useless to brood over what could not be bettered ; and, third, it was hurtful, inasmuch as it prevented the growth of new, hopeful, invigorating thought, and took from his strength, and the quality of his following endeavor. A man's labors must pass like the sunrises and sunsets of the world. The next thing, not the last, must be his care. When he reached home, he would therefore use means to this end of diversion, and not unfrequently would write verses. Here are those he wrote that afternoon.

LET YOUR LIGHT SO SHINE.

Sometimes, O Lord, thou lightest in my head
  A lamp that well might Pharos all the lands ;
Anon the light will neither burn nor spread
  Shrouded in danger gray the beacon stands.

A Pharos ? Oh, dull brain ! Oh, poor quenched lamp,
  Under a bushel, with an earthy smell !
Moldering it lies, in rust and eating damp,
  While the slow oil keeps oozing from its cell !

For me it were enough to be a flower
  Knowing its root in thee was somewhere hid—
To blossom at the far appointed hour,
  And fold in sleep when thou, my Nature, bid.

But hear my brethren crying in the dark !
  Light up my lamp that it may shine abroad.
Fain would I cry—See, brothers ! sisters, mark !
  This is the shining of light's father, God.

CHAPTER VIII.

THE MANOR HOUSE DINING-ROOM.

THE rector never took his eyes off the preacher, but the preacher never saw him. The reason was that he dared not let his eyes wander in the direction of Mrs. Ramshorn ; he was not yet so near perfection but that the sight of her supercilious, unbelieving face, was a reviving cordial to the old Adam, whom he was so anxious to poison with love and prayer. Church over, the rector walked in silence, between the two ladies, to the Manor House. He courted no greetings from the sheep of his neglected flock as he went, and returned those offered with a constrained solemnity. The moment they stood in the hall together, and before the servant who had opened the door to them had quite disappeared, Mrs. Ramshorn, to the indignant consternation of Mrs. Bevis, who was utterly forgotten by both in the colloquy that ensued, turned sharp on the rector, and said,

" There ! what do you say to your curate now ? "

" He *is* enough to set the whole parish by the ears," he answered.

" I told you so, Mr. Bevis ! "

" Only it does not follow that therefore he is in the wrong. Our Lord Himself came not to send peace on earth but a sword."

" Irreverence ill becomes a beneficed clergyman, Mr. Bevis," said Mrs. Ramshorn—who very consistently regarded any practical reference to our Lord as irrelevant, thence naturally as irreverent.

" And, by Jove ! " added the rector, heedless of her remark, and tumbling back into an old college-habit, " I fear he is in the right ; and if he is, it will go hard with you and me at the last day, Mrs. Ramshorn."

" Do you mean to say you are going to let that man turn every thing topsy-turvy, and the congregation out of the church, John Bevis ? "

" I never saw such a congregation in it before, Mrs. Ramshorn."

" It's little better than a low-bred conventicle now, and what it will come to, if things go on like this, God knows."

" That ought to be a comfort," said the rector. " But I hardly know yet where I am. The fellow has knocked the wind out of me with his personalities, and I haven't got my breath yet. Have you a bottle of sherry open ?"

Mrs. Ramshorn led the way to the dining-room, where the early Sunday dinner was already laid, and the decanters stood on the sideboard. The rector poured himself out a large glass of sherry, and drank it off in three mouthfuls.

" Such buffoonery ! such coarseness ! such vulgarity ! such indelicacy !" cried Mrs. Ramshorn, while the parson was still occupied with the sherry. " Not content with talking about himself in the pulpit, he must even talk about his wife ! What's he or his wife in the house of God ? When his gown is on, a clergyman is neither Mr. This nor Mr. That any longer, but a priest of the Church of England, as by law established. My poor Helen ! She has thrown herself away upon a charlatan ! And what will become of her money in the hands of a man with such leveling notions, I dread to think."

" He said something about buying friends with it," said the rector.

" Bribery and corruption must come natural to a fellow who could preach a sermon like that after marrying money !"

" Why, my good madam, would you have a man turn his back on a girl because she has a purse in her pocket ?"

" But to pretend to despise it ! And then, worst of all ! I don't know whether the indelicacy or the profanity was the greater !—when I think of it now, I can scarcely believe I really heard it !—to offer to show his books to every inquisitive fool itching to know *my* niece's fortune ! Well, she shan't see a penny of mine—that I'm determined on."

" You need not be uneasy about the books, Mrs. Ramshorn. You remember the condition annexed ?"

" Stuff and hypocrisy ! He's played his game well ! But time will show."

Mr. Bevis checked his answer. He was beginning to get disgusted with the old cat, as he called her to himself.

He too had made a good speculation in the hymeneomoney-market, otherwise he could hardly have afforded to give up the exercise of his profession. Mrs. Bevis had brought him the nice little property at Owlkirk, where, if he worshiped mammon—and after his curate's sermon he was not at all sure he did not—he worshiped him in a very moderate and gentlemanly fashion. Every body liked the rector, and two or three loved him a little.   If it would be a stretch of the truth to call a man a Christian who never yet in his life had consciously done a thing because it was commanded by Christ, he was not therefore a godless man ; while, through the age-long process of spiritual infiltration, he had received and retained much that was Christian.

The ladies went to take off their bonnets, and their departure was a relief to the rector.   He helped himself to another glass of sherry, and seated himself in the great easy chair formerly approved of the dean, long promoted. But what are easy chairs to uneasy men ?   Dinner, however, was at hand, and that would make a diversion in favor of less disquieting thought.

Mrs. Ramshorn, also, was uncomfortable—too much so to be relieved by taking off her bonnet.   She felt, with no little soreness, that the rector was not with her in her depreciation of Wingfold.   She did her best to play the hostess, but the rector, while enjoying his dinner despite discomfort in the inward parts, was in a mood of silence altogether new both to himself and his companions.   Mrs. Bevis, however, talked away in a soft, continuous murmur.   She was a good-natured, gentle soul, without whose sort the world would be harder for many.   She did not contribute much to its positive enjoyment, but for my part, I can not help being grateful even to a cat that will condescend to purr to me. But she had not much mollifying influence on her hostess, who snarled, and judged, and condemned, nor seemed to enjoy her dinner the less.   When it was over, the ladies went to the drawing-room ; and the rector, finding his company unpleasant, drank but a week-day's allowance of wine, and went to have a look at his horses.

They neighed a welcome the moment his boot struck the stones of the yard, for they loved their master with all the love their strong, timid, patient hearts were as yet capable of.   Satisfied that they were comfortable, for he found them busy with a large feed of oats and chaff and Indian corn, he threw his arm over the back of his favorite, and stood, leaning against her for minutes, half dreaming, half thinking.   As long as they were busy, their munching and grinding soothed him—held him at least in quiescent mood ; the moment it ceased, he seemed to himself to wake up out of a dream.   In that dream, however, he had been more awake than any hour for long years, and had heard and seen many things.   He patted his mare lovingly, then, with a faint sense of rebuked injustice, went into the horse's stall, and patted and stroked him as he had never done before.

He went into the inn, and asked for a cup of tea. He would have had a sleep on Mrs. Pinks's sofa, as was his custom in his study—little study, alas, went on there !—but he had a call to make, and must rouse himself, and that was partly why he had sought the inn. For Mrs. Ramshorn's household was so well ordered that nothing was to be had out of the usual routine. It was like an American country inn, where, if you arrive after supper, you will most likely have to starve till next morning. Her servants, in fact, were her masters, and she dared not go into her own kitchen for a jug of hot water. Possibly it was her dethronement in her own house that made her, with a futile clutching after lost respect, so anxious to rule in the abbey church. As it was, although John Bevis and she had known each other long, and in some poor sense intimately, he would never in her house have dared ask for a cup of tea except it were on the table. But here was the ease of his inn, where the landlady herself was proud to get him what he wanted. She made the tea from her own caddy ; and when he had drunk three cups of it, washed his red face, and re-tied his white neck-cloth, he set out to make his call.

CHAPTER IX.

THE RECTORY DRAWING-ROOM.

The call was upon his curate. It was years since he had entered the rectory. The people who last occupied it, he had scarcely known, and even during its preparation for Wingfold he had not gone near the place. Yet of that house had been his dream as he stood in his mare's stall, and it was with a strange feeling he now approached it. Friends generally took the pleasanter way to the garden door, opening on the churchyard, but Mr. Bevis went round by the lane to the more public entrance.

All his years with his first wife had been spent in that house. She was delicate when he married her, and soon grew sickly and suffering. One after another her children

died as babies. At last came one who lived, and then the
mother began to die. She was one of those lowly women
who apply the severity born of their creed to themselves,
and spend only the love born of the indwelling Spirit upon
their neighbors. She was rather melancholy, but hoped as
much as she could, and when she could not hope did not
stand still, but walked on in the dark. I think when the
sun rises upon them, some people will be astonished to find
how far they have got in the dark.

Her husband, without verifying for himself one of the
things it was his business to teach others, was yet held in
some sort of communion with sacred things by his love for
his suffering wife, and his admiration of her goodness and
gentleness. He had looked up to her, though several
years younger than himself, with something of the same
reverence with which he had regarded his mother, a women
with an element of greatness in her. It was not possible
he should ever have adopted her views, or in any active
manner allied himself with the school whose doctrines she
accepted as the logical embodiment of the gospel, but there
was in him all the time a vague something that was not far
from the kingdom of heaven. Some of his wife's friends
looked upon him as a wolf in the sheepfold ; he was no wolf,
he was only a hireling. Any neighborhood might have
been the better for having such a man as he for the parson
of the parish—only, for one commissioned to be in the
world as he was in the world !—why he knew more about
the will of God as to a horse's legs, than as to the heart
of a man. As he drew near the house, the older and tenderer time came to meet him, and the spirit of his suffering,
ministering wife seemed to overshadow him. Two tears
grew half-way into his eyes :—they were a little bloodshot,
but kind, true eyes. He was not sorry he had married
again, for he and his wife were at peace with each other,
but he had found that the same part of his mind would not
serve to think of the two : they belonged to different zones
of his unexplored world. For one thing, his present wife
looked up to him with perfect admiration, and he, knowing
his own poverty, rather looked down upon her in consequence, though in a loving, gentle, and gentlemanlike way.

He was shown into the same room, looking out on the
churchyard, where in the first months of his married life, he
sat and heard his wife sing her few songs, accompanying
them on the little piano he had saved hard to buy for her,

until she made him love them. It had lasted only through those few months ; after her first baby died, she rarely sang. But all the colors and forms of the room were different, and that made it easier to check the lump rising in his throat. It was the faith of his curate that had thus set his wife before him, although the two would hardly have agreed in any confession narrower than the Apostles' creed.

When Wingfold entered the room, the rector rose, went halfway to meet him, and shook hands with him heartily. They seated themselves, and a short silence followed. But the rector knew it was his part to speak.

"I was in church this morning," he said, with a half-humorous glance right into the clear gray eyes of his curate.

"So my wife tells me," returned Wingfold with a smile.

"You didn't know it then?" rejoined the rector, with now an almost quizzical glance, in which hovered a little doubt. "I thought you were preaching at me all the time."

"God forbid ! " said the curate ; "I was not aware of your presence. I did not even know you were in the town yesterday."

"You must have had some one in your mind's eye. No man could speak as you did this morning, who addressed mere abstract humanity."

"I will not say that individuals did not come up before me ; how can a man help it where he knows every body in his congregation more or less? But I give you my word, sir, I never thought of you."

"Then you might have done so with the greatest pro-priety," returned the rector. "My conscience sided with you all the time. You found me out. I've got a bit of the muscle they call a heart left in me yet, though it *has* got rather leathery.—But what do they mean when they say you are setting the parish by the ears?"

"I don't know, sir. I have heard of no quarreling. I have made some enemies, but they are not very dangerous, and I hope not very bitter ones ; and I have made many more friends, I am sure."

"What they tell me is, that your congregation is divided —that they take sides for and against you, which is a most undesirable thing, surely ! "

"It is indeed ; and yet it may be a thing that, for a time, can not be helped. Was there ever a man with the cure of souls, concerning whom there has not been more or less of such division ? But, if you will have patience with me, sir, I am bold to say, believing in the force and final victory of the truth, there will be more unity by and by."

"I don't doubt it.   But come now!—you are a thoroughly good fellow—that, a blind horse could see in the dimmits—and I'm accountable for the parish—couldn't you draw it a little milder, you know? couldn't you make it just a little less peculiar—only the way of putting it, I mean—so that it should look a little more like what they have been used to? I'm only suggesting the thing, you know—dictating nothing, on my soul, Mr. Wingfold.   I am sure that, whatever you do, you will act according to your own conscience, otherwise I should not venture to say a word, lest I should lead you wrong."

"If you will allow me," said the curate, "I will tell you my whole story; and then if you should wish it, I will resign my curacy, without saying a word more than that my rector thinks it better.   Neither in private shall I make a single remark in a different spirit."

"Let me hear," said the rector.

"Then if you will please take this chair, that I may know that I am not wearying you bodily at least."

The rector did as he was requested, laid his head back, crossed his legs, and folded his hands over his worn waist-coat : he was not one of the neat order of parsons ; he had a not unwholesome disregard of his outermost man, and did not know when he was shabby.   Without an atom of pomposity or air rectorial, he settled himself to listen.

Condensing as much as he could, Wingfold told him how through great doubt, and dismal trouble of mind, he had come to hope in God, and to see that there was no choice for a man but to give himself, heart, and soul, and body, to the love, and will, and care of the Being who had made him. He could no longer, he said, regard his profession as any thing less than a call to use every means and energy at his command for the rousing of men and women from that spiritual sleep and moral carelessness in which he had him-self been so lately sunk.

"I don't want to give up my curacy," he concluded. "Still less do I want to leave Glaston, for there are here some whom I teach and some who teach me.   In all that has given ground for complaint, I have seemed to myself to be but following the dictates of common sense ; if you think me wrong, I have no justification to offer.   We both love God,——"

"How do you know that?" interrupted the rector. "I wish you could make me sure of that."

"I do, I know I do," said the curate earnestly. "I can say no more."

"My dear fellow, I haven't the merest shadow of a doubt of it," returned the rector, smiling. "What I wished was, that you could make me sure *I* do."

"Pardon me, my dear sir, but, judging from sore experience, if I could I would rather make you doubt it; the doubt, even if an utter mistake, would in the end be so much more profitable than any present conviction."

"You have your wish, then, Wingfold: I doubt it very much," replied the rector. "I must go home and think about it all. You shall hear from me in a day or two."

As he spoke Mr. Bevis rose, and stood for a moment like a man greatly urged to stretch his arms and legs. An air of uneasiness pervaded his whole appearance.

"Will you not stop and take tea with us?" said the curate. "My wife will be disappointed if you do not. You have been good to her for twenty years, she says."

"She makes an old man of me," returned the rector musingly. "I remember her such a tiny thing in a white frock and curls. Tell her what we have been talking about, and beg her to excuse me. I *must* go home."

He took his hat from the table, shook hands with Wingfold, and walked back to the inn. There he found his horses bedded, and the hostler away. His coachman was gone too, nobody knew whither.

To sleep at the inn would have given pointed offense, but he would rather have done so than go back to the Manor House to hear his curate abused. With the help of the barmaid, he put the horses to the carriage himself, and to the astonishment of Mrs. Ramshorn and his wife, drew up at the door of the Manor House.

Expostulation on the part of the former was vain. The latter made none: it was much the same to Mrs. Bevis where she was, so long as she was with her husband. Indeed few things were more pleasant to her than sitting in the carriage alone, contemplating the back of Mr. Bevis on the box, and the motion of his elbows as he drove. Mrs. Ramshorn received their adieux very stiffly, and never after mentioned the rector without adding the epithet, "poor man!"

Mrs. Bevis enjoyed the drive; Mr. Bevis did not. The

doubt was growing stronger and stronger all the way, that he had not behaved like a gentleman in his relation to the head of the church. He had naturally, as I have already shown, a fine, honorable, boyish if not childlike nature ; and the eyes of his mind were not so dim with good living as one might have feared from the look of those in his head : in the glass of loyalty he now saw himself a defaulter ; in the scales of honor he weighed and found himself wanting. Of true discipleship was not now the question : he had not behaved like an honorable gentleman to Jesus Christ. It was only in a spasm of terror St. Peter had denied him : John Bevis had for nigh forty years been taking his pay, and for the last thirty at least had done nothing in return. Either Jesus Christ did not care, and then what was the church ?—what the whole system of things called Christianity ?—or he did care, and what then was John Bevis in the eyes of his Master ? When they reached home, he went neither to the stable nor the study, but, without even lighting a cigar, walked out on the neighboring heath, where he found the universe rather gray about him. When he returned he tried to behave as usual, but his wife saw that he scarcely ate at supper, and left half of his brandy and water. She set it down to the annoyance the curate had caused him, and wisely forbore troubling him with questions.

CHAPTER X.

MR. DRAKE'S ARBOR.

WHILE the curate was preaching that same Sunday morning, in the cool cavernous church, with its great lights overhead, Walter Drake—the old minister, he was now called by his disloyal congregation—sat in a little arbor looking out on the river that flowed through the town to the sea. Green grass went down from where he sat to the very water's brink. It was a spot the old man loved, for there his best thoughts came to him. There was in him a good deal of the stuff of which poets are made, and since trouble overtook him, the river had more and more gathered to itself the aspect of that in the Pilgrim's Progress ; and

often, as he sat thus almost on its edge, he fancied himself
waiting the welcome summoms to go home. It was a tidal
river, with many changes. Now it flowed with a full, calm
current, conquering the tide, like life sweeping death with
it down into the bosom of the eternal. Now it seemed to
stand still, as if aghast at the inroad of the awful thing ;
and then the minister would bethink himself that it was the
tide of the eternal rising in the narrow earthly channel :
men, he said to himself, called it *death*, because they did
not know what it was, or the loveliness of its quickening
energy. It fails on their sense by the might of its grand
excess, and they call it by the name of its opposite. A
weary and rather disappointed pilgrim, he thus comforted
himself as he sat.

There a great salmon rose and fell, gleaming like a bolt
of silver in the sun ! There a little waterbeetle scurried
along after some invisible prey. The blue smoke of his pipe
melted in the Sabbath air. The softened sounds of a singing congregation came across gardens and hedges to his
ear. They sang with more energy than grace, and, not for
the first time, he felt they did. Were they indeed singing
to the Lord, he asked himself, or only to the idol Custom ?
A silence came : the young man in the pulpit was giving out
his text, and the faces that had turned themselves up to
Walter Drake as flowers to the sun, were now all turning to
the face of him they had chosen in his stead, " to minister
to them in holy things." He took his pipe from his mouth,
and sat motionless, with his eyes fixed on the ground.

But why was he not at chapel himself ? Could it be that
he yielded to temptation, actually preferring his clay pipe
and the long glide of the river, to the worship, and the
hymns and the sermon ? Had there not been a time when
he judged that man careless of the truth who did not go to
the chapel, and that man little better who went to the
church ? Yet there he sat on a Sunday morning, the church
on one side of him and the chapel on the other, smoking his
pipe ! His daughter was at the chapel ; she had taken
Ducky with her ; the dog lay in the porch waiting for them ;
the cat thought too much of herself to make friends with
her master ; he had forgotten his New Testament on the
study table ; and now he had let his pipe out.

He was not well, it is true, but he was well enough to have
gone. Was he too proud to be taught where he had been
a teacher ? or was it that the youth in his place taught there

doctrines which neither they nor their fathers had known? It could not surely be from resentment that they had super-annuated him in the prime of his old age, with a pared third of his late salary, which nothing but honesty in respect to the small moneys he owed could have prevented him from refusing!

In truth it was impossible the old minister should have any great esteem for the flashy youth, proud of his small Latin and less Greek, a mere unit of the hundreds whom the devil of ambition drives to preaching; one who, whether the doctrines he taught were in the New Testament or not, certainly never found them there, being but the merest dis-ciple of a disciple of a disciple, and fervid in words of which he perceived scarce a glimmer of the divine purport. At the same time, he might have seen points of resemblance between his own early history and that of the callow chirper of divinity now holding forth from his pulpit, which might have tended to mollify his judgment with sympathy.

His people had behaved ill to him, and he could not say he was free from resentment or pride, but he did make for them what excuse lay in the fact that the congregation had been dwindling ever since the curate at the abbey-church began to speak in such a strange outspoken fashion. There now was a right sort of man! he said to himself. No attempted oratory with him! no prepared surprises! no playhouse tricks! no studied graces in wafture of hands and upheaved eyes! And yet at moments when he became possessed with his object rather than subject, every inch of him seemed alive. He was odd—very odd; perhaps he was crazy—but at least he was honest. He had heard him him-self, and judged him well worth helping to what was better, for, alas! notwithstanding the vigor of his preaching, he did not appear to have himself discovered as yet the treasure hid in the field. He was, nevertheless, incomparably the superior of the young man whom, expecting him to *draw*, the deacons of his church, with the members behind them, had substituted for himself, who had for more than fifteen years ministered to them the bread of life.

Bread!—Yes, I think it might honestly be called bread that Walter Drake had ministered. It had not been free from chalk or potatoes: bits of shell and peel might have been found in it, with an occasional bit of dirt, and a hair or two; yes, even a little alum, and that is *bad*, because it tends to destroy, not satisfy the hunger. There was sawdust in it, and parchment-dust, and lumber-dust ; it was ill salted, badly baked, sad ; sometimes it was blue-moldy, and sometimes even maggoty ; but the mass of it was honest flour, and those who did not recoil from the look of it, or recognize the presence of the variety of foreign matter, could live upon it, in a sense, up to a certain pitch of life. But a great deal of it was not of his baking at all—he had been merely the distributor—crumbling down other bakers' loaves and making them up again in his own shapes. In his declining years, however, he had been really beginning to learn the business. Only, in his congregation were many who not merely preferred bad bread of certain kinds, but were incapable of digesting any of high quality.

He would have gone to chapel that morning had the young man been such as he could respect. Neither his doctrine, nor the behavior of the church to himself, would have kept him away. Had he followed his inclination he would have gone to the church, only that would have looked spiteful. His late congregation would easily excuse his non-attendance with them ; they would even pitifully explain to each other why he could not appear just yet ; but to go to church would be in their eyes unpardonable—a declaration of a war of revenge.

There was, however, a reason besides, why Mr. Drake could not go to church that morning, and if not a more serious, it was a much more painful one. Some short time before he had any ground to suspect that his congregation was faltering in its loyalty to him, his daughter had discovered that the chapel butcher, when he sent a piece of meat, invariably charged for a few ounces beyond the weight delivered. Now Mr. Drake was a man of such honesty that all kinds of cheating, down to the most respectable, were abominable to him ; that the man was a professor of religion made his conduct unpardonable in his eyes, and that he was one of his own congregation rendered it insupportable. Having taken pains to satisfy himself of the fact, he declined to deal with him any further, and did not spare to tell him why. The man was far too dishonest to profit by the rebuke save in circumspection and cunning, was revengeful in proportion to the justice of the accusation, and of course brought his influence, which was not small, to bear upon the votes of the church-members in respect of the pastorate.

Had there been another butcher in connection with the

chapel, Mr. Drake would have turned to him, but as there was not, and they could not go without meat, he had to betake himself to the principal butcher in the place, who was a member of the Church of England. Soon after his troubles commenced, and before many weeks were over he saw plainly enough that he must either resign altogether, and go out into the great world of dissent in search of some pastorless flock that might vote him their crook, to be guided by him whither they wanted to go, and whither most of them believed they knew the way as well as he, or accept the pittance offered him. This would be to retire from the forefront of the battle, and take an undistinguished place in the crowd of mere camp-followers ; but, for the sake of honesty, as I have already explained, and with the hope that it might be only for a brief season, he had chosen the latter half of the alternative. And truly it was a great relief not to have to grind out of his poor, weary, groaning mill the two inevitable weekly sermons—labor sufficient to darken the face of nature to the conscientious man. For his people thought themselves intellectual, and certainly were critical. Mere edification in holiness was not enough for them. A large infusion of some polemic element was necessary to make the meat savory and such as their souls loved. Their ambition was not to grow in grace, but in social influence and regard—to glorify their dissent, not the communion of saints. Upon the chief corner-stone they would build their stubble of paltry religionism ; they would set up their ragged tent in the midst of the eternal temple, careless how it blocked up window and stair.

Now last week Mr. Drake had requested his new butcher to send his bill—with some little anxiety, because of the sudden limitation of his income ; but when he saw it he was filled with horror. Amounting only to a very few pounds, causes had come together to make it a large one in comparison with the figures he was accustomed to see. Always feeding some of his flock, he had at this time two sickly, nursing mothers who drew their mortal life from his kitchen ; and, besides, the doctor had, some time ago, ordered a larger amount of animal food for the little Amanda. In fine, the sum at the bottom of that long slip of paper, with the wood-cut of a prize ox at the top of it, small as he would have thought it at one period of his history, was greater than he could imagine how to pay ; and if he went to church, it would be to feel the eye of the butcher and not that of the curate upon him all the time. It was a dismay, a horror to him to have an account rendered which he could not settle, and especially from his new butcher, after he had so severely rebuked the old one. Where was the mighty difference in honesty between himself and the offender? the one claimed for meat he had not sold, the other ordered that for which he could not pay! Would not Mr. Jones imagine he had left his fellow-butcher and come to him because he had run up a large bill for which he was unable to write a check? This was that over which the spirit of the man now brooded by far the most painfully; this it was that made him leave his New Testament in the study, let his pipe out, and look almost lovingly upon the fast-flowing river, because it was a symbol of death.

He had chosen preaching as a profession, just as so many take orders—with this difference from a large proportion of such, that he had striven powerfully to convince himself that he trusted in the merits of the Redeemer. Had he not in this met with tolerable success, he would not have yielded to the wish of his friends and left his father's shop in his native country-town for a dissenting college in the neighborhood of London. There he worked well, and became a good scholar, learning to read in the true sense of the word, that is, to try the spirits as he read. His character, so called, was sound, and his conscience, if not sensitive, was firm and regnant. But he was injured both spiritually and morally by some of the instructions there given. For one of the objects held up as duties before him, was to become capable of rendering himself *acceptable* to a congregation.

Most of the students were but too ready to regard, or at least to treat this object as the first and foremost of duties. The master-duty of devotion to Christ, and obedience to every word that proceeded out of His mouth, was very much treated as a thing understood, requiring little enforcement; while, the main thing demanded of them being sermons in some sense their own—honey culled at least by their own bees, and not bought in jars, much was said about the plan and composition of sermons, about style and elocution, and action—all plainly and confessedly, with a view to pulpit-*success*—the lowest of all low successes, and the most worldly.

These instructions Walter Drake accepted as the wisdom of the holy serpent—devoted large attention to composition,

labored to form his style on the *best models*, and before beginning to write a sermon, always heated the furnace of production with fuel from some exciting or suggestive author :
it would be more correct to say, fed the mill of composition
from some such source ; one consequence of all which was,
that when at last, after many years, he did begin to develop
some individuality, he could not, and never did shake himself free of those weary models ; his thoughts, appearing in
clothes which were not made for them, wore always a certain stiffness and unreality which did not by nature belong
to them, blunting the impressions which his earnestness and
sincerity did notwithstanding make.

Determined to *succeed*, he cultivated eloquence also—
what he supposed eloquence, that is, being, of course, merely
elocution, to attain the right gestures belonging to which
he looked far more frequently into his landlady's mirror,
than for his spiritual action into the law of liberty.   He
had his reward in the success he sought.   But I must make
haste, for the story of worldly success is always a mean tale.
In a few years, and for not a few after, he was a popular
preacher in one of the suburbs of London—a good deal
sought after, and greatly lauded.   He lived in comfort,
indulged indeed in some amount of show ; married a widow
with a large life-annuity, which between them they spent
entirely, and that not altogether in making friends with
everlasting habitations ; in a word, gazed out on the social
landscape far oftener than lifted his eyes to the hills.

After some ten or twelve years, a change began.   They
had three children ; the two boys, healthy and beautiful,
took scarlatina and died ; the poor, sickly girl wailed on.
His wife, who had always been more devoted to her children than her husband, pined, and died also.   Her money
went, if not with her, yet away from him.   His spirits began
to fail him, and his small, puny, peaking daughter did not
comfort him much.   He was capable of true, but not yet of
pure love ; at present his love was capricious.   Little Dora
—a small *Dorothy* indeed in his estimation—had always
been a better child than either of her brothers, but he loved
them the more that others admired them, and her the
less that others pitied her : he did try to love her,
for there was a large element of justice in his nature.
This, but for his being so much occupied with *making himself acceptable* to his congregation, would have given him a
leadership in the rising rebellion against a theology which

crushed the hearts of men by attributing injustice to their God. As it was, he lay at anchor, and let the tide rush past him.

Further change followed—gradual, but rapid. His congregation began to discover that he was not the man he had been. They complained of lack of variety in his preaching ; said he took it too easy; did not study his sermons sufficiently; often spoke extempore, which was a poor compliment to *them ;* did not visit with impartiality, and indeed had all along favored the carriage people. There was a party in the church which had not been cordial to him from the first ; partly from his fault, partly from theirs, he had always made them feel they were of the lower grade ; and from an increase of shops in the neighborhood, this party was now gathering head. Their leaders went so far at length as to hint at a necessity for explanation in regard to the accounts of certain charities administered by the pastor. In these, unhappily, *lacunæ* were patent. In his troubles the pastor had grown careless. But it was altogether to his own loss, for not merely had the money been spent with a rigidity of uprightness, such as few indeed of his accusers exercised in their business affairs, but he had in his disbursements exceeded the contribution committed to his charge. Confident, however, in his position, and much occupied with other thoughts, he had taken no care to set down the particulars of his expenditure, and his enemies did not fail to hint a connection between this fact and the loss of his wife's annuity. Worst of all, doubts of his orthodoxy began to be expressed by the more ignorant, and harbored without examination by the less ignorant.

All at once he became aware of the general disloyalty of his flock, and immediately resigned. Scarcely had he done so when he was invited to Glaston, and received with open arms. There he would heal his wounds, and spend the rest of his days in peace. " He caught a slip or two " in descending, but soon began to find the valley of humiliation that wholesome place which all true pilgrims have ever declared it. Comparative retirement, some sense of lost labor, some suspicion of the worth of the ends for which he had spent his strength, a waking desire after the God in whom he had vaguely believed all the time he was letting the dust of paltry accident inflame his eyes, blistering and deadening his touch with the efflorescent crusts and agaric tumors upon the dry bones of theology, gilding the vane of his chapel instead of cleansing its porch and its floor—these all favored the birth in his mind of the question, whether he had ever entered in at the straight gate himself, or had not merely been standing by its side calling to others to enter in. Was it even as well as this with him? Had he not been more intent on gathering a wretched flock within the rough, wool-stealing, wind-sifting, beggarly hurdles of his church, than on housing true men and women safe in the fold of the true Shepherd? Feeding troughs for the sheep there might be many in the fields, and they might or might not be presided over by servants of the true Shepherd, but the fold they were not! He grew humble before the Master, and the Master began to lord it lovingly over him. He sought His presence, and found Him; began to think less of books and rabbis, yea even, for the time, of Paul and Apollos and Cephas, and to pore and ponder over the living tale of the New Covenant; began to feel that the Lord meant whàt He said, and that His apostles also meant what He said; forgot Calvin a good deal, outgrew the influences of Jonathan Edwards, and began to understand Jesus Christ.

Few sights can be lovelier than that of a man who, having rushed up the staircase of fame in his youth—what matter whether the fame of a paltry world, or a paltry sect of that world!—comes slowly, gently, graciously down in his old age, content to lose that which he never had, and careful only to be honest at last. It had not been so with Walter Drake. He had to come down first to begin to get the good of it, but once down, it was not long ere he began to go up a very different stair indeed. A change took place in him which turned all aims, all efforts, all victories of the world, into the merest, most poverty-stricken trifling. He had been a tarrer and smearer, a marker and shearer of sheep, rather than a pastor; but now he recognized the rod and leaned on the staff of the true Shepherd Who feeds both shepherds and sheep. Hearty were the thanks he offered that he had been staid in his worse than foolish career.

Since then, he had got into a hollow in the valley, and at this moment, as he sat in his summer-house, was looking from a verge abrupt into what seemed a bottomless gulf of humiliation. For his handsome London house, he had little better than a cottage, in which his study was not a quarter of the size of the one he had left; he had sold two-thirds of his books; for three men and four women servants, he had but one old woman and his own daughter to do the work of the house; for all quadrupedal menie, he had but a nondescript canine and a contemptuous feline foundling; from a devoted congregation of comparatively educated people, he had sunk to one in which there was not a person of higher standing than a tradesman, and that congregation had now rejected him as not up to their mark, turning him off to do his best with fifty pounds a year. He had himself heard the cheating butcher remark in the open street that it was quite enough, and more than ever his Master had. But all these things were as nothing in his eyes beside his inability to pay Mr. Jones's bill. He had outgrown his former self, but this kind of misery it would be but deeper degradation to outgrow. All before this had been but humiliation; this was shame. Now first he knew what poverty was! Had God forgotten him? That could not be! that which could forget could not be God. Did he not care then that such things should befall his creatures? Were they but trifles in his eyes? He ceased thinking, gave way to the feeling that God dealt hardly with him, and sat stupidly indulging a sense of grievance—with self-pity, than which there is scarce one more childish or enfeebling in the whole circle of the emotions. Was this what God had brought him nearer to Himself for? was this the end of a ministry in which he had, in some measure at least, denied himself and served God and his fellow? He could bear any thing but shame! That too could he have borne had he not been a teacher of religion—one whose failure must brand him a hypocrite. How mean it would sound— what a reproach to *the cause*, that the congregational minister had run up a bill with a church-butcher which he was unable to pay! It was the shame—the shame he could not bear! Ought he to have been subjected to it?

A humbler and better mood slowly dawned with unconscious change, and he began to ponder with himself wherein he had been misusing the money given him: either he had been misusing it, or God had not given him enough, seeing it would not reach the end of his needs; but he could think only of the poor he had fed, and the child he had adopted, and surely God would overlook those points of extravagance. Still, if he had not the means, he had not the right to do such things. It might not in itself be wrong, but in respect of him it was as dishonest as if he had spent the money on himself—not to mention that it was a thwarting of the counsel of God, who, if He had meant them to be so aided, would have sent him the money to spend upon them honestly. His one excuse was that he could not have foreseen how soon his income was going to shrink to a third. In future he would withhold his hand. But surely he might keep the child? Nay, having once taken her in charge, he must keep the child. It was a comfort, there could be no doubt about that. God had money enough, and certainly He would enable him to do that! Only, why then did He bring him to such poverty?

So round in his mill he went, round and round again, and back to the old evil mood. Either there was no God, or he was a hard-used man, whom his Master did not mind bringing to shame before his enemies! He could not tell which would triumph the more—the church-butcher over dissent, or the chapel-butcher over the church-butcher, and the pastor who had rebuked him for dishonesty! His very soul was disquieted within him. He rose at last with a tear trickling down his cheek, and walked to and fro in his garden.

Things went on nevertheless as if all was right with the world. The Lythe flowed to the sea, and the silver-mailed salmon leaped into the more limpid air. The sun shone gracious over all his kingdom, and his little praisers were loud in every bush. The primroses, earth-born suns, were shining about in every border. The sound of the great organ came from the grand old church, and the sound of many voices from the humble chapel. Only, where was the heart of it all?

CHAPTER XI.

THE CHAMBER AT THE COTTAGE.

MEANWHILE Faber was making a round, with the village of Owlkirk for the end of it. Ere he was half-way thither, his groom was tearing after him upon Niger, with a message from Mrs. Puckridge, which, however, did not overtake him. He opened the cottage-door, and walked up stairs, expecting to find his patient weak, but in the fairest of ways to recover speedily. What was his horror to see her landlady weeping and wringing her hands over the bed, and find the lady lying motionless, with bloodless lips and distended nostrils—to all appearance dead ! Pillows, sheets, blankets, looked one mass of red. The bandage had shifted while she slept, and all night her blood had softly flowed. Hers was one of those peculiar organizations in which, from some cause but dimly conjectured as yet, the blood once set flowing will flow on to death, and even the tiniest wound is hard to stanch. Was the lovely creature gone ? In her wrist he could discern no pulse. He folded back the bed-clothes, and laid his ear to her heart. His whole soul listened. Yes ; there was certainly the faintest flutter. He watched a moment : yes ; he could see just the faintest tremor of the diaphragm.

"Run," he cried, "—for God's sake run and bring me a jug of hot water, and two or three basins. There is just a chance yet ! If you make haste, we may save her. Bring me a syringe. If you haven't one, run from house to house till you get one. Her life depends on it." By this time he was shouting after the hurrying landlady.

In a minute or two she returned.

"Have you got the syringe ?" he cried, the moment he heard her step.

To his great relief she had. He told her to wash it out thoroughly with the hot water, unscrew the top, and take out the piston. While giving his directions, he unbound the arm, enlarged the wound in the vein longitudinally, and re-bound the arm tight below the elbow, then quickly opened a vein of his own, and held the syringe to catch the spout that followed. When it was full, he replaced the piston, telling Mrs. Puckridge to put her thumb on his wound, turned the point of the syringe up and drove a little out to get rid of the air, then, with the help of a probe, inserted the nozzle into the wound, and gently forced in the blood. That done, he placed his own thumbs on the two wounds, and made the woman wash out the syringe in clean hot water. Then he filled it as before, and again forced its contents into the lady's arm. This process he went through repeatedly. Then, listening, he found her heart beating quite perceptibly, though irregularly. Her breath was faintly coming and going. Several times more he repeated the strange dose, then ceased, and was occupied in binding up her arm, when she gave a great shuddering

sigh.   By the time he had finished, the pulse was percepti-
ble at her wrist.   Last of all he bound up his own wound,
from which had escaped a good deal beyond what he had
used.   While thus occupied, he turned sick, and lay down
on the floor.   Presently, however, he grew able to crawl
from the room, and got into the garden at the back of the
house, where he walked softly to the little rude arbor at the
end of it, and sat down as if in a dream.   But in the dream
his soul felt wondrously awake.   He had been tasting death
from the same cup with the beautiful woman who lay there,
coming alive with his life.   A terrible weight was heaved
from his bosom.   If she had died, he would have felt, all
his life long, that he had sent one of the loveliest of
Nature's living dreams back to the darkness and the worm,
long years before her time, and with the foam of the cup of
life yet on her lips.   Then a horror seized him at the pre-
sumptuousness of the liberty he had taken.   What if the
beautiful creature would rather have died than have the
blood of a man, one she neither loved nor knew, in her
veins, and coursing through her very heart !   She must
never know it.

   " I am very grateful," he said to himself ; then smiled and
wondered to whom he was grateful.

   " How the old stamps and colors come out in the brain
when one least expects it ! " he said.   " What I meant was,
How glad I am ! "

   Honest as he was, he did not feel called upon to examine
whether *glad* was really the word to represent the feeling
which the thought of what he had escaped, and of the
creature he had saved from death, had sent up into his consciousness.   Glad he was indeed ! but was there not
mingled with his gladness a touch of something else, very
slight, yet potent enough to make him mean *grateful* when
the word broke from him ? and if there was such a something, where did it come from ?   Perhaps if he had caught
and held the feeling, and submitted it to such a searching
scrutiny as he was capable of giving it, he might have
doubted whether any mother-instilled superstition ever
struck root so deep as the depth from which that seemed at
least to come.   I merely suggest it.   The feeling was a
faint and poor one, and I do not care to reason from it.   I
would not willingly waste upon small arguments, when I see
more and more clearly that our paltriest faults and dishon-
esties need one and the same enormous cure.

But indeed never had Faber less time to examine himself than now, had he been so inclined. With that big wound in it, he would as soon have left a shell in the lady's chamber with the fuse lighted, as her arm to itself. He did not leave the village all day. He went to see another patient in it, and one on its outskirts, but he had his dinner at the little inn where he put up Ruber, and all night long he sat by the bedside of his patient. There the lovely white face, blind like a statue that never had eyes, and the perfect arm, which now and then, with a restless, uneasy, feeble toss, she would fling over the counterpane, the arm he had to watch as the very gate of death, grew into his heart. He dreaded the moment when she would open her eyes, and his might no longer wander at will over her countenance. Again and again in the night he put a hand under her head, and held a cooling draught to her lips ; but not even when she drank did her eyes open : like a child too weak to trust itself, therefore free of all anxiety and fear, she took whatever came, questioning nothing. He sat at the foot of the bed, where, with the slightest movement, he could, through the opening of the curtains, see her perfectly.

By some change of position, he had unknowingly drawn one of them back a little from between her and him, as he sat thinking about her. The candle shone full upon his face, but the other curtain was between the candle and his patient. Suddenly she opened her eyes.

A dream had been with her, and she did not yet know that it was gone. She could hardly be said to *know* any thing. Fever from loss of blood ; uneasiness, perhaps, from the presence in her system of elements elsewhere fashioned and strangely foreign to its economy ; the remnants of sleep and of the dream ; the bewilderment of sudden awaking— all had combined to paralyze her judgment, and give her imagination full career. When she opened her eyes, she saw a beautiful face, and nothing else, and it seemed to her itself the source of the light by which she saw it. Her dream had been one of great trouble ; and when she beheld the shining countenance, she thought it was the face of the Saviour : he was looking down upon her heart, which he held in his hand, and reading all that was written there. The tears rushed to her eyes, and the next moment Faber saw two fountains of light and weeping in the face which had been but as of loveliest marble. The curtain fell between them, and the lady thought the vision had vanished.

The doctor came softly through the dusk to her bedside. He felt her pulse, looked to the bandage on her arm, gave her something to drink, and left the room. Presently Mrs. Puckridge brought her some beef tea.

CHAPTER XII.

THE MINISTER'S GARDEN.

Up and down the garden paced the pastor, stung by the gadflies of debt. If he were in London he could. sell his watch and seals; he had a ring somewhere, too—an antique, worth what now seemed a good deal; but his wife had given him both. Besides, it would cost so much to go to London, and he had no money. Mr. Drew, doubtless, would lend him what he wanted, but he could not bring himself to ask him. If he parted with them in Glaston, they would be put in the watchmaker's window, and that would be a scandal—with the Baptists making head in the very next street! For, notwithstanding the heartless way in which the Congregationalists had treated him, theirs was the cause of scriptural Christianity, and it made him shudder to think of bringing the smallest discredit upon the denomination. The church-butcher was indeed a worse terror to him than Apollyon had been to Christian, for it seemed to his faithlessness that not even the weapon of All-prayer was equal to his discomfiture; nothing could render him harmless but the payment of his bill. He began to look back with something like horror upon the sermons he had preached on honesty; for how would his inability to pay his debts appear in the eyes of those who had heard them? Oh! why had he not paid for every thing as they had it? Then when the time came that he could not pay, they would only have had to go without, whereas now, there was the bill louring at the back of the want!

When Miss Drake returned from the chapel, she found her father leaning on the sun-dial, where she had left him. To all appearance he had not moved. He knew her step but did not stir.

"Father!" she said.

"It is a hard thing, my child," he responded, still without moving, "when the valley of Humiliation comes next the river Death, and no land of Beulah between! I had my good things in my youth, and now I have my evil things."

She laid her hand on his shoulder lovingly, tenderly, worshipfully, but did not speak.

"As you see me now, my Dorothy, my God's-gift, you would hardly believe your father was once a young and popular preacher, ha, ha! Fool that I was! I thought they prized my preaching, and loved me for what I taught them. I thought I was somebody! With shame I confess it! Who were they, or what was their judgment, to fool me in my own concerning myself! Their praise was indeed a fit rock for me to build my shame upon."

"But, father dear, what is even a sin when it is repented of?"

"A shame forever, my child. Our Lord did not cast out even an apostle for his conceit and self-sufficiency, but he let him fall."

"He has not let you fall, father?" said Dorothy, with tearful eyes.

"He is bringing my gray hairs with sorrow and shame to the grave, my child."

"Why, father!" cried the girl, shocked, as she well might be, at his words, "what have I done to make you say that?"

"Done, my darling! *you* done? You have done nothing but righteousness ever since you could do any thing! You have been like a mother to your old father. It is that bill! that horrid butcher's bill!"

Dorothy burst out laughing through her dismay, and wept and laughed together for more than a minute ere she could recover herself.

"Father! you dear father! you're too good to live! Why, there are forks and spoons enough in the house to pay that paltry bill!—not to mention the cream-jug which is, and the teapot which we thought was silver, because Lady Sykes gave it us. Why didn't you tell me what was troubling you, father dear?"

"I can't bear—I never *could* bear to owe money. I asked the man for his bill some time ago. I could have paid it then, though it wouldn't have left me a pound. The moment I looked at it, I felt as if the Lord had forsaken

me. It is easy for you to bear; you are not the one
accountable. I am. And if the pawnbroker or the silver-
smith does stand between me and absolute dishonesty, yet
to find myself in such a miserable condition, with next to
nothing between us and the workhouse, may well make me
doubt whether I have been a true servant of the Lord, for
surely such shall never be ashamed! During these last
days the enemy has even dared to tempt me with the
question, whether after all, these unbelievers may not be
right, and the God that ruleth in the earth a mere pro-
jection of what the conscience and heart bribe the imagination to construct for them!"

"I wouldn't think that before I was driven to it, father,"
said Dorothy, scarcely knowing what she said, for his
doubt shot a poisoned arrow of despair into the very heart
of her heart.

He, never doubting the security of his child's faith, had no
slightest suspicion into what a sore spot his words had carried torture. He did not know that the genius of doubt—
shall I call him angel or demon?—had knocked at her door,
had called through her window; that words dropped by
Faber, indicating that science was against all idea of a God,
and the confidence of their tone, had conjured up in her
bosom hollow fears, faint dismays, and stinging questions.
Ready to trust, and incapable of arrogance, it was hard for
her to imagine how a man like Mr. Faber, upright and kind
and self-denying, could say such things if he did not *know*
them true. The very word *science* appeared to carry an
awful authority. She did not understand that it was only
because science had never come closer to Him than the
mere sight of the fringe of the outermost folds of the taber-
nacle of His presence, that her worshipers dared assert
there was no God. She did not perceive that nothing ever
science could find, could possibly be the God of men; that
science is only the human reflex of truth, and that truth
itself can not be measured by what of it is reflected from the
mirror of the understanding. She did not see that no
incapacity of science to find God, even touched the matter
of honest men's belief that He made His dwelling with the
humble and contrite. Nothing she had learned from her
father either provided her with reply, or gave hope of finding argument of discomfiture; nothing of all that went on
at chapel or church seemed to have any thing to do with
the questions that presented themselves.

Such a rough shaking of so-called faith, has been of end-less service to many, chiefly by exposing the insecurity of all foundations of belief, save that which is discovered in digging with the spade of obedience. Well indeed is it for all honest souls to be thus shaken, who have been building upon doctrines concerning Christ, upon faith, upon exper-iences, upon any thing but Christ Himself, as revealed by Himself and His spirit to all who obey Him, and so reveal-ing the Father—a doctrine just as foolish as the rest to men like Faber, but the power of God and the wisdom of God to such who know themselves lifted out of darkness and an ever-present sense of something wrong—if it be only into twilight and hope.

Dorothy was a gift of God, and the trouble that gnawed at her heart she would not let out to gnaw at her father's.

"There's Ducky come to call us to dinner," she said, and rising, went to meet her.

"Dinner!" groaned Mr. Drake, and would have remained where he was. But for Dorothy's sake he rose and followed her, feeling almost like a repentant thief who had stolen the meal.

CHAPTER XIII.

THE HEATH AT NESTLEY.

On the Monday morning, Mr. Bevis's groom came to the rectory with a note for the curate, begging him and Mrs. Wingfold to dine at Nestley the same day if possible.

"I know," the rector wrote, "Monday is, or ought to be, an idle day with you, and I write instead of my wife, because I want to see you on business. I would have come to you, had I not had reasons for wishing to see you here rather than at Glaston. The earlier you can come and the longer you can stay the better, but you shall go as soon after an early dinner as you please. You are a bee and I am a drone. God bless you. JOHN BEVIS."

The curate took the note to his wife. Things were at once arranged, an answer of ready obedience committed to the groom, and Helen's pony-carriage ordered out.

The curate called every thing Helen's. He had a great contempt for the spirit of men who marry rich wives and then lord it over their money, as if they had done a fine thing in getting hold of it, and the wife had been but keeping it from its rightful owner. They do not know what a confession their whole bearing is, that, but for their wives' money, they would be but the merest, poorest nobodies. So small are they that even that suffices to make them feel big! But Helen did not like it, especially when he would ask her if he might have this or that, or do so and so. Any common man who heard him would have thought him afraid of his wife; but a large-hearted woman would at once have understood, as did Helen, that it all came of his fine sense of truth, and reality, and obligation. Still Helen would have had him forget all such matters in connection with her. They were one beyond obligation. She had given him herself, and what were bank-notes after that? But he thought of her always as an angel who had taken him in, to comfort, and bless, and cherish him with love, that he might the better do the work of his God and hers; therefore his obligation to her was his glory.

"Your ponies go splendidly to-day, Helen," he said, as admiringly he watched how her hands on the reins seemed to mold their movements.

They were the tiniest, daintiest things, of the smallest ever seen in harness, but with all the ways of big horses, therefore amusing in their very grace. They were the delight of the children of Glaston and the villages round.

"Why *will* you call them *my* ponies, Thomas?" returned his wife, just sufficiently vexed to find it easy to pretend to be cross. "I don't see what good I have got by marrying you, if every thing is to be mine all the same!"

"Don't be unreasonable, my Helen!" said the curate, looking into the lovely eyes whose colors seemed a little blown about in their rings. "Don't you see it is my way of feeling to myself how much, and with what a halo about them, they are mine? If I had bought them with my own money, I should hardly care for them. Thank God, they are *not* mine that way, or in any way like that way. *You* are mine, my life, and they are yours—mine therefore because they are about you like your clothes or your watch. They are mine as your handkerchief and your gloves are mine—through worshiping love. Listen to reason. If a thing is yours it is ten times more mine than if I had bought it, for, just because it is yours, I am able to possess it as the meek, and not the land-owners, inherit the earth. It makes *having* such a deep and high—indeed a perfect thing! I take pleasure without an atom of shame in every rich thing you have brought me. Do you think, if you died, and I carried your watch, I should ever cease to feel the watch was yours? Just so they are your ponies; and if you don't like me to say so, you can contradict me every time, you know, all the same."

"I know people will think I am like the lady we heard of the other day, who told her husband the sideboard was hers, not his. Thomas, I *hate* to look like the rich one, when all that makes life worth living for, or fit to be lived, was and is given me by you."

"No, no, no, my darling! don't say that; you terrify me. I was but the postman that brought you the good news."

"Well! and what else with me and the ponies and the money and all that? Did I make the ponies? Or did I even earn the money that bought them? It is only the money my father and brother have done with. Don't make me look as if I did not behave like a lady to my own husband, Thomas."

"Well, my beautiful, I'll make up for all my wrongs by ordering you about as if I were the Marquis of Saluzzo, and you the patient Grisel."

"I wish you would. You don't order me about half enough."

"I'll try to do better. You shall see."

Nestley was a lovely place, and the house was old enough to be quite respectable—one of those houses with a history and a growth, which are getting rarer every day as the ugly temples of mammon usurp their places. It was dusky, cool, and somber—a little shabby, indeed, which fell in harmoniously with its peculiar charm, and indeed added to it. A lawn, not immaculate of the sweet fault of daisies, sank slowly to a babbling little tributary of the Lythe, and beyond were fern-covered slopes, and heather, and furze, and pine-woods. The rector was a sensible Englishman, who objected to have things done after the taste of his gardener instead of his own. He loved grass like a village poet, and would have no flower-beds cut in his lawn. Neither would he have any flowers planted in the summer to be taken up again before the winter. He would have no cockney gardening about his place, he said. Perhaps that was partly why he never employed any but his old cottagers about the grounds ; and the result was that for half the show he had twice the loveliness. His ambition was to have every possible English garden flower.

As soon as his visitors arrived, he and his curate went away together, and Mrs. Wingfold was shown into the drawing-room, where was Mrs. Bevis with her knitting. A greater contrast than that of the two ladies then seated together in the long, low, dusky room, it were not easy to imagine. I am greatly puzzled to think what conscious good in life Mrs. Bevis enjoyed—just as I am puzzled to understand the eagerness with which horses, not hungry, and evidently in full enjoyment of the sun and air and easy exercise, will yet hurry to their stable the moment their heads are turned in the direction of them. Is it that they have no hope in the unknown, and then alone, in all the vicissitudes of their day, know their destination? Would but some good kind widow, of the same type with Mrs. Bevis, without children, tell me wherefore she is unwilling to die ! She has no special friend to whom she unbosoms herself—indeed, so far as any one knows, she has never had any thing of which to unbosom herself. She has no pet— dog or cat or monkey or macaw, and has never been seen to hug a child. She never reads poetry—I doubt if she knows more than the first line of *How doth*. She reads neither novels nor history, and looks at the newspaper as if the type were fly-spots. Yet there she sits smiling ! Why ! oh ! why ? Probably she does not know. Never did question, not to say doubt, cause those soft, square-ended fingers to move one atom less measuredly in the construction of Mrs. Bevis's muffetee, the sole knittable thing her nature seemed capable of. Never was sock seen on her needles ; the turning of the heel was too much for her. That she had her virtues, however, was plain from the fact that her servants staid with her years and years ; and I can, beside, from observation set down a few of them. She never asked her husband what he would have for dinner. When he was ready to go out with her, she was always ready too. She never gave one true reason, and kept back a truer—possibly there was not room for two thoughts at once in her brain. She never screwed down a dependent ; never kept small tradespeople waiting for their money ; never refused a reasonable request. In fact, she was a stuffed bag of virtues ; the bag was of no great size, but neither were the virtues insignificant. There are dozens of sorts of people I should feel a far stronger objection to living with ; but what puzzles me is how she contrives to live with herself, never questioning the comfort of the arrangement, or desiring that it should one day come to an end. Surely she must be deep, and know some secret !

For the other lady, Helen Lingard that was, she had since her marriage altered considerably in the right direction. She used to be a little dry, a little stiff, and a little stately. To the last I should be far from objecting, were it not that her stateliness was of the mechanical sort, belonging to the spine, and not to a soul uplift. Now it had left her spine and settled in a soul that scorned the low and loved the lowly. Her step was lighter, her voice more flexible, her laugh much merrier and more frequent, for now her heart was gay. Her husband praised God when he heard her laugh ; the laugh suggested the praise, for itself rang like praises. She would pull up her ponies in the middle of the street, and at word or sign, the carriage would be full of children. Whoever could might scramble in till it was full. At the least rudeness, the offender would be ordered to the pavement, and would always obey, generally weeping. She would drive two or three times up and down the street with her load, then turn it out, and take another, and another, until as many as she judged fit had had a taste of the pleasure. This she had learned from seeing a costermonger fill his cart with children, and push behind, while the donkey in front pulled them along the street, to the praise and glory of God.

She was overbearing in one thing, and that was submission. Once, when I was in her husband's study, she made a remark on something he had said or written, I forget what, for which her conscience of love immediately smote her. She threw herself on the floor, crept under the writing table at which he sat, and clasped his knees.

" I beg your pardon, husband," she said sorrowfully.

" Helen," he cried, laughing rather oddly, " you will make a consummate idiot of me before you have done."

" Forgive me," she pleaded.

" I can't forgive you. How can I forgive where there is positively nothing to be forgiven ? "

" I don't care what you say ; I know better; you *must* forgive me."

" Nonsense ! "

"Forgive me."

"Do get up. Don't be silly."

"Forgive me. I will lie here till you do."

"But your remark was perfectly true."

"It makes no difference. I ought not to have said it like that. Forgive me, or I will cry."

I will tell no more of it. Perhaps it is silly of me to tell any, but it moved me strangely.

I have said enough to show there was a contrast between the two ladies. As to what passed in the way of talk, that, from pure incapacity, I dare not attempt to report. I did hear them talk once, and they laughed too, but not one salient point could I lay hold of by which afterward to recall their conversation. Do I dislike Mrs. Bevis? Not in the smallest degree. I could read a book I loved in her presence. That would be impossible to me in the presence of Mrs. Ramshorn.

Mrs. Wingfold had developed a great faculty for liking people. It was quite a fresh shoot of her nature, for she had before been rather of a repellent disposition. I wish there were more, and amongst them some of the best of people, similarly changed. Surely the latter would soon be, if once they had a glimpse of how much the coming of the kingdom is retarded by defect of courtesy. The people I mean are slow to *like*, and until they come to *like*, they *seem* to dislike. I have known such whose manner was fit to imply entire disapprobation of the very existence of those upon whom they looked for the first time. They might then have been saying to themselves, "*I* would never have created such people!" Had I not known them, I could not have imagined them lovers of God or man, though they were of both. True courtesy, that is, courtesy born of a true heart, is a most lovely, and absolutely indispensable grace—one that nobody but a Christian can thoroughly develop. God grant us a "coming-on disposition," as Shakespeare calls it. Who shall tell whose angel stands nearer to the face of the Father? Should my brother stand lower in the social scale than I, shall I not be the more tender, and respectful, and self-refusing toward him, that God has placed him there who may all the time be greater than I? A year before, Helen could hardly endure doughy Mrs. Bevis, but now she had found something to like in her, and there was confidence and faith between them. So there they sat, the elder lady meandering on, and Helen, who had taken care to bring some work with her, every now and then casting a bright glance in her face, or saying two or three words with a smile, or asking some simple question. Mrs. Bevis talked chiefly of the supposed affairs and undoubted illness of Miss Meredith, concerning both of which rather strange reports had reached her.

Meantime the gentlemen were walking through the park in earnest conversation. They crossed the little brook and climbed to the heath on the other side. There the rector stood, and turning to his companion, said :

" It's rather late in the day for a fellow to wake up, ain't it, Wingfold ? You see I was brought up to hate fanaticism, and that may have blinded me to something you have seen and got a hold of. I wish I could just see what it is, but I never was much of a theologian. Indeed I suspect I am rather stupid in some things. But I would fain try to look my duty in the face. It's not for me to start up and teach the people, because I ought to have been doing it all this time : I've got nothing to teach them. God only knows whether I haven't been breaking every one of the commandments I used to read to them every Sunday."

" But God does know, sir," said the curate, with even more than his usual respect in his tone, " and that is well, for otherwise we might go on breaking them forever."

The rector gave him a sudden look, full in the face, but said nothing, seemed to fall a thinking, and for some time was silent.

" There's one thing clear," he resumed : " I've been taking pay, and doing no work. I used to think I was at least doing no harm—that I was merely using one of the privileges of my position : I not only paid a curate, but all the repair the church ever got was from me. Now, however, for the first time, I reflect that the money was not given me for that. Doubtless it has been all the better for my congregation, but that is only an instance of the good God brings out of evil, and the evil is mine still. Then, again, there's all this property my wife brought me : what have I done with that ? The kingdom of heaven has not come a hair's-breadth nearer for my being a parson of the Church of England ; neither are the people of England a shade the better that I am one of her land-owners. It is surely time I did something, Wingfold, my boy ! "

" I think it is, sir," answered the curate.

" Then, in God's name, what am I to do ? " returned the rector almost testily.

"Nobody can answer that question but yourself, sir," replied Wingfold.

"It's no use my trying to preach. I could not write a sermon if I took a month to it. If it were a paper on the management of a stable, now, I think I could write that—respectably. I know what I am about there. I could even write one on some of the diseases of horses and bullocks—but that's not what the church pays me for. There's one thing though—it comes over me strong that I should like to read prayers in the old place again. I want to pray, and I don't know how; and it seems as if I could shove in some of my own if I had them going through my head once again. I tell you what : we won't make any fuss about it—what's in a name ?—but from this day you shall be incumbent, and I will be curate. You shall preach—or what you please, and I shall read the prayers or not, just as you please. Try what you can make of me, Wingfold. Don't ask me to do what I can't, but help me to do what I can. Look here—here's what I've been thinking—it came to me last night as I was walking about here after coming from Glaston :—here, in this corner of the parish, we are a long way from church. In the village there, there is no place of worship except a little Methodist one. There isn't one of their—local preachers, I believe they call them—that don't preach a deal better than I could if I tried ever so much. It's vulgar enough sometimes, they tell me, but then they preach, and mean it. Now I might mean it, but I shouldn't preach ;—for what is it to people at work all the week to have a man read a sermon to them ? You might as well drive a nail by pushing it in with the palm of your hand. Those men use the hammer. Ill-bred, conceited fellows, some of them, I happen to know, but they know their business. Now why shouldn't I build a little place here on my own ground, and get the bishop to consecrate it ? I would read prayers for you in the abbey church in the morning, and then you would not be too tired to come and preach here in the evening. I would read the prayers here too, if you liked."

"I think your scheme delightful," answered the curate, after a moment's pause. "I would only venture to suggest one improvement—that you should not have your chapel consecrated. You will find it ever so much more useful. It will then be dedicated to the God of the whole earth, instead of the God of the Church of England."

"Why ! ain't they the same ?" cried the rector, half aghast, as he stopped and faced round on the curate.

" Yes," answered Wingfold ; " and all will be well when the Church of England really recognizes the fact. Meantime its idea of God is such as will not at all fit the God of the whole earth. And that is why she is in bondage. Except she burst the bonds of her own selfishness, she will burst her heart and go to pieces, as her enemies would have her. Every piece will be alive, though, I trust, more or less."

" I don't understand you," said the rector. " What has all that to do with the consecration of my chapel ? "

" If you don't consecrate it," answered Wingfold, " it will remain a portion of the universe, a thoroughfare for all divine influences, open as the heavens to every wind that blows. Consecration—"

Here the curate checked himself. He was going to say —" is another word for congestion,"—but he bethought himself what a wicked thing it would be, for the satisfaction of speaking his mind, to disturb that of his rector, brooding over a good work.

" But," he concluded therefore, " there will be time enough to think about that. The scheme is a delightful one. Apart from it, however, altogether—if you would but read prayers in your own church, it would wonderfully strengthen my hands. Only I am afraid I should shock you sometimes."

" I will take my chance of that. If you do, I will tell you of it. And if I do what you don't like, you must tell me of it. I trust neither of us will find the other incapable of understanding his neighbor's position."

They walked to the spot which the rector had already in his mind as the most suitable for the projected chapel. It was a bit of gently rising ground, near one of the gates, whence they could see the whole of the little village of Owlkirk. One of the nearest cottages was that of Mrs. Puckridge. They saw the doctor ride in at the other end of the street, stop there, fasten his horse to the paling, and go in.

CHAPTER XIV.

No sooner had Faber left the cottage that same morning, than the foolish Mrs. Puckridge proceeded to pour out to the patient, still agitated both with her dream and her waking vision, all the terrible danger she had been in, and the marvelous way in which the doctor had brought her back from the threshold of death. Every drop of the little blood in her body seemed to rush to her face, then back to her heart, leaving behind it a look of terror. She covered her face with the sheet, and lay so long without moving that her nurse was alarmed. When she drew the sheet back, she found her in a faint, and it was with great difficulty she brought her out of it. But not one word could she get from her. She did not seem even to hear what she said. Presently she grew restless, and soon her flushed cheek and bright eye indicated an increase of fever. When Faber saw her, he was much disappointed, perceived at once that something had excited her, and strongly suspected that, for all her promises, Mrs. Puckridge had betrayed the means by which he recovered her.

He said to himself that he had had no choice, but then neither had the lady, and the thing might be hateful to her. She might be in love, and then how she must abominate the business, and detest him ! It was horrible to think of her knowing it. But for knowing it, she would never be a whit the worse, for he never had a day's illness in his life, and knew of no taint in his family.

When she saw him approach her bedside, a look reminding him of the ripple of a sudden cold gust passing with the shadow of a cloud over still water swept across her face. She closed her eyes, and turned a litile from him. What color she had, came and went painfully. Cursing in his heart the faithlessness of Mrs. Puckridge, he assumed his coldest, hardest professional manner, felt her pulse with the gentlest, yet most peremptory inquiry, gave her attendant some authoritative directions, and left her, saying he would call again in the afternoon.

During seven days he visited her twice a day. He had good cause to be anxious, and her recovery was very slow. Once and again appeared threatenings of the primary complaint, while from the tardiness with which her veins refilled, he feared for her lungs. During all these visits, hardly a word beyond the most necessary passed between them. After that time they were reduced to one a day. Ever as the lady grew stronger, she seemed to become colder, and her manner grew more distant. After a fortnight, he again reduced them to one in two days—very unwillingly, for by that time she had come to occupy nearly as much of his thoughts as all the rest of his patients together. She made him feel that his visits were less than welcome to her, except for the help they brought her, allowed him no insight into her character and ways of thinking, behaved to him indeed with such restraint, that he could recall no expression of her face the memory of which drew him to dwell upon it; yet her face and form possessed him with their mere perfection. He had to set himself sometimes to get rid of what seemed all but her very presence, for it threatened to unfit him for the right discharge of his duties. He was haunted with the form to which he had given a renewal of life, as a murderer is haunted with the form of the man he has killed. In those marvelous intervals betwixt sleep and waking, when the soul is like a *camera obscura*, into which throng shapes unbidden, hers had displaced all others, and came constantly—now flashing with feverous radiance, now pale and bloodless as death itself. But ever and always her countenance wore a look of aversion. She seemed in these visions, to regard him as a vile necromancer, who first cast her into the sepulcher, and then brought her back by some hellish art. She had fascinated him. But he would not allow that he was in love with her. A man may be fascinated and hate. A man is not necessarily in love with the woman whose form haunts him. So said Faber to himself; and I can not yet tell whether he was in love with her or not. I do not know where the individuality of love commences—when love begins to be love. He must have been a good way toward that point, however, to have thus betaken himself to denial. He was the more interested to prove himself free, that he feared, almost believed, there was a lover concerned, and that was the reason she hated him so severely for what he had done.

He had long come to the conclusion that circumstances had

straitened themselves around her. Experience had given him a keen eye, and he had noted several things about her dress. For one thing, while he had observed that her under-clothing was peculiarly dainty, he had once or twice caught a glimpse of such an incongruity as he was compelled to set down to poverty. Besides, what reason in which poverty bore no part, could a lady have for being alone in a poor country lodging, without even a maid? Indeed, might it not be the consciousness of the peculiarity of her position, and no dislike to him, that made her treat him with such impenetrable politeness? Might she not well dread being misunderstood!

She would be wanting to pay him for his attendance—and what was he to do? He must let her pay something, or she would consider herself still more grievously wronged by him, but how was he to take the money from her hand? It was very hard that ephemeral creatures of the earth, born but to die, to gleam out upon the black curtain and vanish again, might not, for the brief time the poor yet glorious bubble swelled and throbbed, offer and accept from each other even a few sunbeams in which to dance! Would not the inevitable rain beat them down at night, and "mass them into the common clay"? How then could they hurt each other—why should they fear it—when they were all wandering home to the black, obliterative bosom of their grandmother Night? He well knew a certain reply to such reflection, but so he talked with himself.

He would take his leave as if she were a duchess. But he would not until she made him feel another visit would be an intrusion.

One day Mrs. Puckridge met him at the door, looking mysterious. She pointed with her thumb over her shoulder to indicate that the lady was in the garden, but at the same time nudged him with her elbow, confident that the impartment she had to make would justify the liberty, and led the way into the little parlor.

"Please, sir, and tell me," she said, turning and closing the door, "what I be to do. She says she's got no money to pay neither me nor the doctor, so she give me this, and wants me to sell it. I daren't show it! They'd say I stole it! She declares that if I mention to a living soul where I got it, she'll never speak to me again. In course she didn't mean you, sir, seein' as doctors an' clergymen ain't nobody—leastways nobody to speak on—and I'm sure I beg your

pardon, sir, but my meanin' is as they ain't them as ain't to
be told things. I declare I'm most terrified to set eyes
on the thing!"

She handed the doctor a little morocco case. He opened
it, and saw a ring, which was plainly of value. It was old-
fashioned—a round mass of small diamonds with a good-
sized central one.

"You are quite right," he said. "The ring is far too valuable for you to dispose of. Bring it to my house at four
o'clock, and I will get rid of it for you."

Mrs. Puckridge was greatly relieved, and ended the
interview by leading the way to the back-door. When she
opened it, he saw his patient sitting in the little arbor. She
rose, and came to meet him.

"You see I am quite well now," she said, holding out
her hand.

Her tone was guarded, but surely the ice was melting a
little! Was she taking courage at the near approach of
her deliverance?

She stooped to pick a double daisy from the border.
Prompt as he generally was, he could say nothing: he
knew what was coming next. She spoke while still she
stooped.

"When you come again," she said, "will you kindly let
me know how much I am in your debt?"

As she ended she rose and stood before him, but she
looked no higher than his shirt-studs. She was ashamed to
speak of her indebtedness as an amount that could be
reckoned. The whiteness of her cheek grew warm, which
was all her complexion ever revealed of a blush. It showed
plainer in the deepened darkness of her eyes, and the tremulous increase of light in them.

"I will," he replied, without the smallest response of
confusion, for he had recovered himself. "You will be
careful!" he added. "Indeed you must, or you will never
be strong."

She answered only with a little sigh, as if weakness was
such a weariness! and looked away across the garden-
hedge out into the infinite—into more of it at least I think,
than Faber recognized.

"And of all things," he went on, "wear shoes—every time
you have to step off a carpet—not mere foot-gloves like
those."

"Is this a healthy place, Doctor Faber?" she asked,

looking haughtier, he thought, but plainly with a little trouble in her eyes.

" Decidedly," he answered. " And when you are able to walk on the heath you will find the air invigorating. Only please mind what I say about your shoes.—May I ask if you intend remaining here any time ? "

" I have already remained so much longer than I intended, that I am afraid to say. My plans are now uncertain."

" Excuse me—I know I presume—but in our profession we must venture a little now and then—could you not have some friend with you until you are perfectly strong again ? After what you have come through, it may be years before you are quite what you were. I don't want to frighten you —only to make you careful."

" There is no one," she answered in a low voice, which trembled a little.

" No one— ? " repeated Faber, as if waiting for the end of the sentence. But his heart gave a great bound.

" No one to come to me. I am alone in the world. My mother died when I was a child and my father two years ago. He was an officer. I was his only child, and used to go about with him. I have no friends."

Her voice faltered more and more. When it ceased she seemed choking a cry.

" Since then," she resumed, " I have been a governess. My last situation was in Yorkshire, in a cold part of the county, and my health began to fail me. I heard that Glaston was a warm place, and one where I should be likely to get employment. But I was taken ill on my way there, and forced to stop. A lady in the train told me this was such a sweet, quiet little place, and so when we got to the station I came on here."

Again Faber could not speak. The thought of a lady like her traveling about alone looking for work was frightful ! " And they talk of a God in the world ! " he said to himself—and felt as if he never could forgive Him.

" I have papers to show," she added quietly, as if bethinking herself that he might be taking her for an impostor.

All the time she had never looked him in the face. She had fixed her gaze on the far horizon, but a smile, half pitiful, half proud, flickered about the wonderful curves of her upper lip.

"I am glad you have told me," he said. "I may be of service to you, if you will permit me. I know a great many families about here."

"Oh, thank you!" she cried, and with an expression of dawning hope, which made her seem more beautiful than ever, she raised her eyes and looked him full in the face: it was the first time he had seen her eyes lighted up, except with fever. Then she turned from him, and, apparently lost in relief, walked toward the arbor a few steps distant. He followed her, a little behind, for the path was narrow, his eyes fixed on her exquisite cheek. It was but a moment, yet the very silence seemed to become conscious. All at once she grew paler, shuddered, put her hand to her head, and entering the arbor, sat down. Faber was alarmed. Her hand was quite cold. She would have drawn it away, but he insisted on feeling her pulse.

"You must come in at once," he said.

She rose, visibly trembling. He supported her into the house, made her lie down, got a hot bottle for her feet, and covered her with shawls and blankets.

"You are quite unfit for any exertion yet," he said, and seated himself near her. "You must consent to be an invalid for a while. Do not be anxious. There is no fear of your finding what you want by the time you are able for it. I pledge myself. Keep your mind perfectly easy."

She answered him with a look that dazzled him. Her very eyelids seemed radiant with thankfulness. The beauty that had fixed his regard was now but a mask through which her soul was breaking, assimilating it. His eyes sank before the look, and he felt himself catching his breath like a drowning man. When he raised them again he saw tears streaming down her face. He rose, and saying he would call again in the evening, left the room.

During the rest of his round he did not find it easy to give due attention to his other cases. His custom was to brood upon them as he rode; but now that look and the tears that followed seemed to bewilder him, taking from him all command of his thought.

Ere long the shadow that ever haunts the steps of the angel, Love, the shadow whose name is Beneficence, began to reassume its earlier tyranny. Oh, the bliss of knowing one's self the source of well-being, the stay and protector, the comfort and life, to such a woman! of wrapping her round in days of peace, instead of anxiety and pain and labor!

But ever the thought of her looking up to him as the source of her freedom, was present through it all. What a glory to be the object of such looks as he had never in his dearest dreams imagined ! It made his head swim, even in the very moment while his great Ruber, astonished at what his master required of him that day, rose to some high thorny hedge, or stiff rail. He was perfectly honest ; the consequence he sought was only in his own eyes—and in hers ; there was nothing of vulgar patronage in the feeling ; not an atom of low purpose for self in it. The whole mental condition was nothing worse than the blossom of the dream of his childhood—the dream of being *the* benefactor of his race, of being loved and worshiped for his kindness. But the poison of the dream had grown more active in its blossom. Since then the credit of goodness with himself had gathered sway over his spirit ; and stoical pride in goodness is a far worse and lower thing than delight in the thanks of our fellows. He was a mere slave to his own ideal, and that ideal was not brother to the angel that beholds the face of the Father. Now he had taken a backward step in time, but a forward step in his real history, for again another than himself had a part in his dream. It would be long yet, however, ere he learned so to love goodness as to forget its beauty. To him who *is* good, goodness has ceased to be either object or abstraction ; it is *in* him—a thirst to give ; a solemn, quiet passion to bless ; a delight in beholding well-being. Ah, how we dream and prate of love, until the holy fire of the true divine love, the love that God kindles in a man toward his fellows, burns the shadow of it out !

In the afternoon Mrs. Puckridge appeared with the ring. He took it, told her to wait, and went out. In a few minutes he returned, and, to the woman's astonishment, gave her fifty pounds in notes. He did not tell her he had been to nobody but his own banker. The ring he laid carefully aside, with no definite resolve concerning it, but the great hope of somehow managing that it should return to her one day. The thought shot across his heaven—what a lovely wedding present it would make ! and the meteor drew a long train of shining fancies after it.

CHAPTER XV.

WHEN he called, as he had said, in the evening, she looked much better, and there was even a touch of playfulness in her manner. He could not but hope some crisis had been passed. The money she had received for the ring had probably something to do with it. Perhaps she had not known how valuable the ring was. Thereupon in his conscientiousness he began to doubt whether he had given her its worth. In reality he had exceeded it by a few pounds, as he discovered upon inquiry afterward in London. Anyhow it did not much matter, he said to himself : he was sure to find some way of restoring it to her.

Suddenly she looked up, and said hurriedly :

" I can never repay you, Dr. Faber. No one can do the impossible."

" You can repay me," returned Faber.

" How ? " she said, looking startled.

" By never again thinking of obligation to me."

" You must not ask that of me," she rejoined. " It would not be right."

The tinge of a rose not absolutely white floated over her face and forehead as she spoke.

" Then I shall be content," he replied, " if you will say nothing about it until you are well settled. After that I promise to send you a bill as long as a snipe's."

She smiled, looked up brightly, and said,

" You promise ? "

" I do."

" If you don't keep your promise, I shall have to take severe measures. Don't fancy me without money. I *could* pay you now—at least I think so."

It was a great good sign of her that she could talk about money plainly as she did. It wants a thoroughbred soul to talk *just* right about money. Most people treat money like a bosom-sin : they follow it earnestly, but do not talk about it at all in society.

" I only pay six shillings a week for my lodgings ! " she added, with a merry laugh.

What had become of her constraint and stateliness? Courtesy itself seemed gone, and simple trust in its place ! Was she years younger than he had thought her ? She was hemming something, which demanded her eyes, but every now and then she cast up a glance, and they were black suns unclouding over a white sea. Every look made a vintage in the doctor's heart. There *could* be no man in the case ! Only again, would fifty pounds, with the loss of a family ring, serve to account for such a change ? Might she not have heard from somebody since he saw her yesterday ? In her presence he dared not follow the thought.

Some books were lying on the table which could not well be Mrs. Puckridge's. He took up one : it was *In Memoriam.*

" Do you like Tennyson ? " she asked.

" That is a hard question to answer straight off," he replied.—He had once liked Tennyson, else he would not have answered so.—" Had you asked me if I liked *In Memoriam,*" he went on, " I could more easily have answered you."

" Then, don't you like *In Memoriam ?* "

" No ; it is weak and exaggerated."

" Ah ! you don't understand it. I didn't until after my father died. Then I began to know what it meant, and now think it the most beautiful poem I ever read."

" You are fond of poetry, then ? "

" I don't read much ; but I think there is more in some poetry than in all the prose in the world."

" That is a good deal to say."

" A good deal too much, when I think that I haven't read, I suppose, twenty books in my life—that is, books worth calling books : I don't mean novels and things of that kind. Yet I can not believe twenty years of good reading would make me change my mind about *In Memoriam.* —You don't like poetry ? "

" I can't say I do—much. I like Pope and Crabbe—and —let me see—well, I used to like Thomson. I like the men that give you things just as they are. I do not like the poets that mix themselves up with what they see, and then rave about Nature. I confess myself a lover of the truth beyond all things."

" But are you sure," she returned, looking him gently but

straight in the eyes, " that, in your anxiety not to make
more of things than they are, you do not make less of them
than they are ? "

" There is no fear of that," returned Faber sadly, with an
unconscious shake of the head.   " So long as there is youth
and imagination on that side to paint them,—"

" Excuse me : are you not begging the question ?   Do
they paint, or do they see what they say ?   Some profess to
believe that the child sees more truly than the grown man
—that the latter is the one who paints,—paints out, that is,
with a coarse brush."

" You mean Wordsworth."

" Not him only."

" True ; no end of poets besides.   They all say it now-a-
days."

" But surely, Mr. Faber, if there be a God,—"

" Ah ! " interrupted the doctor, " there *you* beg the question.   Suppose there should be no God, what then ? "

" Then, I grant you, there could be no poetry.   Somebody
says poetry is the speech of hope ; and certainly if there
were no God, there could be no hope."

Faber was struck with what she said, not from any feeling
that there was truth in it, but from its indication of a not
illogical mind. He was on the point of replying that
certain kinds of poetry, and *In Memoriam* in particular,
seemed to him more like the speech of a despair that had
not the courage to confess itself and die ; but he saw she
had not a suspicion he spoke as he did for any thing but
argument, and feared to fray his bird by scattering his
crumbs too roughly. He honestly believed deliverance
from the superstition into which he granted a fine nature
was readier to fall than a common one, the greatest gift one
human being could offer to another ; but at the same time
he could not bear to think of her recoil from such utterance
of his unfaith as he had now almost got into the habit of
making. He bethought himself, too, that he had already mis-
represented himself, in giving her the impression that he was
incapable of enjoying poetry of the more imaginative sort.
He had indeed in his youth been passionately fond of such
verse.   Then came a time in which he turned from it with
a sick dismay. Feelings and memories of agony, which a
word, a line, would rouse in him afresh, had brought him to
avoid it with an aversion seemingly deep-rooted as an instinct,
and mounting even to loathing ; and when at length he cast

from him the semi-beliefs of his education, he persuaded himself that he disliked it for its falsehood. He read his philosophy by the troubled light of wrong and suffering, and that is not the light of the morning, but of a burning house. Of all poems, naturally enough, he then disliked *In Memoriam* the most ; and now it made him almost angry that Juliet Meredith should like so much what he so much disliked. Not that he would have a lady indifferent to poetry. That would argue a lack of poetry in herself, and such a lady would be like a scentless rose. You could not expect, who indeed could wish a lady to be scientific in her ways of regarding things? Was she not the live concentration, the perfect outcome, of the vast poetic show of Nature? In shape, in motion of body and brain, in tone and look, in color and hair, in faithfulness to old dolls and carelessness of hearts, was she not the sublimation, the essence of sunsets, and fading roses, and butterflies, and snows, and running waters, and changing clouds, and cold, shadowy moonlight? He argued thus more now in sorrow than in anger ; for what was the woman but a bubble on the sand of the infinite soulless sea—a bubble of a hundred lovely hues, that must shine because it could not help it, and for the same reason break? She was not to blame. Let her shine and glow, and sparkle, and vanish. For him, he cared for nothing but science—nothing that did not promise one day to yield up its kernel to the seeker. To him science stood for truth, and for truth in the inward parts stood obedience to the laws of Nature. If he was one of a poor race, he would rise above his fellows by being good to them in their misery ; while for himself he would confess to no misery. Let the laws of Nature work—eyeless and heartless as the whirlwind ; he would live his life, be himself, be Nature, and depart without a murmur. No scratch on the face of time, insignificant even as the pressure of a fernleaf upon coal, should tell that he had ever thought his fate hard. He would do his endeavor and die and return to nothing—not then more dumb of complaint than now. Such had been for years his stern philosophy, and why should it now trouble him that a woman thought differently? Did the sound of faith from such lips, the look of hope in such eyes, stir any thing out of sight in his heart? Was it for a moment as if the corner of a veil were lifted, the lower edge of a mist, and he saw something fair beyond? Came there a little glow and flutter out of the old time? "All forget," he said to himself. "I too have forgotten. Why should not Nature forget? Why should I be fooled any more? Is it not enough?"

Yet as he sat gazing, in the broad light of day, through the cottage window, across whose panes waved the little red bells of the common fuchsia, something that had nothing to do with science and yet *was*, seemed to linger and hover over the little garden—something from the very depths of loveliest folly. Was it the refrain of an old song? or the smell of withered rose leaves? or was there indeed a kind of light such as never was on sea or shore?

Whatever it was, it was out of the midst of it the voice of the lady seemed to come—a clear musical voice in common speech, but now veiled and trembling, as if it brooded hearkening over the words it uttered:

> "I wrong the grave with fears untrue:
> Shall love be blamed for want of faith?
> There must be wisdom with great Death:
> The dead shall look me through and through.

> "Be near us when we climb or fall:
> Ye watch, like God, the rolling hours
> With larger other eyes than ours,
>   To make allowance for us all."

She ceased, and the silence was like that which follows sweet music.

"Ah! you think of your father!" he hazarded, and hoped indeed it was her father of whom she was thinking.

She made no answer. He turned toward her in anxiety. She was struggling with emotion. The next instant the tears gushed into her eyes, while a smile seemed to struggle from her lips, and spread a little way over her face. It was inexpressibly touching.

"He was my friend," she said. "I shall never have such love again."

"All is not lost when much is lost," said the doctor, with sad comfort. "There are spring days in winter."

"And *you* don't like poetry!" she said, a sweet playful scorn shining through her tears.

"I spoke but a sober truth," he returned; "—so sober that it seems but the sadder for its truth. The struggle of life is to make the best of things that might be worse."

She looked at him pitifully. For a moment her lips

parted, then a strange look as of sudden bodily pain
crossed her face, her lips closed, and her mouth looked as
if it were locked. She shut the book which lay upon her
knee, and resumed her needlework. A shadow settled upon
her face.

" What a pity such a woman should be wasted in believing lies ! " thought the doctor. " How much better it would
be if she would look things in the face, and resolve to live
as she can, doing her best and enduring her worst, and waiting for the end ! And yet, seeing color is not the thing
itself, and only in the brain whose eye looks upon it, why
should I think it better ? why should she not shine in the
color of her fancy ? why should she grow gray because the
color is only in herself ? We are but bubbles flying from
the round of Nature's mill-wheel. Our joys and griefs are
the colors that play upon the bubbles. Their throbs and
ripples and changes are our music and poetry, and their
bursting is our endless repose. Let us waver and float and
shine in the sun ; let us bear pitifully and be kind ; for the
night cometh, and there an end."

But in the sad silence, he and the lady were perhaps
drifting further and further apart !

" I did not mean," he said, plunging into what came first,
" that I could not enjoy verse of the kind you prefer—as
verse. I took the matter by the more serious handle,
because, evidently, you accepted the tone and the scope of
it. I have a weakness for honesty."

" There is something not right about you, though, Mr.
Faber—if I could find it out," said Miss Meredith. " You
can not mean you enjoy any thing you do not believe in ? "

" Surely there are many things one can enjoy without
believing in them ? "

" On the contrary, it seems to me that enjoying a thing
is only another word for believing in it. If I thought the
sweetest air on the violin had no truth in it, I could not
listen to it a moment longer."

" Of course the air has all the truth it pretends to—the
truth, that is, of the relations of sounds and of intervals—
also, of course, the truth of its relation as a whole to that
creative something in the human mind which gave birth to
it."

" That is not all it pretends. It pretends that the something it gives birth to in the human mind is also a true
thing."

"Is there not then another way also, in which the violin may be said to be true? Its tone throughout is of suffering: does it not mourn that neither what gives rise to it, nor what it gives rise to, is any thing but a lovely vapor— the phantom of an existence not to be lived, only to be dreamed? Does it not mourn that a man, though necessarily in harmony with the laws under which he lives, yet can not be sufficiently conscious of that harmony to keep him from straining after his dream?"

"Ah!" said Miss Meredith, "then there is strife in the kingdom, and it can not stand!"

"There *is* strife in the kingdom, and it can not stand," said the doctor, with mingled assent and assertion. "Hence it is forever falling."

"But it is forever renewed," she objected.

"With what renewal?" rejoined Faber. "What return is there from the jaws of death? The individual is gone. A new consciousness is not a renewal of consciousness."

She looked at him keenly.

"It is hard, is it not?" she said.

"I will not deny that in certain moods it looks so," he answered.

She did not perceive his drift, and was feeling after it.

"Surely," she said, "the thing that ought to be, is the thing that must be."

"How can we tell that?" he returned. "What do we see like it in nature? Whatever lives and thrives—animal or vegetable—or human—it is all one—every thing that lives and thrives, is forever living and thriving on the loss, the defeat, the death of another. There is no unity save absolutely by means of destruction. Destruction is indeed the very center and framework of the sole existing unity. I will not, therefore, as some do, call Nature cruel : what right have I to complain? Nature can not help it. She is no more to blame for bringing me forth, than I am to blame for being brought forth. *Ought* is merely the reflex of *like*. We call ourselves the highest in Nature—and probably we are, being the apparent result of the whole—whence, naturally, having risen, we seek to rise, we feel after something we fancy higher. For as to the system in which we live, we are so ignorant that we can but blunderingly feel our way in it ; and if we knew all its laws, we could neither order nor control, save by a poor subservience. We are the slaves of our circumstance, therefore betake ourselves to dreams of what *ought to be*."

Miss Meredith was silent for a time.

" I can not see how to answer you," she said at length. " But you do not disturb my hope of seeing my father again. We have a sure word of prophecy."

Faber suppressed the smile of courteous contempt that was ready to break forth, and she went on :

" It would ill become me to doubt to-day, as you will grant when I tell you a wonderful fact. This morning I had not money enough to buy myself the pair of strong shoes you told me I must wear. I had nothing left but a few trinkets of my mother's—one of them a ring I thought worth about ten pounds. I gave it to my landlady to sell for me, hoping she would get five for it. She brought me fifty, and I am rich ! "

Her last words trembled with triumph. He had himself been building her up in her foolish faith ! But he took consolation in thinking how easily with a word he could any moment destroy that buttress of her phantom house. It was he, the unbeliever, and no God in or out of her Bible, that had helped her ! It did not occur to him that she might after all see in him only a reed blown of a divine wind.

" I am glad to hear of your good fortune," he answered. " I can not say I see how it bears on the argument. You had in your possession more than you knew."

" Does the length of its roots alter the kind of the plant ? " she asked. " Do we not know in all nature and history that God likes to see things grow ? That must be the best way. It may be the only right way. If that ring was given to my mother against the time when the last child of her race should find herself otherwise helpless, would the fact that the provision was made so early turn the result into a mere chance meeting of necessity and subsidy ? Am I bound to call every good thing I receive a chance, except an angel come down visibly out of the blue sky and give it to me ? That would be to believe in a . God who could not work His will by His own laws. Here I am, free and hopeful—all I needed. Every thing was dark and troubled yesterday ; the sun is up to-day."

" There is a tide in the affairs of men, which taken at the flood leads on to fortune," said the doctor.

" I begin to fear you mean what you say, Mr. Faber.

I hoped it was only for argument's sake," returned Miss Meredith.

She did not raise her eyes from her work this time. Faber saw that she was distressed if not hurt, and that her soul had closed its lips to him. He sprang to his feet, and stood bending before her.

" Miss Meredith," he said, " forgive me. I have offended you."

" You have not offended me," she said quietly.

" Hurt you then, which is worse."

" How should I have got through," she said, as if to herself, and dropped her hands with her work on her knees, "if I had not believed there was One caring for me all the time, even when I was most alone ! "

" Do you never lose that faith ? " asked the doctor.

" Yes ; many and many a time. But it always comes back."

" Comes and goes with your health."

" No—is strongest sometimes when I am furthest from well."

" When you are most feverish," said the doctor. " What a fool I am to go on contradicting her ! " he added to himself.

" I think I know you better than you imagine, Mr. Faber," said Miss Meredith, after just a moment's pause. " You are one of those men who like to represent themselves worse than they are. I at least am bound to think better of you than you would have me. One who lives as you do for other people, can not be so far from the truth as your words."

Faber honestly repudiated the praise, for he felt it more than he deserved. He did try to do well by his neighbor, but was aware of no such devotion as it implied. Of late he had found his work bore him not a little—especially when riding away from Owlkirk. The praise, notwithstanding, sounded sweet from her lips, was sweeter still from her eyes, and from the warmer white of her cheek, which had begun to resume its soft roundness.

" Ah ! " thought the doctor, as he rode slowly home, " were it not for sickness, age, and death, this world of ours would be no bad place to live in. Surely mine is the most needful and the noblest of callings !—to fight for youth, and health, and love; against age, and sickness, and decay ! to fight death to the last, even knowing he must have the best

of it in the end ! to set law against law, and do what poor
thing may be done to reconcile the inexorable with the
desirable ! Who knows—if law be blind, and I am a man
that can see—for at the last, and only at the last do eyes
come in the head of Nature—who knows but I may find out
amongst the blind laws to which I am the eyes, that blind
law which lies nearest the root of life !—Ah, what a dreamer
I should have been, had I lived in the time when great
dreams were possible ! Beyond a doubt I should have sat
brooding over the elixir of life, cooking and mixing, heating
and cooling, watching for the flash in the goblet. We
know so much now, that the range of hope is sadly limited !
A thousand dark ways of what seemed blissful possibility
are now closed to us, because there the light now shines,
and shows naught but despair. Yet why should the thing
be absurd ? Can any one tell *why* this organism we call
man should not go on working forever ? Why should it
not, since its law is change and renewal, go on changing
and renewing forever ? Why should it get tired ? Why
should its law work more feeble, its relations hold less
firmly, after a hundred years, than after ten ? Why should
it grow and grow, then sink and sink ? No one knows a
reason. Then why should it be absurd to seek what shall
encounter the unknown cause, and encountering reveal it ?
Might science be brought to the pitch that such a woman
should live to all the ages, how many common lives
might not well be spared to such an end ! How many
noble ones would not willingly cease for such a consum-
mation—dying that life should be lord, and death no longer
king ! "

Plainly Faber's materialism sprang from no defect in the
region of the imagination ; but I find myself unable to
determine how much honesty, and how much pride and the
desire to be satisfied with himself, had relatively to do with
it. I would not be understood to imply that he had an
unusual amount of pride ; and I am sure he was less easily
satisfied with himself than most are. Most people will
make excuses for themselves which they would neither
make nor accept for their neighbor ; their own failures and
follies trouble them little : Faber was of another sort. As
ready as any other man to discover what could be said on
his side, he was not so ready to adopt it. He required a
good deal of himself. But then he unconsciously compared
himself with his acquaintances, and made what he knew of

them the gauge, if not the measure, of what he required of himself.

It were unintelligible how a man should prefer being the slave of blind helpless Law to being the child of living Wisdom, should believe in the absolute Nothing rather than in the perfect Will, were it not that he does not, can not see the Wisdom or the Will, except he draw nigh thereto.

I shall be answered :

" We do not prefer. We mourn the change which yet we can not resist. We would gladly have the God of our former faith, were it possible any longer to believe in Him."

I answer again :

" Are you sure of what you say ? Do you in reality mourn over your lost faith ? For my part, I would rather disbelieve with you, than have what you have lost. For I would rather have no God than the God whom you suppose me to believe in, and whom therefore I take to be the God in whom you imagine you believed in the days of your ignorance. That those were days of ignorance, I do not doubt ; but are these the days of your knowledge ? The time will come when you will see deeper into your own hearts than now, and will be humbled, like not a few other men, by what you behold."

CHAPER XVI.

THE BUTCHER'S SHOP.

ABOUT four years previous to the time of which I am now writing, and while yet Mr. Drake was in high repute among the people of Cowlane chapel, he went to London to visit an old friend, a woman of great practical benevolence, exercised chiefly toward orphans. Just then her thoughts and feelings were largely occupied with a lovely little girl, the chain of whose history had been severed at the last link, and lost utterly.

A poor woman in Southwark had of her own motion, partly from love to children and compassion for both them and their mothers, partly to earn her own bread with pleasure, established a sort of *crèche* in her two rooms, where mothers who had work from home could bring their children in the morning, and leave them till night. The child had been committed to her charge day after day for some weeks. One morning, when she brought her, the mother seemed out of health, and did not appear at night to take her home. The next day the woman heard she was in the small-pox-hospital. For a week or so, the money to pay for the child came almost regularly, in postage-stamps, then ceased altogether, and the woman heard nothing either from or of the mother. After a fortnight she contrived to go to the hospital to inquire after her. No one corresponding to her description was in the place. The name was a common one, and several patients bearing it had lately died and been buried, while others had recovered and were gone. Her inquiries in the neighborhood had no better success : no one knew her, and she did not even discover where she had lived. She could not bear the thought of taking the child to the work-house, and kept her for six or eight weeks, but she had a sickly son, a grown lad, to support, and in dread lest she should be compelled to give her up to the parish, had applied for counsel to the lady I have mentioned. When Mr. Drake arrived, she had for some time been searching about in vain to find a nest for her.

Since his boys had been taken from him, and the unprized girl left behind had grown so precious, Mr. Drake had learned to love children as the little ones of God. He had no doubt, like many people, a dread of children with unknown antecedents : who could tell what root of bitterness, beyond the common inheritance, might spring up in them ? But all that was known of this one's mother was unusually favorable ; and when his friend took him to see the child, his heart yearned after her. He took her home to Dorothy, and she had grown up such as we have seen her, a wild, roguish, sweet, forgetful, but not disobedient child —very dear to both the Drakes, who called her their duckling.

As we have seen, however, Mr. Drake had in his adversity grown fearful and faint-hearted, and had begun to doubt whether he had a right to keep her. And of course he had not, if it was to be at the expense of his trades-people. But he was of an impetuous nature, and would not give even God time to do the thing that needed time to be done well. He saw a crisis was at hand. Perhaps, however, God saw a spiritual, where he saw a temporal crisis.

Dorothy had a small sum, saved by her mother, so invested as to bring her about twenty pounds a year, and of the last payment she had two pounds in hand. Her father had nothing, and quarter-day was two months off. This was the common knowledge of their affairs at which they arrived as they sat at breakfast on the Monday morning, after the saddest Sunday either of them had ever spent. They had just risen from the table, and the old woman was removing the cloth, when a knock came to the lane-door, and she went to open it, leaving the room-door ajar, whereby the minister caught a glimpse of a blue apron, and feeling himself turning sick, sat down again. Lisbeth re-entered with a rather greasy-looking note, which was of course from the butcher, and Mr. Drake's hand trembled as he opened it. Mr. Jones wrote that he would not have troubled him, had he not asked for his bill; but, if it was quite convenient, he would be glad to have the amount by the end of the week, as he had a heavy payment to make the following Monday. Mr. Drake handed the note to his daughter, rose hastily, and left the room. Dorothy threw it down half-read, and followed him. He was opening the door, his hat in his hand.

"Where are you going in such a hurry, father dear?" she said. "Wait a moment and I'll go with you."

"My child, there is not a moment to lose!" he replied excitedly.

"I did not read all the letter," she returned; "but I think he does not want the money till the end of the week."

"And what better shall we be then?" he rejoined, almost angrily. "The man looks to me, and where will he find himself on Monday? Let us be as honest at least as we can."

"But we may be able to borrow it—or—who knows what might happen?"

"There it is, my dear! Who knows what? We can be sure of nothing in this world."

"And what in the next, father?"

The minister was silent. If God was anywhere, he was here as much as there! That was not the matter in hand, however. He owed the money, and was bound to let the man know that he could not pay it by the end of the week. Without another word to Dorothy, he walked from the house, and, like a man afraid of cowardice, went straight at the object of his dismay. He was out of the lane and well into Pine street before he thought to put on his hat.

From afar he saw the butcher, standing in front of his shop—a tall, thin man in blue. His steel glittered by his side, and a red nightcap hung its tassel among the curls of his gray hair. He was discussing, over a small joint of mutton, some point of economic interest with a country customer in a check-shawl. To the minister's annoyance the woman was one of his late congregation, and he would gladly have passed the shop, had he had the courage. When he came near, the butcher turned from the woman, and said, taking his nightcap by the tassel in rudimentary obeisance.

"At your service, sir."

His courtesy added to Mr. Drake's confusion : it was plain the man imagined he had brought him his money ! Times were indeed changed since his wife used to drive out in her brougham to pay the bills ! Was this what a man had for working in the vineyard the better part of a lifetime ? The property he did not heed. That had been the portion of the messengers of heaven from the first. But the shame ! —what was he to do with that ? Who ever heard of St. Paul not being able to pay a butcher's bill ! No doubt St. Paul was a mighty general, and he but a poor subaltern, but in the service there was no respect of persons. On the other hand, who ever heard of St. Paul having any bills to pay !—or for that matter, indeed, of his marrying a rich wife, and getting into expensive habits through popular-ity ! Who ever heard of his being dependent on a congre-gation ! He accepted help sometimes, but had always his goats'-hair and his tent-making to fall back upon !—Only, after all, was the Lord never a hard master ? Had he not let it come to this ?

Much more of the sort went through his mind in a flash. The country woman had again drawn the attention of the butcher with a parting word.

"You don't want a chicken to-day—do you, Mr. Drake ?" she said, as she turned to go.

"No, thank you, Mrs. Thomson. How is your husband ?"

"Better, I thank you sir. Good morning, sir."

"Mr. Jones," said the minister—and as he spoke, he stepped inside the shop, removed his hat, and wiped his forehead, "I come to you with shame. I have not money enough to pay your bill. Indeed I can not even pay a por-tion of it till next quarter-day."

"Don't mention it, Mr. Drake, sir."

"But your bill on Monday, Mr. Jones!"

"Oh! never mind that. I shall do very well, I dare say. I have a many as owes me a good deal more than you do, sir, and I'm much obliged to you for letting of me know at once. You see, sir, if you hadn't——"

"Yes, I know : I asked for it ! I am the sorrier I can't pay it after all. It is quite disgraceful, but I simply can't help it."

"Disgraceful, sir !" exclaimed Mr. Jones, almost as if hurt : "I wish they thought as you do as has ten times the reason, sir !"

"But I have a request to make," the pastor went on, heedless of the butcher's remark, and pulling out a large and handsome gold watch : "Would you oblige me by taking this watch in security until I do pay you ? It is worth a great deal more than your bill. It would add much to the obligation, if you would put it out of sight somewhere, and say nothing about it. If I should die before paying your bill, you will be at liberty to sell it ; and what is over, after deducting interest, you will kindly hand to my daughter."

Mr. Jones stared with open mouth. He thought the minister had lost his senses.

"What do you make of me, sir ?" he said at last. "You go for to trust me with a watch like that, and fancy I wouldn't trust you with a little bill that ain't been owing three months yet ! You make me that I don't know myself, sir ! Never you mention the bill to me again, sir. I'll ask for it, all in good time. Can I serve you with any thing to-day, sir ?"

"No, I thank you. I must at least avoid adding to my debt."

"I hope what you do have, you'll have of me, sir. I don't mind waiting a goodish bit for my money, but what cuts me to the heart is to see any one as owes me money a goin' over the way, as if 'e 'adn't 'a' found my meat good enough to serve his turn, an' that was why he do it. That does rile me !"

"Take my word for it, Mr. Jones—all the meat we have we shall have of you. But we must be careful. You see I am not quite so—so—"

He stopped with a sickly smile.

"Look ye here, Mr. Drake !" broke in the butcher : "you parsons ain't proper brought up. You ain't learned to take care of yourselves. Now us tradespeople, we're learned from the first to look arter number one, and not on no account to forget which *is* number one. But you parsons, now,—you'll excuse me, sir ; I don't mean no offense ; you ain't brought up to 't, an' it ain't to be expected of you— but it's a great neglect in your eddication, sir ; an' the con- sekence is as how us as knows better 'as to take care on you as don't know no better. I can't say I think much o' them 'senters : they don't stick by their own ; but you're a honest man, sir, if ever there was a honest man as was again' the church, an' ask you for that money, I never will, acause I know when you can pay, it's pay you will. Keep your mind easy, sir : *I* shan't come to grief for lack o' what you owe me ! Only don't you go a starving of yourself, Mr. Drake. I don't hold with that nohow. Have a bit o' meat when you want it, an' don't think over it twice. There ! "

The minister was just able to thank his new friend and no more. He held out his hand to him, forgetful of the grease that had so often driven him from the pavement to the street. The butcher gave it a squeeze that nearly shot it out of his lubricated grasp, and they parted, both better men for the interview.

When Mr. Drake reached home, he met his daughter coming out to find him. He took her hand, led her into the house and up to his study, and closed the door.

" Dorothy," he said, " it is sweet to be humbled. The Spirit can bring water from the rock, and grace from a hard heart. I mean mine, not the butcher's. He has behaved to me as I don't see how any but a Christian could, and that although his principles are scarcely those of one who had given up all for the truth. He is like the son in the parable who said, I go not, but went ; while I, much I fear me, am like the other who said, I go, sir, but went not. Alas ! I have always found it hard to be grateful ; there is something in it unpalatable to the old Adam ; but from the bottom of my heart I thank Mr. Jones, and I will pray God for him ere I open a book. Dorothy, I begin to doubt our way of church-membership. It *may* make the good better ; but if a bad one gets in, it certainly makes him worse. I begin to think too, that every minister ought to be inde- pendent of his flock—I do not mean by the pay of the state, God forbid ! but by having some trade or profession, if no fortune. Still, if I had had the money to pay that bill, I should now be where I am glad not to be—up on my castle-top, instead of down at the gate. He has made me poor that He might send me humility, and that I find unspeakably precious. Perhaps He will send me the money next. But may it not be intended also to make us live more simply—on vegetables perhaps? Do you not remember how it fared with Daniel, Hananiah, Mishael, and Azariah, when they refused the meat and the wine, and ate pulse instead? At the end of ten days their countenances appeared fairer and fatter in flesh than all the children which did eat the portion of the king's meat. Pulse, you know, means peas and beans, and every thing of that kind—which is now proved to be almost as full of nourishment as meat itself, and to many constitutions more wholesome. Let us have a dinner of beans. You can buy haricot beans at the grocer's—can you not? If Ducky does not thrive on them, or they don't agree with you, my Dorothy, you will have only to drop them. I am sure they will agree with me. But let us try, and then the money I owe Mr. Jones, will not any longer hang like a millstone about my neck."

"We will begin this very day," said Dorothy, delighted to see her father restored to equanimity. "I will go and see after a dinner of herbs.—We shall have love with it anyhow, father!" she added, kissing him.

That day the minister, who in his earlier days had been allowed by his best friends to be a little particular about his food, and had been no mean connoisseur in wines, found more pleasure at his table, from lightness of heart, and the joy of a new independence, than he had had for many a day. It added much also to his satisfaction with the experiment, that, instead of sleeping, as his custom was, after dinner, he was able to read without drowsiness even. Perhaps Dorothy's experience was not quite so satisfactory, for she looked weary when they sat down to tea.

CHAPTER XVII.

THE PARLOR AGAIN.

FABER had never made any effort to believe in a divine order of things—indeed he had never made strenuous effort to believe in any thing. It had never at all occurred to him that it might be a duty to believe. He was a kindly and not a repellent man, but when he doubted another, he doubted him ; it never occurred to him that perhaps he ought to believe in that man. There must be a lack of something, where a man's sense of duty urges him mainly to denial. His existence is a positive thing—his main utterance ought to be positive. I would not forget that the nature of a denial may be such as to involve a strong positive.

To Faber it seemed the true and therefore right thing, to deny the existence of any such being as men call God. I heartily admit that such denial may argue a nobler condition than that of the man who will reason for the existence of what he calls a Deity, but omits to order his way after what he professes to believe His will. At the same time, his conclusion that he was not bound to believe in any God, seemed to lift a certain weight off the heart of the doctor— the weight, namely, that gathers partly from the knowledge of having done wrong things, partly from the consciousness of not *being* altogether right. It would be very unfair, however, to leave the impression that this was the origin of all the relief the doctor derived from the conclusion. For thereby he got rid, in a great measure at least, of the notion —horrible in proportion to the degree in which it is actually present to the mind, although, I suspect, it is not, in a true sense, credible to any mind—of a cruel, careless, unjust Being at the head of affairs. That such a notion should exist at all, is mainly the fault of the mass of so-called religious people, for they seem to believe in, and certainly proclaim such a God. In their excuse it may be urged they tell the tale as it was told to them ; but the fault lies in this, that, with the gospel in their hands, they have yet lived in such disregard of its precepts, that they have never discovered their representation of the God of Truth to be such, that the more honest a man is, the less can he accept it. That the honest man, however, should not thereupon set himself to see whether there might not be a true God notwithstanding, whether such a God was not conceivable consistently with things as they are, whether the believers had not distorted the revelation they professed to follow ; especially that he should prefer to believe in some sort of *vitalic* machine, equally void of beneficence and malevolence, existing because it can not help it, and giving birth to all sorts of creatures, men and women included, because it can not help it—must arise from a condition of being, call it spiritual, moral, or mental—I can not be obliging enough to add *cerebral*, because so I should nullify my conclusion, seeing there would be no substance left wherein it could be wrought out—for which the man, I can not but think, will one day discover that he was to blame—for which a living God sees that he is to blame, makes all the excuse he can, and will give the needful punishment to the uttermost lash.

There are some again, to whom the idea of a God perfect as they could imagine Him in love and devotion and truth, seems, they say, too good to be true : such have not yet perceived that no God any thing less than absolutely glorious in loveliness would be worth believing in, or such as the human soul could believe in. But Faber did not belong to this class—still less to that portion of it whose inconsolable grief over the lack of such a God may any day blossom into hope of finding Him. He was in practice at one with that portion of it who, accepting things at their worst, find alleviation for their sorrows in the strenuous effort to make the best of them ; but he sought to content himself with the order of things which, blind and deaf and non-willing, he said had existed for evermore, most likely—the thing was hardly worth discussing ; blind, for we can not see that it sees ; deaf, for we can not hear that it hears ; and without will, for we see no strife, purpose, or change in its going !

There was no God, then, and people would be more comfortable to know it. In any case, as there was none, they ought to know it. As to his certainty of there being none, Faber felt no desire to find one, had met with no proof that there was one, and had reasons for supposing that there was none. He had not searched very long or very wide, or with any eager desire to discover Him, if indeed there should be a God that hid Himself. His genial nature delighted in sympathy, and he sought it even in that whose perfect operation, is the destruction of all sympathy. Who does not know the pleasure of that moment of nascent communion, when argument or expostulation has begun to tell, conviction begins to dawn, and the first faint thrill of response is felt ? But the joy may be either of two very different kinds—delight in victory and the personal success of persuasion, or the ecstasy of the shared vision of truth, in which contact souls come nearer to each other than any closest familiarity can effect. Such a near-ness can be brought about by no negation however genuine, or however evil may be the thing denied.

Sympathy, then, such as he desired, Faber was now bent on finding, or bringing about in Juliet Meredith. He would fain get nearer to her. Something pushed, something drew him toward the lovely phenomenon into which had flow-ered invisible Nature's bud of shapeless protoplasm. He would have her trust him, believe him, love him. If he succeeded, so much the greater would be the value and the pleasure of the conquest, that it had been gained in spite of all her prejudices of education and conscience. And if in the process of finding truth a home in her bosom, he should cause her pain even to agony, would not the tenderness born of their lonely need for each other, be far more con-soling than any mere aspiration after a visionary comforter?

Juliet had been, so far as her father was concerned in her education, religiously brought up. No doubt Captain Meredith was more fervid than he was reasonable, but he was a true man, and in his regiment, on which he brought all his influence to bear, had been regarded with respect, even where not heartily loved. But her mother was one of those weakest of women who can never forget the beauty they once possessed, or quite believe they have lost it, re-maining, even after the very traces of it have vanished, as greedy as ever of admiration. Her maxims and principles, if she could be said to have any of the latter, were not a little opposed to her husband's; but she died when Juliet was only five years old, and the child grew to be almost the companion of her father. Hence it came that she heard much religious conversation, often partaking not a little of the character of discussion and even of dispute. She thus be-came familiar with the forms of a religious belief as narrow as its partisans are numerous. Her heart did not remain uninterested, but she was never in earnest sufficiently to discover what a thing of beggarly elements the system was, and how incapable of satisfying any childlike soul. She never questioned the truth of what she heard, and became skilled in its idioms and arguments and forms of thought. But the more familiar one becomes with any religious system, while yet the conscience and will are unawakened and obedience has not begun, the harder is it to enter into the kingdom of heaven. Such familiarity is a soul-killing experience, and great will be the excuse for some of those sons of religious parents who have gone further toward hell than many born and bred thieves and sinners.

When Juliet came to understand clearly that her new friend did mean thorough-going unbelief, the rejection of *all* the doctrines she had been taught by him whose memory she revered, she was altogether shocked, and for a day and a night regarded him as a monster of wickedness. But her horror was mainly the reflex of that with which her father would have regarded him, and all that was needed to moderate horror to disapproval, was familiarity with his doctrines in the light of his agreeable presence and undeniable good qualities. Thoroughly acquainted as she believed herself with "the plan of salvation," Jesus of Nazareth was to her but the vague shadow of something that was more than a man, yet no man at all. I had nearly said that what He came to reveal had become to her yet more vague from her nebulous notion of Him who was its revelation. Her religion was, as a matter of course, as dusky and uncertain, as the object-center of it was obscure and unrealized. Since her father's death and her comparative isolation, she had read and thought a good deal ; some of my readers may even think she had read and thought to tolerable purposes judging from her answers to Faber in the first serious conversation they had ; but her religion had lain as before in a state of dull quiescence, until her late experience, realizing to her the idea of the special care of which she stood so much in need, awoke in her a keen sense of delight, and if not a sense of gratitude as well, yet a dull desire to be grateful.

The next day, as she sat pondering what had passed between them, altogether unaware of her own weakness, she was suddenly seized with the ambition—in its inward relations the same as his—of converting him to her belief. The purpose justified an interest in him beyond what gratitude obligated, and was in part the cause why she neither shrank from his society, nor grew alarmed at the rapid growth of her intimacy. But they only who love the truth simply and altogether, can really know what they are about.

I do not care to follow the intellectual duel between them. Argument, save that of a man with himself, when council is held between heart, will, imagination, conscience, vision, and intellect, is of little avail or worth. Nothing, however, could have suited Faber's desires better. Under the shadow of such difficulties as the wise man ponders and the fool

flaunts, difficulties which have been difficulties from the
dawn of human thought, and will in new shapes keep returning so long as the human understanding yearns to infold
its origin, Faber brought up an array of arguments utterly
destructive of the wretched theories of forms of religion
which were all she had to bring into the field : so wretched
and false were they—feeblest she found them just where
she had regarded them as invincible—that in destroying
them Faber did even a poor part of the work of a soldier of
God : Mephistopheles describes himself as

> Ein Theil von jener Kraft,
> Die stets das Böse will, und stets das Gute schafft,
> .   .   .   .
> .   .   .   .   der Geist der stets verneint.

For the nature of Juliet's argument I must be content to
refer any curious reader to the false defenses made, and lies
spoken for God, in many a pulpit and many a volume, by the
worshipers of letter and system, who for their sakes " accept
His person," and plead unrighteously for Him. Before the
common sense of Faber, they went down like toys, and
Juliet, without consciously yielding at first, soon came
to perceive that they were worse than worthless—weapons
whose handles were sharper than their blades. She had no
others, nor metal of which to make any ; and what with the
persuasive influence of the man, and the pleasure in the mere
exercise of her understanding, became more and more interested as she saw the drift of his argument, and appre-
hended the weight of what truth lay upon his side. For
even the falsest argument is sustained in virtue of some
show of truth, or perhaps some crumb of reality belonging
to it. The absolute lie, if such be frameable by lips of men,
can look only the blackness of darkness it is. The lie that
can hurt, hurts in the strength of the second lie in which it
is folded—a likeness to the truth. It would have mattered
little that she was driven from line after line of her defense,
had she not, while she seemed to herself to be its champion,
actually lost sight of that for which she thought she was
striving.

It added much to Faber's influence on Juliet, that a tone
of pathos and an element of poetry generally pervaded the
forms of his denial. The tone was the more penetrating
that it veiled the pride behind it all, the pride namely of an
unhealthy conscious individuality, the pride of *self* as self,

which makes a man the center of his own universe, and a mockery to all the demons of the real universe. That man only who rises above the small yet mighty predilection, who sets the self of his own consciousness behind his back, and cherishes only the self of the Father's thought, the angel that beholds the eternal face, that man only is a free and noble being, he only breathes the air of the infinite. Another may well deny the existence of any such Father, any such infinite, for he knows nothing of the nature of either, and his testimony for it would be as worthless as that is which he gives against it.

The nature of Juliet Meredith was true and trusting— but in respect of her mother she had been sown in weakness, and she was not yet raised in strength. Because of his wife, Captain Meredith had more than once had to exchange regiments. But from him Juliet had inherited a certain strength of honest purpose, which had stood him in better stead than the whole sum of his gifts and acquirements, which was by no means despicable.

Late one lovely evening in the early summer, they sat together in the dusky parlor of the cottage, with the window to the garden open. The sweetest of western airs came in, with a faint scent chiefly of damp earth, moss, and primroses, in which, to the pensive imagination, the faded yellow of the sunset seemed to bear a part.

"I am sorry to say we must shut the window, Miss Meredith," said the doctor, rising. "You must always be jealous of the night air. It will never be friendly to you."

"What enemies we have all about us!" she returned with a slight shiver, which Faber attributed to the enemy in question, and feared his care had not amounted to precaution. "It is strange," she went on, "that all things should conspire, or at least rise, against 'the roof and crown of things,' as Tennyson calls us. Are they jealous of us?"

"Clearly, at all events, we are not at home amidst them —not genuinely so," admitted the doctor.

"And yet you say we are sprung of them?" said Juliet.

"We have lifted ourselves above them," rejoined the doctor, "and must conquer them next."

"And until we conquer them," suggested Juliet, "our lifting above them is in vain?"

"For we return to them," assented Faber; and silence fell.—"Yes," he resumed, "it is sad. The upper air is sweet, and the heart of man loves the sun;—"

"Then," interrupted Juliet, "why would you have me willing to go down to the darkness?"

"I would not have you willing. I would have you love the light as you do. We can not but love the light, for it is good; and the sorrow that we must leave it, and that so soon, only makes it dearer. The sense of coming loss is, or ought to be, the strongest of all bonds between the creatures of a day. The sweetest, saddest, most entrancing songs that love can sing, must be but variations on this one theme.—'The morning is clear; the dew mounts heavenward; the odor spreads; the sun looks over the hill; the world breaks into laughter: let us love one another! The sun grows hot, the shadow lies deep; let us sit in it, and remember; the sea lies flashing in green, dulled with purple; the peacock spreads his glories, a living garden of flowers; all is mute but the rush of the stream: let us love one another! The soft evening draws nigh; the dew is coming down again; the air is cool, dusky, and thin; it is sweeter than the morning; other words of death gleam out of the deepening sky; the birds close their wings and hide their heads, for death is near: let us love one another! The night is come, and there is no morrow; it is dark; the end is nigh; it grows cold; in the darkness and the cold we tremble, we sink; a moment and we are no more; ah! ah! beloved! let us love, let us cleave to one another, for we die!'"

But it seems to me, that the pitifulness with which we ought to regard each other in the horror of being the offspring of a love we do not love, in the danger of wandering ever, the children of light, in the midst of darkness, immeasurably surpasses the pitifulness demanded by the fancy that we are the creatures of but a day.

Moved in his soul by the sound of his own words, but himself the harp upon which the fingers of a mightier Nature than he knew were playing a prelude to a grander phantasy than he could comprehend, Faber caught the hand of Juliet where it gleamed white in the gathering gloom. But she withdrew it, saying in a tone which through the darkness seemed to him to come from afar, tinged with mockery.

"You ought to have been a poet—not a doctor, Mr. Faber!"

The jar of her apparent coolness brought him back with a shock to the commonplace. He almost shuddered. It was like a gust of icy wind piercing a summer night.

"I trust the doctor can rule the poet," he said, recovering his self-possession with an effort, and rising.

"The doctor ought at least to keep the poet from falsehood. Is false poetry any better than false religion?" returned Juliet.

"I do not quite see—"

"Your day is not a true picture of life such as you would make it.—Let me see! I will give you one.—Sit down.—Give me time.——'The morning is dark; the mist hangs and will not rise; the sodden leaves sink under the foot; overhead the boughs are bare; the cold creeps into bone and marrow; let us love one another! The sun is buried in miles of vapor; the birds sit mute on the damp twigs; the gathered drizzle slowly drips from the eaves; the wood will not burn in the grate; there is a crust in the larder, no wine in the cellar: let us love one another!'"

"Yes!" cried Faber, again seizing her hand, "let us but love, and I am content!"

Again she withdrew it.

"Nay, but hear my song out," she said, turning her face towards the window.—In the fading light he saw a wild look of pain, which vanished in a strange, bitter smile as she resumed.—"'The ashes of life's volcano are falling; they bepowder my hair; its fires have withered the rose of my lips; my forehead is wrinkled, my cheeks are furrowed, my brows are sullen; I am weary, and discontented, and unlovely: ah, let us love one another! The wheels of time grind on; my heart is sick, and cares not for thee; I care not for myself, and thou art no longer lovely to me; I can no more recall wherefore I desired thee once; I long only for the endless sleep; death alone hath charms: to say, Let us love one another, were now a mockery too bitter to be felt. Even sadness is withered. No more can it make me sorrowful to brood over the days that are gone, or to remember the song that once would have made my heart a fountain of tears. Ah, hah! the folly to think we could love to the end! But I care not; the fancy served its turn; and there is a grave for thee and me—apart or together I care not, so I cease. Thou needst not love me any more; I care not for thy love. I hardly care for the blessed darkness itself. Give me no sweet oblivious antidote, no precious poison such as I once prayed for when I feared the loss of love, that it might open to me the gate of forgetfulness, take me softly in unseen arms, and sink

with me into the during dark.   No ; I will, not calmly, but
in utter indifference, await the end.   I do not love thee ;
but I can eat, and I enjoy my wine, and my rubber of
whist——' "

She broke into a dreadful laugh.   It was all horribly unnatural ! She rose, and in the deepening twilight seemed to
draw herself up far beyond her height, then turned, and
looked out on the shadowy last of the sunset.   Faber rose
also.   He felt her shudder, though she was not within two
arm's-lengths of him.   He sprang to her side.

"Miss Meredith—Juliet—you have suffered ! The world
has been too hard for you ! Let me do all I can to make up
for it ! I too know what suffering is, and my heart is bleeding for you !"

"What ! are you not part of the world ? Are you not her
last-born—the perfection of her heartlessness ?—and will
you act the farce of consolation ? Is it the last stroke of the
eternal mockery ?"

"Juliet," he said, and once more took her hand, "I love
you."

"As a man may !" she rejoined with scorn, and pulled
her hand from his grasp.   "No ! such love as you can give,
is too poor even for me.   Love you I *will* not.   If you
speak to me so again, you will drive me away.   Talk to
me as you will of your void idol.   Tell me of the darkness of
his dwelling, and the sanctuary it affords to poor, tormented,
specter-hunted humanity ; but do not talk to me of love
also, for where your idol is, love can not be."

Faber made a gentle apology, and withdrew—abashed and
hurt—vexed with himself, and annoyed with his failure.

The moment he was gone, she cast herself on the sofa
with a choked scream, and sobbed, and ground her teeth,
but shed no tear.   Life had long been poor, arid, vague ;
now there was not left even the luxury of grief ! Where all
was loss, no loss was worth a tear.

"It were good for me that I had never been born !"
she cried.

But the doctor came again and again, and looked devotion,
though he never spoke of love.   He avoided also for a time
any further pressing of his opinions—talked of poetry, of
science, of nature—all he said tinged with the same sad
glow.   Then by degrees direct denial came up again, and
Juliet scarcely attempted opposition.   Gradually she got
quite used to his doctrine, and as she got used to it, it

seemed less dreadful, and rather less sad. What wickedness could there be in denying a God whom the very works
attributed to him declared not to exist`! Mr. Faber was a
man of science, and knew it. She could see for herself that
it must draw closer the bonds between human beings, to
learn that there was no such power to hurt them or aid them,
or to claim lordship over them, and enslave them to his will.
For Juliet had never had a glimpse of the idea, that in oneness with the love-creating Will, alone lies freedom for the
love created. When Faber perceived that his words had
begun and continued to influence her, he, on his part, grew
more kindly disposed toward her superstitions.

Let me here remark that, until we see God as He is, and
are changed into His likeness, all our beliefs must partake
more or less of superstition ; but if there be a God, the
greatest superstition of all will be found to have consisted
in denying him.

" Do not think me incapable," he said one day, after they
had at length slid back into their former freedom with each
other, " of seeing much that is lovely and gracious in the
orthodox fancies of religion. Much depends, of course,
upon the nature of the person who holds them. No belief
could be beautiful in a mind that is unlovely. A sonnet of
Shakespeare can be no better than a burned cinder in such a
mind as Mrs. Ramshorn's. But there is Mr. Wingfold,
the curate of the abbey-church ! a true, honest man, who
will give even an infidel like me fair play : nothing that
finds acceptance with him can be other than noble, whether
it be true or not. I fear he expects me to come over to
him one day. I am sorry he will be disappointed, for he is
a fellow quite free from the flummery of his profession.
For my part, I do not see why two friends should not consent to respect each other's opinions, letting the one do his
best without a God to hinder him, and the other his best
with his belief in one to aid him. Such a pair might be the
most emulous of rivals in good works."

Juliet returned no satisfactory response to this tentative
remark ; but it was from no objection any longer in her
mind to such a relation in the abstract. She had not yet at
all consented with herself to abandon the faith of her father,
but she did not see, and indeed it were hard for any one in
her condition to see, why a man and a woman, the one denying after Faber's fashion, the other believing after hers,
should not live together, and love and help each other. Of all

valueless things, a merely speculative theology is one of the most valueless. To her, God had never been much more than a name—a name, it is true, that always occurred to her in any vivid moment of her life ; but the Being whose was that name, was vague to her as a storm of sand—hardly so much her father as was the first forgotten ancestor of her line. And now it was sad for her that at such a time of peculiar emotion, when the heart is ready to turn of itself toward its unseen origin, feeling after the fountain of its love, the very occasion of the tide Godward should be an influence destructive of the same. Under the growing fascination of the handsome, noble-minded doctor, she was fast losing what little shadow of faith she had possessed. The theology she had attempted to defend was so faulty, so unfair to God, that Faber's atheism had an advantage over it as easy as it was great. His unbelief was less selfish than Juliet's faith ; consequently her faith sank, as her conscience rose meeting what was true in Faber's utterances. How could it be otherwise when she opposed lies uttered for the truth, to truths uttered for the lie ? the truth itself she had never been true enough to look in the face. As her arguments, yea the very things she argued for, went down before him, her faith, which, to be faith, should have been in the living source of all true argument, found no object, was swept away like the uprooted weed it was, and whelmed in returning chaos.

"If such is your God," he said, "I do Him a favor in denying His existence, for His very being would be a disgrace to Himself. At times, as I go my rounds, and think of the horrors of misery and suffering before me, I feel as if I were out on a campaign against an Evil supreme, the Author of them all. But when I reflect that He must then actually create from very joy in the infliction and sight of agony, I am ashamed of my foolish and cruel, though but momentary imagination, and—'There can be no such being !' I say. "I but labor in a region of inexorable law, blind as Justice herself ; law that works for good in the main, and whose carelessness of individual suffering it is for me, and all who know in any way how, to supplement with the individual care of man for his fellow-men, who, either from Nature's own necessity, or by neglect or violation of her laws, find themselves in a sea of troubles." For Nature herself, to the man who will work in harmony with her, affords the means of alleviation, of restoration even— **who knows if not of something better still ?**—the means, that is, of encountering the ills that result from the breach of her own laws ; and the best the man who would help his fellows can do, is to search after and find such other laws, whose applied operation will restore the general conduction, and render life after all an endurable, if not a desirable thing."

"But you can do nothing with death," said Juliet.

"Nothing—yet—alas ! "

"Is death a law, or a breach of law, then ? " she asked.

"That is a question I can not answer."

"In any case, were it not better to let the race die out, instead of laboriously piecing and patching at a too old garment, and so leave room for a new race to come up, which the fruit of experience, both sweet and bitter, left behind in books, might enable to avoid like ruin ? "

"Ages before they were able to read our books, they would have broken the same laws, found the same evils, and be as far as we are now beyond the help of foregone experiences : they would have the experience itself, of whose essence it is, that it is still too late."

"Then would not the kindest thing be to poison the race —as men on the prairies meet fire with fire—and so with death foil Death and have done with dying ? "

"It seems to me better to live on in the hope that some-one may yet—in some far-off age it may only be, but what a thing if it should be !—discover the law of death, learn how to meet it, and, with its fore-runners, disease and decay, banish it from the world. Would you crush the dragonfly, the moth, or the bee, because its days are so few ? Rather would you not pitifully rescue them, that they might enjoy to their natural end the wild intoxication of being ? "

"Ah, but they are happy while they live ! "

"So also are men—all men—for parts of their time. How many, do you think, would thank me for the offered poison ? "

Talk after talk of this kind, which the scope of my history forbids me to follow, took place between them, until at length Juliet, generally silenced, came to be silenced not unwillingly. All the time, their common humanity, each perceiving that the other had suffered, was urging to mutual consolation. And all the time, that mysterious force, inscru-table as creation itself, which draws the individual man and woman together, was mightily at work between them—a force which, terrible as is the array of its attendant shadows, will at length appear to have been one of the most powerful in the redemption of the world. But Juliet did nothing, said nothing, to attract Faber. He would have cast himself before her as a slave begging an owner, but for something in her carriage which constantly prevented him. At one time he read it as an unforgotten grief, at another as a cherished affection, and trembled at the thought of the agonies that might be in store for him.

Weeks passed, and he had not made one inquiry after a situation for her. It was not because he would gladly have prolonged the present arrangement of things, but that he found it almost impossible to bring himself to talk about her. If she would but accept him, he thought—then there would be no need ! But he dared not urge her—mainly from fear of failure, not at all from excess of modesty, seeing he soberly believed such love and devotion as his, worth the acceptance of any woman—even while he believed also, that to be loved of a true woman was the one only thing which could make up for the enormous swindle of life, in which man must ever be a sorrow to himself, as ever lagging behind his own child, his ideal. Even for this, the worm that must forever lie gnawing in the heart of humanity, it would be consolation enough to pluck together the roses of youth ; they had it in their own power to die while their odor was yet red. Why did she repel him ? Doubtless, he concluded over and over again, because, with her lofty ideal of love, a love for this world only seemed to her a love not worth the stooping to take. If he could but persuade her that the love offered in the agony of the fire must be a nobler love than that whispered from a bed of roses, then perhaps, dissolved in confluent sadness and sweetness, she would hold out to him the chalice of her heart, and the one pearl of the world would yet be his—a woman all his own—pure as a flower, sad as the night, and deep as nature unfathomable.

He had a grand idea of woman. He had been built with a goddess-niche in his soul, and thought how he would worship the woman that could fill it. There was a time when she must, beyond question, be one whose radiant mirror had never reflected form of man but his : now he would be content if for him she would abjure and obliterate her past. To make the woman who had loved forget utterly, was a greater victory, he said, than to wake love in

the heart of a girl, and would yield him a finer treasure, a
richer conquest. Only, pure as snow she must be—pure as
the sun himself ! Paul Faber was absolutely tyrannous in
his notions as to feminine purity. Like the diamond shield
of Prince Arthur, Knight of Magnificence, must be the
purity that would satisfy this lord of the race who could
live without a God ! Was he then such a master of purity
himself ? one so immaculate that in him such aspiration
was no presumption ? Was what he knew himself to be,
an idea to mate with his unspotted ideal ? The notion men
have of their own worth, and of claims founded thereon, is
amazing ; most amazing of all is what a man will set up to
himself as the standard of the woman he will marry. What
the woman may have a right to claim, never enters his
thought. He never doubts the right or righteousness of
aspiring to wed a woman between whose nature and his
lies a gulf, wide as between an angel praising God, and a
devil taking refuge from him in a swine. Never a shadow
of compunction crosses the leprous soul, as he stretches
forth his arms to infold the clean woman ! Ah, white dove !
thou must lie for a while among the pots. If only thy
mother be not more to blame than the wretch that acts but
after his kind ! He does not die of self-loathing ! how
then could he imagine the horror of disgust with which a
glimpse of him such as he is would blast the soul of the
woman ?" Yet has he—what is it ?—the virtue ? the pride ?
or the cruel insolence ?—to shrink with rudest abhorrence
from one who is, in nature and history and ruin, his fitting
and proper mate ! To see only how a man will be content
to be himself the thing which he scorns another for being,
might well be enough to send any one crying to the God
there may be, to come between him and himself. Lord !
what a turning of things upside down there will be one
day ! What a setting of lasts first, and firsts last !

CHAPTER XVIII.

THE PARK AT NESTLEY.

JUST inside the park, on a mossy knoll, a little way from the ancient wrought-iron gate that opened almost upon the one street of Owlkirk, the rector dug the foundation of his chapel—an oblong Gothic hall, of two squares and a half, capable of seating all in the parish nearer to it than to the abbey church. In his wife's eyes, Mr. Bevis was now an absolute saint, for not only had he begun to build a chapel in his own grounds, but to read prayers in his own church ! She was not the only one, however, who remarked how devoutly he read them, and his presence was a great comfort to Wingfold. He often objected to what his curate preached—but only to his face, and seldom when they were not alone. There was policy in this restraint : he had come to see that in all probability he would have to give in—that his curate would most likely satisfy him that he was right. The relation between them was marvelous and lovely. The rector's was a quiet awakening, a gentle second birth almost in old age. But then he had been but a boy all the time, and a very good sort of boy. He had acted in no small measure according to the light he had, and time was of course given him to grow in. It is not the world alone that requires the fullness of its time to come, ere it can receive a revelation ; the individual also has to pass through his various stages of Pagan, Guebre, Moslem, Jew, Essene—God knows what all —before he can begin to see and understand the living Christ. The child has to pass through all the phases of lower animal life ; when. change is arrested, he is born a monster ; and in many a Christian the rudiments of former stages are far from extinct—not seldom revive, and for the time seem to reabsorb the development, making indeed a monstrous show.

"For myself,"—I give a passage from Wingfold's notebook, written for his wife's reading—" I feel sometimes as if I were yet a pagan, struggling hard to break through where I see a glimmer of something better, called Christianity. In any case what I have, can be but a foretaste of what I have yet to *be ;* and if so, then indeed is there a glory laid

up for them that will have God, the *I* of their *I*, to throne
it in the temple he has built, to pervade the life he has
lifed out of himself. My soul is now as a chaos with a hungry
heart of order buried beneath its slime, that longs and longs
for the moving of the breath of God over its water and
mud."

The foundation-stone of the chapel was to be laid with
a short and simple ceremony, at which no clergy but themselves were to be present.   The rector had not consented,
and the curate had not urged, that it should remain uncon-
secrated ; it was therefore uncertain, so far at least as
Wingfold knew, whether it was to be chapel or lecture hall.
In either case it was for the use and benefit of the villagers,
and they were all invited to be present. A few of the
neighbors who were friends of the rector and his wife, were
also invited, and among them was Miss Meredith.

Mr. and Mrs. Bevis had long ere now called upon her,
and found her, as Mrs. Bevis said, fit for any society. She
had lunched several times with them, and, her health being
now greatly restored, was the readier to accept the present
invitation, that she was growing again anxious about
employment.

Almost every one was taken with her sweet manner,
shaded with sadness. At one time self-dissatisfaction had
made her too anxious to please : in the mirror of other
minds she sought a less unfavorable reflection of herself.
But trouble had greatly modified this tendency, and taken
the too-much out of her courtesy.

She and Mrs. Puckridge went together, and Faber, calling soon after, found the door locked.   He saw the gathering in the park, however, had heard something about the
ceremony, concluded they were assisting, and, after a little
questioning with himself, led his horse to the gate, made
fast the reins to it, went in, and approached the little assembly.   Ere he reached it, he saw them kneel, whereupon he
made a circuit and got behind a tree, for he would not willingly seem rude, and he dared not be hypocritical.   Thence
he descried Juliet kneeling with the rest, and could not help
being rather annoyed.   Neither could he help being a little
struck with the unusual kind of prayer the curate was making ; for he spoke as to the God of workmen, the God of
invention and creation, who made the hearts of his creatures
so like his own that they must build and make.

When the observance was over, and the people were

scattering in groups, till they should be summoned to the repast prepared for them, the rector caught sight of the doctor, and went to him.

"Ha, Faber !" he cried, holding out his hand, "this *is* kind of you ! I should hardly have expected you to be present on such an occasion !"

"I hoped my presence would not offend you," answered the doctor. "I did not presume to come closer than just within earshot of your devotions. Neither must you think me unfriendly for keeping aloof."

"Certainly not. I would not have you guilty of irreverence."

"That could hardly be, if I recognized no presence."

"There was at least," rejoined Mr. Bevis, "the presence of a good many of your neighbors, to whom you never fail to recognize your duty, and that is the second half of religion : would it not have showed want of reverence toward them, to bring an unsympathetic presence into the midst of their devotion ?"

"That I grant," said the doctor.

"But it may be," said the curate, who had come up while they talked, "that what you, perhaps justifiably, refuse to recognize as irreverence, has its root in some fault of which you are not yet aware."

"Then I'm not to blame for it," said Faber quietly.

"But you might be terribly the loser by it."

"That is, you mean, if there should be One to whom reverence is due ?"

"Yes."

"Would that be fair, then—in an All-wise, that is, toward an ignorant being ?"

"I think not. Therefore I look for something to reveal it to you. But, although I dare not say you are to blame, because that would be to take upon myself the office of a judge, which is God's alone, He only being able to give fair play, I would yet have you search yourself, and see whether you may not come upon something which keeps you from giving full and honest attention to what some people, as honest as yourself, think they see true. I am speaking only from my knowledge of myself, and the conviction that we are all much alike. What if you should discover that you do not really and absolutely disbelieve in a God ?—that the human nature is not capable of such a disbelief ?—that your unbelief has been only indifference and irreverence—and that to a Being grander and nobler and fairer than numan heart can conceive?"

"If it be so, let Him punish me," said the doctor gravely.

"If it be so, He will," said the curate solemnly, "—and you will thank Him for it—after a while. The God of my belief is too good not to make Himself known to a man who loves what is fair and honest, as you do."

The doctor was silent.

While they were talking thus, two ladies had left the others and now approached them—Mrs. Wingfold and Miss Meredith. They had heard the last few sentences, and seeing two clergymen against one infidel, hastened with the generosity of women to render him what aid they might.

"I am sure Mr. Faber is honest," said Helen.

"That is much to say for any man," returned the curate.

"If any man is, then," adjected Juliet.

"That is a great *If*," rejoined Wingfold. "—Are *you* honest, Helen?" he added, turning to his wife.

"No," she answered; "but I am honester than I was a year ago."

"So am I," said her husband; "and I hope to be honester yet before another is over. It's a big thing to say, *I am honest.*"

Juliet was silent, and Helen, who was much interested with her, turned to see how she was taking it. Her lips were as white as her face. Helen attributed the change to anger, and was silent also. The same moment the rector moved toward the place where the luncheon-tables were, and they all accompanied him, Helen still walking, in a little anxiety, by Juliet's side. It was some minutes before the color came back to her lips; but when Helen next addressed her, she answered as gently and sweetly as if the silence had been nothing but an ordinary one.

"You will stay and lunch with us, Mr. Faber?" said the rector. "There can be no hypocrisy in that—eh?"

"Thank you," returned the doctor heartily; "but my work is waiting me, and we all agree that *must* be done, whatever our opinions as to the ground of the obligation."

"And no man can say you don't do it," rejoined the curate kindly. "That's one thing we do agree in, as you say: let us hold by it, Faber, and keep as good friends as we can, till we grow better ones."

Faber could not quite match the curate in plain speaking: the pupil was not up with his master yet.

"Thank you, Wingfold," he returned, and his voice was not free of emotion, though Juliet alone felt the tremble of the one vibrating thread in it. "—Miss Meredith," he went on, turning to her, "I have heard of something that perhaps may suit you : will you allow me to call in the evening, and talk it over with you ?"

"Please do," responded Juliet eagerly. "Come before post-time if you can. It may be necessary to write."

"I will. Good morning."

He made a general bow to the company and walked away, cutting off the heads of the dandelions with his whip as he went. All followed with their eyes his firm, graceful figure, as he strode over the grass in his riding-boots and spurs.

"He's a fine fellow that !" said the rector. "—But, bless me !" he added, turning to his curate, "how things change ! If you had told me a year ago, the day would come when I should call an atheist a fine fellow, I should almost have thought you must be one yourself ! Yet here I am saying it—and never in my life so much in earnest to be a Christian ! How is it, Wingfold, my boy ?"

"He who has the spirit of his Master, will speak the truth even of his Master's enemies," answered the curate. "To this he is driven if he does not go willingly, for he knows his Master loves his enemies. If you see Faber a fine fellow, you say so, just as the Lord would, and try the more to save him. A man who loves and serves his neighbor, let him speak ever so many words against the Son of Man, is not sinning against the Holy Ghost. He is still open to the sacred influence—the virtue which is ever going forth from God to heal. It is the man who in the name of religion opposes that which he sees to be good, who is in danger of eternal sin."

"Come, come, Wingfold ! whatever you do, don't misquote," said the rector.

"I don't say it is the right reading," returned the curate, "but I can hardly be convicted of misquoting, so long as it is that of the two oldest manuscripts we have."

"You always have the better of me," answered the rector. "But tell me—are not the atheists of the present day a better sort of fellows than those we used to hear of when we were young ?"

"I do think so. But, as one who believes with his whole soul, and strives with his whole will, I attribute their betterness to the growing influences of God upon the race through them that have believed. And I am certain of this, that, whatever they are, it needs but time and continued unbelief to bring them down to any level from whatever height. They will either repent, or fall back into the worst things, believing no more in their fellow-man and the duty they owe him—of which they now rightly make so much, and yet not half enough—than they do in God and His Christ. But I do not believe half the bad things Christians have said and written of atheists. Indeed I do not believe the greater number of those they have called such, were atheists at all. I suspect that worse dishonesty, and greater injustice, are to be found among the champions, lay and cleric, of religious opinion, than in any other class. If God were such a One as many of those who would fancy themselves His apostles, the universe would be but a huge hell. Look at certain of the so-called religious newspapers, for instance. Religious! Their tongue is set on fire of hell. It may be said that they are mere money-speculations; but what makes them pay? Who buys them? To please whom do they write? Do not many buy them who are now and then themselves disgusted with them? Why do they not refuse to touch the unclean things? Instead of keeping the commandment, 'that he who loveth God love his brother also,' these, the prime channels of Satanic influence in the Church, powerfully teach, that He that loveth God must abuse his brother—or he shall be himself abused."

"I fancy," said the rector, "they would withhold the name of brother from those they abuse."

"No; not always."

"They would from an unbeliever."

"Yes. But let them then call him an enemy, and behave to him as such—that is, love him, or at least try to give him the fair play to which the most wicked of devils has the same right as the holiest of saints. It is the vile falsehood and miserable unreality of Christians, their faithlessness to their Master, their love of their own wretched sects, their worldliness and unchristianity, their talking and not doing, that has to answer, I suspect, for the greater part of our present atheism."

"I have seen a good deal of Mr. Faber of late," Juliet said, with a slight tremor in her voice, "and he seems to me incapable of falling into those vile conditions I used to hear attributed to atheists."

"The atheism of some men," said the curate, "is a

nobler thing than the Christianity of some of the foremost of so-called and so-believed Christians, and I may not doubt they will fare better at the last."

The rector looked a little blank at this, but said nothing. He had so often found, upon reflection, that what seemed extravagance in his curate was yet the spirit of Scripture, that he had learned to suspend judgment.

Miss Meredith's face glowed with the pleasure of hearing justice rendered the man in whom she was so much interested, and she looked the more beautiful. She went soon after luncheon was over, leaving a favorable impression behind her. Some of the ladies said she was much too fond of the doctor; but the gentlemen admired her spirit in standing up for him. Some objected to her paleness; others said it was not paleness, but fairness, for her eyes and hair were as dark as the night; but all agreed, that whatever it was to be called, her complexion was peculiar— some for that very reason judging it the more admirable, and others the contrary. Some said she was too stately, and attributed her carriage to a pride to which, in her position, she had no right, they said. Others judged that she needed such a bearing the more for self-defense, especially if she had come down in the world. Her dress, it was generally allowed, was a little too severe—some thought, in its defiance of the fashion, assuming. No one disputed that she had been accustomed to good society, and none could say that she had made the slightest intrusive movement toward their circle. Still, why was it that nobody knew any thing about her?

CHAPTER XIX.

THE RECTORY.

THE curate and his wife had a good deal of talk about Juliet as they drove home from Nestley. Much pleased with herself, they heard from their hostess what she had learned of her history, and were the more interested. They must find her a situation, they agreed, where she would feel at home; and in the meantime would let her understand that, if she took up her abode in Glaston, and were so inclined, the town was large enough to give a good hope of finding a few daily engagements.

Before they left Nestley, Helen had said to Mrs. Bevis that she would like to ask Miss Meredith to visit them for a few days.

"No one knows much about her," remarked Mrs. Bevis, feeling responsible.

"She can't be poison," returned Helen. "And if she were, she couldn't hurt us. That's the good of being husband and wife : so long as you are of one mind, you can do almost any thing."

When Faber called upon Juliet in the evening, nothing passed between them concerning the situation at which he had hinted. When he entered she was seated as usual in the corner of the dingy little couch, under the small window looking into the garden, in the shadow. She did not rise, but held out her hand to him. He went hastily up to her, took the hand she offered, sat down beside her, and at once broke into a full declaration of his love—now voluble, now hesitating, now submissive, now persuasive, but humblest when most passionate. Whatever the man's conceit, or his estimate of the thing he would have her accept, it was in all honesty and modesty that he offered her the surrender of the very citadel of his being—alas, too " empty, swept, and garnished ! " Juliet kept her head turned from him ; he felt the hand he held tremble, and every now and then make a faint struggle to escape from his ; but he could not see that her emotion was such as hardly to be accounted for either by pleasure at the hearing of welcome words, or sorrow that her reply must cause pain. He ceased at length, and with eyes of longing sought a glimpse of her face, and caught one. Its wild, waste expression frightened him. It was pallid like an old sunset, and her breath came and went stormily. Three times, in a growing agony of effort, her lips failed of speech. She gave a sudden despairing cast of her head sideways, her mouth opened a little as if with mere helplessness, she threw a pitiful glance in his face, burst into a tumult of sobs, and fell back on the couch. Not a tear came to her eyes, but such was her trouble that she did not even care to lift her hand to her face to hide the movements of its rebellious muscles. Faber, bewildered, but, from the habits of his profession, master of himself, instantly prepared her something, which she took obediently ;

and as soon as she was quieted a little, mounted and rode away : two things were clear—one, that she could not be indifferent to him ; the other, that, whatever the cause of her emotion, she would for the present be better without him. He was both too kind and too proud to persist in presenting himself.

The next morning Helen drew up her ponies at Mrs. Puckridge's door, and Wingfold got out and stood by their heads, while she went in to call on Miss Meredith.

Juliet had passed a sleepless night, and greatly dreaded the next interview with Faber. Helen's invitation, therefore, to pay them a few days' visit, came to her like a redemption : in their house she would have protection both from Faber and from herself. Heartily, with tears in her eyes, she accepted it ; and her cordial and grateful readiness placed her yet a step higher in the regard of her new friends. The acceptance of a favor may be the conferring of a greater. Quickly, hurriedly, she put up "her bag of needments," and with a sad, sweet smile of gentle apology, took the curate's place beside his wife, while he got into the seat behind.

Juliet, having been of late so much confined to the house, could not keep back the tears called forth by the pleasure of the rapid motion through the air, the constant change of scene, and that sense of human story which haunts the mind in passing unknown houses and farms and villages. An old thatched barn works as directly on the social feeling as the ancient castle or venerable manor-seat ; many a simple house will move one's heart like a poem ; many a cottage like a melody. When at last she caught sight of the great church-tower, she clapped her hands with delight. There was a place in which to wander and hide ! she thought—in which to find refuge and rest, and coolness and shadow ! Even for Faber's own sake she would not believe that faith a mere folly which had built such a pile as that ! Surely there was some way of meeting the terrible things he said—if only she could find it !

"Are you fastidious, Miss Meredith, or willing to do any thing that is honest ?" the curate asked rather abruptly, leaning forward from the back seat.

"If ever I was fastidious," she answered, "I think I am pretty nearly cured. I should certainly like my work to be so far within my capacity as to be pleasant to me."

"Then there is no fear," answered the curate. "The people who don't get on, are those that pick and choose upon false principles. They generally attempt what they are unfit for, and deserve their failures.—Are you willing to teach little puds and little tongues ? "

" Certainly."

" Tell me what you are able to do ? "

" I would rather not. You might think differently when you came to know me. But you can ask me any questions you please. I shan't hide my knowledge, and I can't hide my ignorance."

" Thank you," said the curate, and leaned back again in his seat.

After luncheon, Helen found to her delight that, although Juliet was deficient enough in the mechanics belonging to both voice and instrument, she could yet sing and play with expression and facility, while her voice was one of the loveliest she had ever heard. When the curate came home from his afternoon attentions to the ailing of his flock, he was delighted to hear his wife's report of her gifts.

" Would you mind reading a page or two aloud ? " he said to their visitor, after they had had a cup of tea. " I often get my wife to read to me."

She consented at once. He put a volume of Carlyle into her hand. She had never even tasted a book of his before, yet presently caught the spirit of the passage, and read charmingly.

In the course of a day or two they discovered that she was sadly defective in spelling, a paltry poverty no doubt, yet awkward for one who would teach children. In grammar and arithmetic also the curate found her lacking. Going from place to place with her father, she had never been much at school, she said, and no one had ever compelled her to attend to the dry things. But nothing could be more satisfactory than the way in which she now, with the help of the curate and his wife, set herself to learn ; and until she should have gained such proficiency as would enable them to speak of her acquirements with confidence, they persuaded her, with no great difficulty, to continue their guest. Wingfold, who had been a tutor in his day, was well qualified to assist her, and she learned with wonderful rapidity.

The point that most perplexed Wingfold with her was that, while very capable of perceiving and admiring the good, she was yet capable of admiring things of altogether inferior quality. What did it mean ? Could it arise from an excess of productive faculty, not yet sufficiently differenced from

the receptive ?   One could imagine such an excess ready to
seize the poorest molds, flow into them, and endow them
for itself with attributed life and power.   He found also that
she was familiar with the modes of thought and expression
peculiar to a certain school of theology—embodiments from
which, having done their good, and long commenced doing
their evil, Truth had begun to withdraw itself, consuming as
it withdrew.   For the moment the fire ceases to be the life
of the bush in which it appears, the bush will begin to be
consumed.   At the same time he could perfectly recognize
the influence of Faber upon her.   For not unfrequently, the
talk between the curate and his wife would turn upon some
point connected with the unbelief of the land, so much more
active, though but seemingly more extensive than heretofore ;
when she would now make a remark, now ask a question, in
which the curate heard the doctor as plainly as if the words
had come direct from his lips : those who did not believe
might answer so and so—might refuse the evidence—might
explain the thing differently.   But she listened well, and
seemed to understand what they said.   The best of her un-
doubtedly appeared in her music, in which she was funda-
mentally far superior to Helen, though by no means so well
trained, taught or practiced in it ; whence Helen had the unspeakable delight, one which only a humble, large and lofty
mind can ever have, of consciously ministering to the growth
of another in the very thing wherein that other is naturally
the superior.   The way to the blessedness that is in music,
as to all other blessednesses, lies through weary labors, and
the master must suffer with the disciple ; Helen took Juliet
like a child, set her to scales and exercises, and made her
practice hours a day.

CHAPTER XX.

AT THE PIANO.

WHEN Faber called on Juliet, the morning after the last
interview recorded, and found where she was gone, he did
not doubt she had taken refuge with her new friends from
his importunity, and was at once confirmed in the idea he

had cherished through the whole wakeful night, that the cause of her agitation was nothing else than the conflict between her heart and a false sense of duty, born of prejudice and superstition. She was not willing to send him away, and yet she dared not accept him. Her behavior had certainly revealed any thing but indifference, and therefore must not make him miserable. At the same time if it was her pleasure to avoid him, what chance had he of seeing her alone at the rectory? The thought made him so savage that for a moment he almost imagined his friend had been playing him false.

" I suppose he thinks every thing fair in religion, as well as in love and war ! " he said to himself. " It's a mighty stake, no doubt—a soul like Juliet's ! "

He laughed scornfully. It was but a momentary yielding to the temptation of injustice, however, for his conscience told him at once that the curate was incapable of any thing either overbearing or underhand. He would call on her as his patient, and satisfy himself at once how things were between them. At best they had taken a bad turn.

He judged it better, however, to let a day or two pass. When he did call, he was shown into the drawing-room, where he found Helen at the piano, and Juliet having a singing-lesson from her. Till then he had never heard Juliet's song voice. A few notes of it dimly reached him as he approached the room, and perhaps prepared him for the impression he was about to receive : when the door opened, like a wind on a more mobile sea, it raised sudden tumult in his soul. Not once in his life had he ever been agitated in such fashion ; he knew himself as he had never known himself. It was as if some potent element, undreamed of before, came rushing into the ordered sphere of his world, and shouldered its elements from the rhythm of their going. It was a full contralto, with pathos in the very heart of it, and it seemed to wrap itself round his heart like a serpent of saddest splendor, and press the blood from it up into his eyes. The ladies were too much occupied to hear him announced, or note his entrance, as he stood by the door, absorbed, entranced.

Presently he began to feel annoyed, and proceeded thereupon to take precautions with himself. For Juliet was having a lesson of the severest kind, in which she accepted every lightest hint with the most heedful attention, and conformed thereto with the sweetest obedience ; whence it

came that Faber, the next moment after fancying he had
screwed his temper to stoic pitch, found himself passing
from displeasure to indignation, and thence almost to fury,
as again and again some exquisite tone, that went thrilling
through all his being, discovering to him depths and recesses
hitherto unimagined, was unceremoniously, or with briefest
apology, cut short for the sake of some suggestion from
Helen. Whether such suggestion was right or wrong, was
to Faber not of the smallest consequence : it was in itself a
sacrilege, a breaking into the house of life, a causing of that
to cease whose very being was its justification. Mrs. Wingfold ! she was not fit to sing in the same chorus with her !
Juliet was altogether out of sight of her. He had heard
Mrs. Wingfold sing many a time, and she could no more
bring out a note like one of those she was daring to
criticise, than a cat could emulate a thrush !

"Ah, Mr. Faber !—I did not know you were there," said
Helen at length, and rose. "We were so busy we never
heard you."

If she had looked at Juliet, she would have said *I* instead
of *we*. Her kind manner brought Faber to himself a little.

"Pray, do not apologize," he said. "I could have listened
forever."

"I don't wonder. It is not often one hears notes like
those. Were you aware what a voice you had saved to the
world ?"

"Not in the least. Miss Meredith leaves her gifts to be
discovered."

"All good things wait the seeker," said Helen, who had
taken to preaching since she married the curate, some of
her half-friends said ; the fact being that life had grown to
her so gracious, so happy, so serious, that she would not
unfrequently say a thing worth saying.

In the interstices of this little talk, Juliet and Faber had
shaken hands, and murmured a conventional word or two.

"I suppose this is a professional visit ?" said Helen.
"Shall I leave you with your patient ?"

As she put the question, however, she turned to Juliet.

"There is not the least occasion," Juliet replied, a little
eagerly, and with a rather wan smile. "I am quite well,
and have dismissed my doctor."

Faber was in the mood to imagine more than met the ear,
and the words seemed to him of cruel significance. A flush
of anger rose to his forehead, and battled with the paleness

of chagrin. He said nothing. But Juliet saw and understood. Instantly she held out her hand to him again, and
supplemented the offending speech with the words,

" —but, I hope, retained my friend ? "

The light rushed again into Faber's eyes, and Juliet
repented afresh, for the words had wrought too far in the
other direction.

" That is," she amended, " if Mr. Faber will condescend
to friendship, after having played the tyrant so long."

" I can only aspire to it," said the doctor.

It sounded mere common compliment, the silliest thing
between man and woman, and Mrs. Wingfold divined nothing more : she was not quick in such matters. Had she
suspected, she might, not knowing the mind of the lady
have been a little perplexed. As it was, she did not leave
the room, and presently the curate entered, with a newspaper in his hand.

" They're still at it, Faber," he said, " with their heated
liquids and animal life ! "

" I need not ask which side you take," said the doctor,
not much inclined to enter upon any discussion.

" I take neither," answered the curate. " Where is the
use, or indeed possibility, so long as the men of science themselves are disputing about the facts of experiment ? It will
be time enough to try to understand them, when they are
agreed and we know what the facts really are. Whatever
they may turn out to be, it is but a truism to say they must
be consistent with all other truth, although they may entirely
upset some of our notions of it."

" To which side then do you lean, as to the weight of the
evidence ? " asked Faber, rather listlessly.

He had been making some experiments of his own in the
direction referred to. They were not so complete as he
would have liked, for he found a large country practice
unfriendly to investigation ; but, such as they were, they
favored the conclusion that no form of life appeared where
protection from the air was thorough.

" I take the evidence," answered the curate, " to be in
favor of what they so absurdly call spontaneous generation."

" I am surprised to hear you say so," returned Faber.
" The conclusions necessary thereupon, are opposed to all
your theology."

" Must I then, because I believe in a living Truth, be

myself an unjust judge ? " said the curate. " But indeed
the conclusions are opposed to no theology I have any
acquaintance with ; and if they were, it would give me no
concern.   Theology is not my origin, but God.   Nor do I
acknowledge any theology but what Christ has taught, and
has to teach me.   When, and under what circumstances,
life comes first into human ken, can not affect His lessons of
trust and fairness.   If I were to play tricks with the truth,
shirk an argument, refuse to look a fact in the face, I should
be ashamed to look Him in the face.   What he requires of
his friends is pure, open-eyed truth."

" But how," said the doctor, " can you grant spontaneous
generation, and believe in a Creator ? "

" I said the term was an absurd one," rejoined the curate.

" Never mind the term then : you admit the fact ? " said
Faber.

" What fact ? " asked Wingfold.

" That in a certain liquid, where all life has been destroyed, and where no contact with life is admitted, life of
itself appears," defined the doctor.

" No, no ; I admit nothing of the sort," cried Wingfold.
" I only admit that the evidence seems in favor of believing that in some liquids that have been heated to a high
point, and kept from the air, life has yet appeared.   How
can I tell whether *all* life already there was first destroyed ?
whether a yet higher temperature would not have destroyed
yet more life ?   What if the heat, presumed to destroy all
known germs of life in them, should be the means of developing other germs, further removed ?   Then as to *spon-
taneity*, as to life appearing of itself, that question involves
something beyond physics.   Absolute life can exist only of
and by itself, else were it no perfect thing ; but will you
say that a mass of protoplasm—that *proto* by the way is a
begged question—exists by its own power, appears by its
own will ?   Is it not rather there because it can not help it ? "

" It is there in virtue of the life that is in it," said Faber.

" Of course ; that is a mere truism," returned Wingfold,
" equivalent to, It lives in virtue of life.   There is nothing
spontaneous in that.   Its life must in some way spring from
the true, the original, the self-existent life."

" There you are begging the whole question," objected
the doctor.

" No ; not the whole," persisted the curate ; " for I fancy
you will yourself admit there is some blind driving law be-

hind the phenomenon. But now I will beg the whole question, if you like to say so, for the sake of a bit of purely metaphysical argument : the law of life behind, if it be spontaneously existent, can not be a blind, deaf, unconscious law ; if it be unconscious of itself, it can not be spontaneous ; whatever is of itself must be God, and the source of all non-spontaneous, that is, all other existence."

" Then it has been only a dispute about a word ?" said Faber.

" Yes, but a word involving a tremendous question," answered Wingfold.

" Which I give up altogether," said the doctor, " asserting that there is *nothing* spontaneous, in the sense you give the word—the original sense I admit. From all eternity a blind, unconscious law has been at work, producing."

" I say, an awful living Love and Truth and Right, creating children of its own," said the curate—" and there is our difference."

" Yes," assented Faber.

" Anyhow, then," said Wingfold, " so far as regards the matter in hand, all we can say is, that under such and such circumstances life *appears—whence*, we believe differently ; *how*, neither of us can tell—perhaps will ever be able to tell. I can't talk in scientific phrase like you, Faber, but truth is not tied to any form of words."

" It is well disputed," said the doctor, " and I am inclined to grant that the question with which we started does not immediately concern the great differences between us."

It was rather hard upon Faber to have to argue when out of condition and with a lady beside to whom he was longing to pour out his soul—his antagonist a man who never counted a sufficing victory gained, unless his adversary had had light and wind both in his back. Trifling as was the occasion of the present skirmish, he had taken his stand on the lower ground. Faber imagined he read both triumph and pity in Juliet's regard, and could scarcely endure his position a moment longer.

" Shall we have some music ?" said Wingfold. " —I see the piano open. Or are you one of those worshipers of work, who put music in the morning in the same category with looking on the wine when it is red ?"

" Theoretically, no ; but practically, yes," answered Faber, " —at least for to-day. I shouldn't like poor Widow

Mullens to lie listening to the sound of that old water-wheel,
till it took up its parable against the faithlessness of men in
general, and the doctor in particular.   I can't do her much
good, poor old soul, but I can at least make her fancy herself of consequence enough not to be forgotten."

The curate frowned a little—thoughtfully—but said nothing, and followed his visitor to the door. When he returned,
he said,

"I wonder what it is in that man that won't let him
believe !"

"Perhaps he will yet, some day," said Juliet, softly.

"He will ; he must," answered the curate. "He always
reminds me of the young man who had kept the law, and
whom our Lord loved.   Surely he must have been one of
the first that came and laid his wealth at the apostles' feet !
May not even that half of the law which Faber tries to keep,
be school-master enough to lead him to Christ ?—But come,
Miss Meredith ; now for our mathematics !"

Every two or three days the doctor called to see his late
patient.   She wanted looking after, he said.   But not once
did he see her alone.   He could not tell from their behavior whether she or her hostess was to blame for his recur-
ring disappointment ; but the fact was, that his ring at the
door-bell was the signal to Juliet not to be alone.

CHAPTER XXI.

THE PASTOR'S STUDY.

HAPPENING at length to hear that visitors were expected,
Juliet, notwithstanding the assurances of her hostess that
there was plenty of room for her, insisted on finding lodgings, and taking more direct measures for obtaining employment.   But the curate had not been idle in her affairs, and
had already arranged for her with some of his own people
who had small children, only he had meant she should not
begin just yet.   He wanted her both to be a little stronger,
and to have got a little further with one or two of her studies.
And now, consulting with Helen, he broached a new idea on
the matter of her lodgment.

A day or two before Jones, the butcher, had been talking to him about Mr. Drake—saying how badly his congregation had behaved to him, and in what trouble he had come to him, because he could not pay his bill. The good fellow had all this time never mentioned the matter ; and it was from growing concern about the minister that he now spoke of it to the curate.

"We don't know all the circumstances, however, Mr. Jones," the curate replied ; "and perhaps Mr. Drake himself does not think so badly of it as you do. He is a most worthy man. Mind you let him have whatever he wants. I'll see to you. Don't mention it to a soul."

" Bless your heart and liver, sir !" exclaimed the butcher, " he's ten times too much of a gentleman to do a kindness to. I couldn't take no liberty with that man—no, not if he was 'most dead of hunger. He'd eat the rats out of his own 'cellar, I do believe, before he'd accept what you may call a charity ; and for buying when he knows he can't pay, why he'd beg outright before he'd do that. What he do live on now I can't nohow make out—and that's what doos make me angry with him—as if a honest tradesman didn't know how to behave to a gentleman ! Why, they tell me, sir, he did use to drive his carriage and pair in London ! And now he's a doin' of his best to live on nothink at all ! —leastways, so they tell me—seein' as how he'd have 'em believe he was turned a—what's it they call it !—a—a—a wegetablarian !—that's what he do, sir ! But I know better. He may be eatin' grass like a ox, as did that same old king o' Israel as growed the feathers and claws in consequence ; and I don't say he ain't ; but one thing I'm sure of, and that is, that if he be, it's by cause he can't help it. Why, sir, I put it to you—no gentleman would—if he could help it.— Why don't he come to me for a bit o' wholesome meat ?" he went on in a sorely injured tone. " He knows I'm ready for anythink in reason ! Them peas an' beans an' cabbages an' porridges an' carrots an' turmits—why, sir, they ain't nothink at all but water an' wind. I don't say as they mayn't keep a body alive for a year or two, but, bless you, there's nothink in them ; and the man'll be a skelinton long before he's dead an' buried ; an' I shed jest like to know where's the good o' life on sich terms as them !"

Thus Jones, the butcher—a man who never sold bad meat, never charged for an ounce more than he delivered, and when he sold to the poor, considered them. In buying and selling he had a weakness for giving the fair play he demanded. He had a little spare money somewhere, but he did not make a fortune out of hunger, retire early, and build churches. A local preacher once asked him if he knew what was the plan of salvation. He answered with the utmost innocence, cutting him off a great lump of leg of beef for a family he had just told him was starving, that he hadn't an idea, but no Christian could doubt it was all right.

The curate, then, pondering over what Mr. Jones had told him, had an idea ; and now he and his wife were speedily of one mind as to attempting an arrangement for Juliet with Miss Drake. What she would be able to pay would, they thought, ease them a little, while she would have the advantage of a better protection than a lodging with more humble people would afford her. Juliet was willing for any thing they thought best.

Wingfold therefore called on the minister, to make the proposal to him, and was shown up to his study—a mere box, where there was just room for a chair on each side of the little writing-table. The walls from top to bottom were entirely hidden with books.

Mr. Drake received him with a touching mixture of sadness and cordiality, and heard in silence what he had to say.

" It is very kind of you to think of us, Mr. Wingfold," he replied, after a moment's pause. " But I fear the thing is impossible. Indeed, it is out of the question. Circumstances are changed with us. Things are not as they once were."

There had always been a certain negative virtue in Mr. Drake, which only his friends were able to see, and only the wisest of them to set over against his display—this, namely, that he never attempted to gain credit for what he knew he had not. As he was not above show, I can not say he was safely above false show, for he who is capable of the one is still in danger of the other ; but he was altogether above deception : that he scorned. If, in his time of plenty he liked men to be aware of his worldly facilities, he now, in the time of his poverty, preferred that men should be aware of the bonds in which he lived. His nature was simple, and loved to let in the daylight. Concealment was altogether alien to him. From morning to night anxious, he could not bear to be supposed of easy heart. Some men think poverty such a shame that they would rather be judged absolutely mean than confess it. Mr. Drake's openness may have

sprung from too great a desire for sympathy; or from a
diseased honesty—I can not tell; I will freely allow that if
his faith had been as a grain of mustard seed, he would not
have been so haunted with a sense of his poverty, as to be
morbidly anxious to confess it. He would have known that
his affairs were in high charge : and that, in the full flow
of the fountain of prosperity, as well as in the scanty,
gravelly driblets from the hard-wrought pump of poverty, the
supply came all the same from under the throne of God,
and he would not have *felt* poor. A man ought never to
feel rich for riches, nor poor for poverty. The perfect man
must always feel rich, because God is rich.

"The fact is," Mr. Drake went on, "we are very poor—
absolutely poor, Mr. Wingfold—so poor that I may not even
refuse the trifling annuity my late congregation will dole
out to me."

"I am sorry to know it," said the curate.

"But I must take heed of injustice," the pastor resumed ;
"I do not think they would have treated me so had they
not imagined me possessed of private means. The pity now
is that the necessity which would make me glad to fall in
with your kind proposal itself renders the thing impracti-
cable. Even with what your friend would contribute to the
housekeeping we could not provide a table fit for her. But
Dorothy ought to have the pleasure of hearing your kind
proposition : if you will allow me I will call her."

Dorothy was in the kitchen, making pastry—for the rare
treat of a chicken pudding : they had had a present of a
couple of chickens from Mrs. Thomson—when she heard
her father's voice calling her from the top of the little stair.
When Lisbeth opened the door to the curate she was on her
way out, and had not yet returned ; so she did not know
any one was with him, and hurried up with her arms bare.

She recoiled half a step when she saw Mr. Wingfold,
then went frankly forward to welcome him, her hands in
her white pinafore.

"It's only flour," she said, smiling.

"It is a rare pleasure now-a-days to catch a lady at work "
said Wingfold. "My wife always dusts my study for me.
I told her I would not have it done except she did it—just
to have the pleasure of seeing her at it. My conviction is,
that only a lady can become a thorough servant."

"Why don't you have lady-helps then ?" said Dorothy.

"Because I don't know where to find them. Ladies are

scarce ; and any thing almost would be better than a house-ful of half-ladies."

"I think I understand," said Dorothy thoughtfully.

Her father now stated Mr. Wingfold's proposal—in the tone of one sorry to be unable to entertain it.

"I see perfectly why you think we could not manage it, papa," said Dorothy. "But why should not Miss Meredith lodge with us in the same way as with Mrs. Puckridge? She could have the drawing-room and my bedroom, and her meals by herself. Lisbeth is wretched for want of dinners to cook."

"Miss Meredith would hardly relish the idea of turning you out of your drawing-room," said Wingfold.

"Tell her it may save us from being turned out of the house. Tell her she will be a great help to us," returned Dorothy eagerly.

"My child," said her father, the tears standing in his eyes, "your reproach sinks into my very soul."

"My reproach, father!" repeated Dorothy aghast. "How you do mistake me! I can't say with you that the will of God is every thing ; but I can say that far less than your will—your ability—will always be enough for me."

"My child," returned her father, "you go on to rebuke me! You are immeasurably truer to me than I am to my God.—Mr. Wingfold, you love the Lord, else I would not confess my sin to you : of late I have often thought, or at least felt as if He was dealing hardly with me. Ah, my dear sir ! you are a young man : for the peace of your soul serve God so, that, by the time you are my age, you may be sure of Him. I try hard to put my trust in Him, but my faith is weak. It ought by this time to have been strong. I always want to see the way He is leading me—to under-stand something of what He is doing with me or teaching me, before I can accept His will, or get my heart to consent not to complain. It makes me very unhappy. I begin to fear that I have never known even the beginning of confi-dence, and that faith has been with me but a thing of the understanding and the lips."

He bowed his head on his hands. Dorothy went up to him and laid a hand on his shoulder, looking unspeakably sad. A sudden impulse moved the curate.

"Let us pray," he said, rising, and kneeled down.

It was a strange, unlikely thing to do ; but he was an

unlikely man, and did it. The others made haste to kneel also.

"God of justice," he said, " Thou knowest how hard it is for us, and Thou wilt be fair to us. We have seen no visions ; we have never heard the voice of Thy Son, of whom those tales, so dear to us, have come down the ages ; we have to fight on in much darkness of spirit and of mind, both from the ignorance we can not help, and from the fault we could have helped ; we inherit blindness from the error of our fathers ; and when fear, or the dread of shame, or the pains of death, come upon us, we are ready to despair, and cry out that there is no God, or, if there be, He has forgotten His children. There are times when the darkness closes about us like a wall, and Thou appearest nowhere, either in our hearts, or in the outer universe ; we can not tell whether the things we seemed to do in Thy name, were not mere hypocrisies, and our very life is but a gulf of darkness. We cry aloud, and our despair is as a fire in our bones to make us cry ; but to all our crying and listening, there seems neither hearing nor answer in the boundless waste. Thou who knowest Thyself God, who knowest Thyself that for which we groan, Thou whom Jesus called Father, we appeal to Thee, not as we imagine Thee, but as Thou seest Thyself, as Jesus knows Thee, to Thy very self we cry—help us, O Cause of us ! O Thou from whom alone we are this weakness, through whom alone we can become strength, help us—be our Father. We ask for nothing beyond what Thy Son has told us to ask. We beg for no signs or wonders, but for Thy breath upon our souls, Thy spirit in our hearts. We pray for no cloven tongues of fire—for no mighty rousing of brain or imagination ; but we do, with all our power of prayer, pray for Thy spirit ; we do not even pray to know that it is given to us ; let us, if so it pleases Thee, remain in doubt of the gift for years to come—but lead us thereby. Knowing ourselves only as poor and feeble, aware only of ordinary and common movements of mind and soul, may we yet be possessed by the spirit of God, led by His will in ours. For all things in a man, even those that seem to him the commonest and least uplifted, are the creation of Thy heart, and by the lowly doors of our wavering judgment, dull imagination, luke-warm love, and palsied will, Thou canst enter and glorify all. Give us patience because our hope is in Thee, not in ourselves. Work Thy will in us, and our prayers are ended. Amen."

They rose. The curate said he would call again in the evening, bade them good-by, and went. Mr. Drake turned to his daughter and said—

" Dorothy, that's not the way I have been used to pray or hear people pray ; nevertheless the young man seemed to speak very straight up to God. It appears to me there was another spirit there with his. I will humble myself before the Lord. Who knows but he may lift me up ! "

" What can my father mean by saying that perhaps God will lift him up ? " said Dorothy to herself when she was alone. " It seems to me if I only knew God was anywhere, I should want no other lifting up. I should then be lifted up above every thing forever."

Had she said so to the curate, he would have told her that the only way to be absolutely certain of God, is to see Him as He is, and for that we must first become absolutely pure in heart. For this He is working in us, and perfection and vision will flash together. Were conviction possible without that purity and that vision, I imagine it would work evil in us, fix in their imperfection our ideas, notions, feelings, concerning God, give us for His glory the warped reflection of our cracked and spotted and rippled glass, and so turn our worship into an idolatry.

Dorothy was a rather little woman, with lightish auburn hair, a large and somewhat heavy forehead, fine gray eyes, small well-fashioned features, a fair complexion on a thin skin, and a mouth that would have been better in shape if it had not so often been informed of trouble. With this trouble their poverty had nothing to do ; that did not weigh upon her as a straw. She was proud to share her father's lot, and could have lived on as little as any laboring woman with seven children. She was indeed a trifle happier since her father's displacement, and would have been happier still had he found it within the barest possibility to decline the annuity allotted him ; for, as far back as she could remember, she had been aware of a dislike to his position—partly from pride it may be, but partly also from a sense of the imperfection of the relation between him and his people—one in which love must be altogether predominant, else is it hateful—and chiefly because of a certain sordid element in the community —a vile way of looking at sacred things through the spectacles of mammon, more evident—I only say more evident —in dissenting than in Church of England communities, because of the pressure of expenses upon them. Perhaps

the impossibility of regarding her father's church with reverence, laid her mind more open to the cause of her trouble
—such doubts, namely, as an active intellect, nourished on
some of the best books, and disgusted with the weak fervor
of others rated high in her hearing, had been suggesting for
years before any words of Faber's reached her. The more
her devout nature longed to worship, the more she found it
impossible to worship that which was presented for her love
and adoration. She believed entirely in her father, but she
knew he could not meet her doubts, for many things made
it plain that he had never had such himself. An ordinary
mind that has had doubts, and has encountered and over-
come them, or verified and found them the porters of the
gates of truth, may be profoundly useful to any mind similarly assailed ; but no knowledge of books, no amount of
logic, no degree of acquaintance with the wisest conclusions
of others, can enable a man who has not encountered skep-
ticism in his own mind, to afford any essential help to those
caught in the net. For one thing, such a man will be incapable of conceiving the possibility that the net may be the
net of The Fisher of Men.

Dorothy, therefore, was sorely oppressed. For a long
time her life had seemed withering from her, and now that
her father was fainting on the steep path, and she had no
water to offer him, she was ready to cry aloud in bitterness
of spirit.

She had never heard the curate preach—had heard talk
of his oddity on all sides, from men and women no more
capable of judging him than the caterpillar of judging the
butterfly—which yet it must become. The draper, who
understood him, naturally shrunk from praising to her
the teaching for which he not unfrequently deserted that of
her father, and she never looked in the direction of him with
any hope. Yet now, the very first time she had heard him
speak out of the abundance of his heart, he had left behind
him a faint brown ray of hope in hers. It was very peculiar
of him to break out in prayer after such an abrupt fashion
—in the presence of an older minister than himself—and
praying for him too ! But there was such an appearance of
reality about the man ! such a simplicity in his look ! such
a directness in his petitions ! such an active fervor of hope
in his tone—without an atom of what she had heard called
unction ! His thought and speech appeared to arise from
no separated sacred mood that might be assumed and laid

aside, but from present faith and feeling, from the absolute point of life at that moment being lived by him. It
was an immediate appeal to a hearing, and understanding,
and caring God, whose breath was the very air His creatures breathed, the element of their life; an utter acknowledgment of His will as the bliss of His sons and daughters! Such was the shining of the curate's light, and it
awoke hope in Dorothy.

In the evening he came again as he had said, and brought
Juliet. Each in the other, Dorothy and she recognized
suffering, and in a very few moments every thing was
arranged between them. Juliet was charmed with the simplicity and intentness of Dorothy; in Juliet's manner and
carriage, Dorothy at once recognized a breeding superior to
her own, and at once laid hold of the excellence by acknowledging it. In a moment she made Juliet understand how
things were, and Juliet saw as quickly that she must assent
to the arrangement proposed. But she had not been with
them two days, when Dorothy found the drawing-room as
open to her as before she came, and far more pleasant.

While the girls were talking below, the two clergymen sat
again in the study.

"I have taken the liberty," said the curate, "of bringing
an old book I should like you to look at, if you don't mind
—chiefly for the sake of some verses that pleased me much
when I read them first, and now please me more when I
read them for the tenth time. If you will allow me, I will
read them to you."

Mr. Drake liked good poetry, but did not much relish
being called upon to admire, as he imagined he was now.
He assented, of course, graciously enough, and soon found
his mistake.

This is the poem Wingfold read:

CONSIDER THE RAVENS.

Lord, according to Thy words,
I have considered Thy birds;
And I find their life good,
And better the better understood;
Sowing neither corn nor wheat,
They have all that they can eat;
Reaping no more than they sow,
They have all they can stow;
Having neither barn nor store,
Hungry again, they eat more.

Considering, I see too that they
Have a busy life, and plenty of play ;
In the earth they dig their bills deep,
And work well though they do not heap ;
Then to play in the air they are not loth,
And their nests between are better than both.

But this is when there blow no storms ;
When berries are plenty in winter, and worms ;
When their feathers are thick, and oil is enough
To keep the cold out and the rain off :
If there should come a long hard frost,
Then it looks as Thy birds were lost.

But I consider further, and find
A hungry bird has a free mind ;
He is hungry to-day, not to-morrow ;
Steals no comfort, no grief doth borrow ;
This moment is his, Thy will hath said it,
The next is nothing till Thou hast made it.

The bird has pain, but has no fear,
Which is the worst of any gear ;
When cold and hunger and harm betide him,
He gathers them not to stuff inside him ;
Content with the day's ill he has got,
He waits just, nor haggles with his lot ;
Neither jumbles God's will
With driblets from his own still.

But next I see, in my endeavor,
Thy birds here do not live forever ;
That cold or hunger, sickness or age,
Finishes their earthly stage ;
The rook drops without a stroke,
And never gives another croak ;
Birds lie here, and birds lie there,
With little feathers all astare ;
And in Thy own sermon, Thou
That the sparrow falls dost allow.

It shall not cause me any alarm,
For neither so comes the bird to harm,
Seeing our Father, Thou hast said,
Is by the sparrow's dying bed ;
Therefore it is a blessed place,
And the sparrow in high grace.

It cometh therefore to this, Lord ;
I have considered Thy word,
And henceforth will be Thy bird.

By the time Wingfold ceased, the tears were running

down the old man's face. When he saw that, the curate rose at once, laid the book on the table, shook hands with him, and went away. The minister laid his head on the table, and wept.

Juliet had soon almost as much teaching as she could manage. People liked her, and children came to love her a little. A good report of her spread. The work was hard, chiefly because it included more walking than she had been accustomed to ; but Dorothy generally walked with her, and to the places furthest off, Helen frequently took her with her ponies, and she got through the day's work pretty well. The fees were small, but they sufficed, and made life a little easier to her host and his family. Amanda got very fond of her, and, without pretending to teach her, Juliet taught her a good deal. On Sundays she went to church ; and Dorothy, although it cost her a struggle to face the imputation of resentment, by which the chapel-people would necessarily interpret the change, went regularly with her, in the growing hope of receiving light from the curate. Her father also not unfrequently accompanied her.

CHAPTER XXII.

TWO MINDS.

ALL this time poor Faber, to his offer of himself to Juliet, had received no answer but a swoon—or something very near it. Every attempt he made to see her alone at the rectory had been foiled ; and he almost came to the conclusion that the curate and his wife had set themselves to prejudice against himself a mind already prejudiced against his principles. It added to his uneasiness that, as he soon discovered, she went regularly to church. He knew the power and persuasion of Wingfold, and looked upon his influence as antagonistic to his hopes. Pride, anger, and fear were all at work in him ; but he went on calling, and did his best to preserve an untroubled demeanor. Juliet imagined no change in his feelings, and her behavior to him was not such as to prevent them from deepening still.

Every time he went it was with a desperate resolution of

laying his hand on the veil in which she had wrapped herself, but every time he found it impossible, for one reason or another, to make a single movement toward withdrawing it. Again and again he tried to write to her, but the haunting suspicion that she would lay his epistle before her new friends, always made him throw down his pen in a smothering indignation. He found himself compelled to wait what opportunity chance or change might afford him.

When he learned that she had gone to live with the Drakes, it was a relief to him; for although he knew the minister was far more personal in his hostility than Wingfold, he was confident his influence over her would not be so great; and now he would have a better chance, he thought, of seeing her alone. Meantime he took satisfaction in knowing that he did not neglect a single patient, and that in no case had he been less successful either as to diagnosis or treatment because of his trouble. He pitied himself just a little as a martyr to the truth, a martyr the more meritorious that the truth to which he sacrificed himself gave him no hope for the future, and for the present no shadow of compensation beyond the satisfaction of not being deceived. It remains a question, however, which there was no one to put to Faber—whether he had not some amends in relief from the notion, vaguely it may be, yet unpleasantly haunting many minds—of a Supreme Being —a Deity—putting forth claims to obedience—an uncomfortable sort of phantom, however imaginary, for one to have brooding above him, and continually coming between him and the freedom of an else empty universe. To the human soul as I have learned to know it, an empty universe would be as an exhausted receiver to the lungs that thirst for air; but Faber liked the idea: how he would have liked the reality remains another thing. I suspect that what we call damnation is something as near it as it can be made; itself it can not be, for even the damned must live by God's life. Was it, I repeat, no compensation for his martyrdom to his precious truth, to know that to none had he to render an account? Was he relieved from no misty sense of a moral consciousness judging his, and ready to enforce its rebuke—a belief which seems to me to involve the highest idea, the noblest pledge, the richest promise of our nature? There may be men in whose turning from implicit to explicit denial, no such element of relief is concerned—I can not tell; but although the structure of Paul Faber's life had in it material of noble sort, I doubt if he was one of such.

The summer at length reigned lordly in the land. The roses were in bloom, from the black purple to the warm white. Ah, those roses! He must indeed be a God who invented the roses. They sank into the red hearts of men and women, caused old men to sigh, young men to long, and women to weep with strange ecstatic sadness. But their scent made Faber lonely and poor, for the rose-heart would not open its leaves to him.

The winds were soft and odor-laden. The wide meadows through which flowed the river, seemed to smite the eye with their greenness; and the black and red and white kine bent down their sleek necks among the marsh-marigolds and the meadow-sweet and the hundred lovely things that border the level water-courses, and fed on the blessed grass. Along the banks, here with nets, there with rod and line, they caught the gleaming salmon, and his silver armor flashed useless in the sun. The old pastor sat much in his little summer-house, and paced his green walk on the border of the Lythe; but in all the gold of the sunlight, in all the glow and the plenty around him, his heart was oppressed with the sense of his poverty. It was not that he could not do the thing he would, but that he could not meet and rectify the thing he had done. He could behave, he said to himself, neither as a gentleman nor a Christian, for lack of money; and, worst of all, he could not get rid of a sense of wrong—of rebellious heavings of heart, of resentments, of doubts that came thick upon him—not of the existence of God, nor of His goodness towards men in general, but of His kindness to himself. Logically, no doubt, they were all bound in one, and the being that could be unfair to a beetle could not be God, could not make a beetle; but our feelings, especially where a wretched self is concerned, are notably illogical.

The morning of a glorious day came in with saffron, gold, and crimson. The color sobered, but the glory grew. The fleeting dyes passed, but the azure sky, the white clouds, and the yellow fire remained. The larks dropped down to their breakfast. The kine had long been busy at theirs, for they had slept their short night in the midst of their food. Every thing that could move was in motion, and what could not move was shining, and what could not shine was feeling warm. But the pastor was tossing restless. He had a troubled night. The rent of his house fell due with the miserable pittance allowed him by the church ; but the hard thing was not that he had to pay nearly the whole of the latter to meet the former, but that he must first take it. The thought of that burned in his veins like poison. But he had no choice. To refuse it would be dishonest ; it would be to spare or perhaps indulge his feelings at the expense of the guiltless. He must not kill himself, he said, because he had insured his life, and the act would leave his daughter nearly destitute. Yet how was the insurance longer to be paid? It *was* hard, with all his faults, to be brought to this ! It *was* hard that he who all his life had been urging people to have faith, should have his own turned into a mockery.

Here heart and conscience together smote him. Well might his faith be mocked, for what better was it than a mockery itself ! Where was this thing he called his faith ? Was he not cherishing, talking flat unbelief ?—as much as telling God he did *not* trust in Him ? Where was the faithlessness of which his faithlessness complained ? A phantom of its own ! Yea, let God be true and every man a liar ! Had the hour come, and not the money ? A fine faith it was that depended on the very presence of the help !—that required for its existence that the supply should come before the need !—a fine faith in truth, which still would follow in the rear of sight !—But why then did God leave him thus without faith ? Why did not God make him able to trust ? He had prayed quite as much for faith as for money. His conscience replied, " That is your part—the thing you will not do. If God put faith into your heart without your stirring up your heart to believe, the faith would be God's and not yours. It is true all is God's ; he made this you call *me*, and made it able to believe, and gave you Himself to believe in ; and if after that He were to make you believe without you doing your utmost part, He would be making you down again into a sort of holy dog, not making you grow a man like Christ Jesus His Son "—" But I have tried hard to trust in Him," said the little self.—" Yes, and then fainted and ceased," said the great self, the conscience.

Thus it went on in the poor man's soul. Ever and anon he said to himself, " Though He slay me, yet will I trust in Him," and ever and anon his heart sickened afresh, and he said to himself, " I shall go down to the grave with shame, and my memorial will be debts unpaid, for the Lord hath forsaken me." All the night he had lain wrestling with fear and doubt : fear was hard upon him, but doubt was much harder. "If I could but trust," he said, "I could endure any thing."

In the splendor of the dawn, he fell into a troubled sleep, and a more troubled dream, which woke him again to misery. Outside his chamber, the world was rich in light, in song, in warmth, in odor, in growth, in color, in space ; inside, all was to him gloomy, groanful, cold, musty, ungenial, dingy, confined ; yet there was he more at ease, shrunk from the light, and in the glorious morning that shone through the chinks of his shutters, saw but an alien common day, not the coach of his Father, come to carry him yet another stage toward his home. He was in want of nothing at the moment. There were no holes in the well-polished shoes that seemed to keep ghostly guard outside his chamber-door. The clothes that lay by his bedside were indeed a little threadbare, but sound and spotless. The hat that hung in the passage below might have been much shabbier without necessarily indicating poverty. His walking-stick had a gold knob like any earl's. If he did choose to smoke a church-warden, he had a great silver-mounted meerschaum on his mantle-shelf. True, the butcher's shop had for some time contributed nothing to his dinners, but his vegetable diet agreed with him. He would himself have given any man time, would as soon have taken his child by the throat as his debtor, had worshiped God after a bettering fashion for forty years at least, and yet would not give God time to do His best for him—the best that perfect love, and power limited only by the lack of full consent in the man himself, could do.

His daughter always came into his room the first thing in the morning. It was plain to her that he had been more restless than usual, and at sight of his glazy red-rimmed eyes and gray face, her heart sank within her. For a moment she was half angry with him, thinking in herself that if she believed as he did, she would never trouble her heart about any thing : her head should do all the business. But with his faith, she would have done just the same as he. It is one thing to be so used to certain statements and modes of thought that you take all for true, and quite another so to believe the heart of it all, that you are in essential and imperturbable peace and gladness because of it. But oh, how the poor girl sighed for the freedom of a God to trust in ! She could content herself with the husks the swine ate, if she only knew that a Father sat at the home-heart of the universe, wanting to have her. Faithful in her faithlessness, she did her best to comfort her *believing* father : beyond the love that offered it, she had but cold comfort to give. He did not listen to a word she said, and she left him at last with a sigh, and went to get him his breakfast. When she returned, she brought him his letters with his tea and toast. He told her to take them away : she might open them herself if she liked ; they could be nothing but bills ! She might take the tray too ; he did not want any breakfast : what right had he to eat what he had no money to pay for ! There would be a long bill at the baker's next ! What right had any one to live on other people ! Dorothy told him she paid for every loaf as it came, and that there was no bill at the baker's, though indeed he had done his best to begin one. He stretched out his arms, drew her down to his bosom, said she was his only comfort, then pushed her away, turned his face to the wall, and wept. She saw it would be better to leave him, and, knowing in this mood he would eat nothing, she carried the tray with her. A few moments after, she came rushing up the stair like a wind, and entered his room swiftly, her face "white with the whiteness of what is dead."

CHAPTER XXIII.

THE MINISTER'S BEDROOM.

The next day, in the afternoon, old Lisbeth appeared at the rectory, with a hurried note, in which Dorothy begged Mr. Wingfold to come and see her father. The curate rose at once and went. When he reached the house, Dorothy, who had evidently been watching for his arrival, herself opened the door.

"What's the matter ?" he asked. "Nothing alarming, I hope ? "

"I hope not," she answered. There was a strange light

well. " But I am a little alarmed about him.   He has suffered much of late. Ah, Mr. Wingfold, you don't know how good he is ! Of course, being no friend to the church——"

" I don't wonder at that, the church is so little of a friend to herself," interrupted the curate, relieved to find her so composed, for as he came along he had dreaded something terrible.

" He wants very much to see you.   He thinks perhaps you may be able to help him.   I am sure if you can't nobody can.   But please don't heed much what he says about himself.   He is feverish and excited.   There is such a thing— is there not ?—as a morbid humility ? I don't mean a false humility, but one that passes over into a kind of self disgust."

" I know what you mean," answered the curate, laying down his hat : he never took his hat into a sick-room.

Dorothy led the way up the narrow creaking stairs.

It was a lowly little chamber in which the once popular preacher lay—not so good as that he had occupied when a boy, two stories above his father's shop.   That shop had been a thorn in his spirit in the days of his worldly success, but again and again this morning he had been remembering it as a very haven of comfort and peace.   He almost forgot himself into a dream of it once ; for one blessed moment, through the upper half of the window he saw the snow falling in the street, while he sat inside and half under the counter, reading Robinson Crusoe ! Could any thing short of heaven be so comfortable ?

As the curate stepped in, a grizzled head turned toward him a haggard face with dry, bloodshot eyes, and a long hand came from the bed to greet him.

" Ah, Mr. Wingfold ! " cried the minister, " God has forsaken me. If He had only forgotten me, I could have borne that, I think ; for, as Job says, the time would have come when He would have had a desire to the work of His hands. But He has turned His back upon me, and taken His free Spirit from me. He has ceased to take His own way, to do His will with me, and has given me my way and my will. Sit down, Mr. Wingfold. You can not comfort me, but you are a true servant of God, and I will tell you my sorrow. I am no friend to the church, as you know, but——"

" So long as you are a friend of its Head, that goes for little with me," said the curate.   " But if you will allow me, I should like to say just one word on the matter."

He wished to try what a diversion of thought might do ; not that he foolishly desired to make him forget his trouble, but that he knew from experience any gap might let in comfort.

" Say on, Mr. Wingfold. I am a worm and no man."

" It seems, then, to me a mistake for any community to spend precious energy upon even a just finding of fault with another. The thing is, to trim the lamp and clean the glass of our own, that it may be a light to the world. It is just the same with communities as with individuals. The community which casts if it be but the mote out of its own eye, does the best thing it can for the beam in its neighbor's. For my part, I confess that, so far as the clergy form and represent the Church of England, it is and has for a long time been doing its best—not its worst, thank God—to serve God and Mammon."

" Ah ! that's my beam ! " cried the minister. " I have been serving Mammon assiduously. I served him not a little in the time of my prosperity, with confidence and show, and then in my adversity with fears and complaints. Our Lord tells us expressly that we are to take no thought for the morrow, because we can not serve God and Mammon. I have been taking thought for a hundred morrows, and that not patiently, but grumbling in my heart at His dealings with me. Therefore now He has cast me off."

" How do you know that He has cast you off ? "asked the curate.

" Because He has given me my own way with such a vengeance. I have been pulling, pulling my hand out of His, and He has let me go, and I lie in the dirt."

" But you have not told me your grounds for concluding so."

" Suppose a child had been crying and fretting after his mother for a spoonful of jam," said the minister, quite gravely, " and at last she set him down to a whole pot— what would you say to that ? "

" I should say she meant to give him a sharp lesson, perhaps a reproof as well—certainly not that she meant to cast him off," answered Wingfold, laughing. " But still I do not understand."

" Have you not heard then ? Didn't Dorothy tell you ? "

" She has told me nothing."

" Not that my old uncle has left me a hundred thousand pounds and more ? "

The curate was on the point of saying, " I am very glad
to hear it," when the warning Dorothy had given him
returned to his mind, and with it the fear that the pastor
was under a delusion—that, as a rich man is sometimes not
unnaturally seized with the mania of imagined poverty, so
this poor man's mental barometer had, from excess of
poverty, turned its index right round again to riches.

" Oh !" he returned, lightly and soothingly, " perhaps it
is not so bad as that.   You may have been misinformed.
There may be some mistake."

" No, no !" returned the minister ; " it is true, every word
of it.   You shall see the lawyers' letter.   Dorothy has it, I
think.   My uncle was an ironmonger in a country town, got
on, and bought a little bit of land in which he found iron.
I knew he was flourishing, but he was a churchman and a
terrible Tory, and I never dreamed he would remember me.
There had been no communication between our family and
his for many years. He must have fancied me still a flourishing London minister, with a rich wife ! If he had had a
suspicion of how sorely I needed a few pounds, I can not
believe he would have left me a farthing.   He did not save
his money to waste it on bread and cheese, I can fancy him
saying."

Although a look almost of despair kept coming and going
upon his face, he lay so still, and spoke so quietly and col-
lectedly, that Wingfold began to wonder whether there
might not be some fact in his statement.   He did not well
know what to say.

" When I heard the news from Dorothy—she read the
letter first," Mr. Drake went on, " —old fool that I was
I was filled with such delight that, although I could not
have said whether I believed or not, the very idea of the
thing made me weep. Alas ! Mr. Wingfold, I have had visions of God in which the whole world would not have
seemed worth a salt tear !   And now !——I jumped out of
bed, and hurried on my clothes, but by the time I came to
kneel at my bedside, God was away.   I could not speak a
word to Him !   I had lost all the trouble that kept me
crying after Him like a little child at his mother's heels, the
bond was broken and He was out of sight.   I tried to be
thankful, but my heart was so full of the money, it lay like
a stuffed bag.   But I dared not go even to my study till I
had prayed.   I tramped up and down this little room,
thinking more about paying my butcher's bill than any thing

else. I would give him a silver snuff-box ; but as to God and His goodness my heart felt like a stone ; I *could not* lift it up. All at once I saw how it was : He had heard my prayers in anger ! Mr. Wingfold, the Lord has sent me this money as He sent the quails to the Israelites : while it was yet, as it were, between my teeth, He smote me with hard-ness of heart. O my God ! how shall I live in the world with a hundred thousand pounds instead of my Father in heaven ! If it were only that He had hidden His face, I should be able to pray somehow ! He has given me over to the Mammon I was worshiping ! Hypocrite that I am ! how often have I not pointed out to my people, while yet I dwelt in the land of Goshen, that to fear poverty was the same thing as to love money, for that both came of lack of faith in the living God ! Therefore has He taken from me the light of His countenance, which yet, Mr. Wingfold, with all my sins and shortcomings, yea, and my hypocrisy, is the all in all to me ! "

He looked the curate in the face with such wild eyes as convinced him that, even if perfectly sane at present, he was in no small danger of losing his reason.

"Then you would willingly give up this large fortune," he said, "and return to your former condition ? "

"Rather than not be able to pray—I would ! I would ! " he cried ; then paused and added, " —if only He would give me enough to pay my debts and not have to beg of other people."

Then, with a tone suddenly changed to one of agonized effort, with clenched hands, and eyes shut tight, he cried vehemently, as if in the face of a lingering unwillingness to encounter again the miseries through which he had been passing.

"No, no, Lord ! Forgive me. I will not think of con-ditions. Thy will be done ! Take the money and let me be a debtor and a beggar if Thou wilt, only let me pray to Thee ; and do Thou make it up to my creditors."

Wingfold's spirit was greatly moved. Here was victory ! Whether the fortune was a fact or fancy, made no feature of difference. He thanked God and took courage. The same instant the door opened, and Dorothy came in hesi-tating, and looking strangely anxious. He threw her a face-question. She gently bowed her head, and gave him a letter with a broad black border which she held in her hand.

He read it. No room for rational doubt was left. He folded it softly, gave it back to her, and rising, kneeled down by the bedside, near the foot, and said—

"Father, whose is the fullness of the earth, I thank Thee that Thou hast set my brother's heel on the neck of his enemy. But the suddenness of Thy relief from holy poverty and evil care, has so shaken his heart and brain, or rather, perhaps, has made him think so keenly of his lack of faith in his Father in heaven, that he fears Thou hast thrown him the gift in disdain, as to a dog under the table, though never didst Thou disdain a dog, and not given it as to a child, from Thy hand into his. Father, let Thy spirit come with the gift, or take it again, and make him poor and able to pray."—Here came an *amen*, groaned out as from the bottom of a dungeon.—"Pardon him, Father," the curate prayed on, "all his past discontent and the smallness of his faith. Thou art our Father, and Thou knowest us tenfold better than we know ourselves ; we pray Thee not only to pardon us, but to make all righteous excuse for us, when we dare not make any for ourselves, for Thou art the truth. We will try to be better children. We will go on climbing the mount of God through all the cloudy darkness that swaths it, yea, even in the face of the worst terrors—that when we reach the top, we shall find no one there."—Here Dorothy burst into sobs.—"Father ! " thus the curate ended his prayer, "take pity on Thy children. Thou wilt not give them a piece of bread, in place of a stone—to poison them ! The egg Thou givest will not be a serpent's. We are Thine, and Thou art ours : in us be Thy will done ! Amen."

As he rose from his knees, he saw that the minister had turned his face to the wall, and lay perfectly still. Rightly judging that he was renewing the vain effort to rouse, by force of the will, feelings which had been stunned by the strange shock, he ventured to try a more authoritative mode of address.

"And now, Mr. Drake, you have got to spend this money," he said, "and the sooner you set about it the better. Whatever may be your ideas about the principal, you are bound to spend at least every penny of the income."

The sad-hearted man stared at the curate.

"How is a man to do any thing whom God has forsaken ?" he said.

"If He had forsaken you, for as dreary work as it would be, you would have to try to do your duty notwithstanding.

But He has not forsaken you. He has given you a very sharp lesson, I grant, and as such you must take it, but that is the very opposite of forsaking you. He has let you know what it is not to trust in Him, and what it would be to have money that did not come from His hand. You did not conquer in the fight with Mammon when you were poor, and God has given you another chance : He expects you to get the better of him now you are rich. If God had forsaken you, I should have found you strutting about and glorying over imagined enemies."

"Do you really think that is the mind of God toward me ?" cried the poor man, starting half up in bed. "*Do* you think so ?" he repeated, staring at the curate almost as wildly as at first, but with a different expression.

"I do," said Wingfold ; " and it will be a bad job indeed if you fail in both trials. But that I am sure you will not. It is your business now to get this money into your hands as soon as possible, and proceed to spend it."

"Would there be any harm in ordering a few things from the tradespeople ?" asked Dorothy.

"How should there be ?" returned Wingfold.

"Because, you see," answered Dorothy, "we can't be sure of a bird in the bush."

"Can you be sure of it in your hands ? It may spread its wings when you least expect it. But Helen will be delighted to take the risk—up to a few hundreds," he added laughing.

"Somebody may dispute the will : they do sometimes," said Dorothy.

"They do very often," answered Wingfold. "It does not look likely in the present case ; but our trust must be neither in the will nor in the fortune, but in the living God. You have to get all the *good* out of this money you can. If you will walk over to the rectory with me now, while your father gets up, we will carry the good news to my wife, and she will lend you what money you like, so that you need order nothing without paying for it."

"Please ask her not to tell any body," said Mr. Drake. "I shouldn't like it talked about before I understand it myself."

"You are quite right. If I were you I would tell nobody yet but Mr. Drew. He is a right man, and will help you to bear your good fortune. I have always found good fortune harder to bear than bad."

Dorothy ran to put her bonnet on. The curate went back to the bedside. Mr. Drake had again turned his face to the wall.

"Sixty years of age !" he was murmuring to himself.

"Mr. Drake," said Wingfold, "so long as you bury yourself with the centipedes in your own cellar, instead of going out into God's world, you are tempting Satan and Mammon together to come and tempt you. Worship the God who made the heaven and the earth, and the sea and the mines of iron and gold, by doing His will in the heart of them. Don't worship the poor picture of Him you have got hanging up in your closet ;—worship the living power beyond your ken. Be strong in Him whose is your strength, and all strength. Help Him in His work with His own. Give life to His gold. Rub the canker off it, by sending it from hand to hand. You must rise and bestir yourself. I will come and see you again to-morrow. Good-by for the present."

He turned away and walked from the room. But his hand had scarcely left the lock, when he heard the minister alight from his bed upon the floor.

"He'll do !" said the curate to himself, and walked down the stair.

When he got home, he left Dorothy with his wife, and going to his study, wrote the following verses, which had grown in his mind as he walked silent beside her :—

WHAT MAN IS THERE OF YOU?

The homely words, how often read !
  How seldom fully known !
" Which father of you, asked for bread,
  Would give his son a stone ? "

How oft has bitter tear been shed,
  And heaved how many a groan,
Because Thou wouldst not give for bread
  The thing that was a stone !

How oft the child Thou wouldst have fed,
  Thy gift away has thrown !
He prayed, Thou heardst, and gav'st the bread :
  He cried, it is a stone !

Lord, if I ask in doubt or dread
  Lest I be left to moan—
I am the man who, asked for bread,
  Would give his son a stone.

As Dorothy returned from the rectory, where Helen had

made her happier than all the money by the kind words she said to her, she stopped at Mr. Jones' shop, and bought of him a bit of loin of mutton.

"Shan't I put it down, miss?" he suggested, seeing her take out her purse.—Helen had just given her the purse: they had had great fun, with both tears and laughter over it.

"I would rather not—thank you very much," she replied with a smile.

He gave her a kind, searching glance, and took the money.

That day Juliet dined with them. When the joint appeared, Amanda, who had been in the kitchen the greater part of the morning, clapped her hands as at sight of an old acquaintance.

"Dere it comes! dere it comes!" she cried.

But the minister's grace was a little longer than she liked, for he was trying hard to feel grateful. I think some people mistake pleasure and satisfaction for thankfulness: Mr. Drake was not so to be taken in. Ere long, however, he found them a good soil for thankfulness to grow in.—So Amanda fidgeted not a little, and the moment the grace was over—

"Now 'en! now 'en!" she almost screamed, her eyes sparkling with delight. "'Iss is dinner!—'Ou don't have dinner every day, Miss Mellidif!"

"Be quiet, Ducky," said her aunt, as she called her. "You mustn't make any remarks."

"Ducky ain't makin' no marks," returned the child, looking anxiously at the table-cloth, and was quiet but not for long.

"Lisbef say surely papa's sip come home wif 'e nice dinner!" she said next.

"No, my ducky," said Mr. Drake: "it was God's ship that came with it."

"Dood sip!" said the child.

"It will come one day and another, and carry us all home," said the minister.

"Where Ducky's yeal own papa and mamma yive in a big house, papa?" asked Amanda, more seriously.

"I will tell you more about it when you are older," said Mr. Drake. "Now let us eat the dinner God has sent us." He was evidently far happier already, though his daughter could see that every now and then his thoughts were away;

she hoped they were thanking God. Before dinner was over, he was talking quite cheerfully, drawing largely from his stores both of reading and experience. After the child was gone, they told Juliet of their good fortune. She congratulated them heartily, then looked a little grave, and said—

"Perhaps you would like me to go?"

"What!" said Mr. Drake; "does your friendship go no further than that? Having helped us so much in adversity, will you forsake us the moment prosperity looks in at the window?"

Juliet gave one glance at Dorothy, smiled, and said no more. For Dorothy, she was already building a castle for Juliet—busily.

CHAPTER XXIV.

JULIET'S CHAMBER.

AFTER tea, Mr. Drake and Dorothy went out for a walk together—a thing they had not once done since the church-meeting of acrid memory in which had been decreed the close of the minister's activity, at least in Glaston. It was a lovely June twilight; the bats were flitting about like the children of the gloamin', and the lamps of the laburnum and lilac hung dusky among the trees of Osterfield Park.

Juliet, left all but alone in the house, sat at her window, reading. Her room was on the first floor, but the dining-room beneath it was of low pitch, and at the lane-door there were two steps down into the house, so that her window was at no great height above the lane. It was open, but there was little to be seen from it, for immediately opposite rose a high old garden-wall, hiding every thing with its gray bulk, lovelily blotted with lichens and moss, brown and green and gold, except the wall-flowers and stone-crop that grew on its coping, and a running plant that hung down over it, like a long fringe worn thin. Had she put her head out of the window, she would have seen in the one direction a cow-house, and in the other the tall narrow iron gate of the garden—and that was all. The twilight deepened as

she read, until the words before her began to play hide and
seek ; they got worse and worse, until she was tired of
catching at them ; and when at last she stopped for a moment, they were all gone like a troop of fairies, and her
reading was ended. She closed the book, and was soon
dreaming awake ; and the twilight world was the globe in
which the dream-fishes came and went—now swelling up
strange and near, now sinking away into the curious distance.

Her mood was broken by the sound of hoofs, which she
almost immediately recognized as those of the doctor's red
horse—great hoofs falling at the end of long straight-flung
steps. Her heart began to beat violently, and confident in
the protection of the gathering night, she rose and looked
cautiously out toward the side on which was the approach.
In a few moments, round the furthest visible corner, and past
the gate in the garden-wall, swung a huge shadowy form—
gigantic in the dusk. She drew back her head, but ere she
could shape her mind to retreat from the window, the solid
gloom hurled itself thundering past, and she stood trembling
and lonely, with the ebb of Ruber's paces in her ears—and
in her hand a letter. In a minute she came to herself, closed
her window, drew down the blind, lighted a candle, set it on the
window-sill, and opened the letter. It contained these verses,
and nothing more :—

> My morning rose in laughter—
>   A gold and azure day.
> Dull clouds came trooping after,
>   Livid, and sullen gray.
>
> At noon, the rain did batter,
>   And it thundered like a hell :
> I sighed, it is no matter,
>   At night I shall sleep as well.
>
> But I longed with a madness tender
>   For an evening like the morn,
> That my day might die in splendor,
>   Not folded in mist forlorn—
>
> Die like a tone elysian,
>   Like a bee in a cactus-flower,
> Like a day-surprised vision,
>   Like a wind in a summer shower.
>
> Through the vaulted clouds about me
>   Broke trembling an azure space :

Was it a dream to flout me—
  Or was it a perfect face?

The sky and the face together
  Are gone, and the wind blows fell.
But what matters a dream or the weather?
  At night it will all be well.

For the day of life and labor,
  Of ecstasy and pain,
Is only a beaten tabor,
  And I shall not dream again.

But as the old Night steals o'er me,
  Deepening till all is dead,
I shall see thee still before me
  Stand with averted head.

And I shall think, Ah sorrow!
  The *might* that never was *may!*
The night that has no morrow!
  And the sunset all in gray!

Juliet laid her head on her hands and wept.

"Why should I not let him have his rosy sunset?" she thought. "It is all he hopes for—cares for, I think—poor fellow! Am I not good enough to give him that? What does it matter about me, if it is all but a vision that flits between heaven and earth, and makes a passing shadow on human brain and nerves?—a tale that is telling—then a tale that is told! Much the good people make out of their better faith! Should *I* be troubled to learn that it was indeed a lasting sleep? If I were dead, and found myself waking, should I want to rise, or go to sleep again? Why should not I too dare to hope for an endless rest? Where would be the wrong to any? If there be a God, He will have but to wake me to punish me hard enough. Why should I not hope at least for such a lovely thing? Can any one help desiring peace? Oh, to sleep, and sleep, and wake no more forever and ever! I would not hasten the sleep; the end will surely come, and why should we not enjoy the dream a little longer—at least while it is a good dream, and the tossing has not begun? There would always be a time. Why wake before our time out of the day into the dark nothing? I should always want to see what to-morrow and to-morrow and to-morrow would bring—that is, so long as he loved me. He is noble, and sad, and beautiful, and gracious!—but would he—could he love me to the end—even if—? Why should we not make the best of what we have? Why should we not make life as happy to ourselves and to others as we can—however worthless, however arrant a cheat it may be? Even if there be no such thing as love, if it be all but a lovely vanity, a bubble-play of color, why not let the bubble-globe swell, and the tide of its ocean of color flow and rush and mingle and change? Will it not break at last, and the last come soon enough, when of all the glory is left but a tear on the grass? When we dream a pleasant dream, and know it is but a dream, we will to dream on, and quiet our minds that it may not be scared and flee: why should we not yield to the stronger dream, that it may last yet another sweet, beguiling moment? Why should he not love me—kiss me? Why should we not be sad together, that we are not and can not be the real man and woman we would—that we are but the forms of a dream—the fleeting shadows of the night of Nature?—mourn together that the meddlesome hand of fate should have roused us to consciousness and aspiration so long before the maturity of our powers that we are but a laughter—no—a scorn and a weeping to ourselves? We could at least sympathize with each other in our common misery— bear with its weakness, comfort its regrets, hide its mortifications, cherish its poor joys, and smooth the way down the steepening slope to the grave! Then, if in the decrees of blind fate, there should be a slow, dull procession toward perfection, if indeed some human God be on the way to be born, it would be grand, although we should know nothing of it, to have done our part fearless and hopeless, to have lived and died that the triumphant Sorrow might sit throned on the ever dying heart of the universe. But never, never would I have chosen to live for that! Yes, one might choose to be born, if there were suffering one might live or die to soften, to cure! That would be to be like Paul Faber. To will to be born for that would be grand indeed!"

In paths of thought like these her mind wandered, her head lying upon her arms on the old-fashioned, wide-spread window-sill. At length, weary with emotion and weeping, she fell fast asleep, and slept for some time.

The house was very still. Mr. Drake and Dorothy were in no haste to return. Amanda was asleep, and Lisbeth was in the kitchen—perhaps also asleep.

Juliet woke with a great start. Arms were around her from behind, lifting her from her half-prone position of sorrowful rest. With a terrified cry, she strove to free herself.

"Juliet, my love! my heart! be still, and let me speak,"
said Faber.   His voice trembled as if full of tears.   "I can
bear this no longer.   You are my fate.   I never lived till I
knew you. I shall cease to live when I know for certain that
you turn from me."

Juliet was like one half-drowned, just lifted from the
water, struggling to beat it away from eyes and ears and
mouth.

"Pray leave me, Mr. Faber," she cried, half-terrified,
half-bewildered, as she rose and turned toward him.   But
while she pushed him away with one hand, she unconsciously clasped his arm tight with the other.   "You have
no right to come into my room, and surprise me—startle
me so! Do go away.   I will come to you."

"Pardon, pardon, my angel! Do not speak so loud,"
he said, falling on his knees, and clasping hers.

"Do go away," persisted Juliet, trying to remove his
grasp.   "What will they think if they find us—you here.
They know I am perfectly well."

"You drive me to liberties that make me tremble, Juliet.
Everywhere you avoid me.   You are never to be seen without some hateful protector.   Ages ago I put up a prayer
to you—one of life or death to me, and, like the God you
believe in, you have left it unanswered.   You have no pity
on the sufferings you cause me! If your God *be* cruel,
why should you be cruel too?   Is not one tormentor enough
in your universe?   If there be a future let us go on together
to find it.   If there be not, let us yet enjoy what of life may
be enjoyed.   My past is a sad one——"

Juliet shuddered.

"Ah, my beautiful, you too have suffered!" he went on.
"Let us be angels of mercy to each other, each helping the
other to forget! My griefs I should count worthless if I
might but erase yours."

"I would I could say the same!" said Juliet, but only in
her heart.

"Whatever they may have been," he continued, "my
highest ambition shall be to make you forget them.   We
will love like beings whose only eternity is the moment.
Come with me, Juliet; we will go down into the last darkness
together, loving each other—and then peace.   At least there is
no eternal hate in my poor, ice-cold religion, as there is in
yours.   I am not suffering alone, Juliet.   All whom it is
my work to relieve, are suffering from your unkindness.

For a time I prided myself that I gave every one of them as full attention as before, but I can not keep it up. I am defeated. My brain seems deserting me. I mistake symptoms, forget cases, confound medicines, fall into incredible blunders. My hand trembles, my judgment wavers, my will is undecided. Juliet, you are ruining me."

"He saved my life," said Juliet to herself, "and that it is which has brought him to this. He has a claim to me. I am his property. He found me a castaway on the shore of Death, and gave me *his* life to live with. He must not suffer where I can prevent it."—She was on the point of yielding.

The same moment she heard a step in the lane approaching the door.

"If you love me, do go now, dear Mr. Faber," she said. "I will see you again. Do not urge me further to-night.— Ah, I wish! I wish!" she added, with a deep sigh, and ceased.

The steps came up to the door. There came a knock at it. They heard Lisbeth go to open it. Faber rose.

"Go into the drawing-room," said Juliet. "Lisbeth may be coming to fetch me; she must not see you here."

He obeyed. Without a word he left the chamber, and went into the drawing-room. He had been hardly a moment there, when Wingfold entered. It was almost dark, but the doctor stood against the window, and the curate knew him.

"Ah, Faber!" he said, "it is long since I saw you. But each has been about his work, I suppose, and there could not be a better reason."

"Under different masters, then," returned Faber, a little out of temper.

"I don't exactly think so. All good work is done under the same master."

"Pooh! Pooh!"

"Who is your master, then?"

"My conscience. Who is yours?"

"The Author of my conscience."

"A legendary personage!"

"One who is every day making my conscience harder upon me. Until I believed in Him, my conscience was dull and stupid—not half-awake, indeed."

"Oh! I see! You mean my conscience is dull and stupid."

" I do not. But if you were once lighted up with the
light of the world, you would pass just such a judgment on
yourself.   I can't think you so different from myself, as
that that shouldn't be the case ; though most heartily I
grant you do your work ten times better than I did.   And
all the time I thought myself an honest nan !   I wasn't. A
man may honestly think himself honest, and a fresh week's
experience may make him doubt it altogether.   I sorely
want a God to make me honest."

Here Juliet entered the room, greeted Mr. Wingfold, and
then shook hands with Faber.   He was glad the room was
dark.

" What do you think, Miss Meredith—is a man's conscience enough for his guidance ? " said the curate.

" I don't know any thing about a man's conscience,"
answered Juliet.

" A woman's then ? " said the curate.

" What else has she got ? " returned Juliet.

The doctor was inwardly cursing the curate for talking
shop.   Only, if a man knows nothing so good, so beautiful,
so necessary, as the things in his shop, what else ought he
to talk—especially if he is ready to give them without money
and without price ?   The doctor would have done better to
talk shop too.

" Of course he has nothing else," answered the curate ;
" and if he had, he must follow his conscience all the
same."

" There you are, Wingfold !—always talking paradoxes ! "
said Faber.

" Why, man ! you may only have a blundering boy to
guide you, but if he is your only guide, you must follow
him.   You don't therefore call him a sufficient guide ! "

" What a logomachist you are !   If it is a horn lantern
you've got, you needn't go mocking at it."

" The lantern is not the light.   Perhaps you can not
change your horn for glass, but what if you could better
the light ?   Suppose the boy's father knew all about the
country, but you never thought it worth while to send the
lad to him for instructions ? "

" Suppose I didn't believe he had a father ?   Suppose he
told me he hadn't ? "

" Some men would call out to know if there was any body
in the house to give the boy a useful hint."

" Oh bother !   I'm quite content with my fellow."

"Well, for my part I should count my conscience, were it ten times better than it is, poor company on any journey. Nothing less than the living Truth ever with me can make existence a peace to me,—that's the joy of the Holy Ghost, Miss Meredith.—What if you should find one day, Faber, that, of all facts, the thing you have been so coolly refusing was the most precious and awful?"

Faber had had more than enough of it. There was but one thing precious to him; Juliet was the perfect flower of nature, the apex of law, the last presentment of evolution, the final reason of things! The very soul of the world stood there in the dusk, and there also stood the foolish curate, whirling his little vortex of dust and ashes between him and her!

"It comes to this," said Faber; "what you say moves nothing in me. I am aware of no need, no want of that Being of whom you speak. Surely if in Him I did live and move and have my being, as some old heathen taught your Saul of Tarsus, I should in one mode or another be aware of Him!"

While he spoke, Mr. Drake and Dorothy had come into the room. They stood silent.

"That is a weighty word," said Wingfold. "But what if you feel His presence every moment, only do not recognize it as such?"

"Where would be the good of it to me then?"

"The good of it to you might lie in the blinding. What if any further revelation to one who did not seek it would but obstruct the knowledge of Him? Truly revealed, the word would be read untruly—even as The Word has been read by many in all ages. Only the pure in heart, we are told, shall see Him. The man who, made by Him, does not desire Him—how should he know Him?"

"Why don't I desire Him then?—I don't."

"That is for you to find out."

"I do what I know to be right; even on your theory I ought to get on," said Faber, turning from him with a laugh.

"I think so too," replied Wingfold. "Go on, and prosper. Only, if there be untruth in you alongside of the truth—? It might be, and you are not awake to it. It is marvelous what things can co-exist in a human mind."

"In that case, why should not your God help me?"

"Why not? I think he will. But it may *have* to be in a way you will not like."

" Well, well ! good night.   Talk is but talk, whatever be the subject of it.—I beg your pardon," he added, shaking hands with the minister and his daughter ; " I did not see you come in.   Good night."

" I won't allow that talk is only talk, Faber," Wingfold called after him with a friendly laugh. Then turning to Mr. Drake, " Pardon me," he said, " for treating you with so much confidence. I saw you come in, but believed you would rather have us end our talk than break it off."

" Certainly.   But I can't help thinking you grant him too much, Mr. Wingfold," said the minister seriously.

" I never find I lose by giving, even in argument," said the curate. " Faber rides his hobby well, but the brute is a sorry jade.   He will find one day she has not a sound joint in her whole body."

The man who is anxious to hold every point, will speedily bring a question to a mere dispute about trifles, leaving the real matter, whose elements may appeal to the godlike in every man, out in the cold.   Such a man, having gained his paltry point, will crow like the bantam he is, while the other, who may be the greater, perhaps the better man, although in the wrong, is embittered by his smallness, and turns away with increased prejudice.   Human nature can hardly be blamed for its readiness to impute to the case the shallowness of its pleader.   Few men do more harm than those who, taking the right side, dispute for personal victory, and argue, as they are sure then to do, ungenerously.   But even genuine argument for the truth is not preaching the gospel, neither is he whose unbelief is thus assailed, likely to be brought thereby into any mood but one unfit for receiving it.   Argument should be kept to books ; preachers ought to have nothing to do with it—at all events in the pulpit. There let them hold forth light, and let him who will, receive it, and him who will not, forbear.   God alone can convince, and till the full time is come for the birth of the truth in a soul, the words of even the Lord Himself are not there potent.

" The man irritates me, I confess," said Mr. Drake.   " I do not say he is self-satisfied, but he is very self-suffi-cient."

" He is such a good fellow," said Wingfold, " that I think God will not let him go on like this very long.   I think we shall live to see a change upon him.   But much as I esteem and love the man, I can not help a suspicion that he has a great lump of pride somewhere about him, which has not a little to do with his denials."

Juliet's blood seemed seething in her veins as she heard her lover thus weighed, and talked over ; and therewith came the first rift of a threatened breach betwixt her heart and the friends who had been so good to her. He had done far more for her than any of them, and mere loyalty seemed to call upon her to defend him ; but she did not know how, and, dissatisfied with herself as well as indignant with them, she maintained an angry silence.

CHAPTER XXV.

OSTERFIELD PARK.

It was a long time since Mr. Drake and Dorothy had had such a talk together, or had spent such a pleasant evening as that on which they went into Osterfield Park to be alone with a knowledge of their changed fortunes. The anxiety of each, differing so greatly from that of the other, had tended to shut up each in loneliness beyond the hearing of the other ; so that, while there was no breach in their love, it was yet in danger of having long to endure

> " an expansion,
> Like gold to airy thinness beat."

But this evening their souls rushed together. The father's anxiety was chiefly elevated ; the daughter's remained much what it was before ; yet these anxieties no longer availed to keep them apart.

Each relation of life has its peculiar beauty of holiness ; but that beauty is the expression of its essential truth, and the essence itself is so strong that it bestows upon its embodiment even the power of partial metamorphosis with all other vital relations. How many daughters have in the devotion of their tenderness, become as mothers to their own fathers ! Who has not known some sister more of a wife to a man than she for whose sake he neglected her ? But it will take the loves of all the relations of life gathered in one, to shadow the love which, in the kingdom of heaven,

is recognized as due to each from each human being *per se.*
It is for the sake of the essential human, that all human
relations and all forms of them exist—that we may learn
what it is, and become capable of loving it aright.

Dorothy would now have been as a mother to her father,
had she had but a good hope, if no more, of finding her Father
in heaven. She was not at peace enough to mother any
body. She had indeed a grasp of the skirt of His robe—
only she could not be sure it was not the mere fringe of a
cloud she held. Not the less was her father all her care, and
pride, and joy. Of his faults she saw none : there was
enough of the noble and generous in him to hide them from
a less partial beholder than a daughter. They had never
been serious in comparison with his virtues. I do not
mean that every fault is not so serious that a man must be
willing to die twenty deaths to get rid of it ; but that, relatively to the getting rid of it, a fault is serious or not, in proportion to the depth of its root, rather than the amount of
its foliage. Neither can that be the worst-conditioned fault,
the man's own suspicion of which would make him hang his
head in shame ; those are his worst faults which a man will
start up to defend ; those are the most dangerous moral
diseases whose symptoms are regarded as the signs of
health.

Like lovers they walked out together, with eyes only for
each other, for the good news had made them shy—through
the lane, into the cross street, and out into Pine street, along
which they went westward, meeting the gaze of the low sun,
which wrapped them round in a veil of light and dark, for
the light made their eyes dark, so that they seemed feeling
their way out of the light into the shadow.

"This is like life," said the pastor, looking down at the
precious face beside him : "our eyes can best see from under
the shadow of afflictions."

"I would rather it were from under the shadow of God's
wings," replied Dorothy timidly.

"So it is ! so it is ! Afflictions are but the shadow of His
wings," said her father eagerly. "Keep there, my child, and
you will never need the afflictions I have needed. I have
been a hard one to save."

But the child thought within herself, "Alas, father ! you
have never had any afflictions which you or I either could
not bear tenfold better than what I have to bear." She was
perhaps right. Only she did not know that when she got

through, all would be transfigured with the light of her resurrection, just as her father's poverty now was in the light of his plenty.

Little more passed between them in the street. All the way to the entrance of the park they were silent. There they exchanged a few words with the sweet-faced little dwarf-woman that opened the gate, and those few words set the currents of their thoughts singing yet more sweetly as they flowed. They entered the great park, through the trees that bordered it, still in silence, but when they reached the wide expanse of grass, with its clumps of trees and thickets, simul-taneously they breathed a deep breath of the sweet wind, and the fountains of their deeps were broken up. The evening was lovely, they wandered about long in delight, and much was the trustful converse they held. It was getting dark before they thought of returning.

The father had been telling the daughter how he had mourned and wept when his boys were taken from him, never thinking at all of the girl who was left him.

"And now," he said, " I would not part with my Dorothy to have them back the finest boys in the world. What would my old age be without you, my darling ?"

Dorothy's heart beat high. Surely there must be a Father in heaven too ! They walked a while in a great silence, for the heart of each was full. And all the time scarce an allu-sion had been made to the money.

As they returned they passed the new house, at some dis-tance, on the highest point in the park. It stood unfinished, with all its windows boarded up.

" The walls of that house," said Mr. Drake, " were scarcely above ground when I came to Glaston. So they had been for twenty years, and so they remained until, as you remem-ber, the building was recommenced some three or four years ago. Now, again, it is forsaken, and only the wind is at home in it."

" They tell me the estate is for sale," said Dorothy. " Those building-lots, just where the lane leads into Pine street, I fancy belong to it."

" I wish," returned her father, "they would sell me that tumble-down place in the hollow they call the Old House of Glaston. I shouldn't mind paying a good sum for it. What a place it would be to live in ! And what a pleasure there would be in the making of it once more habitable, and watch-ing order dawn out of neglect ! "

"It would be delightful," responded Dorothy. "When I was a child, it was one of my dreams that that house was my papa's—with the wild garden and all the fruit, and the terrible lake, and the ghost of the lady that goes about in the sack she was drowned in. But would you really buy it, father, if you could get it?"

"I think I should, Dorothy," answered Mr. Drake.

"Would it not be damp—so much in the hollow? Is it not the lowest spot in the park?"

"In the park—yes; for the park drains into it. But the park lies high; and you must note that the lake, deep as it is—very deep, yet drains into the Lythe. For all they say of no bottom to it, I am nearly sure the deepest part of the lake is higher than the surface of the river. If I am right, then we could, if we pleased, empty the lake altogether—not that I should like the place nearly so well without it. The situation is charming—and so sheltered!—looking full south—just the place to keep open house in!"

"That is just like you, father!" cried Dorothy, clapping her hands once and holding them together as as she looked up at him. "The very day you are out of prison, you want to begin to keep an open house!—Dear father!"

"Don't mistake me, my darling. There was a time, long ago, after your mother was good enough to marry me, when —I am ashamed to confess it even to you, my child—I did enjoy making a show. I wanted people to see, that, although I was a minister of a sect looked down upon by the wealthy priests of a worldly establishment, I knew how to live after the world's fashion as well as they. That time you will scarcely recall, Dorothy?"

"I remember the coachman's buttons," answered Dorothy.

"Well! I suppose it will be the same with not a few times and circumstances we may try to recall in the other world. Some insignificant thing will be all, and fittingly too, by which we shall be able to identify them.—I liked to give nice dinner parties, and we returned every invitation we accepted. I took much pains to have good wines, and the right wines with the right dishes, and all that kind of thing—though I dare say I made more blunders than I knew. Your mother had been used to that way of living, and it was no show in her as it was in me. Then I was proud of my library and the rare books in it. I delighted in showing them, and talking over the rarity of this edition, the tallness of that copy, the binding, and such-like follies. And where was the wonder, seeing I served religion so much in the same way—descanting upon the needlework that clothed the king's daughter, instead of her inward glory ! I do not say always, for I had my better times. But how often have I not insisted on the mint and anise and cummin, and forgotten the judgment, mercy and faith ! How many sermons have I not preached about the latchets of Christ's shoes, when I might have been talking about Christ himself ! But now I do not want a good house to make a show with any more : I want to be hospitable. I don't call giving dinners being hospitable. I would have my house a hiding-place from the wind, a covert from the tempest. That would be to be hospitable. Ah ! if your mother were with us, my child ! But you will be my little wife, as you have been for so many years now.—God keeps open house ; I should like to keep open house.—I wonder does any body ever preach hospitality as a Christian duty ? "

" I hope you won't keep a butler, and set up for grand, father," said Dorothy.

" Indeed I will not, my child. I would not run the risk of postponing the pleasure of the Lord to that of inhospitable servants. I will look to you to keep a warm, comfortable, welcoming house, and such servants only as shall be hospitable in heart and behavior, and make no difference between the poor and the rich."

" I can't feel that any body is poor," said Dorothy, after a pause, " except those that can't be sure of God.—They are so poor ! " she added.

" You are right, my child ! " returned her father. " It was not my poverty—it was not being sure of God that crushed me.—How long is it since I was poor, Dorothy ? "

" Two days, father—not two till to-morrow morning."

" It looks to me two centuries. My mind is at ease, and I have not paid a debt yet ! How vile of me to want the money in my own hand, and not be content it should be in God's pocket, to come out just as it was wanted ! Alas ! I have more faith in my uncle's leavings than in my Father's generosity ! But I must not forget gratitude in shame. Come, my child—no one can see us—let us kneel down here on the grass and pray to God who is in yon star just twinkling through the gray, and in my heart and in yours, my child."

I will not give the words of the minister's prayer. The words are not the prayer. Mr. Drake's words were common-

place, with much of the conventionality and platitude of
prayer-meetings. He had always objected to the formality
of the Prayer-book, but the words of his own prayers without
book were far more formal ; the prayer itself was in the
heart, not on the lips, and was far better than the words.
But poor Dorothy heard only the words, and they did not
help her. They seemed rather to freeze than revive her
faith, making her feel as if she never could believe in the
God of her father. She was too unhappy to reason well, or
she might have seen that she was not bound to measure God
by the way her father talked to him—that the form of the
prayer had to do with her father, not immediately with God
—that God might be altogether adorable, notwithstanding
the prayers of all heathens and of all saints.

Their talk turned again upon the Old House of Glaston.
"If it be true, as I have heard ever since I came," said
Mr. Drake, "that Lord de Barre means to pull down the
house and plow up the garden, and if he be so short of
money as they say, he might perhaps take a few thousands
for it. The Lythe bounds the estate, and there makes a
great loop, so that a portion might be cut off by a straight
line from one arm of the curve to the other, which would
be quite outside the park. I will set some inquiry on foot.
I have wished for a long time to leave the river, only we
had a lease. The Old House is nothing like so low as the
one we are in now. Besides, as I propose, we should have
space to build, if we found it desirable, on the level of the
park."

When they reached the gate on their return, a second
dwarfish figure, a man, pigeon-chested, short-necked, and
asthmatic—a strange, gnome-like figure, came from the
lodge to open it. Every body in Glaston knew Polwarth the
gatekeeper.

"How is the asthma to-night, Mr. Polwarth?" said the
pastor. He had not yet got rid of the tone in which in his
young days he had been accustomed to address the poor of
his flock—a tone half familiar, half condescending. To big
ships barnacles will stick—and may add weeks to the length
of a voyage too.

"Not very bad, thank you, Mr. Drake. But, bad or not,
it is always a friendly devil," answered the little man.

"I am ast——— a little surprised to hear you use such
——— express yourself so, Mr. Polwarth," said the minister.

The little man laughed a quiet, huskily melodious, gently merry laugh.

"I am not original in the idea, and scarcely so in my way of expressing it. I am sorry you don't like it, Mr. Drake," he said. "I found it in the second epistle to the Corinthians last night, and my heart has been full of it ever since. It is surely no very bad sign if the truth should make us merry at a time! It ought to do so, I think, seeing merriment is one of the lower forms of bliss."

"I am at a loss to understand you, Mr. Polwarth," said the minister.

"I beg your pardon, Mr. Drake. I will come to the point. In the passage I refer to St. Paul says: 'There was given to me a thorn in the flesh, the messenger of Satan to buffet me, lest I should be exalted above measure :'—am I not right in speaking of such a demon as a friendly one? He was a gift from God."

"I had not observed—that is, I had not taken particular notice of the unusual combination of phrases in the passage," answered Mr. Drake. "It is a very remarkable one, certainly. I remember no other in which a messenger of Satan is spoken of as being *given* by God."

"Clearly, sir, St. Paul accepted him as something to be grateful for, so soon as his mission was explained to him; and after that, who is to say what may not be a gift of God! It won't do to grumble at any thing—will it, sir?— when it may so unexpectedly turn out to be *given* to us by God. I begin to suspect that never, until we see a thing plainly a gift of God, can we be sure that we see it right. I am quite certain the most unpleasant things may be such gifts. I should be glad enough to part with this asthma of mine, if it pleased God it should depart from me ; but would I yield a fraction of what it has brought me, for the best lungs in England? I trow not ! "

"You are a happy man, Mr. Polwarth—if you can say that and abide by it."

"I *am* a happy man, sir. I don't know what would come of me sometimes, for very gladness, if I hadn't my good friend, the asthma-devil, to keep me down a bit Good night, sir," he added, for Mr. Drake was already moving away.

He felt superior to this man, set him down as forward, did not quite approve of him. Always ready to judge involuntarily from externals, he would have been shocked to discover how much the deformity of the man, which caused him discomfort, prejudiced him also against him. Then Polwarth seldom went to a place of worship, and when he did, went to church ! A cranky, visionary, talkative man, he was in Mr. Drake's eyes. He set him down as one of those mystical interpreters of the Word, who are always searching it for strange things, whose very insight leads them to vagary, blinding them to the relative value of things. It is amazing from what a mere fraction of fact concerning him, a man will dare judge the whole of another man. In reality, little Polwarth could have carried big Drake to the top of any hill Difficulty, up which, in his spiritual pilgrimage, he had yet had to go panting and groaning—and to the top of many another besides, within sight even of which the minister would never come in this world.

" He is too ready with his spiritual experience, that little man !—too fond of airing it," said the minister to his daughter. " I don't quite know what to make of him. He is a favorite with Mr. Wingfold ; but my experience makes me doubtful. I suspect prodigies."

Now Polwarth was not in the habit of airing his religious experiences ; but all Glaston could see that the minister was in trouble, and he caught at the first opportunity he had of showing his sympathy with him, offering him a share of the comfort he had just been receiving himself. He smiled at its apparent rejection, and closed the gate softly, saying to himself that the good man would think of it yet, he was sure.

Dorothy took little interest in Polwarth, little therefore in her father's judgment of him. But, better even than Wingfold himself, that poor physical failure of a man could have helped her from under every gravestone that was now crushing the life out of her—not so much from superiority of intellect, certainly not from superiority of learning, but mainly because he was alive all through, because the life eternal pervaded every atom of his life, every thought, every action. Door nor window of his being had a lock to it ! All of them were always on the swing to the wind that bloweth where it listeth. Upon occasions when most would seek refuge from the dark sky and gusty weather of trouble, by hiding from the messengers of Satan in the deepest cellar of their hearts, there to sit grumbling, Polwarth always went out into the open air. If the wind was rough, there was none the less life in it : the breath of God, it was rough to blow the faults from him, genial to put fresh energy in him ; if the rain fell, it was the water of cleansing and growth. Misfortune he would not know by that name : there was no *mis* but in himself, and that the messenger of Satan was there to buffet. So long as God was, all was right. No wonder the minister then was incapable of measuring the gate-keeper ! But Polwarth was right about him—as he went home he pondered the passage to which he had referred him, wondering whether he was to regard the fortune sent him as a messenger of Satan given to buffet him.

CHAPTER XXVI.

THE SURGERY DOOR.

THAT Juliet loved Faber as she had at one time resolved never to love man, she no longer attempted to conceal from herself ; but she was far from being prepared to confess the discovery to him. His atheism she satisfactorily justified herself in being more ready to pity than to blame. There were difficulties ! There were more than difficulties ! Not a few of them she did not herself see how to get over ! If her father had been alive, then indeed !—children must not break their parents' hearts. But if, as *appeared* the most likely thing, that father, tenderly as she had loved him, was gone from her forever, if life was but a flash across from birth to the grave, why should not those who loved make the best of it for each other during that one moment "brief as the lightning in the collied night"? They must try to be the more to one another, and the time was so short. All that Faber had ever pleaded was now blossoming at once in her thought. She had not a doubt that he loved her—as would have been enough once at all events. A man of men he was !—noble, unselfish, independent, a ruler of himself, a benefactor of his race ! What right had those *believers* to speak of him as they did ? In any personal question he was far their superior. That they undervalued him, came all of their narrow prejudices ! He was not of their kind, therefore he must be below them ! But there were first that should be last, and last first !

She felt herself no whit worthy of him. She believed herself not for a moment comparable to him !   But his infinite
chivalry, gentleness, compassion, would be her refuge !
Such a man would bear with her weaknesses, love her love,
and forgive her sins !   If he took her God from her, he
must take His place, and be a God-like man to her !   Then,
if there should be any further truth discoverable, why indeed, as himself said, should they not discover it together ?
Could they be as likely to discover it apart, and distracted
with longing ?   She must think about it a little longer,
though.   She could not make up her mind the one way,
and would not the other.   She would wait and see.   She
dared not yet.   Something might turn up to decide her.   If
she could but see into his heart for a moment !

All this later time, she had been going to church every
Sunday, and listening to sermons in which the curate poured
out the energy of a faith growing stronger day by day ; but
not a word he said had as yet laid hold of one root-fiber
of her being.   She judged, she accepted, she admired,
she refused, she condemned, but she never *did*.   To many
souls hell itself seems a less frightful alternative than the
agony of resolve, of turning, of being born again ; but Juliet
had never got so far as that : she had never yet looked the
thing required of her in the face.   She came herself to
wonder that she had made any stand at all against the arguments of Faber.   But how is it that any one who has been
educated in Christianity, yet does not become the disciple
of Jesus Christ, avoids becoming an atheist ?   To such the
whole thing must look so unlike what it really is !   Does he
prefer to keep half believing the revelation, in order to
attribute to it elements altogether unlovely, and so justify
himself in refusing it ?   Were it not better to reject it altogether if it be not fit to be believed in ?   If he be unable to
do that, if he dare not proclaim an intellectual unbelief, if
some reverence for father or mother, some inward drawing
toward the good thing, some desire to keep an open door
of escape, prevent, what a hideous folly is the moral disregard !   " The thing is true, but I don't mind it ! "   What is
this acknowledged heedlessness, this apologetic arrogance ?
Is it a timid mockery, or the putting forth of a finger in the
very face of the Life of the world ?   I know well how foolish words like these must seem to such as Faber, but for
such they are not written ; they are written for the men and
women who close the lids of but half-blinded eyes, and

thInk they do God service by not denying that there is not
a sun in the heavens. There may be some denying Christ
who shall fare better than they, when He comes to judge
the world with a judgment which even those whom He sends
from Him shall confess to be absolutely fair—a judgment
whose very righteousness may be a consolation to some
upon whom it falls heavily.

That night Juliet hardly knew what she had said to Faber,
and longed to see him again. She slept little, and in the morning was weary and exhausted. But he had set her the grand
example of placing work before every thing else, and she
would do as he taught her. So, in the name of her lover,
and in spite of her headache, she rose to her day's duty.
Love delights to put on the livery of the loved.

After breakfast, as was their custom, Dorothy walked
with her to the place where she gave her first lesson. The
nearest way led past the house of the doctor ; but hitherto, as often as she could frame fitting reason, generally
on the ground that they were too early, and must make a
little longer walk of it, Juliet had contrived to avoid turning the corner of Mr. Drew's shop. This day, however,
she sought no excuse, and they went the natural road. She
wanted to pass his house—to get a glimpse of him if she
might.

As they approached it, they were startled by a sudden
noise of strife. The next instant the door of the surgery,
which was a small building connected with the house by a
passage, flew open, and a young man was shot out. He
half jumped, half fell down the six or eight steps, turned at
once, and ran up again. He had rather a refined look, notwithstanding the annoyance and resentment that discom-
posed his features. The mat had caught the door and he
was just in time to prevent it from being shut in his face.

" I will *not* submit to such treatment, Mr. Faber," cried
the youth. " It is not the part of a gentleman to forget that
another is one."

" To the devil with your *gentleman !* " they heard the doctor shout in a rage, from behind the half-closed door. " The
less said about the gentleman the better, when the man is
nowhere ! "

" Mr. Faber, I will allow no man to insult me," said the
youth, and made a fierce attempt to push the door open.

" You are a wretch below insult," returned the doctor ;
and the next moment the youth staggered again down the

steps, this time to fall, in awkward and ignominious fashion, half on the pavement, half in the road.

Then out on the top of the steps came Paul Faber, white with wrath, too full of indignation to see person or thing except the object of it.

" You damned rascal ! " he cried. " If you set foot on my premises again, it will be at the risk of your contemptible life."

" Come, come, Mr. Faber ! this won't do," returned the youth, defiantly, as he gathered himself up. " I don't want to make a row, but—"

" *You* don't want to make a row, you puppy ! Then *I* do. You don't come into my house again. I'll have your traps turned out to you.—Jenkins !—You had better leave the town as fast as you can, too, for this won't be a secret."

" You'll allow me to call on Mr. Crispin first ? "

" Do. Tell him the truth, and see whether he'll take the thing up ! If I were God, I'd damn you ! "

" Big words from you, Faber ! " said the youth with a sneer, struggling hard to keep the advantage he had in temper. " Every body knows you don't believe there is any God."

" Then there ought to be, so long as such as you 'ain't got your deserts. *You* set up for a doctor ! I would sooner lose all the practice I ever made than send *you* to visit woman or child, you heartless miscreant ! "

The epithet the doctor really used here was stronger and more contemptuous, but it is better to take the liberty of substituting this.

" What have I done then to let loose all this Billingsgate ? " cried the young man indignantly. " I have done nothing the most distinguished in the profession haven't done twenty times over."

" I don't care a damn. What's the profession to humanity ! For a wonder the public is in the right on this question, and I side with the public. The profession may go to—Turkey ! "—Probably Turkey was not the place he had intended to specify, but at the moment he caught sight of Juliet and her companion.—" There ! " he concluded, pointing to the door behind him, " you go in and put your things up—*and be off*."

Without another word, the young man ascended the steps, and entered the house.

Juliet stood staring, motionless and white. Again and

again Dorothy would have turned back, but Juliet grasped
her by the arm, stood as if frozen to the spot, and would
not let her move. She *must* know what it meant. And all
the time a little crowd had been gathering, as it well might,
even in a town no bigger than Glaston, at such uproar in
its usually so quiet streets. At first it was all women, who
showed their interest by a fixed regard of each speaker in
the quarrel in turn, and a confused staring from one to the
other of themselves. No handle was yet visible by which
to lay hold of the affair. But the moment the young man
re-entered the surgery, and just as Faber was turning to go
after him, out, like a bolt, shot from the open door a long-
legged, gaunt mongrel dog, in such a pitiful state as I will
not horrify my readers by attempting to describe. It is
enough to say that the knife had been used upon him with
a ghastly freedom. In an agony of soundless terror the
poor animal, who could never recover the usage he had had,
and seemed likely to tear from himself a part of his body at
every bound, rushed through the spectators, who scattered
horror-stricken from his path. Ah, what a wild waste look
the creature had !—as if his spirit within him were wan with
dismay at the lawless invasion of his humble house of life.
A cry, almost a shriek, rose from the little crowd, to which
a few men had now added themselves. The doctor came
dashing down the steps in pursuit of him. The same instant, having just escaped collision with the dog, up came
Mr. Drew. His round face flamed like the sun in a fog
with anger and pity and indignation. He rushed straight
at the doctor, and would have collared him. Faber flung
him from him without a word, and ran on. The draper
reeled, but recovered himself, and was starting to follow,
when Juliet, hurrying up, with white face and flashing eyes,
laid her hand on his arm, and said, in a voice of whose
authoritative tone she was herself unconscious,

"Stop, Mr. Drew."

The draper obeyed, but stood speechless with anger, not
yet doubting it was the doctor who had so misused the dog.

"I have been here from the first," she went on. "Mr.
Faber is as angry as you are.—Please, Dorothy, will you
come ?—It is that assistant of his, Mr. Drew ! He hasn't
been with him more than three days."

With Dorothy beside her, Juliet now told him, loud
enough for all to hear, what they had heard and seen.

"I must go and beg his pardon," said the draper. "I

had no right to come to such a hasty conclusion. I hope he will not find it hard to forgive me."

"You did no more than he would have done in your place," replied Juliet. "—But," she added, "where is the God of that poor animal, Mr. Drew?"

"I expect He's taken him by this time," answered the draper. "But I must go and find the doctor."

So saying, he turned and left them. The ladies went also, and the crowd dispersed. But already rumors, as evil as discordant, were abroad in Glaston to the prejudice of Faber, and at the door of his godlessness was from all sides laid the charge of cruelty.

How difficult it is to make prevalent the right notion of any thing! But only a little reflection is required to explain the fact. The cause is, that so few people give themselves the smallest trouble to understand what is told them. The first thing suggested by the words spoken is taken instead of the fact itself, and to that as a ground-plan all that follows is fitted. People listen so badly, even when not sleepily, that the wonder is any thing of consequence should ever be even approximately understood. How appalling it would be to one anxious to convey a meaning, to see the shapes his words assumed in the mind of his listening friend! For, in place of falling upon the table of his perception, kept steady by will and judgment, he would see them tumble upon the sounding-board of his imagination, ever vibrating, and there be danced like sand into all manner of shapes, according to the tune played by the capricious instrument. Thus, in Glaston, the strangest stories of barbarity and cruelty were now attributed to a man entirely incapable of them. He was not one of the foul seekers after knowledge, and if he had had a presentiment of the natural tendency of his opinions, he would have trembled at the vision, and set himself to discover whether there might not be truth in another way of things.

As he went about in the afternoon amongst his sick and needy, the curate heard several of these ill reports. Some communicated them to ease their own horror, others in the notion of pleasing the believer by revolting news of the unbeliever. In one house he was told that the poor young man whom Dr. Faber had enticed to be his assistant, had behaved in the most gentlemanly fashion, had thrown up his situation, consenting to the loss of his salary, rather than connive at the horrors of cruelty in which the doctor claimed

his help. Great moan was made over the pity that such a
nice man should be given to such abominations ; but where
was the wonder, some said, seeing he was the enemy of God,
that he should be the enemy of the beasts God had made ?
Much truth, and many wise reflections were uttered, only
they were not " as level as the cannon to his blank," for they
were pointed at the wrong man.

There was one thing in which Wingfold differed from
most of his parishioners : he could hear with his judgment,
and make his imagination lie still. At the same time, in
order to arrive the more certainly at the truth, in any matter
presented to him, he would, in general, listen to the end of
what any body had to say. So doing he let eagerness ex-
haust itself, and did not by opposition in the first heat of
narration, excite partisan interest, or wake malevolent
caution. If the communication was worthy, he thus got all
the worth of it ; if it was evil, he saw to the bottom of it,
and discovered, if such were there, the filthy reptile in the
mud beneath, which was setting the whole ugly pool in commotion. By this deliberateness he also gave the greater
weight to what answer he saw fit to give at last—sometimes
with the result of considerable confusion of face to the nar-
rator. In the present instance, he contented himself with
the strongest assurance that the whole story was a mistake
so far as it applied to Mr. Faber, who had, in fact, dismissed
his assistant for the very crime of which they accused himself. The next afternoon, he walked the whole length of
Pine street with the doctor, conversing all the way.

Nor did he fail to turn the thing to advantage. He had
for some time been awaiting a fit opportunity for instructing
his people upon a point which he thought greatly neglected :
here was the opportunity, and he made haste to avail himself of it.

CHAPTER XXVII.

THE GROANS OF THE INARTICULATE.

THE rest of the week was rainy, but Sunday rose a day
of perfect summer. As the curate went up the pulpit-stair,
he felt as if the pulse of all creation were beating in unison

with his own ; for to-day he was the speaker for the speech-less, the interpreter of groans to the creation of God.

He read, *Are not two sparrows sold for a farthing? and one of them shall not fall on the ground without your Father*, and said :

"My friends, doth God care for sparrows? Or saith He it altogether for our sakes, and not at all for the sparrows? No, truly ; for indeed it would be nothing to us if it were not every thing to the sparrows. The word can not reach our door except through the sparrow's nest. For see ! what comfort would it be to us to be told we were of more value than ever so many sparrows, if their value was noth-ing—if God only knew and did not care for them ? The saying would but import that we were of more value than just nothing. Oh, how skillful is unbelief to take all the color and all the sweetness and all the power out of the words of The Word Himself ! How many Christians are there not who take the passage to mean that not a sparrow can fall to the ground without the *knowledge* of its Creator ! A mighty thing that for the sparrow ! If such a Christian seemed to the sparrow the lawful interpreter of the spar-row's Creator, he would make an infidel of the sparrow. What Christ-like heart, what heart of loving man, could be content to take all the comfort to itself, and leave none for the sparrows ? Not that of our mighty brother Paul. In his ears sounded, in his heart echoed, the cries of all the creation of God. Their groanings that could not be uttered, roused the response of his great compassion. When Christ was born in the heart of Paul, the whole crea-tion of God was born with him ; nothing that could feel could he help loving ; in the trouble of the creatures' trou-bles, sprang to life in his heart the hope, that all that could groan should yet rejoice, that on the lowest servant in the house should yet descend the fringe of the robe that was cast about the redeemed body of the Son. *He* was no pettifogging priest standing up for the rights of the superior ! An exclusive is a self-excluded Christian. They that shut the door will find themselves on the wrong side of the door they have shut. They that push with the horn and stamp with the hoof, can not be admitted to the fold. St. Paul would acknowledge no distinctions. He saw every wall—of seclusion, of exclusion, of partition, broken down. Jew and Greek, barbarian, Scythian, bond and free—all must come in to his heart. Mankind was not enough to fill that divine space, enlarged to infinitude by the presence of the Christ : angels, principalities, and powers, must share in its conscious splendor. Not yet filled, yet unsatisfied with beings to love, Paul spread forth his arms to the whole groaning and troubled race of animals. Whatever could send forth a sigh of discomfort, or heave a helpless limb in pain, he took to the bosom of his hope and affection—yea, of his love and faith : on them, too, he saw the cup of Christ's heart overflow. For Paul had heard, if not from His own, yet from the lips of them that heard Him speak, the words, *Are not five sparrows sold for two farthings, and not one of them is forgotten before God?* What if the little half-farthing things bear their share, and always have borne, in that which is behind of the sufferings of Christ ? In any case, not one of them, not one so young that it topples from the edge of its nest, unable to fly, is forgotten by the Father of men. It shall not have a lonely deathbed, for the Father of Jesus will be with it. It *must* be true. It is indeed a daring word, but less would not be enough for the hearts of men, for the glory of God, for the need of the sparrow. I do not close my eyes to one of a thousand seemingly contradictory facts. I misdoubt my reading of the small-print notes, and appeal to the text, yea, beyond the text, even to the God of the sparrows Himself.

" I count it as belonging to the smallness of our faith, to the poorness of our religion, to the rudimentary condition of our nature, that our sympathy with God's creatures is so small. Whatever the narrowness of our poverty-stricken, threadbare theories concerning them, whatever the inhospitality and exclusiveness of our mean pride toward them, we can not escape admitting that to them pain is pain, and comfort is comfort ; that they hunger and thirst ; that sleep restores and death delivers them : surely these are ground enough to the true heart wherefore it should love and cherish them—the heart at least that believes with St. Paul, that they need and have the salvation of Christ as well as we. Right grievously, though blindly, do they groan after it.

" The ignorance and pride which is forever sinking us toward them, are the very elements in us which mislead us in our judgment concerning them, causing us to imagine them not upon a lower merely, but upon an altogether dif- ferent footing in creation from our own. The same things we call by one name in us, and by another in them. How

jealous have not men been as to allowing them any share
worthy the name of reason! But you may see a greater
difference in this respect between the lowest and the highest at a common school, than you will between them and
us. A pony that has taught itself without hands to pump
water for its thirst, an elephant that puts forth its mighty
lip to lift the moving wheel of the heavy wagon over the
body of its fallen driver, has rather more to plead on the
score of intellect than many a schoolboy. Not a few of
them shed tears. A bishop, one of the foremost of our
scholars, assured me that once he saw a certain animal
laugh while playing off a practical joke on another of a different kind from himself. I do not mention the kind of
animal, because it would give occasion for a silly articulate
joke, far inferior to his practical one. I go further, and say,
that I more than suspect a rudimentary conscience in every
animal. I care not how remotely rudimentary. There
must be in the moral world absolute and right potent ger-
minal facts which lie infinitudes beyond the reach of any
moral microscope, as in the natural world beyond the most
powerful of lenses. Yet surely in this respect also, one may
see betwixt boys at the same school greater differences than
there are betwixt the highest of the animals and the lowest
of the humans. If you plead for time for the boy to develop
his poor rudimentary mollusk of a conscience, take it and
heartily welcome—but grant it the animals also. With
some of them it may need millions of years for any thing I
know. Certainly in many human beings it never comes
plainly into our ken all the time they walk the earth. Who
shall say how far the vision of the apostle reached? but
surely the hope in which he says God Himself subjected the
creature to vanity, must have been an infinite hope : I will
hope infinitely. That the Bible gives any ground for the
general fancy that at death an animal ceases to exist, is but
the merest dullest assumption. Neither is there a single
scientific argument, so far as I know, against the continued
existence of the animals, which would not tell equally
against human immortality. My hope is, that in some way,
concerning which I do not now choose to speculate, there
may be progress, growth, for them also. While I believe
for myself, I *must* hope for them. This much at least seems
clear—and I could press the argument further : if not one
of them is forgotten before God—and one of them yet
passes out of being—then is God the God of the dead and

not of the living ! But we praise Thee, we bless Thee, we worship Thee, we glorify Thee, we give thanks to Thee for Thy great glory, O Lord God, heavenly King, God the Father almighty ! Thy universe is life, life and not death. Even the death which awoke in the bosom of Sin, Thy Son, opposing Himself to its hate, and letting it spend its fury upon Him, hath abolished. I know nothing, therefore care little, as to whether or not it may have pleased God to bring man up to the hill of humanity through the swamps and thickets of lower animal nature, but I do care that I should not now any more approach that level, whether once rightly my own or not. For what is honor in the animals, would be dishonor in me. Not the less may such be the punishment, perhaps redemption, in store for some men and women. For aught I know, or see unworthy in the thought, the self-sufficing exquisite, for instance, may one day find himself chattering amongst fellow apes in some monkey-village of Africa or Burmah. Nor is the supposition absurd, though at first sight it may well so appear. Let us remember that we carry in us the characteristics of each and every animal. There is not one fiercest passion, one movement of affection, one trait of animal economy, one quality either for praise or blame, existing in them that does not exist in us. The relationship can not be so very distant. And if theirs be so freely in us, why deny them so much we call ours ? Hear how one of the ablest doctors of the English church, John Donne, Dean of St. Paul's in the reign of James the first, writes :—

> Man is a lump where all beasts kneaded be ;
> Wisdom makes him an ark where all agree ;
> The fool, in whom these beasts do live at jar,
> Is sport to others, and a theater ;
> Nor scapes he so, but is himself their prey ;
> All which was man in him, is eat away ;
> And now his beasts on one another feed,
> Yet couple in anger, and new monsters breed.
> How happy's he which hath due place assigned
> To his beasts, and disaforested his mind !
> Impaled himself to keep them out, not in ;
> Can sow, and dares trust corn where they have been ;
> Can use his horse, goat, wolf, and every beast,
> And is not ass himself to all the rest !
> Else man not only is the herd of swine,
> But he's those devils, too, which did incline
> Them to an headlong rage, and made them worse ;
> For man can add weight to heaven's heaviest curse.

" It astonishes me, friends, that we are not more terrified at ourselves. Except the living Father have brought order, harmony, a world, out of His chaos, a man is but a cage of unclean beasts, with no one to rule them, however fine a gentleman he may think himself. Even in this fair, well-ordered England of ours, at Kirkdale, in Yorkshire, was discovered, some fifty years ago, a great cavern that had once been a nest of gigantic hyenas, evidenced by their own broken bones, and the crushed bones of tigers, elephants, bears, and many other creatures. See to what a lovely peace the Creating Hand has even now brought our England, far as she is yet from being a province in the kingdom of Heaven ; but see also in her former condition a type of the horror to which our souls may festering sink, if we shut out His free spirit, and have it no more moving upon the face of our waters. And when I say a type, let us be assured there is no type worth the name which is not poor to express the glory or the horror it represents.

" To return to the animals : they are a care to God ! they occupy part of His thoughts ; we have duties toward them, owe them friendliness, tenderness. That God should see us use them as we do is a terrible fact—a severe difficulty to faith. For to such a pass has the worship of Knowledge— an idol vile even as Mammon himself, and more cruel— arrived, that its priests, men kind as other men to their own children, kind to the animals of their household, kind even to some of the wild animals, men who will scatter crumbs to the robins in winter, and set water for the sparrows on their house-top in summer, will yet, in the worship of this their idol, in their greed after the hidden things of the life of the flesh, without scruple, confessedly without compunction, will, I say, dead to the natural motions of the divine element in them, the inherited pity of God, subject innocent, helpless, appealing, dumb souls to such tortures whose bare description would justly set me forth to the blame of cruelty toward those who sat listening to the same. Have these living, moving, seeing, hearing, feeling creatures, who could not be but by the will and the presence of Another any more than ourselves—have they no rights in this their compelled existence ? Does the most earnest worship of an idol excuse robbery with violence extreme to obtain the sacrifices he loves ? Does the value of the thing that may be found there justify me in breaking into the house of another's life ? Does his ignorance of the existence of that which I seek

alter the case ? Can it be right to water the tree of knowledge with blood, and stir its boughs with the gusts of bitter
agony, that we may force its flowers into blossom before
their time ? Sweetly human must be the delights of knowledge so gained ! grand in themselves, and ennobling in their
tendencies ! Will it justify the same as a noble, a laudable,
a worshipful endeavor to cover it with the reason or pretext
—God knows which—of such love for my own human kind
as strengthens me to the most ruthless torture of their poorer
relations, whose little treasure I would tear from them that
it may teach me how to add to their wealth ? May my God
give me grace to prefer a hundred deaths to a life gained by
the suffering of one simplest creature. He holds his life as
I hold mine by finding himself there where I find myself.
Shall I quiet my heart with the throbs of another heart ?
soothe my nerves with the agonized tension of a system ?
live a few days longer by a century of shrieking deaths ? It
were a hellish wrong, a selfish, hateful, violent injustice. An
evil life it were that I gained or held by such foul means !
How could I even attempt to justify the injury, save on the
plea that I am already better and more valuable than he ;
that I am the stronger ; that the possession of all the
pleasures of human intelligence gives me the right to turn
the poor innocent joys of his senses into pains before which,
threatening my own person, my very soul would grow gray
with fear ? Or let me grant what many professional men
deny utterly, that some knowledge of what is called practical
value to the race has been thus attained—what can be its
results at best but the adding of a cubit to the life ? Grant
that it gave us an immortal earthly existence, one so happy
that the most sensual would never wish for death : what
would it be by such means to live forever ? God in Heaven !
who, what is the man who would dare live a life wrung from
the agonies of tortured innocents ? Against the will of my
Maker, live by means that are an abhorrence to His soul !
Such a life must be all in the flesh ! the spirit could have
little share therein. Could it be even a life of the flesh that
came of treason committed against essential animality ? It
could be but an abnormal monstrous existence, that sprang,
toadstool-like, from the blood-marsh of cruelty—a life
neither spiritual nor fleshey, but devilish.

"It is true we are above the creatures—but not to keep
them down ; they are for our use and service, but neither to
be trodden under the foot of pride, nor misused as ministers,

at their worst cost of suffering, to our inordinate desires of ease. After no such fashion did God give them to be our helpers in living. To be tortured that we might gather ease ! none but a devil could have made them for that ! When I see a man who professes to believe not only in a God, but such a God as holds His court in the person of Jesus Christ, assail with miserable cruelty the scanty, lovely, timorous lives of the helpless about him, it sets my soul aflame with such indignant wrath, with such a sense of horrible incongruity and wrong to every harmony of Nature, human and divine, that I have to make haste and rush to the feet of the Master, lest I should scorn and hate where He has told me to love. Such a wretch, not content that Christ should have died to save men, will tear Christ's living things into palpitating shreds, that he may discover from them how better to save the same men. Is this to be in the world as He was in the world ! Picture to yourselves one of these Christian inquirers erect before his class of students : knife in hand, he is demonstrating to them from the live animal, so fixed and screwed and wired that he cannot find for his agony even the poor relief of a yelp, how this or that writhing nerve or twitching muscle operates in the business of a life which his demonstration has turned from the gift of love into a poisoned curse ; picture to yourself such a one so busied, suddenly raising his eyes and seeing the eyes that see him ! the eyes of Him who, when He hung upon the cross, knew that He suffered for the whole creation of His Father, to lift it out of darkness into light, out of wallowing chaos into order and peace ! Those eyes watching him, that pierced hand soothing his victim, would not the knife fall from his hand in the divine paralysis that shoots from the heart and conscience ? Ah me ! to have those eyes upon me in any wrong-doing ! One thing only could be worse—*not* to have them upon me—to be left with my devils.

"You all know the immediate cause of the turning of our thoughts in this direction—the sad case of cruelty that so unexpectedly rushed to light in Glaston. So shocked was the man in whose house it took place that, as he drove from his door the unhappy youth who was guilty of the crime, this testimony, in the righteous indignation of his soul, believing, as you are aware, in no God and Father of all, broke from him with curses—' There ought to be a God to punish such cruelty.'—' Begone,' he said. ' Never would I commit woman or child into the hands of a willful author of suffering.'

" We are to rule over the animals ; the opposite of rule is torture, the final culmination of anarchy. We slay them, and if with reason, then with right. Therein we do them no wrong. Yourselves will bear me witness however and always in this place, I have protested that death is no evil, save as the element of injustice may be mingled therein. The sting of death is sin. Death, righteously inflicted, I repeat, is the reverse of an injury.

" What if there is too much lavishment of human affection upon objects less than human ! it hurts less than if there were none. I confess that it moves with strange discomfort one who has looked upon swarms of motherless children, to see in a childless house a ruined dog, overfed, and snarling with discomfort even on the blessed throne of childhood, the lap of a woman. But even that is better than that the woman should love no creature at all—infinitely better ! It may be she loves as she can. Her heart may not yet be equal to the love of a child, may be able only to cherish a creature whose oppositions are merely amusing, and whose presence, as doubtless it seems to her, gives rise to no responsibilities. Let her love her dog—even although her foolish treatment of him should delay the poor animal in its slow trot towards canine perfection : she may come to love him better ; she may herself through him advance to the love and the saving of a child—who can tell ? But do not mistake me ; there are women with hearts so divinely insatiable in loving, that in the mere gaps of their untiring ministration of humanity, they will fondle any living thing capable of receiving the overflow of their affection. Let such love as they will ; they can hardly err. It is not of such that I have spoken.

" Again, to how many a lonely woman is not life made endurable, even pleasant, by the possession and the love of a devoted dog ! The man who would focus the burning glass of science upon the animal, may well mock at such a mission, and speak words contemptuous of the yellow old maid with her yellow ribbons and her yellow dog. Nor would it change his countenance or soften his heart to be assured that that withered husk of womanhood was lovely once, and the heart in it is loving still ; that she was reduced to all but misery by the self-indulgence of a brother, to whom the desolation of a sister was but a pebble to pave the way to his pleasures ; that there is no one left her now to love, or to be grateful for her love, but the creature

which he regards merely as a box of nature's secrets, worthy
only of being rudely ransacked for what it may contain, and
thrown aside when shattered in the search.   A box he is
indeed, in which lies inclosed a shining secret !—a truth too
radiant for the eyes of such a man as he ; the love of a living God is in him and his fellows, ranging the world in
broken incarnation, ministering to forlorn humanity in
dumb yet divine service.   Who knows, in their great silence,
how germane with ours may not be their share in the groanings that can not be uttered !

   " Friends, there must be a hell.   If we leave scripture
and human belief aside, science reveals to us that nature has
her catastrophes—that there is just so much of the failed
cycle, of the unrecovered, the unbalanced, the incompleted,
the fallen-short, in her motions, that the result must be collision, shattering resumption, the rage of unspeakable fire.
Our world and all the worlds of the system, are, I suppose,
doomed to fall back at length into their parent furnace.
Then will come one end and another beginning.   There is
many an end and many a beginning.   At one of those ends,
and that not the furthest, must surely lie a hell, in which, of
all sins, the sin of cruelty, under whatever pretext committed, will receive its meed from Him with whom there is no
respect of persons, but who giveth to every man according
to his works.   Nor will it avail him to plead that in life he
never believed in such retribution ; for a cruelty that would
have been restrained by a fear of hell was none the less
hellworthy.

   " But I will not follow this track.   The general conviction of humanity will be found right against any conclusions calling themselves scientific, that go beyond the scope
or the reach of science.   Neither will I presume to suggest
the operation of any *lex talionis* in respect of cruelty.   I
know little concerning the salvation by fire of which St. Paul
writes in his first epistle to the Corinthians ; but I say this,
that if the difficulty of curing cruelty be commensurate with
the horror of its nature, then verily for the cruel must the
furnace of wrath be seven times heated.   Ah ! for them,
poor injured ones, the wrong passes away !   Friendly,
lovely death, the midwife of Heaven, comes to their relief,
and their pain sinks in precious peace.   But what is to be
done for our brother's soul, bespattered with the gore of
innocence ?   Shall the cries and moans of the torture
he inflicted haunt him like an evil smell ?   Shall

the phantoms of exquisite and sickening pains float lambent about the fingers, and pass and repass through the heart and brain, that sent their realities quivering and burning into the souls of the speechless ones? It has been said somewhere that the hell for the cruel man would be to have the faces of all the creatures he had wronged come staring round him, with sad, weary eyes. But must not the divine nature, the pitiful heart of the universe, have already begun to reassert itself in him, before that would hurt him? Upon such a man the justice in my heart desires this retribution—to desire more would be to be more vile than he ; to desire less would not be to love my brother :—that the soul capable of such deeds shall be compelled to know the nature of its deeds in the light of the absolute Truth—that the eternal fact shall flame out from the divine region of its own conscience until it writhe in the shame of being itself, loathe as absolute horror the deeds which it would now justify, and long for deliverance from that which it has made of itself. The moment the discipline begins to blossom, the moment the man begins to thirst after confession and reparation, then is he once more my brother ; then from an object of disgust in spite of pity, he becomes a being for all tender, honest hearts in the universe of God to love, cherish, revere.

"Meantime, you who behold with aching hearts the wrongs done to the lower brethren that ought to be cherished as those to whom less has been given, having done all, stand comforted in the thought that not one of them suffers without the loving, caring, sustaining presence of the great Father of the universe, the Father of men, the God and Father of Jesus Christ, the God of the sparrows and the ravens and the oxen—yea, of the lilies of the field."

As might be expected, Mrs. Ramshorn was indignant. What right had he to desecrate a pulpit of the Church of England by misusing it for the publication of his foolish fancies about creatures that had not reason ! Of course nobody would think of being cruel to them, poor things ! But there was that silly man talking about them as if they were better Christians than any of them ! He was intruding into things he had not seen, vainly puffed up by his fleshly mind.

The last portion of these remarks she made in the hearing of her niece, who carried it home for the amusement of

her husband.   He said he could laugh with a good conscience, for the reading of the passage, according to the
oldest manuscripts we have, was not "the things he hath
not seen," but "the things he hath seen," and he
thought it meant—haunting the visible, the sensuous,
the fleshly, so, for the satisfaction of an earthly
imagination, in love with embodiment for its own sake,
worshiping angels, and not keeping hold of the invisible,
the real, the true—the mind, namely, and spirit of the living
Christ, the Head.

" Poor auntie," replied Helen, " would hold herself quite
above the manuscripts.   With her it is the merest sectarianism and radicalism to meddle with the text as appointed to
be read in churches.   What was good enough for the dean,
must be far more than good enough for an unbeneficed
curate ! "

But the rector, who loved dogs and horses, was delighted
with the sermon.

Faber's whole carriage and conduct in regard to the
painful matter was such as to add to Juliet's confidence in
him.   Somehow she grew more at ease in his company, and
no longer took pains to avoid him.

CHAPTER XXVIII.

COW-LANE-CHAPEL.

By degrees Mr. Drake's mind grew quiet, and accommo-
dated itself to the condition of the new atmosphere in which
at first it was so hard for him to draw spiritual breath.   He
found himself again able to pray, and while he bowed his
head lower before God, he lifted up his heart higher toward
him. His uncle's bequest presenting no appropriative difficulties, he at once set himself to be a faithful and wise steward
of the grace of God, to which holy activity the return of his
peace was mainly owing.   Now and then the fear would
return that God had sent him the money in displeasure, that
He had handed him over all his principal, and refused to be
his banker any more ; and the light-winged, haunting dread
took from him a little even of the blameless pleasure that

naturally belonged to the paying of his debts. Also he now became plainly aware of a sore fact which he had all his life dimly suspected—namely, that there was in his nature a spot of the leprosy of avarice, the desire to accumulate. Hence he grew almost afraid of his money, and his anxiety to spend it freely and right, to keep it flowing lest it should pile up its waves and drown his heart, went on steadily increasing. That he could hoard now if he pleased gave him just the opportunity of burning the very possibility out of his soul. It is those who are unaware of their proclivities, and never pray against them, that must be led into temptation, lest they should forever continue capable of evil. When a man could do a thing, then first can he abstain from doing it. Now, with his experience of both poverty and riches, the minister knew that he must make them both follow like hounds at his heel. If he were not to love money, if, even in the free use of it, he were to regard it with honor, fear its loss, forget that it came from God, and must return to God through holy channels, he must sink into a purely contemptible slave. Where would be the room for any further repentance ? He would have had every chance, and failed in every trial the most opposed ! He must be lord of his wealth ; Mammon must be the slave, not Walter Drake. Mammon must be more than his brownie, more than his Robin Goodfellow ; he must be the subject Djin of a holy spell—holier than Solomon's wisdom, more potent than the stamp of his seal. At present he almost feared him as a Caliban to whom he might not be able to play Prospero, an Ufreet half-escaped from his jar, a demon he had raised, for whom he must find work, or be torn by him into fragments. The slave must have drudgery, and the master must take heed that he never send him alone to do love's dear service.

" I am sixty," he said to himself, " and I have learned to begin to learn." Behind him his public life looked a mere tale that is told ; his faith in the things he had taught had been little better than that which hangs about an ancient legend. He had been in a measure truthful ; he had endeavored to act upon what he taught ; but alas ! the accidents of faith had so often been uppermost with him, instead of its eternal fundamental truths ! How unlike the affairs of the kingdom did all that church-business look to him now !—the rich men ruling—the poor men grumbling ! In the whole assembly including himself, could he honestly

say he knew more than one man that sought the kingdom
of Heaven *first?* And yet he had been tolerably content,
until they began to turn against himself !—What better could
they have done than get rid of him ? The whole history of
their relation appeared now as a mess of untruth shot
through with threads of light. Now, now, he would strive
to enter in at the strait gate : the question was not of
pushing others in. He would mortify the spirit of worldly
judgments and ambitions : he would be humble as the servant of Christ.

Dorothy's heart was relieved a little. She could read her
father's feelings better than most wives those of their husbands, and she knew he was happier. But she was not herself happier. She would gladly have parted with all the
money for a word from any quarter that could have assured
her there was a God in Heaven who *loved*. But the teaching
of the curate had begun to tell upon her. She had begun
to have a faint perception that if the story of Jesus Christ
was true, there might be a Father to be loved, and being
might be a bliss. The poorest glimmer of His loveliness
gives a dawn to our belief in a God ; and a small amount
indeed of a genuine knowledge of Him will serve to neutral-
ize the most confident declaration that science is against
the idea of a God—an utterance absolutely false. Scientific
men may be unbelievers, but it is not from the teaching of
science. Science teaches that a man must not say he knows
what he does not know ; not that what a man does not
know he may say does not exist. I will grant, however,
and willingly, that true science is against Faber's idea of
other people's idea of a God. I will grant also that the
tendency of one who exclusively studies science is certainly
to deny what no one has proved, and he is uninterested in
proving ; but that is the fault of the man and his lack of
science, not of the science he has. If people understood
better the arrogance of which they are themselves guilty,
they would be less ready to imagine that a strong assertion
necessarily implies knowledge. Nothing can be known
except what is true. A negative may be *fact*, but can not
be *known* except by the knowledge of its opposite. I believe
also that nothing can be really *believed*, except it be true.
But people think they believe many things which they do not
and can not in the real sense.

When, however, Dorothy came to concern herself about
the will of God, in trying to help her father to do the best

with their money, she began to reap a little genuine comfort, for then she found things begin to explain themselves a little. The more a man occupies himself in doing the works of the Father—the sort of thing the Father does, the easier will he find it to believe that such a Father is at work in the world.

In the curate Mr. Drake had found not only a man he could trust, but one to whom, young as he was, he could look up ; and it was a trait in the minister nothing short of noble, that he did look up to the curate—perhaps without knowing it. He had by this time all but lost sight of the fact, once so monstrous, so unchristian in his eyes, that he was the paid agent of a government-church ; the sight of the man's own house, built on a rock in which was a well of the water of life, had made him nearly forget it. In his turn he could give the curate much ; the latter soon discovered that he knew a great deal more about Old Testament criticism, church-history, and theology—understanding by the last the records of what men had believed and argued about God—than he did. They often disagreed and not seldom disputed ; but while each held the will and law of Christ as the very foundation of the world, and obedience to Him as the way to possess it after its idea, how could they fail to know that they were brothers? They were gentle with each other for the love of Him whom in eager obedience they called Lord.

The moment his property was his availably, the minister betook himself to the curate.

" Now," he said—he too had the gift of going pretty straight, though not quite so straight as the curate—" Now, Mr. Wingfold, tell me plainly what you think the first thing I ought to do with this money toward making it a true gift of God. I mean, what can I do with it for somebody else— some person or persons to whom money in my hands, not in theirs, may become a small saviour ? "

" You want, in respect of your money," rejoined the curate, " to be in the world as Christ was in the world, setting right what is wrong in ways possible to you, and not counteracting His ? You want to do the gospel as well as preach it ? "

" That is what I mean—or rather what I wish to mean. You have said it.—What do you count the first thing I should try to set right ? "

" I should say *injustice*. My very soul revolts against the talk about kindness to the poor, when such a great part of their misery comes from the injustice and greed of the rich."

" I well understand," returned Mr. Drake, "that a man's first business is to be just to his neighbor, but I do not so clearly see when he is to interfere to make others just. Our Lord would not settle the division of the inheritance between the two brothers."

" No, but he gave them a lesson concerning avarice, and left that to work. I don't suppose any body is unjust for love of injustice. I don't understand the pure devilish very well—though I have glimpses into it. Your way must be different from our Lord's in form, that it may be the same in spirit : you have to work with money ; His father had given Him none. In His mission He was not to use all means —only the best. But even He did not attack individuals to *make* them do right ; and if you employ your money in doing justice to the oppressed and afflicted, to those shorn of the commonest rights of humanity, it will be the most powerful influence of all to wake the sleeping justice in the dull hearts of other men. It is the business of any body who can, to set right what any body has set wrong. I will give you a special instance, which has been in my mind all the time. Last spring—and it was the same the spring before, my first in Glaston—the floods brought misery upon every family in what they call the Pottery here. How some of them get through any wet season I can not think ; but Faber will tell you what a multitude of sore throats, cases of croup, scarletfever, and diphtheria, he has to attend in those houses every spring and autumn. They are crowded with laborers and their families, who, since the railway came, have no choice but live there, and pay a much heavier rent in proportion to their accommodation than you or I do—in proportion to the value of the property, immensely heavier. Is it not hard ? Men are their brothers' keepers indeed—but it is in chains of wretchedness they keep them. Then again—I am told that the owner of these cottages, who draws a large yearly sum from them, and to the entreaties of his tenants for really needful repairs, gives nothing but promises, is one of the most influential attendants of a chapel you know, where, Sunday after Sunday, the gospel is preached. If this be true, here again is a sad wrong : what can those people think of religion so represented ? "

" I am a sinful man," exclaimed the pastor. " That

Barwood is one of the deacons. He is the owner of the chapel as well as the cottages. I ought to have spoken to him years ago.—But," he cried, starting to his feet, " the property is for sale ! I saw it in the paper this very morning ! Thank God ! "—He caught up his hat.—" I shall have no choice but buy the chapel too," he added, with a queer, humorous smile ; "—it is part of the property.— Come with me, my dear sir. We must see to it directly. You will speak : I would rather not appear in the affair until the property is my own ; but I will buy those houses, please God, and make them such as His poor sons and daughters may live in without fear or shame."

The curate was not one to give a cold bath to enthusiasm. They went out together, got all needful information, and within a month the title-deeds were in Mr. Drake's possession.

When the rumor reached the members of his late congregation that he had come in for a large property, many called to congratulate him, and such congratulations are pretty sure to be sincere. But he was both annoyed and amused when—it was in the morning during business hours—Dorothy came and told him, not without some show of disgust, that a deputation from the church in Cow-lane was below.

" We've taken the liberty of calling, in the name of the church, to congratulate you, Mr. Drake," said their leader, rising with the rest as the minister entered the dining-room.

" Thank you," returned the minister quietly.

" I fancy," said the other, who was Barwood himself, with a smile such as heralds the facetious, " you will hardly condescend to receive our little gratuity now ? "

" I shall not require it, gentlemen."

" Of course we should never have offered you such a small sum, if we hadn't known you were independent of us."

" Why then did you offer it at all ? " asked the minister.

" As a token of our regard."

" The regard could not be very lively that made no inquiry as to our circumstances. My daughter had twenty pounds a year ; I had nothing. We were in no small peril of simple starvation."

" Bless my soul ! we hadn't an idea of such a thing, sir ! Why didn't you tell us ? "

Mr. Drake smiled, and made no other reply.

" Well, sir," resumed Barwood, after a very brief pause,

for he was a man of magnificent assurance, " as it's all
turned out so well, you'll let bygones be bygones, and give
us a hand?"

" I am obliged to you for calling," said Mr. Drake,
"—especially to you, Mr. Barwood, because it gives me an
opportunity of confessing a fault of omission on my part
toward you."

Here the pastor was wrong. Not having done his duty
when he ought, he should have said nothing now it was
needless for the wronged, and likely only to irritate the
wrong-doer.

" Don't mention it, pray," said Mr. Barwood. " This is
a time to forget every thing."

" I ought to have pointed out to you, Mr. Barwood,"
pursued the minister, " both for your own sake and that of
those poor families, your tenants, that your property in this
lower part of the town was quite unfit for the habitation of
human beings."

" Don't let your conscience trouble you on the score of
that neglect," answered the deacon, his face flushing with
anger, while he tried to force a smile : " I shouldn't have paid
the least attention to it if you had. My firm opinion has
always been that a minister's duty is to preach the gospel,
not meddle in the private affairs of the members of his
church ; and if you knew all, Mr. Drake, you would not
have gone out of your way to make the remark. But that's
neither here nor there, for it's not the business as we've
come upon.—Mr. Drake, it's a clear thing to every one as
looks into it, that the cause will never prosper so long as
that's the chapel we've got. We did think as perhaps a
younger man might do something to counteract church-
influences ; but there don't seem any sign of betterment
yet. In fact, thinks looks worse. No, sir ! it's the chapel
as is the stumbling-block. What has religion got to do with
what's ugly and dirty ! A place that any lady or gentleman, let he or she be so much of a Christian, might turn up
the nose and refrain the foot from ! No ! I say ; what we
want is a new place of worship. Cow-lane is behind the
age—and *that* musty ! uw !"

" With the words of truth left sticking on the walls?"
suggested Mr. Drake.

" Ha ! ha ! ha !—Good that ! " exclaimed several.

But the pastor's face looked stern, and the voices dropped
into rebuked silence.

" At least you'll allow, sir," persisted Barwood, " that the house of God ought to be as good as the houses of his people. It stands to reason. Depend upon it, He won't give us no success till we give Him a decent house. What ! are we to dwell in houses of cedar, and the ark of the Lord in a tent ? That's what it comes to, sir ! "

The pastor's spiritual gorge rose at this paganism in Jew clothing.

" You think God loves newness and finery better than the old walls where generations have worshiped ? " he said.

" I make no doubt of it, sir," answered Barwood. " What's generations to him ! He wants the people drawn to His house ; and what there is in Cow-lane to draw is more than I know."

" I understand you wish to sell the chapel," said Mr. Drake. " Is it not rather imprudent to bring down the value of your property before you have got rid of it ? "

Barwood smiled a superior smile. He considered the bargain safe, and thought the purchaser a man who was certain to pull the chapel down.

" I know who the intending purchaser is," said Mr. Drake, " and—— "

Barwood's countenance changed : he bethought himself that the conveyance was not completed, and half started from his chair.

" You would never go to do such an unneighborly act," he cried, " as—— "

" —As conspire to bring down the value of a property the moment it had passed out of my hands ?—I would not, Mr. Barwood ; and this very day the intending purchaser shall know of your project."

Barwood locked his teeth together, and grinned with rage. He jumped from his seat, knocked it over in getting his hat from under it, and rushed out of the house. Mr. Drake smiled, and looking calmly round on the rest of the deacons, held his peace. It was a very awkward moment for them. At length one of them, a small tradesman, ventured to speak. He dared make no allusion to the catastrophe that had occurred. It would take much reflection to get hold of the true weight and bearing of what they had just heard and seen, for Barwood was a mighty man among them.

" What we were thinking, sir," he said, "—and you will please to remember, Mr. Drake, that I was always on your side, and it's better to come to the point ; there's a strong party of us in the church, sir, that would like to have you back, and we was thinking if you would condescend to help us, now as you're so well able to, sir, toward a new chapel, now as you have the means, as well as the will, to do God service, sir, what with the chapel-building society, and every man-jack of us setting our shoulder to the wheel, and we should all do our very best, we should get a nice, new, I won't say showy, but attractive—that's the word, attractive place—not gaudy, you know, I never would give in to that, but ornamental too—and in a word, attractive—that's it—a place to which the people would be drawn by the look of it outside, and kep' by the look of it inside—a place as would make the people of Glaston say, ' Come, and let us go up to the house of the Lord,'—if, with your help, sir, we had such a place, then perhaps you would condescend to take the reins again, sir, and we should then pay Mr. Rudd as your assistant, leaving the whole management in your hands—to preach when you pleased, and leave it alone when you didn't.—There, sir ! I think that's much the whole thing in a nut-shell."

" And now will you tell me what result you would look for under such an arrangement ? "

" We should look for the blessing of a little success ; it's a many years since we was favored with any."

" And by success you mean——? "

" A large attendance of regular hearers in the morning—not a seat to let !—and the people of Glaston crowding to hear the word in the evening, and going away because they can't get a foot inside the place ! That's the success *I* should like to see."

" What ! would you have all Glaston such as yourselves ! " exclaimed the pastor indignantly. " Gentlemen, this is the crowning humiliation of my life ! Yet I am glad of it, because I deserve it, and it will help to make and keep me humble. I see in you the wood and hay and stubble with which, alas ! I have been building all these years ! I have been preaching dissent instead of Christ, and there you are ! —dissenters indeed—but can I—can I call you Christians ? Assuredly do I believe the form of your church that or- dained by the apostles, but woe is me for the material whereof it is built ! Were I to aid your plans with a single penny in the hope of withdrawing one inhabitant of Glaston from the preaching of Mr. Wingfold, a man who speaks the truth and fears nobody, as I, alas ! have feared you, because of your dullness of heart and slowness of understanding, I should be doing the body of Christ a grievous wrong. I have been as one beating the air in talking to you against episcopacy when I ought to have been preaching against dishonesty ; eulogizing congregationalism, when I ought to have been training you in the three abiding graces, and chiefly in the greatest of them, charity. I have taken to pieces and put together for you the plan of salvation, when I ought to have spoken only of Him who is the way and the life. I have been losing my life, and helping you to lose yours. But go to the abbey church, and there a man will stir you up to lay hold upon God, will teach you to know Christ, each man for himself and not for another. Shut up your chapel, put off your scheme for a new one, go to the abbey church, and be filled with the finest of the wheat. Then should this man depart, and one of the common episcopal train, whose God is the church, and whose neighbor is the order of the priesthood, come to take his place, and preach against dissent as I have so foolishly preached against the church—then, and not until then, will the time be to gather together your savings and build yourselves a house to pray in. Then, if I am alive, as I hope I shall not be, come, and I will aid your purpose liberally. Do not mistake me ; I believe as strongly as ever I did that the constitution of the Church of England is all wrong ; that the arrogance and assumption of her priesthood is essentially opposed to the very idea of the kingdom of Heaven ; that the Athanasian creed is unintelligible, and where intelligible, cruel ; but where I find my Lord preached as only one who understands Him can preach Him, and as I never could preach Him, and never heard Him preached before, even faults great as those shall be to me as merest accidents. Gentlemen, every thing is pure loss—chapels and creeds and churches—all is loss that comes between us and Christ—individually, masterfully. And of unchristian things one of the most unchristian is to dispute and separate in the name of Him whose one object was, and whose one victory will be unity.—Gentlemen, if you should ever ask me to preach to you, I will do so with pleasure."

They rose as one man, bade him an embarrassed good morning, and walked from the room, some with their heads thrown back, other hanging them forward in worshipful shame. The former spread the rumor that the old minister had gone crazy, the latter began to go now and then to church.

I may here mention, as I shall have no other opportunity, that a new chapel was not built ; that the young pastor soon left the old one ; that the deacons declared themselves unable to pay the rent ; that Mr. Drake took the place into his own hands, and preached there every Sunday evening, but went always in the morning to hear Mr. Wingfold. There was kindly human work of many sorts done by them in concert, and each felt the other a true support.   When the pastor and the parson chanced to meet in some lowly cottage, it was never with embarrassment or apology, as if they served two masters, but always with hearty and glad greeting, and they always went away together.   I doubt if wickedness does half as much harm as sectarianism, whether it be the sectarianism of the church or of dissent, the sectarianism whose virtue is condescension, or the sectarianism whose vice is pride.   Division has done more to hide Christ from the view of men, than all the infidelity that has ever been spoken.   It is the half-Christian clergy of every denomination that are the main cause of the so-called failure of the Church of Christ.   Thank God, it has not failed so miserably as to succeed in the estimation or to the satisfaction of any party in it.

But it was not merely in relation to forms of church government that the heart of the pastor now in his old age began to widen.   It is foolish to say that after a certain age a man can not alter.   That some men can not—or will not, (God only can draw the line between those two *nots*) I allow ; but the cause is not age, and it is not universal. The man who does not care and ceases to grow, becomes torpid, stiffens, is in a sense dead ; but he who has been growing all the time need never stop ; and where growth is, there is always capability of change : growth itself is a succession of slow, melodious, ascending changes.

The very next Sunday after the visit of their deputation to him, the church in Cow-lane asked their old minister to preach to them.   Dorothy, as a matter of course, went with her father, although, dearly as she loved him, she would have much preferred hearing what the curate had to say.   The pastor's text was, *Ye pay tithe of mint and anise and cummin, and have omitted the weightier matters of the law—judgment, mercy, and faith.*   In his sermon he enforced certain of the dogmas of a theology which once expressed more truth than falsehood, but now at least *conveys* more falsehood than truth, because of the

changed conditions of those who teach and those who
hear it ; for, even where his faith had been vital enough to
burst the verbally rigid, formal, and indeed spiritually vulgar theology he had been taught, his intellect had not been
strong enough to cast off the husks. His expressions, as-
sertions, and arguments, tying up a bundle of mighty truth
with cords taken from the lumber-room and the ash-pit,
grazed severely the tenderer nature of his daughter. When
they reached the house, and she found herself alone with
her father in his study, she broke suddenly into passionate
complaint—not that he should so represent God, seeing, for
what she knew, He might indeed be such, but that, so repre-
senting God, he should expect men to love Him. It was not
often that her sea, however troubled in its depths, rose into
such visible storm. She threw herself upon the floor with
a loud cry, and lay sobbing and weeping. Her father was
terribly startled, and stood for a moment as if stunned ;
then a faint slow light began to break in upon him, and he
stood silent, sad, and thoughtful. He knew that he loved
God, yet in what he said concerning Him, in the impression
he gave of Him, there was that which prevented the best
daughter in the world from loving her Father in Heaven !
He began to see that he had never really thought about
these things ; he had been taught them but had never
turned them over in the light, never perceived the fact, that,
however much truth might be there, there also was what at
least looked like a fearful lie against God. For a moment
he gazed with keen compassion on his daughter as she lay,
actually writhing in her agony, then kneeled beside her, and
laying his hand upon her, said gently :

"Well, my dear, if those things are not true, my saying
them will not make them so."

She sprung to her feet, threw her arms about his neck,
kissed him, and left the room. The minister remained upon
his knees.

CHAPTER XXIX.

THE DOCTOR'S HOUSE.

THE holidays came, and Juliet took advantage of them to escape from what had begun to be a bondage to her— the daily intercourse with people who disapproved of the man she loved. In her thoughts even she took no intellectual position against them with regard to what she called doctrine, and Faber superstition. Her father had believed as they did ; she clung to his memory ; perhaps she believed as he did ; she could not tell. There was time yet wherein to make up her mind. She had certainly believed so once, she said to herself, and she might so believe again. She would have been at first highly offended, but the next moment a little pleased at being told that in reality she had never believed one whit more than Faber, that she was at present indeed incapable of believing. Probably she would have replied, " Then wherein am I to blame ? " But although a woman who sits with her child in her arms in the midst of her burning house, half asleep, and half stifled and dazed with the fierce smoke, may not be to blame, certainly the moment she is able to excuse herself she is bound to make for the door. So long as men do not feel that they are in a bad condition and in danger of worse, the message of deliverance will sound to them as a threat. Yea, the offer of absolute well-being upon the only possible conditions of the well-being itself, must, if heard at all, rouse in them a discomfort whose cause they attribute to the message, not to themselves ; and immediately they will endeavor to justify themselves in disregarding it. There are those doing all they can to strengthen themselves in unbelief, who, if the Lord were to appear plainly before their eyes, would tell Him they could not help it, for He had not until then given them ground enough for faith, and when He left them, would go on just as before, except that they would speculate and pride themselves on the vision. If men say, " We want no such deliverance," then the Maker of them must either destroy them as vile things for whose existence He is to Himself accountable, or compel them to change. If they say, " We choose to be destroyed," He, as their Maker, has a choice in the matter too. Is He not free to say, " You

can not even slay yourselves, and I choose that you shall
know the death of living without Me ; you shall learn to
choose to live indeed. I choose that you shall know what *I
know* to be good " ? And however much any individual
consciousness may rebel, surely the individual consciousness
which called that other into being, and is the Father of that
being, fit to be such because of Himself He is such, has a
right to object that by rebellion His creature should destroy
the very power by which it rebels, and from a being capable
of a divine freedom by partaking of the divine nature,
should make of itself the merest slave incapable of will of any
sort ! Is it a wrong to compel His creature to soar aloft
into the ether of its origin, and find its deepest, its only
true self ? It is God's knowing choice of life against man's
ignorant choice of death.

But Juliet knew nothing of such a region of strife in the
human soul. She had no suspicion what an awful swamp
lay around the prison of her self-content—no, self-discon-
tent—in which she lay chained. To her the one good and
desirable thing was the love and company of Paul Faber.
He was her saviour, she said to herself, and the woman who
could not love and trust and lean upon such a heart of
devotion and unselfishness as his, was unworthy of the
smallest of his thoughts. He was nobility, generosity, justice itself ! If she sought to lay her faults bare to him, he
would but fold her to his bosom to shut them out from her
own vision ! He would but lay his hand on the lips of confession, and silence them as unbelievers in his perfect affection ! He was better than the God the Wingfolds and
Drakes believed in, with whom humiliation was a condition
of acceptance !

She told the Drakes that, for the air of Owlkirk, she was
going to occupy her old quarters with Mrs. Puckridge during the holidays. They were not much surprised, for they
had remarked a change in her manner, and it was not long
unexplained : for, walking from the Old House together
one evening rather late, they met her with the doctor in a
little frequented part of the park. When she left them,
they knew she would not return ; and her tears betrayed
that she knew it also.

Meantime the negotiation for the purchase of the Old
House of Glaston was advancing with slow legal sinuosity.
Mr. Drake had offered the full value of the property, and
the tender seemed to be regarded not unfavorably. But

his heart and mind were far more occupied with the humbler property he had already secured in the town : that was now to be fortified against the incursions of the river, with its attendant fevers and agues.   A survey of the ground had satisfied him that a wall at a certain point would divert a great portion of the water, and this wall he proceeded at once to build.   He hoped in the end to inclose the ground altogether, or at least to defend it at every assailable point, but there were many other changes imperative, with difficulties such that they could not all be coped with at once. The worst of the cottages must be pulled down, and as they were all even over-full, he must contrive to build first. Nor until that was done, could he effect much toward rendering the best of them fit for human habitation.

Some of the householders in the lower part of the adjoining street shook their heads when they saw what the bricklayers were about.   They had reason to fear they were turning the water more upon them ; and it seemed a wrong that the wretched cottages which had from time immemorial been accustomed to the water, should be now protected from it at the cost of respectable houses !   It did not occur to them that it might be time for Lady Fortune to give her wheel a few inches of a turn.   To common minds, custom is always right so long as it is on their side.

In the meantime the chapel in the park at Nestley had been advancing, for the rector, who was by nature no dawdler where he was interested, had been pushing it on ; and at length on a certain Sunday evening in the autumn, the people of the neighborhood having been invited to attend, the rector read prayers in it, and the curate preached a sermon.   At the close of the service the congregation was informed that prayers would be read there every Sunday evening, and that was all.   Mrs. Bevis, honest soul, the green-mantled pool of whose being might well desire a wind, if only from a pair of bellows, to disturb its repose, for not a fish moved to that end in its sunless deeps—I say deeps, for such there must have been, although neither she nor her friends were acquainted with any thing there but shallows—was the only one inclined to grumble at the total absence of ceremonial pomp : she did want her husband to have the credit of the great deed.

About the same time it was that Juliet again sought the cottage at Owlkirk, with the full consciousness that she went there to meet her fate.   Faber came to see her every day, and both Ruber and Niger began to grow skinny. But I have already said enough to show the nature and course of the stream, and am not bound to linger longer over its noise among the pebbles. Some things are interesting rather for their results than their process, and of such I confess it is to me the love-making of these two.— "What! were they not human?" Yes: but with a truncated humanity—even shorn of its flower-buds, and full only of variegated leaves. It shall suffice therefore to say that, in a will-less sort of a way, Juliet let the matter drift; that, although she withheld explicit consent, she yet at length allowed Faber to speak as if she had given it; that they had long ceased to talk about God or no God, about life and death, about truth and superstition, and spoke only of love, and the days at hand, and how they would spend them; that they poured out their hearts in praising and worshiping each other; and that, at last, Juliet found herself as firmly engaged to be Paul's wife, as if she had granted every one of the promises he had sought to draw from her, but which she had avoided giving in the weak fancy that thus she was holding herself free. It was perfectly understood in all the neighborhood that the doctor and Miss Meredith were engaged. Both Helen and Dorothy felt a little hurt at her keeping an absolute silence toward them concerning what the country seemed to know; but when they spoke of it to her, she pointedly denied any engagement, and indeed although helplessly drifting toward marriage, had not yet given absolute consent even in her own mind. She dared not even then regard it as inevitable. Her two friends came to the conclusion that she could not find the courage to face disapproval, and perhaps feared expostulation.

"She may well be ashamed of such an unequal yoking!" said Helen to her husband.

"There is no unequal yoking in it that I see," he returned. "In the matter of faith, what is there to choose between them? I see nothing. They may carry the yoke straight enough. If there *be* one of them further from the truth than the other, it must be the one who says, *I go sir*, and goes not. Between *don't believe* and *don't care*, *I* don't care to choose. Let them marry and God bless them. It will be good for them—for one thing if for no other—it is sure to bring trouble to both."

"Indeed, Mr. Wingfold!" returned Helen playfully.

"So that is how you regard marriage!—Sure to bring trouble!"

She laid her head on his shoulder.

"Trouble to every one, my Helen, like the gospel itself; more trouble to you than to me, but none to either that will not serve to bring us closer to each other," he answered. "But about those two—well, I am both doubtful and hopeful. At all events I can not wish them not to marry. I think it will be for both of them a step nearer to the truth. The trouble will, perhaps, drive them to find God. That any one who had seen and loved our Lord, should consent to marry one, whatever that one was besides, who did not at least revere and try to obey Him, seems to me impossible. But again I say there is no such matter involved between them.—Shall I confess to you, that, with all her frankness, all her charming ways, all the fullness of the gaze with which her black eyes look into yours, there is something about Juliet that puzzles me? At times I have thought she must be in some trouble, out of which she was on the point of asking me to help her; at others I have fancied she was trying to be agreeable against her inclination, and did not more than half approve of me. Sometimes, I confess, the shadow of a doubt crosses me: is she altogether a true woman? But that vanishes the moment she smiles. I wish she could have been open with me. I could have helped her, I am pretty sure. As it is, I have not got one step nearer the real woman than when first I saw her at the rector's."

"I know," said Helen. "But don't you think it may be that she has never yet come to know any thing about herself —to perceive either fact or mystery of her own nature? If she is a stranger to herself, she cannot reveal herself —at least of her own will—to those about her. She is just what I was, Thomas, before I knew you—a dull, sleepy-hearted thing that sat on her dignity. Be sure she has not an idea of the divine truth you have taught me to see under-lying creation itself—namely, that every thing possessed owes its very value as possession to the power which that possession gives of parting with it."

"You are a pupil worth having, Helen!—even if I had had to mourn all my days that you would not love me."

"And now you have said your mind about Juliet," Helen went on, "allow me to say that I trust her more than I do Faber. I do not for a moment imagine him consciously dishonest, but he makes too much show of his honesty for me. I can not help feeling that he is selfish—and can a selfish man be honest?"

"Not thoroughly. I know that only too well, for I at all events am selfish, Helen."

"I don't see it ; but if you are, you know it, and hate it, and strive against it. I do not think he knows it, even when he says that every body is selfish. Only, what better way to get rid of it than to love and marry?"

"Or to confirm it," said Wingfold thoughtfully.

"I shouldn't wonder a bit if they're married already!" said Helen.

She was not far from wrong, although not quite right. Already Faber had more than hinted at a hurried marriage, as private as could be compassed. It was impossible of course, to be married at church. That would be to cast mockery on the marriage itself, as well as on what Faber called his *beliefs*. The objection was entirely on Faber's side, but Juliet did not hint at the least difference of feeling in the matter. She let every thing take its way now.

At length having, in a neighboring town, arranged all the necessary preliminaries, Faber got one of the other doctors in Glaston to attend to his practice for three weeks, and went to take a holiday. Juliet left Owlkirk the same day. They met, were lawfully married, and at the close of the three weeks, returned together to the doctor's house.

The sort of thing did not please Glaston society, and although Faber was too popular as a doctor to lose position by it, Glaston was slow in acknowledging that it knew there was a lady at the head of his house. Mrs. Wingfold and Miss Drake, however, set their neighbors a good example, and by degrees there came about a dribbling sort of recognition. Their social superiors stood the longest aloof—chiefly because the lady had been a governess, and yet had behaved so like one of themselves ; they thought it well to give her a lesson. Most of them, however, not willing to offend the leading doctor in the place, yielded and called. Two elderly spinsters and Mrs. Ramshorn did not. The latter declared she did not believe they were married. Most agreed they were the handsomest couple ever seen in that quarter, and looked all right.

Juliet returned the calls made upon her, at the proper retaliatory intervals, and gradually her mode of existence fell into routine. The doctor went out every day, and was out most of the day, while she sat at home and worked or read. She had to amuse herself, and sometimes found life duller than when she had to earn her bread—when, as she went from place to place, she might at any turn meet Paul upon Ruber or Niger. Already the weary weed of the commonplace had begun to show itself in the marriage garden—a weed which, like all weeds, requires only neglect for perfect development, when it will drive the lazy Eve who has never made her life worth *living*, to ask whether life be worth *having*. She was not a great reader. No book had ever yet been to her a well-spring of life ; and such books as she liked best it was perhaps just as well that she could not easily procure in Glaston ; for, always ready to appreciate the noble, she had not moral discernment sufficient to protect her from the influence of such books as paint poor action in noble color. For a time also she was stinted in her natural nourishment : her husband had ordered a grand piano from London for her, but it had not yet arrived ; and the first touch she laid on the tall spinster-looking one that had stood in the drawing-room for fifty years, with red silk wrinkles radiating from a gilt center, had made her shriek. If only Paul would buy a yellow gig, like his friend Dr. May of Broughill, and take her with him on his rounds ! Or if she had a friend or two to go and see when he was out !— friends like what Helen or even Dorothy might have been : she was not going to be hand-in-glove with any body that didn't like her Paul ! She missed church too—not the prayers, much ; but she did like hearing what she counted a good sermon, that is, a lively one. Her husband wanted her to take up some science, but if he had considered that, with all her gift in music, she expressed an utter indifference to thorough bass, he would hardly have been so foolish.

CHAPTER XXX.

THE PONY-CARRIAGE.

ONE Saturday morning the doctor was called to a place a good many miles distant, and Juliet was left with the prospect of being longer alone than usual. She felt it almost sultry although so late in the season, and could not rest in the

house. She pretended to herself she had some shopping to
do in Pine Street, but it was rather a longing for air and
motion that sent her out. Also, certain thoughts which she
did not like, had of late been coming more frequently, and
she found it easier to avoid them in the street. They were
not such as troubled her from being hard to think out.
Properly speaking, she *thought* less now than ever. She
often said nice things, but they were mostly the mere gracious movements of a nature sweet, playful, trusting, fond of
all beautiful things, and quick to see artistic relation where
her perception reached.

As she turned the corner of Mr. Drew's shop, the house-
door opened, and a lady came out. It was Mr. Drew's
lodger. Juliet knew nothing about her, and was not aware
that she had ever seen her ; but the lady started as if she
recognized her. To that kind of thing Juliet was accustomed, for her style of beauty was any thing but common.
The lady's regard however was so fixed that it drew hers,
and as their eyes met, Juliet felt something, almost a physical
pain, shoot through her heart. She could not understand it,
but presently began to suspect, and by degrees became quite
certain that she had seen her before, though she could not tell
where. The effect the sight of her had had, indicated some
painful association, which she must recall before she could
be at rest. She turned in the other direction, and walked
straight from the town, that she might think without eyes
upon her.

Scene after scene of her life came back as she searched to
find some circumstance associated with that face. Once and
again she seemed on the point of laying hold of something,
when the face itself vanished and she had that to recall, and
the search to resume from the beginning. In the process
many painful memories arose, some, connected with her
mother, unhappy in themselves, others, connected with her
father, grown unhappy from her marriage ; for thereby she
had built a wall between her thoughts and her memories of
him ; and, if there should be a life beyond this, had hol-
lowed a gulf between them forever.

Gradually her thoughts took another direction.—Could it
be that already the glamuor had begun to disperse, the roses
of love to wither, the magic to lose its force, the common
look of things to return ? Paul was as kind, as courteous, as
considerate as ever, and yet there was a difference. Her
heart did not grow wild, her blood did not rush to her face,

when she heard the sound of his horse's hoofs in the street, though she knew them instantly. Sadder and sadder grew her thoughts as she walked along, careless whither.

Had she begun to cease loving ? No. She loved better than she knew, but she must love infinitely better yet. The first glow was gone—already : she had thought it would not go, and was miserable. She recalled that even her honeymoon had a little disappointed her. I would not be mistaken as implying that any of these her reflections had their origin in what was *peculiar* in the character, outlook, or speculation of herself or her husband. The passion of love is but the vestibule—the pylon—to the temple of love. A garden lies between the pylon and the adytum. They that will enter the sanctuary must walk through the garden. But some start to see the roses already withering, sit down and weep and watch their decay, until at length the aged flowers hang drooping all around them, and lo ! their hearts are withered also, and when they rise they turn their backs on the holy of holies, and their feet toward the gate.

Juliet was proud of her Paul, and loved him as much as she was yet capable of loving. But she had thought they were enough for each other, and already, although she was far from acknowledging it to herself, she had, in the twilight of her thinking, begun to doubt it. Nor can she be blamed for the doubt. Never man and woman yet succeeded in being all in all to each other.

It were presumption to say that a lonely God would be enough for Himself, seeing that we can know nothing of God but as He is our Father. What if the Creator Himself is suf-ficient to Himself in virtue of His self-existent *creatorship ?* Let my reader think it out. The lower we go in the scale of creation, the more independent is the individual. The richer and more perfect each of a married pair is in the other relations of life, the more is each to the other. For us, the children of eternal love, the very air our spirits breathe, and without which they can not live, is the eternal life ; for us, the brothers and sisters of a countless family, the very space in which our souls can exist, is the love of each and every soul of our kind.

Such were not Juliet's thoughts. To her such would have seemed as unreal as unintelligible. To her they would have looked just what some of my readers will pronounce them, not in the least knowing what they are. She was suddenly roused from her painful reverie by the pulling up of Helen's ponies, with much clatter and wriggling recoil, close beside her, making more fuss with their toy-carriage than the mightiest of tractive steeds with the chariot of pomp.

"Jump in, Juliet," cried their driver, addressing her with the greater *abandon* that she was resolved no stiffness on her part should deposit a grain to the silting up of the channel of former affection. She was one of the few who understand that no being can afford to let the smallest love-germ die.

Juliet hesitated. She was not a little bewildered with the sudden recall from the moony plains of memory, and the demand for immediate action. She answered uncertainly, trying to think what was involved.

"I know your husband is not waiting you at home," pursued Helen. "I saw him on Ruber, three fields off, riding away from Glaston. Jump in, dear. You can make up that mind of yours in the carriage as well as upon the road. I will set you down wherever you please. My husband is out too, so the slaves can take their pleasure."

Juliet could not resist, had little inclination to do so, yielded without another word, and took her place beside Helen, a little shy of being alone with her, yet glad of her company. Away went the ponies, and as soon as she had got them settled to their work, Helen turned her face toward Juliet.

"I *am* so glad to see you!" she said.

Juliet's heart spoke too loud for her throat. It was a relief to her that Helen had to keep her eyes on her charge, the quickness of whose every motion rendered watchfulness right needful.

"Have you returned Mrs. Bevis's call yet!" asked Helen.

"No," murmured Juliet. "I haven't been able yet."

"Well, here is a good chance. Sit where you are, and you will be at Nestley in half an hour, and I shall be the more welcome. You are a great favorite there!"

"How kind you are!" said Juliet, the tears beginning to rise. "Indeed, Mrs. Wingfold,——"

"You *used* to call me Helen!" said that lady, pulling up her ponies with sudden energy, as they shied at a bit of paper on the road, and nearly had themselves and all they drew in the ditch.

"May I call you so still?"

"Surely! What else?"

"You are too good to me!" said Juliet, and wept out-right.

"My dear Juliet," returned Helen, "I will be quite plain with you, and that will put things straight in a moment. Your friends understand perfectly why you have avoided them of late, and are quite sure it is from no unkindness to any of them. But neither must you imagine we think hardly of you for marrying Mr. Faber. We detest his opinions so much that we feel sure if you saw a little further into them, neither of you would hold them."

"But I don't—that is, I——"

"You don't know whether you hold them or not: I understand quite well. My husband says in your case it does not matter much; for if you had ever really believed in Jesus Christ, you could not have done it. At all events now the thing is done, there is no question about it left. Dear Juliet, think of us as your friends still, who will always be glad to see you, and ready to help you where we can."

Juliet was weeping for genuine gladness now. But even as she wept, by one of those strange movements of our being which those who have been quickest to question them wonder at the most, it flashed upon her where she had seen the lady that came from Mr. Drew's house, and her heart sunk within her, for the place was associated with that portion of her history which of all she would most gladly hide from herself. During the rest of the drive she was so silent, that Helen at last gave up trying to talk to her. Then first she observed how the clouds had risen on all sides and were meeting above, and that the air was more still and sultry than ever.

Just as they got within Nestley-gate, a flash of lightning, scarcely followed by a loud thunder-clap, shot from over-head. The ponies plunged, reared, swayed asunder from the pole, nearly fell, and recovered themselves only to dart off in wild terror. Juliet screamed.

"Don't be frightened, child," said Helen. "There is no danger here. The road is staight and there is nothing on it. I shall soon pull them up. Only don't cry out: that will be as little to their taste as the lightning."

Juliet caught at the reins.

"For God's sake, don't do that!" cried Helen, balking her clutch. "You will kill us both."

Juliet sunk back in her seat. The ponies went at full speed along the road. The danger was small, for the park was upon both sides, level with the drive, in which there was a slight ascent. Helen was perfectly quiet, and went on gradually tightening her pull upon the reins. Before they reached the house, she had entirely regained her command of them. When she drew up to the door, they stood quite steady, but panting as if their little sides would fly asunder. By this time Helen was red as a rose ; her eyes were flashing, and a smile was playing about her mouth ; but Juliet was like a lily on which the rain has been falling all night : her very lips were bloodless. When Helen turned and saw her, she was far more frightened than the ponies could make her.

" Why, Juliet, my dear ! " she said, " I had no thought you were so terrified ! What would your husband say to me for frightening you so ! But you are safe now."

A servant came to take the ponies. Helen got out first, and gave her hand to Juliet.

" Don't think me a coward, Helen," she said. " It was the thunder. I never could bear thunder."

" I should be far more of a coward than you are, Juliet," answered Helen, " if I believed, or even feared, that just a false step of little Zephyr there, or one plunge more from Zoe, might wipe out the world, and I should never more see the face of my husband."

She spoke eagerly, lovingly, believingly. Juliet shivered, stopped, and laid hold of the baluster rail. Things had been too much for her that day. She looked so ill that Helen was again alarmed, but she soon came to herself a little, and they went on to Mrs. Bevis's room. She received them most kindly, made Mrs. Faber lie on the sofa, covered her over, for she was still trembling, and got her a glass of wine. But she could not drink it, and lay sobbing in vain endeavor to control herself.

Meantime the clouds gathered thicker and thicker : the thunder-peal that frightened the ponies had been but the herald of the storm, and now it came on in earnest. The rain rushed suddenly on the earth, and as soon as she heard it, Juliet ceased to sob. At every flash, however, although she lay with her eyes shut, and her face pressed into the pillow, she shivered and moaned.—" Why should one," thought Helen, " who is merely and only the child of Nature, find herself so little at home with her ? " Presently Mr. Bevis came running in from the stable, drenched in crossing to the house. As he passed to his room, he opened the door of his wife's, and looked in.

"I am glad to see you safely housed, ladies," he said. "You must make up your minds to stay where you are. It will not clear before the moon rises, and that will be about midnight. I will send John to tell your husbands that you are not cowering under a hedge, and will not be home to-night."

He was a good weather-prophet. The rain went on. In the evening the two husbands appeared, dripping. They had come on horseback together, and would ride home again after dinner. The doctor would have to be out the greater part of the Sunday, and would gladly leave his wife in such good quarters ; the curate would walk out to his preaching in the evening, and drive home with Helen after it, taking Juliet, if she should be able to accompany them.

After dinner, when the ladies had left them, between the two clergymen and the doctor arose the conversation of which I will now give the substance, leaving the commencement, and taking it up at an advanced point.

"Now tell me," said Faber, in the tone of one satisfied he must be allowed in the right, "which is the nobler—to serve your neighbor in the hope of a future, believing in a God who will reward you, or to serve him in the dark, obeying your conscience, with no other hope than that those who come after you will be the better for you ?"

"I allow most heartily," answered Wingfold, "and with all admiration, that it is indeed grand in one hopeless for himself to live well for the sake of generations to come, which he will never see, and which will never hear of him. But I will not allow that there is any thing grand in being hopeless for one's self, or in serving the Unseen rather than those about you, seeing it is easier to work for those who can not oppose you, than to endure the contradiction of sinners. But I know you agree with me that the best way to assist posterity is to be true to your contemporaries, so there I need say no more—except that the hopeless man can do the least for his fellows, being unable to give them any thing that should render them other than hopeless themselves ; and if, for the grandeur of it, a man were to cast away his purse in order to have the praise of parting with the two mites left in his pocket, you would simply say the man was a fool. This much seems to me clear, that, if there be no God, it may be nobler to be able to live without one ; but, if there be a God, it must be nobler not to be able to live without Him. The moment, however, that nobility becomes the object in any action, that moment the nobleness of the action vanishes. The man who serves his fellow that he may himself be noble, misses the mark. He alone who follows the truth, not he who follows nobility, shall attain the noble. A man's nobility will, in the end, prove just commensurate with his humanity—with the love he bears his neighbor—not the amount of work he may have done for him. A man might throw a lordly gift to his fellow, like a bone to a dog, and damn himself in the deed. You may insult a dog by the way you give him his bone."

" I dispute nothing of all that," said Faber—while good Mr. Bevis sat listening hard, not quite able to follow the discussion ; " but I know you will admit that to do right from respect to any reward whatever, hardly amounts to doing right at all."

" I doubt if any man ever did or could do a thing worthy of passing as in itself good, for the sake of a reward," rejoined Wingfold. " Certainly, to do good for something else than good, is not good at all. But perhaps a reward may so influence a low nature as to bring it a little into contact with what is good, whence the better part of it may make some acquaintance with good. Also, the desire of the approbation of the Perfect, might nobly help a man who was finding his duty hard, for it would humble as well as strengthen him, and is but another form of the love of the good. The praise of God will always humble a man, I think."

" There you are out of my depth," said Faber. " I know nothing about that."

" I go on then to say," continued the curate, " that a man may well be strengthened and encouraged by the hope of being made a better and truer man, and capable of greater self-forgetfulness and devotion. There is nothing low in having respect to such a reward as that, is there ? "

" It seems to me better," persisted the doctor, " to do right for the sake of duty, than for the sake of any goodness even that will come thereby to yourself."

" Assuredly, if self in the goodness, and not the goodness itself be the object," assented Wingfold. " When a duty lies before one, self ought to have no part in the gaze we fix upon it ; but when thought reverts upon himself, who would avoid the wish to be a better man ? The man who will not do a thing for duty, will never get so far as to derive any help from the hope of goodness. But duty itself is only a stage toward something better. It is but the impulse, God-given I believe, toward a far more vital contact with the truth. We shall one day forget all about duty, and do every thing from the love of the loveliness of it, the satisfaction of the rightness of it. What would you say to a man who ministered to the wants of his wife and family only from duty? Of course you wish heartily that the man who neglects them would do it from any cause, even were it fear of the whip ; but the strongest and most operative sense of duty would not satisfy you in such a relation. There are depths within depths of righteousness. Duty is the only path to freedom, but that freedom is the love that is beyond and prevents duty."

"But," said Faber, "I have heard you say that to take from you your belief in a God would be to render you incapable of action. Now, the man—I don't mean myself, but the sort of a man for whom I stand up—does act, does his duty, without the strength of that belief : is he not then the stronger ?—Let us drop the word *noble*."

"In the case supposed, he would be the stronger—for a time at least," replied the curate. "But you must remember that to take from me the joy and glory of my life, namely the belief that I am the child of God, an heir of the Infinite, with the hope of being made perfectly righteous, loving like God Himself, would be something more than merely reducing me to the level of a man who had never loved God, or seen in the possibility of Him any thing to draw him. I should have lost the mighty dream of the universe ; he would be what and where he chose to be, and might well be the more capable. Were I to be convinced there is no God, and to recover by the mere force of animal life from the prostration into which the conviction cast me, I should, I hope, try to do what duty was left me, for I too should be filled, for a time at least, with an endless pity for my fellows ; but all would be so dreary, that I should be almost paralyzed for serving them, and should long for death to do them and myself the only good service. The thought of the generations doomed to be born into a sunless present, would almost make me join any conspiracy to put a stop to the race. I should agree with Hamlet that the whole thing had better come to an end. Would it necessarily indicate a lower nature, or condition, or habit of thought, that, having cherished such hopes, I should, when I lost them, be more troubled than one who never had had them ? "

" Still," said Faber, " I ask you to allow that a nature which can do without help is greater than a nature which can not."

" If the thing done were the same, I should allow it," answered the curate ; " but the things done will prove altogether different. And another thing to be noted is, that, while the need of help might indicate a lower nature, the capacity for receiving it must indicate a higher. The mere fact of being able to live and act in more meager spiritual circumstances, in itself proves nothing : it is not the highest nature that has the fewest needs. The highest nature is the one that has the most necessities, but the fewest of its own making. He is not the greatest man who is the most independent, but he who thirsts most after a conscious harmony with every element and portion of the mighty whole ; demands from every region thereof its influences to perfect his individuality ; regards that individuality as his kingdom, his treasure, not to hold but to give ; sees in his Self the one thing he can devote, the one precious means of freedom by its sacrifice, and that in no contempt or scorn, but in love to God and his children, the multitudes of his kind. By dying ever thus, ever thus losing his soul, he lives like God, and God knows him, and he knows God. This is too good to be grasped, but not too good to be true. The highest is that which needs the highest, the largest that which needs the most ; the finest and strongest that which to live must breath essential life, self-willed life, God Himself. It follows that it is not the largest or the strongest nature that will feel a loss the least. An ant will not gather a grain of corn the less that his mother is dead, while a boy will turn from his books and his play and his dinner because his bird is dead : is the ant, therefore, the stronger nature ? "

" Is it not weak to be miserable ? " said the doctor.

" Yes—without good cause," answered the curate. " But you do not know what it would be to me to lose my faith in my God. My misery would be a misery to which no assurance of immortality or of happiness could bring any thing but tenfold misery—the conviction that I should never be good myself, never have any thing to love absolutely, never be able to make amends for the wrongs I had done. Call such a feeling selfish if you will : I can not help it. I can not count one fit for existence to whom such things would be no grief. The worthy existence must hunger after good. The largest nature must have the mightiest hunger. Who calls a man selfish because he is hungry? He is selfish if he broods on the pleasures of eating, and would not go without his dinner for the sake of another ; but if he had no hunger, where would be the room for his self-denial? Besides, in spiritual things, the only way to give them to your neighbors is to hunger after them yourself. There each man is a mouth to the body of the whole creation. It can not be selfishness to hunger and thirst after righteousness, which righteousness is just your duty to your God and your neighbor. If there be any selfishness in it, the very answer to your prayer will destroy it."

"There you are again out of my region," said Faber. "But answer me one thing : is it not weak to desire happiness?"

"Yes ; if the happiness is poor and low," rejoined Wingfold. "But the man who would choose even the grandeur of duty before the bliss of the truth, must be a lover of himself. Such a man must be traveling the road to death. If there be a God, truth must be joy. If there be not, truth may be misery.—But, honestly, I know not one advanced Christian who tries to obey for the hope of Heaven or the fear of hell. Such ideas have long vanished from such a man. He loves God ; he loves truth ; he loves his fellow, and knows he must love him more. You judge of Christianity either by those who are not true representatives of it, and are indeed, less of Christians than yourself ; or by others who, being intellectually inferior, perhaps even stupid, belie Christ with their dull theories concerning Him. Yet the latter may have in them a noble seed, urging them up heights to you at present unconceived and inconceivable ; while, in the meantime, some of them serve their generation well, and do as much for those that are to come after as you do yourself."

"There is always weight as well as force in what you urge, Wingfold," returned Faber. "Still it looks to me just a cunningly devised fable—I will not say of the priests, but of the human mind deceiving itself with its own hopes and desires."

"It may well look such to those who are outside of it, and it must at length appear such to all who, feeling in it any claim upon them, yet do not put it to the test of their obedience."

"Well, you have had your turn, and now we are having ours—you of the legends, we of the facts."

" No," said Wingfold, " we have not had our turn, and you
have been having yours for a far longer time than we. But
if, as you profess, you are *doing* the truth you see, it belongs
to my belief that you will come to see the truth you do not
see.   Christianity is not a failure ; for to it mainly is the
fact owing that here is a class of men which, believing in no
God, yet believes in duty toward men.   Look here : if
Christianity be the outcome of human aspiration, the natural
growth of the human soil, is it not strange it should be
such an utter failure as it seems to you ? and as such a
natural growth, it must be a failure, for if it were a success,
must not you be the very one to see it ? If it is false, it is
worthless, or an evil : where then is your law of development, if the highest result of that development is an evil to
the nature and the race ? "

" I do not grant it the highest result," said Faber.   " It is
a failure—a false blossom, with a truer to follow."

" To produce a superior architecture, poetry, music ? "

" Perhaps not.   But a better science."

" Are the architecture and poetry and music parts of the
failure ? "

" Yes—but they are not altogether a failure, for they lay
some truth at the root of them all.   Now we shall see what
will come of turning away from every thing we do not
know."

" That is not exactly what you mean, for that would be
never to know any thing more.   But the highest you have
in view is immeasurably below what Christianity has always
demanded of its followers."

" But has never got from them, and never will.   Look at the
wars, the hatreds, to which your *gospel* has given rise ! Look
at Calvin and poor Servetus ! Look at the strifes and divis-
ions of our own day ! Look at the religious newspapers ! "

" All granted.   It is a chaos, the motions of whose organization must be strife.   The spirit of life is at war with
the spasmatical body of death.   If Christianity be not
still in the process of development, it is the saddest of all
failures."

" The fact is, Wingfold, your prophet would have been
King of the race if He had not believed in a God."

" I dare not speak the answer that rises to my lips," said
Wingfold.   " But there is more truth in what you say than
you think, and more of essential lie also.   My answer is,
that the faith of Jesus in His God and Father is, even now,

saving me, setting me free from my one horror, selfishness ;
making my life an unspeakable boon to me, letting me
know its roots in the eternal and perfect ; giving me such
love to my fellow, that I trust at last to love him as Christ
has loved me.   But I do not expect you to understand me.
He in whom I believe said that a man must be born again to
enter into the kingdom of Heaven."

The doctor laughed.

" You then *are* one of the double-born, Wingfold ? " he
said.

" I believe, I think, I hope so," replied the curate, very
gravely.

" And you, Mr. Bevis ? "

" I don't know.   I wish.   I doubt," answered the rector,
with equal solemnity.

" Oh, never fear ! " said Faber, with a quiet smile, and
rising, left the clergymen together.

But what a morning it was that came up after the storm !
All night the lightning had been flashing itself into peace,
and gliding further and further away. Bellowing and growl-
ing the thunder had crept with it ; but long after it could
no more be heard, the lightning kept gleaming up, as if
from a sea of flame behind the horizon.   The sun brought
a glorious day, and looked larger and mightier than before.
To Helen, as she gazed eastward from her window, he
seemed ascending his lofty pulpit to preach the story of
the day named after him—the story of the Sun-day ; the
rising again in splendor of the darkened and buried Sun of
the universe, with whom all the worlds and all their hearts
and suns arose.   A light steam was floating up from the
grass, and the raindrops were sparkling everywhere.   The
day had arisen from the bosom of the night ; peace and
graciousness from the bosom of the storm ; she herself from
the grave of her sleep, over which had lain the turf of the
darkness ; and all was fresh life and new hope.   And
through it all, reviving afresh with every sign of Nature's
universal law of birth, was the consciousness that her life,
her own self, was rising from the dead, was being new-born
also.   She had not far to look back to the time when all
was dull and dead in her being : when the earthquake
came, and the storm, and the fire ; and after them the still
small voice, breathing rebuke, and hope, and strength.   Her
whole world was now radiant with expectation.   It was
through her husband the change had come to her, but he

was not the rock on which she built. For his sake she could go to hell—yea, cease to exist ; but there was One whom she loved more than him—the one One whose love was the self-willed cause of all love, who from that love had sent forth her husband and herself to love one another ; whose heart was the nest of their birth, the cradle of their growth, the rest of their being. Yea, more than her husband she loved Him, her elder Brother, by whom the Father had done it all, the Man who lived and died and rose again so many hundred years ago. In Him, the perfect One, she hoped for a perfect love to her husband, a perfect nature in herself. She knew how Faber would have mocked at such a love, the very existence of whose object she could not prove, how mocked at the notion that His life even now was influencing hers. She knew how he would say it was merely love and marriage that had wrought the change ; but while she recognized them as forces altogether divine, she knew that not only was the Son of Man behind them, but that it was her obedience to Him and her confidence in Him that had wrought the red heart of the change in her. She knew that she would rather break with her husband altogether, than to do one action contrary to the known mind and will of that Man. Faber would call her faith a mighty, perhaps a lovely illusion : her life was an active waiting for the revelation of its object in splendor before the universe. The world seemed to her a grand march of resurrections—out of every sorrow springing the joy at its heart, without which it could not have been a sorrow ; out of the troubles, and evils, and sufferings, and cruelties that clouded its history, ever arising the human race, the sons of God, redeemed in Him who had been made subject to death that He might conquer Death for them and for his Father— a succession of mighty facts, whose meanings only God can evolve, only the obedient heart behold.

On such a morning, so full of resurrection, Helen was only a little troubled not to be one of her husband's congregation : she would take her New Testament, and spend the sunny day in the open air. In the evening he was coming, and would preach in the little chapel. If only Juliet might hear him too ! But she would not ask her to go.

Juliet was better, for fatigue had compelled sleep. The morning had brought her little hope, however, no sense of resurrection. A certain dead thing had begun to move in its coffin ; she was utterly alone with it, and it made the world

feel a tomb around her. Not all resurrections are the resurrection of life, though in the end they will be found, even
to the lowest birth of the power of the enemy, to have contributed thereto. She did not get up to breakfast ; Helen
persuaded her to rest, and herself carried it to her. But
she rose soon after, and declared herself quite well.

The rector drove to Glaston in his dog-cart to read
prayers. Helen went out into the park with her New Testament and George Herbert. Poor Juliet was left with Mrs.
Bevis, who happily could not be duller than usual, although
it was Sunday. By the time the rector returned, bringing
his curate with him, she was bored almost beyond endurance. She had not yet such a love of wisdom as to be able
to bear with folly. The foolish and weak are the most easily
disgusted with folly and weakness which is not of their own
sort, and are the last to make allowances for them. To
spend also the evening with the softly smiling old woman,
who would not go across the grass after such a rain the
night before, was a thing not to be contemplated. Juliet
borrowed a pair of galoshes, and insisted on going to the
chapel. In vain the rector and his wife dissuaded her.
Neither Helen nor her husband said a word.

CHAPTER XXXI

A CONSCIENCE.

THE chapel in the park at Nestley, having as yet received
no color, and having no organ or choir, was a cold, uninteresting little place. It was neat, but had small beauty,
and no history. Yet even already had begun to gather in
the hearts of two or three of the congregation a feeling of
quiet sacredness about it : some soft airs of the spirit-wind
had been wandering through their souls as they sat there
and listened. And a gentle awe, from old associations
with lay worship, stole like a soft twilight over Juliet as she
entered. Even the antral dusk of an old reverence may
help to form the fitting mood through which shall slide un-
hindered the still small voice that makes appeal to what of
God is yet awake in the soul. There were present about a
score of villagers, and the party from the house.

Clad in no vestments of office, but holding in his hand the New Testament, which was always held either there or in his pocket, Wingfold rose to speak. He read :

"*Beware ye of the leaven of the Pharisees, which is hypocrisy. For there is nothing covered, that shall not be revealed ; neither hid, that shall not be known.*"

Then at once he began to show them, in the simplest interpretation, that the hypocrite was one who pretended to be what he was not ; who tried or consented to look other and better than he was. That a man, from unwillingness to look at the truth concerning himself, might be but half-consciously assenting to the false appearance, would, he said, nowise serve to save him from whatever of doom was involved in this utterance of our Lord concerning the crime. These words of explanation and caution premised, he began at the practical beginning, and spoke a few forceful things on the necessity of absolute truth as to fact in every communication between man and man, telling them that, so far as he could understand His words recorded, our Lord's objection to swearing lay chiefly in this, that it encouraged untruthfulness, tending to make a man's yea less than yea, his nay other than nay. He said that many people who told lies every day, would be shocked when they discovered that they were liars ; and that their lying must be discovered, for the Lord said so. Every untruthfulness was a passing hypocrisy, and if they would not come to be hypocrites out and out, they must begin to avoid it by speaking every man the truth to his neighbor. If they did not begin at once to speak the truth, they must grow worse and worse liars. The Lord called hypocrisy *leaven*, because of its irresistible, perhaps as well its unseen, growth and spread ; he called it the leaven *of the Pharisees*, because it was the all-pervading quality of their being, and from them was working moral dissolution in the nation, eating like a canker into it, by infecting with like hypocrisy all who looked up to them.

"Is it not a strange drift, this of men," said the curate, "to hide what is, under the veil of what is not ? to seek refuge in lies, as if that which *is* not, could be an armor of adamant ? to run from the daylight for safety, deeper into the cave ? In the cave house the creatures of the night— the tigers and hyenas, the serpent and the old dragon of the dark ; in the light are true men and women, and the clear-eyed angels. But the reason is only too plain ; it is,

alas ! that they are themselves of the darkness and not of
the light. They do not fear their own. They are more
comfortable with the beasts of darkness than with the
angels of light. They dread the peering of holy eyes into
their hearts ; they feel themselves naked and fear to be
ashamed, therefore cast the garment of hypocrisy about
them. They have that in them so strange to the light that
they feel it must be hidden from the eye of day, as a thing
hideous, that is, a thing to be hidden. But the hypocrisy is
worse than all it would hide. That they have to hide again,
as a more hideous thing still.

" God hides nothing. His very work from the beginning
is *revelation*—a casting aside of veil after veil, a showing
unto men of truth after truth. On and on, from fact to
fact divine He advances, until at length in His Son Jesus, He
unveils His very face. Then begins a fresh unveiling, for
the very work of the Father is the work the Son Himself has
to do—to reveal. His life was the unveiling of Himself,
and the unveiling of the Son is still going on, and is that for
the sake of which the world exists. When He is unveiled,
that is, when we know the Son, we shall know the Father
also. The whole of creation, its growth, its history, the
gathering total of human existence, is an unveiling of the
Father. He is the life, the eternal life, the *Only*. I see it—
ah ! believe me—I see it as I can not say it. From month
to month it grows upon me. The lovely home-light, the
one essence of peaceful being, is God Himself.

" He loves light and not darkness, therefore shines, therefore reveals. True, there are infinite gulfs in Him, into
which our small vision can not pierce, but they are gulfs of
light, and the truths there are invisible only through excess
of their own clarity. There is a darkness that comes of
effulgence, and the most veiling of all veils is the light.
That for which the eye exists is light, but *through*
light no human eye can pierce.—I find myself beyond
my depth. I am ever beyond my depth, afloat in an
infinite sea ; but the depth of the sea knows me, for
the ocean of my being is God.—What I would say is
this, that the light is not blinding because God would hide,
but because the truth is too glorious for our vision. The
effulgence of Himself God veiled that He might unveil it—
in his Son. Inter-universal spaces, æons, eternities—what
word of vastness you can find or choose—take unfathomable darkness itself, if you will, to express the infinitude of

God, that original splendor existing only to the consciousness of God Himself—I say He hides it not, but is revealing
it ever, forever, at all cost of labor, yea of pain to Himself.
His whole creation is a sacrificing of Himself to the being
and well-being of His little ones, that, being wrought out at
last into partakers of His divine nature, that nature may be
revealed in them to their divinest bliss. He brings hidden
things out of the light of His own being into the light of
ours.

"But see how different *we* are—until we learn of Him!
See the tendency of man to conceal his treasures, to claim
even truth as his own by discovery, to hide it and be proud
of it, gloating over that which he thinks he has in himself,
instead of groaning after the infinite of God! We would
be forever heaping together possessions, dragging things
into the cave of our finitude, our individual self, not perceiving that the things which pass that dreariest of doors,
whatever they may have been, are thenceforth but ' straws,
small sticks, and dust of the floor.' When a man would
have a truth in thither as if it were of private interpretation,
he drags in only the bag which the truth, remaining outside, has burst and left.

"Nowhere are such children of darkness born as in the
caves of hypocrisy; nowhere else can a man revel with
such misshapen hybrids of religion and sin. But, as one
day will be found, I believe, a strength of physical light before which even solid gold or blackest marble becomes transparent, so is there a spiritual light before which all veils of
falsehood shall shrivel up and perish and cease to hide; so
that, in individual character, in the facts of being, in
the densest of Pharisaical hypocrisy, there is nothing
covered that shall not be revealed, nothing hid that shall
not be known.

"If then, brother or sister, thou hast that which would be
hidden, make haste and drag the thing from its covert into
the presence of thy God, thy Light, thy Saviour, that, if it be
in itself good, it may be cleansed; if evil, it may be stung
through and through with the burning arrows of truth, and
perish in glad relief. For the one bliss of an evil thing is to
perish and pass; the evil thing, and that alone, is the natural
food of Death—nothing else will agree with the monster. If
we have such foul things, I say, within the circumference of
our known selves, we must confess the charnel-fact to ourselves and to God; and if there be any one else who has a

claim to know it, to that one also must we confess, casting
out the vile thing that we may be clean.   Let us make haste
to open the doors of our lips and the windows of our humility, to let out the demon of darkness, and in the angels of
light—so abjuring the evil.   Be sure that concealment is
utterly, absolutely hopeless.   If we do not thus ourselves
open our house, the day will come when a roaring blast of
His wind, or the flame of His keen lightning, will destroy
every defense of darkness, and set us shivering before the
universe in our naked vileness ; for there is nothing covered
that shall not be revealed, neither hid that shall not be known.
Ah ! well for man that he can not hide !   What vaults of
uncleanness, what sinks of dreadful horrors, would not the
souls of some of us grow !   But for every one of them, as
for the universe, comes the day of cleansing.   Happy they
who hasten it ! who open wide the doors, take the broom in
the hand, and begin to sweep !   The dust may rise in clouds ;
the offense may be great ; the sweeper may pant and choke,
and weep, yea, grow faint and sick with self-disgust ; but
the end will be a clean house, and the light and wind of
Heaven shining and blowing clear and fresh and sweet
through all its chambers.   Better so, than have a hurricane
from God burst in doors and windows, and sweep from his
temple with the besom of destruction every thing that loveth
and maketh a lie.   Brothers, sisters, let us be clean.   The
light and the air around us are God's vast purifying furnace ;
out into it let us cast all hypocrisy.   Let us be open-hearted,
and speak every man the truth to his neighbor.   Amen."

The faces of the little congregation had been staring all
the time at the speaker's, as the flowers of a little garden
stare at the sun.   Like a white lily that had begun to fade,
that of Juliet had drawn the eyes of the curate, as the
whitest spot always will.   But it had drawn his heart also.
Had her troubles already begun, poor girl ? he thought.
Had the sweet book of marriage already begun to give out
its bitterness ?

It was not just so.   Marriage was good to her still.   Not
yet, though but a thing of this world, as she and her husband
were agreed, had it begun to grow stale and wearisome.   She
was troubled.   It was with no reaction against the opinions
to which she had practically yielded ; but not the less had
the serpent of the truth bitten her, for it can bite through
the gauze of whatever opinions or theories.   Conscious, persistent wrong may harden and thicken the gauze to a quilted

armor, but even through that the sound of its teeth may
wake up Don Worm, the conscience, and then is the baser
nature between the fell incensed points of mighty opposites.
It avails a man little to say he does not believe this or that,
if the while he can not rest because of some word spoken.
True speech, as well as true scripture, is given by inspiration
of God ; it goes forth on the wind of the Spirit, with the
ministry of fire. The sun will shine, and the wind will blow,
the floods will beat, and the fire will burn, until the yielding
soul, re-born into childhood, spreads forth its hands and
rushes to the Father.

It was dark, and Juliet took the offered arm of the rector
and walked with him toward the house. Both were silent,
for both had been touched. The rector was busy tumbling
over the contents now of this now of that old chest and
cabinet in the lumber-room of his memory, seeking for things
to get rid of by holy confession ere the hour of proclamation
should arrive. He was finding little yet beyond boyish esca-
pades, and faults and sins which he had abjured ages ago
and almost forgotten. His great sin, of which he had already
repented, and was studying more and more to repent—that
of undertaking holy service for the sake of the loaves and the
fishes—then, in natural sequence, only taking the loaves and
the fishes, and doing no service in return, did not come under
the name of hypocrisy, being indeed a crime patent to the
universe, even when hidden from himself. When at length
the heavy lids of his honest sleepy-eyed nature arose, and he
saw the truth of his condition, his dull, sturdy soul had gathered itself like an old wrestler to the struggle, and hardly
knew what was required of it, or what it had to overthrow,
till it stood panting over its adversary.

Juliet also was occupied—with no such search as the rector's, hardly even with what could be called thought, but
with something that must either soon cause the keenest
thought, or at length a spiritual callosity : somewhere in her
was a motion, a something turned and twisted, ceased and
began again, boring like an auger ; or was it a creature that
tried to sleep, but ever and anon started awake, and with
fretful claws pulled at its nest in the fibers of her heart ?

The curate and his wife talked softly all the way back to
the house.

" Do you really think," said Helen, " that every fault one
has ever committed will one day be trumpeted out to the
universe ? "

"That were hardly worth the while of the universe," answered her husband. "Such an age-long howling of evil stupidities would be enough to turn its brain with ennui and disgust. Nevertheless, the hypocrite will certainly know himself discovered and shamed, and unable any longer to hide himself from his neighbor. His past deeds also will be made plain to all who, for further ends of rectification, require to know them. Shame will then, I trust, be the first approach of his redemption."

Juliet, for she was close behind them, heard his words and shuddered.

"You are feeling it cold, Mrs. Faber," said the rector, and, with the fatherly familiarity of an old man, drew her cloak better around her.

"It is not cold," she faltered ; "but somehow the night-air always makes me shiver."

The rector pulled a muffler from his coat-pocket, and laid it like a scarf on her shoulders.

"How kind you are !" she murmured. "I don't deserve it."

"Who deserves any thing ?" said the rector. "I less, I am sure, than any one I know. Only, if you will believe my curate, you have but to ask, and have what you need."

"I wasn't the first to say that, sir," Wingfold struck in, turning his head over his shoulder.

"I know that, my boy," answered Mr. Bevis ; "but you were the first to make me want to find its true.—I say, Mrs. Faber, what if it should turn out after all, that there was a grand treasure hid in your field and mine, that we never got the good of because we didn't believe it was there and dig for it ? What if this scatter-brained curate of mine should be right when he talks so strangely about our living in the midst of calling voices, cleansing fires, baptizing dews, and *won't* hearken, won't be clean, won't give up our sleep and our dreams for the very bliss for which we cry out in them !"

The old man had stopped, taken off his hat, and turned toward her. He spoke with such a strange solemnity of voice that it could hardly have been believed his by those who knew him as a judge of horses and not as a reader of prayers. The other pair had stopped also.

"I should call it very hard," returned Juliet, "to come so near it and yet miss it."

"Especially to be driven so near it against one's will, and yet succeed in getting past without touching it," said the curate, with a flavor of asperity. His wife gently pinched his arm, and he was ashamed.

When they reached home, Juliet went straight to bed—or at least to her room for the night.

"I say, Wingfold," remarked the rector, as they sat alone after supper, "that sermon of yours was above your congregation."

"I am afraid you are right, sir. I am sorry. But if you had seen their faces as I did, perhaps you would have modified the conclusion."

"I am very glad I heard it, though," said the rector.

They had more talk, and when Wingfold went up stairs, he found Helen asleep. Annoyed with himself for having spoken harshly to Mrs. Faber, and more than usually harassed by a sense of failure in his sermon, he threw himself into a chair, and sat brooding and praying till the light began to appear. Out of the reeds shaken all night in the wind, rose with the morning this bird :—

THE SMOKE.

Lord, I have laid my heart upon Thy altar,
　　But can not get the wood to burn ;
It hardly flares ere it begins to falter,
　　And to the dark return.

Old sap, or night-fallen dew, has damped the fuel ;
　　In vain my breath would flame provoke ;
Yet see—at every poor attempt's renewal
　　To Thee ascends the smoke.

'Tis all I have—smoke, failure, foiled endeavor,
　　Coldness, and doubt, and palsied lack ;
Such as I have I send Thee ;—perfect Giver,
　　Send Thou Thy lightning back.

In the morning, as soon as breakfast was over, Helen's ponies were brought to the door, she and Juliet got into the carriage, Wingfold jumped up behind, and they returned to Glaston. Little was said on the way, and Juliet seemed strangely depressed. They left her at her own door.

"What did that look mean ?" said Wingfold to his wife, the moment they were round the corner of Mr. Drew's shop.

"You saw it then ?" returned Helen. "I did not think you had been so quick."

" I saw what I could not help taking for relief," said the curate, " when the maid told her that her husband was not at home."

They said no more till they reached the rectory, where Helen followed her husband to his study.

" He can't have turned tyrant already ! " she said, resuming the subject of Juliet's look. " But she's afraid of him."

" It did look like it," rejoined her husband. " Oh, Helen, what a hideous thing fear of her husband must be for a woman, who has to spend not her days only in his presence, but her nights by his side ! I do wonder so many women dare to be married. They would need all to have clean consciences."

" Or no end of faith in their husbands," said Helen. " If ever I come to be afraid of you, it will be because I have done something very wrong indeed."

" Don't be too sure of that, Helen," returned Wingfold. " There are very decent husbands as husbands go, who are yet unjust, exacting, selfish. The most devoted of wives are sometimes afraid of the men they yet consider the very models of husbands. It is a brutal shame that a woman should feel afraid, or even uneasy, instead of safe, beside her husband."

" You are always on the side of the women, Thomas," said his wife ; " and I love you for it somehow—I can't tell why."

" You make a mistake to begin with, my dear : you don't love me because I am on the side of the women, but because I am on the side of the wronged. If the man happened to be the injured party, and I took the side of the woman, you would be down on me like an avalanche."

" I dare say. But there is something more in it. I don't think I am altogether mistaken. You don't talk like most men. They have such an ugly way of asserting superiority, and sneering at women ! That you never do, and as a woman I am grateful for it."

The same afternoon Dorothy Drake paid a visit to Mrs. Faber, and was hardly seated before the feeling that something was wrong arose in her. Plainly Juliet was suffering —from some cause she wished to conceal. Several times she seemed to turn faint, hurriedly fanned herself, and drew a deep breath. Once she rose hastily and went to the window, as if struggling with some oppression, and returned looking very pale.

Dorothy was frightened.

"What is the matter, dear?" she said.

"Nothing," answered Juliet, trying to smile. "Perhaps I took a little cold last night," she added with a shiver.

"Have you told your husband?" asked Dorothy.

"I haven't seen him since Saturday," she answered quietly, but a pallor almost deathly overspread her face.

"I hope he will soon be home," said Dorothy. "Mind you tell him how you feel the instant he comes in."

Juliet answered with a smile, but that smile Dorothy never forgot. It haunted her all the way home. When she entered her chamber, her eyes fell upon the petal of a monthly rose, which had dropped from the little tree in her window, and lay streaked and crumpled on the black earth of the flower-pot : by one of those queer mental vagaries in which the imagination and the logical faculty seem to combine to make sport of the reason—"How is it that smile has got here before me?" she said to herself.

She sat down and thought. Could it be that Juliet had, like herself, begun to find there could be no peace without the knowledge of an absolute peace? If it were so, and she would but let her know it, then, sisters at least in sorrow and search, they would together seek the Father of their spirits, if haply they might find Him ; together they would cry to Him—and often : it might be He would hear them, and reveal Himself. Her heart was sore all day, thinking of that sad face. Juliet, whether she knew it or not, was, like herself, in trouble because she had no God.

The conclusion shows that Dorothy was far from hopeless. That she could believe the lack of a God was the cause unknown to herself of her friend's depression, implies an assurance of the human need of a God, and a hope there might be One to be found. For herself, if she could but find Him, she felt there would be nothing but bliss evermore. Dorothy then was more hopeful than she herself knew. I doubt if absolute hopelessness is ever born save at the word, *Depart from me.* Hope springs with us from God Himself, and, however down-beaten, however sick and nigh unto death, will evermore lift its head and rise again.

She could say nothing to her father. She loved him—oh, how dearly! and trusted him, where she could trust him at all!—oh, how perfectly! but she had no confidence in his understanding of herself. The main cause whence arose his insufficiency and her lack of trust was, that all his faith in God was as yet scarcely more independent of thought-forms, word-shapes, dogma and creed, than that of the Catholic or Calvinist. How few are there whose faith is simple and mighty in the Father of Jesus Christ, waiting to believe all that He will reveal to them! How many of those who talk of faith as the one needful thing, will accept as sufficient to the razing of the walls of partition between you and them, your heartiest declaration that you believe *in Him* with the whole might of your nature, lay your soul bare to the revelation of His spirit, and stir up your will to obey Him?—And then comes *your* temptation—to exclude, namely, from your love and sympathy the weak and boisterous brethren who, after the fashion possible to them, believe in your Lord, because they exclude you, and put as little confidence in your truth as in your insight. If you do know more of Christ than they, upon you lies the heavier obligation to be true to them, as was St. Paul to the Judaizing Christians, whom these so much resemble, who were his chief hindrance in the work his Master had given him to do. In Christ we must forget Paul and Apollos and Cephas, pope and bishop and pastor and presbyter, creed and interpretation and theory. Careless of their opinions, we must be careful of themselves—careful that we have salt in ourselves, and that the salt lose not its savor, that the old man, dead through Christ, shall not, vampire-like, creep from his grave and suck the blood of the saints, by whatever name they be called, or however little they may yet have entered into the freedom of the gospel that God is light, and in Him is no darkness at all.

How was Dorothy to get nearer to Juliet, find out her trouble, and comfort her?

"Alas!" she said to herself, "what a thing is marriage in separating friends!"

CHAPTER XXXII.

THE OLD HOUSE OF GLASTON.

THE same evening Dorothy and her father walked to the Old House. Already the place looked much changed. The very day the deeds were signed, Mr. Drake, who was not the man to postpone action a moment after the time for it was come, had set men at work upon the substantial repairs. The house was originally so well built that these were not so heavy as might have been expected, and when completed they made little show of change. The garden, however, looked quite another thing, for it had lifted itself up from the wilderness in which it was suffocated, reviving like a repentant soul reborn. Under its owner's keen watch, its ancient plan had been rigidly regarded, its ancient features carefully retained. The old bushes were well trimmed, but as yet nothing live, except weeds, had been uprooted. The hedges and borders, of yew and holly and box, tall and broad, looked very bare and broken and patchy; but now that the shears had, after so long a season of neglect, removed the gathered shade, the naked stems and branches would again send out the young shoots of the spring, a new birth would begin everywhere, and the old garden would dawn anew. For all his lack of sympathy with the older forms of religious economy in the country, a thing, alas! too easy to account for, the minister yet loved the past and felt its mystery. He said once in a sermon—and it gave offense to more than one of his deacons, for they scented in it *Germanism*,—" The love of the past, the desire of the future, and the enjoyment of the present, make an eternity, in which time is absorbed, its lapse lapses, and man partakes of the immortality of his Maker. In each present personal being, we have the whole past of our generation inclosed, to be re-developed with endless difference in each individuality. Hence perhaps it comes that, every now and then, into our consciousnesses float strange odors of feeling, strange tones as of bygone affections, strange glimmers as of forgotten truths, strange mental sensations of indescribable sort and texture. Friends, I should be a terror to myself, did I not believe that wherever my dim consciousness may come to itself, God is there."

Dorothy would have hastened the lighter repairs inside the house as well, so as to get into it as soon as possible ; but her father very wisely argued that it would be a pity to get the house in good condition, and then, as soon as they went into it, and began to find how it could be altered better to suit their tastes and necessities, have to destroy a great part of what had just been done. His plan, therefore, was to leave the house for the winter, now it was weather-tight, and with the first of the summer partly occupy it as it was, find out its faults and capabilities, and have it gradually repaired and altered to their minds and requirements. There would in this way be plenty of time to talk about every thing, even to the merest suggestion of fancy, and discover what they would really like.

But ever since the place had been theirs, Dorothy had been in the habit of going almost daily to the house, with her book and her work, sitting now in this, now in that empty room, undisturbed by the noises of the workmen, chiefly outside : the foreman was a member of her father's church, a devout man, and she knew every one of his people. She had taken a strange fancy to those empty rooms : perhaps she felt them like her own heart, waiting for something to come and fill them with life. Nor was there any thing to prevent her, though the work was over for a time, from indulging herself in going there still, as often as she pleased, and she would remain there for hours, sometimes nearly the whole day. In her present condition of mind and heart, she desired and needed solitude : she was one of those who when troubled rush from their fellows, and, urged by the human instinct after the divine, seek refuge in loneliness—the cave on Horeb, the top of Mount Sinai, the closet with shut door—any lonely place where, unseen, and dreading no eye, the heart may call aloud to the God hidden behind the veil of the things that do appear.

How different, yet how fit to merge in a mutual sympathy, were the thoughts of the two, as they wandered about the place that evening ! Dorothy was thinking her commonest thought—how happy she could be if only she knew there was a Will central to the universe, willing all that came to her—good or seeming-bad—a Will whom she might love and thank for *all* things. He would be to her no God whom she could thank only when He sent her what was pleasant. She must be able to thank Him for every thing, or she could thank Him for nothing.

Her father was saying to himself he could not have believed the lifting from his soul of such a gravestone of debt, would have made so little difference to his happiness. He fancied honest Jones, the butcher, had more mere pleasure from the silver snuff-box he had given him, than he had himself from his fortune. Relieved he certainly was, but the relief was not happiness. His debt had been the stone that blocked up the gate of Paradise : the stone was rolled away, but the gate was not therefore open. He seemed for the first time beginning to understand what he had so often said, and in public too, and had thought he understood, that God Himself, and not any or all of His gifts, is the life of a man. He had got rid of the dread imagination that God had given him the money in anger, as He had given the Israelites the quails, nor did he find that the possession formed any barrier between him and God : his danger now seemed that of forgetting the love of the Giver in his anxiety to spend the gift according to His will.

" You and I ought to be very happy, my love," he said, as now they were walking home.

He had often said so before, and Dorothy had held her peace ; but now, with her eyes on the ground, she rejoined, in a low, rather broken voice,

" Why, papa ? "

" Because we are lifted above the anxiety that was crushing us into the very mud," he answered, with surprise at her question.

" It never troubled me so much as all that," she answered. " It is a great relief to see you free from it, father ; but otherwise, I can not say that it has made much difference to me."

" My dear Dorothy," said the minister, " it is time we should understand each other. Your state of mind has for a long time troubled me ; but while debt lay so heavy upon me, I could give my attention to nothing else. Why should there be any thing but perfect confidence between a father and daughter who belong to each other alone in all the world ? Tell me what it is that so plainly oppresses you. What prevents you from opening your heart to me ? You can not doubt my love."

" Never for one moment, father," she answered, almost eagerly, pressing to her heart the arm on which she leaned. " I know I am safe with you because I am yours, and yet

somehow I can not get so close to you as I would.   Some·
thing comes between us, and prevents me."

"What is it, my child?   I will do all and every thing I
can to remove it."

"You, dear father!   I don't believe ever child had such
a father."

"Oh yes, my dear! many have had better fathers, but
none better than I hope one day by the grace of God to be
to you.   I am a poor creature, Dorothy, but I love you as
my own soul.   You are the blessing of my days, and my
thoughts brood over you in the night : it would be in utter
content, if I only saw you happy.   If your face were
acquainted with smiles, my heart would be acquainted
with gladness."

For a time neither said any thing more.   The silent
tears were streaming from Dorothy's eyes.   At length she
spoke.

"I wonder if I could tell you what it is without hurting
you, father!" she said.

"I can hear any thing from you, my child," he answered.

"Then I will try.   But I do not think I shall ever quite
know my father on earth, or be quite able to open my heart
to him, until I have found my Father in Heaven."

"Ah, my child! is it so with you?   Do you fear you have
not yet given yourself to the Saviour?   Give yourself now.
His arms are ever open to receive you."

"That is hardly the point, father.—Will you let me ask
you any question I please?"

"Assuredly, my child."   He always spoke, though quite
unconsciously, with a little of the *ex-cathedral* tone.

"Then tell me, father, are you just as sure of God as
you are of me standing here before you?"

She had stopped and turned, and stood looking him full
in the face with wide, troubled eyes.

Mr. Drake was silent.   Hateful is the professional, contemptible is the love of display, but in his case they floated
only as vapors in the air of a genuine soul.   He was a true
man, and as he could not say *yes*, neither would he hide his
no in a multitude of words—at least to his own daughter :
he was not so sure of God as he was of that daughter, with
those eyes looking straight into his !   Could it be that he
never had believed in God at all?   The thought went
through him with a great pang.   It was as if the moon
grew dark above him, and the earth withered under his

feet. He stood before his child like one whose hypocrisy had been proclaimed from the housetop.

" Are you vexed with me, father?" said Dorothy sadly.

" No, my child," answered the minister, in a voice of unnatural composure. " But you stand before me there like the very thought started out of my soul, alive and visible, to question its own origin."

" Ah, father !" cried Dorothy, " let us question our origin."

The minister never even heard the words.

" That very doubt, embodied there in my child, has, I now know, been haunting me, dogging me behind, ever since I began to teach others," he said, as if talking in his sleep. " Now it looks me in the face. Am I myself to be a cast-away ?—Dorothy, I am *not* sure of God—not as I am sure of you, my darling."

He stood silent. His ear expected a low-voiced, sorrowful reply. He started at the tone of gladness in which Dorothy cried—

" Then, father, there is henceforth no cloud between us, for we are in the same cloud together ! It does not divide us, it only brings us closer to each other. Help me, father : I am trying hard to find God. At the same time, I confess I would rather not find Him, than find Him such as I have sometimes heard you represent Him."

" It may well be," returned her father—the *ex-cathedral*, the professional tone had vanished utterly for the time, and he spoke with the voice of an humble, true man—" it may well be that I have done Him wrong ; for since now at my age I am compelled to allow that I am not sure of Him, what more likely than that I may have been cherishing wrong ideas concerning Him, and so not looking in the right direction for finding Him ?"

" Where did you get your notions of God, father—those, I mean, that you took with you to the pulpit ? "

A year ago even, if he had been asked the same question, he would at once have answered, " From the Word of God ;" but now he hesitated, and minutes passed before he began a reply. For he saw now that it was not from the Bible *he* had gathered them, whence soever they had come at first. He pondered and searched—and found that the real answer eluded him, hiding itself in a time beyond his earliest memory. It seemed plain, therefore, that the source whence first he began to draw those notions, right or wrong, must be the talk and behavior of the house in which he was born, the words and carriage of his father and mother and their friends. Next source to that came the sermons he heard on Sundays, and the books given him to read. The Bible was one of those books, but from the first he read it through the notions with which his mind was already vaguely filled, and with the comments of his superiors around him. Then followed the books recommended at college, this author and that, and the lectures he heard there upon the attributes of God and the plan of salvation. The spirit of commerce in the midst of which he had been bred, did not occur to him as one of the sources.

But he had perceived enough. He opened his mouth and bravely answered her question as well as he could, not giving the Bible as the source from which he had taken any one of the notions of God he had been in the habit of presenting.

"But mind," he added, "I do not allow that therefore my ideas must be incorrect. If they be second-hand, they may yet be true. I do admit that where they have continued only second-hand, they can have been of little value to me."

"What you allow, then, father," said Dorothy, "is that you have yourself taken none of your ideas direct from the fountain-head?"

"I am afraid I must confess it, my child—with this modification, that I have thought many of them over a good deal, and altered some of them not a little to make them fit the molds of truth in my mind."

"I am so glad, father!" said Dorothy. "I was positively certain, from what I knew of you—which is more than any one else in this world, I do believe—that some of the things you said concerning God never could have risen in your own mind."

"They might be in the Bible for all that," said the minister, very anxious to be and speak the right thing. "A man's heart is not to be trusted for correct notions of God."

"Nor yet for correct interpretation of the Bible, I should think," said Dorothy.

"True, my child," answered her father with a sigh, "—except as it be already a Godlike heart. The Lord says a bramble-bush can not bring forth grapes."

"The notions you gathered of God from other people, must have come out of their hearts, father?"

" Out of somebody's heart ? "

" Just so," answered Dorothy.

" Go on, my child," said her father. " Let me understand clearly your drift."

" I have heard Mr. Wingfold say," returned Dorothy, " that however men may have been driven to form their ideas of God before Christ came, no man can, with thorough honesty, take the name of a Christian, whose ideas of the Father of men are gathered from any other field than the life, thought, words, deeds, of the only Son of that Father. He says it is not from the Bible as a book that we are to draw our ideas of God, but from the living Man into whose presence that book brings us, Who is alive now, and gives His spirit that they who read about Him may understand what kind of being He is, and why He did as He did, and know Him, in some possible measure, as He knows Himself. —I can only repeat the lesson like a child."

" I suspect," returned the minister, "that I have been greatly astray.   But after this, we will seek our Father together, in our Brother, Jesus Christ."

It was the initiation of a daily lesson together in the New Testament, which, while it drew their hearts closer to each other, drew them, with growing delight, nearer and nearer to the ideal of humanity, Jesus Christ, in whom shines the glory of its Father.

A man may look another in the face for a hundred years and not know him.   Men *have* looked Jesus Christ in the face, and not known either Him or his Father. It was needful that He should appear, to begin the knowing of Him, but speedily was His visible presence taken away, that it might not become, as assuredly it would have become, a veil to hide from men the Father of their spirits.   Do you long for the assurance of some sensible sign ?   Do you ask why no intellectual proof is to be had ?   I tell you that such would but delay, perhaps altogether impair for you, that better, that best, that only vision, into which at last your world must blossom—such a contact, namely, with the heart of God Himself, such a perception of His being, and His absolute oneness with you, the child of His thought, the individuality softly parted from His spirit, yet living still and only by His presence and love, as, by its own radiance, will sweep doubt away forever.   Being then in the light and knowing it, the lack of intellectual proof concerning that which is too high for it, will trouble you no more than would your inability to silence a metaphysician who declared that you had no real existence. It is for the sake of such vision as God would give that you are denied such vision as you would have. The Father of our spirits is not content that we should know Him as we now know each other. There is a better, closer, nearer than any human way of knowing, and to that He is guiding us across all the swamps of our unteachableness, the seas of our faithlessness, the desert of our ignorance. It is so very hard that we should have to wait for that which we can not yet receive? Shall we complain of the shadows cast upon our souls by the hand and the napkin polishing their mirrors to the receiving of the more excellent glory! Have patience, children of the Father. Pray always and do not faint. The mists and the storms and the cold will pass—the sun and the sky are for evermore. There were no volcanoes and no typhoons but for the warm heart of the earth, the soft garment of the air, and the lordly sun over all. The most loving of you can not imagine how one day the love of the Father will make you love even your own.

Much trustful talk passed between father and daughter as they walked home: they were now nearer to each other than ever in their lives before.

"You don't mind my coming out here alone, papa?" said Dorothy, as, after a little chat with the gate-keeper, they left the park. "I have of late found it so good to be alone! I think I am beginning to learn to think."

"Do in every thing just as you please, my child," said her father. "I can have no objection to what you see good. Only don't be so late as to make me anxious."

"I like coming early," said Dorothy. "These lovely mornings make me feel as if the struggles of life were over, and only a quiet old age were left."

The father looked anxiously at his daughter. Was she going to leave him? It smote him to the heart that he had done so little to make her life a blessed one. How hard no small portion of it had been! How worn and pale she looked! Why did she not show fresh and bright like other young women—Mrs. Faber for instance? He had not guided her steps into the way of peace! At all events he had not led her home to the house of wisdom and rest! Too good reason why—he had not himself yet found that home! Henceforth, for her sake as well as his own, he would besiege the heavenly grace with prayer.

The opening of his heart in confessional response to his daughter, proved one of those fresh starts in the spiritual life, of which a man needs so many as he climbs to the heavenly gates.

CHAPTER XXXIII.

PAUL FABER'S DRESSING-ROOM.

FABER did not reach home till a few minutes before the dinner hour. He rode into the stable-yard, entered the house by the surgery, and went straight to his dressing-room ; for the roads were villianous, and Ruber's large feet had made a wonderful sight of his master, who re-spected his wife's carpet. At the same time he hoped, as it was so near dinner-time, to find her in her chamber. She had, however, already made her toilet, and was waiting his return in the drawing-room. Her heart made a false motion and stung her when she heard his steps pass the door and go up stairs, for generally he came to greet her the moment he entered the house.—Had he seen any body !—Had he heard any thing ? It was ten dreadful minutes before he came down, but he entered cheerily, with the gathered warmth of two days of pent-up affection. She did her best to meet him as if nothing had happened. For indeed what had happened—except her going to church ? If nothing had taken place since she saw him—since she knew him—why such perturbation ? Was marriage a slavery of the very soul, in which a wife was bound to confess every thing to her husband, even to her most secret thoughts and feelings ? Or was a husband lord not only over the present and future of his wife, but over her past also ? Was she bound to dis-close every thing that lay in that past ? If Paul made no claim upon her beyond the grave, could he claim back upon the dead past before he knew her, a period over which she had now no more control than over that when she would be but a portion of the material all ?

But whatever might be Paul's theories of marriage or claims upon his wife, it was enough for her miserable unrest that she was what is called a living soul, with a history, and what has come to be called a conscience—a something, that is, as most people regard it, which has the power, and uses it, of making uncomfortable.

The existence of such questions as I have indicated reveals that already between her and him there showed space, separation, non-contact : Juliet was too bewildered with misery to tell whether it was a cleft of a hair's breadth, or a gulf across which no cry could reach ; this moment it seemed the one, the next the other. The knowledge which caused it had troubled her while he sought her love, had troubled her on to the very eve of her surrender. The deeper her love grew the more fiercely she wrestled with the evil fact. A low moral development and the purest resolve of an honest nature afforded her many pleas, and at length she believed she had finally put it down. She had argued that, from the opinions themselves of Faber, the thing could not consistently fail to be as no thing to him. Even were she mistaken in this conclusion, it would be to wrong his large nature, his generous love, his unselfish regard, his tender pitifulness, to fail of putting her silent trust in him. Besides, had she not read in the newspapers the utterance of a certain worshipful judge on the bench that no man had any thing to do with his wife's ante-nuptial history ? The contract then was certainly not retrospective. What in her remained unsatisfied after all her arguments, reasons, and appeals to common sense and consequences, she strove to strangle, and thought, hoped, she had succeeded. She willed her will, made up her mind, yielded to Paul's solicitations, and put the whole painful thing away from her.

The step taken, the marriage over, nothing could any more affect either fact. Only, unfortunately for the satisfaction and repose she had desired and expected, her love to her husband had gone on growing after they were married. True she sometimes fancied it otherwise, but while the petals of the rose were falling, its capsule was filling ; and notwithstanding the opposite tendency of the deoxygenated atmosphere in which their thoughts moved, she had begun already to long after an absolute union with him. But this growth of her love, and aspiration after its perfection, although at first they covered what was gone by with a deepening mist of apparent oblivion, were all the time bringing it closer to her consciousness—out of the far into the near. And now suddenly that shape she knew of, lying in the bottom of the darkest pool of the stagnant Past, had been stung into life by a wind of words that swept through

Nestley chapel, had stretched up a hideous neck and threatening head from the deep, and was staring at her with sodden eyes : henceforth she knew that the hideous Fact had its appointed place between her and her beautiful Paul, the demon of the gulfy cleft that parted them.

The moment she spoke in reply to his greeting her husband also felt something dividing them, but had no presentiment of its being any thing of import.

" You are over-tired, my love," he said, and taking her hand, felt her pulse. It was feeble and frequent.

" What have they been doing to you, my darling ?" he asked. " Those little demons of ponies running away again ? "

" No," she answered, scarce audibly.

" Something has gone wrong with you," he persisted. " Have you caught cold ? None of the old symptoms, I hope ? "

" None, Paul. There is nothing the matter," she answered, laying her head lightly, as if afraid of the liberty she took, upon his shoulder. His arm went round her waist.

" What is it, then, my wife ? " he said tenderly.

" Which would you rather have, Paul—have me die, or do something wicked ? "

" Juliet, this will never do ! " he returned quietly but almost severely. " You have been again giving the reins to a morbid imagination. Weakness and folly only can come of that. It is nothing better than hysteria."

" No, but tell me, dear Paul," she persisted pleadingly. " Answer my question. Do, please."

" There is no such question to be answered," he returned. " You are not going to die, and I am yet more certain you are not going to do any thing wicked. Are you now ? "

" No, Paul. Indeed I am not. But——"

" I have it ! " he exclaimed. " You went to church at Nestley last night ! Confound them all with their humbug ! You have been letting their infernal nonsense get a hold of you again ! It has quite upset you—that, and going much too long without your dinner. What *can* be keeping it ? " He left her hurriedly and rang the bell. " You must speak to the cook, my love. She is getting out of the good habits I had so much trouble to teach her. But no—no ! you shall not be troubled with *my* servants. I will speak to her myself. After dinner I will read you some of my

favorite passages in Montaigne.   No, you shall read to me :
your French is so much better than mine."

Dinner was announced and nothing more was said.   Paul
ate well, Juliet scarcely at all, but she managed to hide
from him the offense.   They rose together and returned to
the drawing-room.

The moment Faber shut the door Juliet turned in the
middle of the room, and as he came up to her said, in a
voice much unlike her own :

"Paul, if I *were* to do any thing very bad, as bad as could
be, would you forgive me ? "

"Come, my love," expostulated Faber, speaking more
gently than before, for he had had his dinner, "surely you
are not going to spoil our evening with any more such nonsense ! "

"Answer me, Paul, or I shall think you do not love me,"
she said, and the tone of her entreaty verged upon demand.
"Would you forgive me if I had done something *very* bad ? "

"Of course I should," he answered, with almost irritated
haste, "—that is, if I could ever bring myself to allow any
thing you did was wrong.   Only, you would witch me out
of opinion and judgment and every thing else with two
words from your dear lips."

"Should I, Paul ? " she said ; and lifting her face from
his shoulder, she looked up in his from the depths of two
dark fountains full of tears. . Never does the soul so nearly
identify itself with matter as when revealing itself through
the eyes ; never does matter so nearly lose itself in spiritual
absorption, as when two eyes like Juliet's are possessed and
glorified by the rush of the soul through their portals.
Faber kissed eyes and lips and neck in a glow of delight.
She was the vision of a most blessed dream, and she was
his, all and altogether his !   He never thought then how his
own uncreed and the prayer-book were of the same mind
that Death would one day part them.   There is that in every
high and simple feeling that stamps it with eternity.   For my
own part I believe that, if life has not long before twinned
any twain, Death can do nothing to divide them.   The
nature of each and every pure feeling, even in the man who
may sin away the very memory of it, is immortal ; and who
knows from under what a depth of ashes the love of the
saving God may yet revive it !

The next moment the doctor was summoned.   When he
returned, Juliet was in bed, and pretended to be asleep.

In the morning she appeared at the breakfast table so pale, so worn, so troubled, that her husband was quite anxious about her. All she would confess to was, that she had not slept well, and had a headache. Attributing her condition to a nervous attack, he gave her some medicine, took her to the drawing-room, and prescribed the new piano, which he had already found the best of all sedatives for her. She loathed the very thought of it—could no more have touched it than if the ivory keys had been white hot steel. She watched him from the window while he mounted his horse, but the moment the last red gleam of Ruber vanished, she flung her arms above her head, and with a stifled cry threw herself on a couch, stuffed her handkerchief into her mouth, and in fierce dumb agony, tore it to shreds with hands and teeth. Presently she rose, opened the door almost furtively, and stole softly down the stair, looking this way and that, like one intent on some evil deed. At the bottom she pushed a green baize-covered door, peeped into a passage, then crept on tiptoe toward the surgery. Arrived there she darted to a spot she knew, and stretched a trembling hand toward a bottle full of a dark-colored liquid. As instantly she drew it back, and stood listening with bated breath and terrified look. It *was* a footstep approaching the outer door of the surgery ! She turned and fled from it, still noiseless, and never stopped till she was in her own room. There she shut and locked the door, fell on her knees by the bedside, and pressed her face into the coverlid. She had no thought of praying. She wanted to hide, only to hide. Neither was it from old habit she fell upon her knees, for she had never been given to kneeling. I can not but think, nevertheless, that there was a dumb germ of prayer at the heart of the action—that falling upon her knees, and that hiding of her face. The same moment something took place within her to which she could have given no name, which she could have represented in no words, a something which came she knew not whence, was she knew not what, and went she knew not whither, of which indeed she would never have become aware except for what followed, but which yet so wrought, that she rose from her knees saying to herself, with clenched teeth and burning eyes, " I *will* tell him."

As if she had known the moment of her death near, she began mechanically to set every thing in order in the room, and as she came to herself she was saying, " Let him kill

me. I wish he would. I am quite willing to die by his
hand. He will be kind, and do it gently. He knows so
many ways ! "

It was a terrible day. She did not go out of her room
again. Her mood changed a hundred times. The resolve
to confess alternated with wild mockery and laughter, but
still returned. She would struggle to persuade herself that
her whole condition was one of foolish exaggeration, of
senseless excitement about nothing—the merest delirium of
feminine fastidiousness ; and the next instant would turn
cold with horror at a fresh glimpse of the mere fact. What
could the wretched matter be to him now—or to her ? Who
was the worse, or had ever been the worse but herself ? And
what did it amount to ? What claim had any one, what
claim could even a God, if such a being there were, have
upon the past which had gone from her, was no more in any
possible sense within her reach than if it had never been ?
Was it not as if it had never been ? Was the woman to be
hurled—to hurl herself into misery for the fault of the girl ?
It was all nonsense—a trifle at worst—a disagreeable trifle,
no doubt, but still a trifle ! Only would to God she had
died rather—even although then she would never have
known Paul !—Tut ! she would never have thought of it
again but for that horrid woman that lived over the draper's
shop ! All would have been well if she had but kept from
thinking about it ! Nobody would have been a hair the
worse then !—But, poor Paul !—to be married to such a
woman as she !

If she were to be so foolish as let him know, how would
it strike Paul ? What would he think of it ? Ought she not
to be sure of that before she committed herself—before she
uttered the irrevocable words ? Would he call it a trifle, or
would he be ready to kill her ? True, he had no right, he
could have no right to know ; but how horrible that there
should be any thought of right between them ! still worse,
any thing whatever between them that he had no right to
know ! worst of all, that she did not belong to him so utterly
that he must have a right to know *every* thing about her !
She *would* tell him all ! She would ! she would ! she had
no choice ! she must !—But she need not tell him now. She
was not strong enough to utter the necessary words. But
that made the thing very dreadful ! If she could not speak
the words, how bad it must really be !—Impossible to tell
her Paul ! That was pure absurdity.—Ah, but she *could* not !

She would be certain to faint—or fall dead at his feet. That would be well!—Yes! that would do! She would take a wine-glass full of laudanum just before she told him; then, if he was kind, she would confess the opium, and he could save her if he pleased; if he was hard, she would say nothing, and die at his feet. She had hoped to die in his arms—all that was left of eternity. But her life was his, he had saved it with his own—oh horror! that it should have been to disgrace him!—and it should not last a moment longer than it was a pleasure to him.

Worn out with thought and agony, she often fell asleep—only to start awake in fresh misery, and go over and over the same torturing round. Long before her husband appeared, she was in a burning fever. When he came, he put her at once to bed, and tended her with a solicitude as anxious as it was gentle. He soothed her to sleep, and then went and had some dinner.

On his return, finding, as he had expected, that she still slept, he sat down by her bedside, and watched. Her slumber was broken with now and then a deep sigh, now and then a moan. Alas, that we should do the things that make for moan!—but at least I understand why we are left to do them: it is because we can. A dull fire was burning in her soul, and over it stood the caldron of her history, and it bubbled in sighs and moans.

Faber was ready enough to attribute every thing human to a physical origin, but as he sat there pondering her condition, recalling her emotion and strange speech of the night before, and watching the state she was now in, an uneasiness began to gather—undefined, but other than concerned her health. Something must be wrong somewhere. He kept constantly assuring himself that at worst it could be but some mere moleheap, of which her lovelily sensitive organization, under the influence of a foolish preachment, made a mountain. Still, it was a huge disorder to come from a trifle! At the same time who knew better than he upon what a merest trifle nervous excitement will fix the attention! or how to the mental eye such a speck will grow and grow until it absorb the universe! Only a certain other disquieting thought, having come once, would keep returning—that, thoroughly as he believed himself acquainted with her mind, he had very little knowledge of her history. He did not know a single friend of hers, had never met a person who knew any thing of her family, or had even an acquaintance with her earlier than his own. The thing he most dreaded was, that the shadow of some old affection had returned upon her soul, and that, in her excessive delicacy, she heaped blame upon herself that she had not absolutely forgotten it. He flung from him in scorn every slightest suggestion of blame. *His* Juliet! his glorious Juliet! Bah!—But he must get her to say what the matter was—for her own sake; he must help her to reveal her trouble, whatever it might be—else how was he to do his best to remove it! She should find he knew how to be generous!

Thus thinking, he sat patient by her side, watching until the sun of her consciousness should rise and scatter the clouds of sleep. Hour after hour he sat, and still she slept, outwearied with the rack of emotion. Morning had begun to peer gray through the window-curtains, when she woke with a cry.

She had been dreaming. In the little chapel in Nestley Park, she sat listening to the curate's denouncement of hypocrisy, when suddenly the scene changed: the pulpit had grown to a mighty cloud, upon which stood an arch-angel with a trumpet in his hand. He cried that the hour of the great doom had come for all who bore within them the knowledge of any evil thing neither bemoaned before God nor confessed to man. Then he lifted the great silver trumpet with a gleam to his lips, and every fiber of her flesh quivered in expectation of the tearing blast that was to follow; when instead, soft as a breath of spring from a bank of primroses, came the words, uttered in the gentlest of sorrowful voices, and the voice seemed that of her unbelieving Paul: "I will arise and go to my Father." It was no wonder, therefore, that she woke with a cry. It was one of indescribable emotion. When she saw his face bending over her in anxious love, she threw her arms round his neck, burst into a storm of weeping, and sobbed.

"Oh Paul! husband! forgive me. I have sinned against you terribly—the worst sin a woman can commit. Oh Paul! Paul! make me clean, or I am lost."

"Juliet, you are raving," he said, bewildered, a little angry, and at her condition not a little alarmed. For the confession, it was preposterous: they had not been many weeks married! "Calm yourself, or you will give me a lunatic for a wife!" he said. Then changing his tone, for his heart rebuked him, when he saw the ashy despair that spread over her face and eyes, "Be still, my precious," he went on. "All is well. You have been dreaming, and are not yet quite awake. It is the morphia you had last night ! Don't look so frightened. It is only your husband. No one else is near you."

With the tenderest smile he sought to reassure her, and would have gently released himself from the agonized clasp of her arms about his neck, that he might get her something. But she tightened her hold.

"Don't leave me, Paul," she cried. "I was dreaming, but I am wide awake now, and know only too well what I have done."

"Dreams are nothing. The will is not in them," he said.

But the thought of his sweet wife even dreaming a thing to be repented of in such dismay, tore his heart. For he was one of the many—not all of the purest—who cherish an ideal of woman which, although indeed poverty-stricken and crude, is to their minds of snowy favor, to their judgment of loftiest excellence. I trust in God that many a woman, despite the mud of doleful circumstance, yea, even the defilement that comes first from within, has risen to a radiance of essential innocence ineffably beyond that whose form stood white in Faber's imagination. For I see and understand a little how God, giving righteousness, makes pure of sin, and that verily —by no theological quibble of imputation, by no play with words, by no shutting of the eyes, no oblivion, willful or irresistible, but by very fact of cleansing, so that the consciousness of the sinner becomes glistering as the raiment of the Lord on the mount of His transfiguration. I do not expect the Pharisee who calls the sinner evil names, and drags her up to judgment, to comprehend this ; but, woman, cry to thy Father in Heaven, for He can make thee white, even to the contentment of that womanhood which thou hast thyself outraged.

Faber unconsciously prided himself on the severity of his requirements of woman, and saw his own image reflected in the polish of his ideal ; and now a fear whose presence he would not acknowledge began to gnaw at his heart, a vague suggestion's horrid image, to which he would yield no space, to flit about his brain.

"Would to God it were a dream, Paul !" answered the stricken wife.

"You foolish child ! " returned the nigh trembling husband, "how can you expect me to believe, married but yesterday, you have already got tired of me ! "

"Tired of you, Paul! I should desire no other eternal paradise than to lie thus under your eyes forever."

"Then for my sake, my darling wife, send away this extravagance, this folly, this absurd fancy that has got such a hold of you. It will turn to something serious if you do not resist it. There can be no truth in it, and I am certain that one with any strength of character can do much at least to prevent the deeper rooting of a fixed idea." But as he spoke thus to her, in his own soul he was as one fighting the demons off with a fan. "Tell me what the mighty matter is," he went on, "that I may swear to you I love you the more for the worst weakness you have to confess."

"Ah, my love!" returned Juliet, "how like you are now to the Paul I have dreamed of so often! But you will not be able to forgive me. I have read somewhere that men never forgive—that their honor is before their wives with them. Paul! if you should not be able to forgive me, you must help me to die, and not be cruel to me."

"Juliet, I will not listen to any more such foolish words. Either tell me plainly what you mean, that I may convince you what a goose you are, or be quiet and go to sleep again."

"*Can* it be that after all it does not signify so much?" she said aloud, but only to herself, meditating in the light of a little glow-worm of hope. "Oh if it could be so! And what is it really so much? I have not murdered any body! —I *will* tell you, Paul!"

She drew his head closer down, laid her lips to his ear, gave a great gasp, and whispered two or three words.

He started up, sundering at once the bonds of her clasped hands, cast one brief stare at her, turned, walked, with a great quick stride to his dressing-room, entered, and closed the door.

As if with one rush of a fell wind, they were ages, deserts, empty star-spaces apart! She was outside the universe, in the cold frenzy of infinite loneliness. The wolves of despair were howling in her. But Paul was in the next room! There was only the door between them! She sprung from her bed and ran to a closet. The next moment she appeared in her husband's dressing-room.

Paul sat sunk together in his chair, his head hanging forward, his teeth set, his whole shape, in limb and feature, carrying the show of profound, of irrecoverable injury. He started to his feet when she entered. She did not once lift her eyes to his face, but sunk on her knees before him, hurriedly slipped her night-gown from her shoulders to her waist, and over her head, bent toward the floor, held up to him a riding-whip.

They were baleful stars that looked down on that naked world beneath them.

To me scarce any thing is so utterly pathetic as the back. That of an animal even is full of sad suggestion. But the human back!—It is the other, the dark side of the human moon; the blind side of the being, defenseless, and exposed to every thing; the ignorant side, turned toward the abyss of its unknown origin; the unfeatured side, eyeless and dumb and helpless—the enduring animal of the marvelous commonwealth, to be given to the smiter, and to bend beneath the burden—lovely in its patience and the tender forms of its strength.

An evil word, resented by the lowest of our sisters, rushed to the man's lips, but died there in a strangled murmur.

" Paul ! " said Juliet, in a voice from whose tone it seemed as if her soul had sunk away, and was crying out of a hollow place of the earth, " take it—take it. Strike me."

He made no reply—stood utterly motionless, his teeth clenched so hard that he could not have spoken without grinding them. She waited as motionless, her face bowed to the floor, the whip held up over her head.

" Paul ! " she said again, " you saved my life once : save my soul now. Whip me and take me again."

He answered with only a strange unnatural laugh through his teeth.

" Whip me and let me die then," she said.

He spoke no word. She spoke again. Despair gave her both insight and utterance—despair and great love, and the truth of God that underlies even despair.

" You pressed me to marry you," she said : " what was I to do? How could I tell you? And I loved you so ! I persuaded myself I was safe with you—you were so generous. You would protect me from every thing, even my own past. In your name I sent it away, and would not think of it again. I said to myself you would not wish me to tell you the evil that had befallen me. I persuaded myself you loved me enough even for that. I held my peace trusting you. Oh my husband ! my Paul ! my heart is crushed. The dreadful thing has come back. I thought it was gone from me, and now it will not leave me any more. I am a horror to myself. There is no one to punish and forgive me but you. Forgive me, my husband. You are the God to whom I pray. If you pardon me I shall be content even with myself. I shall seek no other pardon; your favor is all I care for. If you take me for clean, I *am* clean for all the world. You can make me clean—you only. Do it, Paul; do it, husband. Make me clean that I may look women in the face. Do, Paul, take the whip and strike me. I long for my deserts at your hand. Do comfort me. I am waiting the sting of it, Paul, to know that you have forgiven me. If I should cry out, it will be for gladness.—Oh, my husband,"—here her voice rose to an agony of entreaty—"I was but a girl—hardly more than a child in knowledge—I did not know what I was doing. He was much older than I was, and I trusted him!—O my God! I hardly know what I knew and what I did not know: it was only when it was too late that I woke and understood. I hate myself. I scorn myself. But am I to be wretched forever because of that one fault, Paul? Will you not be my saviour and forgive me my sin? Oh, do not drive me mad. I am only clinging to my reason. Whip me and I shall be well. Take me again, Paul. I will not, if you like, even fancy myself your wife any more. I will be your slave. You shall do with me whatever you will. I will obey you to the very letter. Oh beat me and let me go."

She sunk prone on the floor, and clasped and kissed his feet.

He took the whip from her hand.

Of course a man can not strike a woman! He may tread her in the mire; he may clasp her and then scorn her; he may kiss her close, and then dash her from him into a dung-heap, but he must not strike her—that would be unmanly! Oh! grace itself is the rage of the pitiful Othello to the forbearance of many a self-contained, cold-blooded, self-careful slave, that thinks himself a gentleman! Had not Faber been even then full of his own precious self, had he yielded to her prayer or to his own wrath, how many hours of agony would have been saved them both!—"What! would you have had him really strike her?" I would have had him do *any thing* rather than choose himself and reject his wife: make of it what you will. Had he struck once, had he seen the purple streak rise in the snow, that instant his pride-frozen heart would have melted into a torrent of grief ; he would have flung himself on the floor beside her, and in an agony of pity over her and horror at his own sacrilege, would have clasped her to his bosom, and baptized her in the tears of remorse and repentance ; from that moment they would have been married indeed.

When she felt him take the whip, the poor lady's heart gave a great heave of hope ; then her flesh quivered with fear. She closed her teeth hard, to welcome the blow without a cry. Would he give her many stripes? Then the last should be welcome as the first. Would it spoil her skin? What matter if it was his own hand that did it !

A brief delay—long to her ! then the hiss, as it seemed, of the coming blow ! But instead of the pang she awaited, the sharp ring of breaking glass followed : he had thrown the whip through the window into the garden. The same moment he dragged his feet rudely from her embrace, and left the room. The devil and the gentleman had conquered. He had spared her, not in love, but in scorn. She gave one great cry of utter loss, and lay senseless.

CHAPTER XXXIV.

THE BOTTOMLESS POOL.

She came to herself in the gray dawn. She was cold as ice —cold to the very heart, but she did not feel the cold: there was nothing in her to compare it against ; her very being was frozen. The man who had given her life had thrown her from him. He cared less for her than for the tortured dog. She was an outcast, defiled and miserable. Alas ! alas ! this was what came of speaking the truth—of making confession ! The cruel scripture had wrought its own fulfillment, made a mock of her, and ruined her husband's peace. She knew poor Paul would never be himself again! She had carried the snake so long harmless in her bosom only to let it at last creep from her lips into her husband's ear, sting the vital core of her universe, and blast it forever ! How foolish she had been !—What was left her to do ? What would her husband have her to do ? Oh misery ! he cared no more what she did or did not do. She was alone—utterly alone ! But she need not live.

Dimly, vaguely, the vapor of such thoughts as these passed through her despairing soul, as she lifted herself from the floor and tottered back to her room. Yet even then, in the very midst of her freezing misery, there was, although she had not yet begun to recognize it, a nascent comfort in that she had spoken and confessed. She would not really have taken back her confession. And although the torture was greater, yet was it more endurable than that she had been suffering before. She had told him who had a right to know.—But, alas! what a deception was that dream of the trumpet and the voice! A poor trick to entrap a helpless sinner!

Slowly, with benumbed fingers and trembling hands, she dressed herself : that bed she would lie in no more, for she had wronged her husband. Whether before or after he was her husband, mattered nothing. To have ever called him husband was the wrong. She had seemed that she was not, else he would never have loved or sought her ; she had outraged his dignity, defiled him ; he had cast her off, and she could not, would not blame him. Happily for her endurance of her misery, she did not turn upon her idol and cast him from his pedestal ; she did not fix her gaze upon his failure instead of her own ; she did not espy the contemptible in his conduct, and revolt from her allegiance.

But was such a man then altogether the ideal of a woman's soul? Was he a fit champion of humanity who would aid only within the limits of his pride? who, when a despairing creature cried in soul-agony for help, thought first and only of his own honor? The notion men call their honor is the shadow of righteousness, the shape that is where the light is not, the devil that dresses as nearly in angel-fashion as he can, but is none the less for that a sneak and a coward.

She put on her cloak and bonnet : the house was his, not hers. He and she had never been one : she must go and meet her fate. There was one power, at least, the key to the great door of liberty, which the weakest as well as the strongest possessed : she could die. Ah, how welcome would Death be now ! Did he ever know or heed the right time to come, without being sent for—without being compelled? In the meantime her only anxiety was to get out of the house : away from Paul she would understand more precisely what she had to do. With the feeling of his angry presence, she could not think. Yet how she loved him—

strong in his virtue and indignation ! She had not yet begun to pity herself, or to allow to her heart that he was hard upon her.

She was leaving the room when a glitter on her hand caught her eye : the old diamond disk, which he had bought of her in her trouble, and restored to her on her wedding-day, was answering the herald of the sunrise. She drew it off : he must have it again. With it she drew off also her wedding-ring. Together she laid them on the dressing table, turned again, and with noiseless foot and desert heart went through the house, opened the door, and stole into the street. A thin mist was waiting for her. A lean cat, gray as the mist, stood on the steps of the door opposite. No other living thing was to be seen. The air was chill. The autumn rains were at hand. But her heart was the only desolation.

Already she knew where she was going. In the street she turned to the left.

Shortly before, she had gone with Dorothy, for the first time, to see the Old House, and there had had rather a narrow escape. Walking down the garden they came to the pond or small lake, so well known to the children of Glaston as bottomless. Two stone steps led from the end of the principal walk down to the water, which was, at the time, nearly level with the top of the second. On the upper step Juliet was standing, not without fear, gazing into the gulf, which was yet far deeper than she imagined, when, without the smallest preindication, the lower step suddenly sank. Juliet sprung back to the walk, but turned instantly to look again. She saw the stone sinking, and her eyes opened wider and wider, as it swelled and thinned to a great, dull, wavering mass, grew dimmer and dimmer, then melted away and vanished utterly. With "stricken look," and fright-filled eyes, she turned to Dorothy, who was a little behind her, and said,

"How will you be able to sleep at night? I should be always fancying myself sliding down into it through the darkness."

To this place of terror she was now on the road. When consciousness returned to her as she lay on the floor of her husband's dressing-room, it brought with it first the awful pool and the sinking stone. She seemed to stand watching it sink, lazily settling with a swing this way and a sway that, into the bosom of the earth, down and down, and still

down.   Nor did the vision leave her as she came more to
herself.   Even when her mental eyes were . at length quite
open to the far more frightful verities of her condition, half
of her consciousness was still watching the ever sinking
stone ; until at last she seemed to understand that it was
showing her a door out of her misery, one easy to open.

She went the same way into the park that Dorothy had
then taken her—through a little door of privilege which she
had shown her how to open, and not by the lodge.   The
light was growing fast, but the sun was not yet up.   With
feeble steps but feverous haste she hurried over the grass.
Her feet were wet through her thin shoes.   Her dress was
fringed with dew.   But there was no need for taking care
of herself now ; she felt herself already beyond the reach of
sickness.   The still pond would soon wash off the dew.

Suddenly, with a tremor of waking hope, came the thought
that, when she was gone from his sight, the heart of her
husband would perhaps turn again toward her a little.   For
would he not then be avenged ? would not his justice be
satisfied ?   She had been well drilled in the theological lie,
that punishment is the satisfaction of justice.

" Oh, now I thank you, Paul ! " she said, as she hastened
along.   " You taught me the darkness, and made me brave
to seek its refuge.   Think of me sometimes, Paul.   I will
come back to you if I can—but no, there is no coming
back, no greeting more, no shadows even to mingle their
loves, for in a dream there is but one that dreams.   I shall
be the one that does not dream.   There is nothing where I
am going—not even the darkness—nothing but nothing.
Ah, would I were in it now !   Let me make haste.   All
will be one, for all will be none when I am there.   Make you
haste too, and come into the darkness, Paul.   It is soothing and soft and cool.   It will wash away the sin of the
girl and leave you a — — nothing."

While she was hurrying toward the awful pool, her husband sat in his study, sunk in a cold fury of conscious disgrace—not because of his cruelty, not because he had cast a
woman into hell—but because his honor, his self-satisfaction in his own fate, was thrown to the worms.   Did he fail
thus in consequence of having rejected the common belief ?
No ; something far above the *common* belief it must be,
that would have enabled him to act otherwise.   But had he
known the Man of the gospel, he could not have left her.
He would have taken her to his sorrowful bosom, wept with

her, forgotten himself in pitiful grief over the spot upon her whiteness; he would have washed her clean with love and husband-power. He would have welcomed his shame as his hold of her burden, whereby to lift it, with all its misery and loss, from her heart forever. Had Faber done so as he was, he would have come close up to the gate of the kingdom of Heaven, for he would have been like-minded with Him who sought not His own. His honor, for-sooth! Pride is a mighty honor! His pride was great indeed, but it was not grand! Nothing reflected, nothing whose object is self, has in it the poorest element of grandeur. Our selves are ours that we may lay them on the altar of love. Lying there, bound and bleeding and burn-ing if need be, they are grand indeed—for they are in their noble place, and rejoicing in their fate. But this man was miserable, because, the possessor of a priceless jewel, he had found it was not such as would pass for flawless in the judgment of men—judges themselves unjust, whose very hearts were full of bribes. He sat there an injured hus-band, a wronged, woman-cheated, mocked man—he in whose eyes even a smutch on her face would have lowered a woman—who would not have listened to an angel with a broken wing-feather!

Let me not be supposed to make a little of Juliet's loss! What that amounted to, let Juliet feel!—let any woman say, who loves a man, and would be what that man thinks her! But I read, and think I understand, the words of the per-fect Purity: "Neither do I condemn thee: go and sin no more."

CHAPTER XXXV.

A HEART.

If people were both observant and memorious, they would cease, I fancy, to be astonished at coincidences. Rightly regarded, the universe is but one coincidence—only where will has to be developed, there is need for human play, and room for that must be provided in its spaces. The works of God being from the beginning, and all his beginnings invisible either from greatness or smallness or nearness or remoteness, numberless coincidences may pass in every man's history, before he becomes capable of know-ing either the need or the good of them, or even of noting them.

The same morning there was another awake and up early. When Juliet was about half-way across the park, hurrying to the water, Dorothy was opening the door of the empty house, seeking solitude that she might find the one Dweller therein. She went straight to one of the upper rooms look-ing out upon the garden, and kneeling prayed to her Unknown God. As she knelt, the first rays of the sunrise visited her face. That face was in itself such an embodied prayer, that had any one seen it, he might, when the beams fell upon it, have imagined he saw prayer and answer meet. It was another sunrise Dorothy was looking for, but she started and smiled when the warm rays touched her; they too came from the home of answers. As the daisy mimics the sun, so is the central fire of our system but a flower that blossoms in the eternal effulgence of the unapproachable light.

The God to whom we pray is nearer to us than the very prayer itself ere it leaves the heart; hence His answers may well come to us through the channel of our own thoughts. But the world too being itself one of His thoughts, He may also well make the least likely of His creatures an angel of His own will to us. Even the blind, if God be with him, that is, if he knows he is blind and does not think he sees, may become a leader of the blind up to the narrow gate. It is the blind who says *I see*, that leads his fellow into the ditch.

The window near which Dorothy kneeled, and toward which in the instinct for light she had turned her face, looked straight down the garden, at the foot of which the greater part of the circumference of the pond was visible. But Dorothy, busy with her prayers, or rather with a weight of hunger and thirst, from which like a burst of lightning skyward from the overcharged earth, a prayer would now and then break and rush heavenward, saw nothing of the outer world: between her and a sister soul in mortal agony, hung the curtains of her eyelids. But there were no shutters to her ears, and in at their portals all of a sudden darted a great and bitter cry, as from a heart in the gripe of a fierce terror. She had been so absorbed, and it so startled and shook her, that she never could feel certain whether the cry she heard was of this world or not. Half-asleep one hears

such a cry, and can not tell whether it entered his consciousness by the ear, or through some hidden channel of
the soul. Assured that waking ears heard nothing, he
remains, it may be, in equal doubt, whether it came from
the other side of life or was the mere cry of a dream.
Before Dorothy was aware of a movement of her will, she
was on her feet, and staring from the window. Something
was lying on the grass beyond the garden wall, close to the
pond : it looked like a woman. She darted from the house,
out of the garden, and down the other side of the wall.
When she came nearer she saw it was indeed a woman,
evidently insensible. She was bare-headed. Her bonnet was
floating in the pond; the wind had blown it almost to the middle of it. Her face was turned toward the water. One hand
was in it. The bank overhung the pond, and with a single
movement more she would probably have been beyond help
from Dorothy. She caught her by the arm, and dragged
her from the brink, before ever she looked in her face.
Then to her amazement she saw it was Juliet. She opened
her eyes, and it was as if a lost soul looked out of them
upon Dorothy—a being to whom the world was nothing, so
occupied was it with some torment, which alone measured
its existence—far away, although it hung attached to the
world by a single hook of brain and nerve.

" Juliet, my darling ! " said Dorothy, her voice trembling
with the love which only souls that know trouble can feel for
the troubled, " come with me. I will take care of you."

At the sound of her voice, Juliet shuddered. Then a better
light came into her eyes, and feebly she endeavored to get
up. With Dorothy's help she succeeded, but stood as if
ready to sink again to the earth. She drew her cloak about
her, turned and stared at the water, turned again and stared
at Dorothy, at last threw herself into her arms, and sobbed
and wailed. For a few moments Dorothy held her in a close
embrace. Then she sought to lead her to the house, and
Juliet yielded at once. She took her into one of the lower
rooms, and got her some water—it was all she could get for
her, and made her sit down on the window-seat. It seemed
a measureless time before she made the least attempt to
speak ; and again and again when she began to try, she
failed. She opened her mouth, but no sounds would come.
At length, interrupted with choking gasps, low cries of despair, and long intervals of sobbing, she said something like
this :

"I was going to drown myself. When I came in sight of the water, I fell down in a half kind of faint. All the time I lay, I felt as if some one was dragging me nearer and nearer to the pool. Then something came and drew me back—and it was you, Dorothy. But you ought to have left me. I am a wretch. There is no room for me in this world any more." She stopped a moment, then fixing wide eyes on Dorothy's, said, "Oh Dorothy, dear! there are awful things in the world! as awful as any you ever read in a book!"

"I know that, dear. But oh! I am sorry if any of them have come your way. Tell me what is the matter. I *will* help you if I can."

"I dare not; I dare not! I should go raving mad if I said a word about it."

"Then don't tell me, my dear. Come with me up stairs; there is a warmer room there—full of sunshine; you are nearly dead with cold. I came here this morning, Juliet, to be alone and pray to God; and see what He has sent me! You, dear! Come up stairs. Why, you are quite wet! You will get your death of cold!"

"Then it would be all right. I would rather not kill myself if I could die without. But it must be somehow."

"We'll talk about it afterward. Come now."

With Dorothy's arm round her waist, Juliet climbed trembling to the warmer room. On a rickety wooden chair, Dorothy made her sit in the sunshine, while she went and gathered chips and shavings and bits of wood left by the workmen. With these she soon kindled a fire in the rusty grate. Then she took off Juliet's shoes and stockings, and put her own upon her. She made no resistance, only her eyes followed Dorothy's bare feet going to and fro, as if she felt something was wrong, and had not strength to inquire into it.

But Dorothy's heart rebuked her for its own lightness. It had not been so light for many a day. It seemed as if God was letting her know that He was there. She spread her cloak on a sunny spot of the floor, made Juliet lie down upon it, put a bundle of shavings under her head, covered her with her own cloak, which she had dried at the fire, and was leaving the room

"Where are you going, Dorothy?" cried Juliet, seeming all at once to wake up.

"I am going to fetch your husband, dear," answered Dorothy.

She gave a great cry, rose to her knees, and clasped Dorothy round hers.

"No, no, no!" she screamed. "You shall not. If you do, I swear I will run straight to the pond."

Notwithstanding the wildness of her voice and look, there was an evident determination in both.

"I will do nothing you don't like, dear," said Dorothy. "I thought that was the best thing I could do for you."

"No! no! no! any thing but that!"

"Then of course I won't. But I must go and get you something to eat."

"I could not swallow a mouthful; it would choke me. And where would be the good of it, when life is over!"

"Don't talk like that, dear. Life can't be over till it is taken from us."

"Ah, you would see it just as I do, if you knew all!"

"Tell me all, then."

"Where is the use, when there is no help?"

"No help!" echoed Dorothy.—The words she had so often uttered in her own heart, coming from the lips of another, carried in them an incredible contradiction.—Could God make or the world breed the irreparable?—"Juliet," she went on, after a little pause, "I have often said the same myself, but——"

"You!" interrupted Juliet; "you who always professed to believe!"

Dorothy's ear could not distinguish whether the tone was of indignation or of bitterness.

"You never heard me, Juliet," she answered, "profess any thing. If my surroundings did so for me, I could not help that. I never dared say I believed any thing. But I hope—and, perhaps," she went on with a smile, "seeing Hope is own sister to Faith, she may bring me to know her too some day. Paul says——"

Dorothy had been brought up a dissenter, and never said *St.* this one or that, any more than the Christians of the New Testament.

At the sound of the name, Juliet burst into tears, the first she shed, for the word *Paul*, like the head of the javelin torn from the wound, brought the whole fountain after it. She cast herself down again, and lay and wept. Dorothy kneeled beside her, and laid a hand on her shoulder. It was the only way she could reach her at all.

"You see," she said at last, for the weeping went on and

on, "there is nothing will do you any good but your husband."

"No, no; he has cast me from him forever!" she cried, in a strange wail that rose to a shriek.

"The wretch!" exclaimed Dorothy, clenching a fist whose little bones looked fierce through the whitened skin.

"No," returned Juliet, suddenly calmed, in a voice almost severe; "it is I who am the wretch, to give you a moment in which to blame him. He has done nothing but what is right."

"I don't believe it."

"I deserved it."

"I am sure you did not. I would believe a thousand things against him before I would believe one against you, my poor white queen!" cried Dorothy, kissing her hand.

She snatched it away, and covered her face with both hands.

"I should only need to tell you one thing to convince you," she sobbed from behind them.

"Then tell it me, that I may not be unjust to him."

"I can not."

"I won't take your word against yourself," returned Dorothy determinedly. "You will have to tell me, or leave me to think the worst of him." She was moved by no vulgar curiosity: how is one to help without knowing? "Tell me, my dear," she went on after a little; "tell me all about it, and in the name of the God in whom I hope to believe, I promise to give myself to your service."

Thus adjured, Juliet found herself compelled. But with what heart-tearing groans and sobs, with what intervals of dumbness, in which the truth seemed unutterable for despair and shame, followed by what hurrying of wild confession, as if she would cast it from her, the sad tale found its way into Dorothy's aching heart, I will not attempt to describe. It is enough that at last it was told, and that it had entered at the wide-open, eternal doors of sympathy. If Juliet had lost a husband, she had gained a friend, and that was something—indeed no little thing—for in her kind the friend was more complete than the husband. She was truer, more entire—in friendship nearly perfect. When a final burst of tears had ended the story of loss and despair, a silence fell.

"Oh, those men! those men!" said Dorothy, in a low voice of bitterness, as if she knew them and their ways well, though never had kiss of man save her father lighted on her cheek. "—My poor darling!" she said after another pause, "—and he cast you from him!—I suppose a woman's heart," she went on after a third pause, "can never make up for the loss of a man's, but here is mine for you to go into the very middle of, and lie down there."

Juliet had, as she told her story, risen to her knees. Dorothy was on hers too, and as she spoke she opened wide her arms, and clasped the despised wife to her bosom. None but the arms of her husband, Juliet believed, could make her alive with forgiveness, yet she felt a strange comfort in that embrace. It wrought upon her as if she had heard a far-off whisper of the words: *Thy sins be forgiven thee*. And no wonder: there was the bosom of one of the Lord's clean ones for her to rest upon! It was her first lesson in the mighty truth that sin of all things is mortal, and purity alone can live for evermore.

CHAPTER XXXVI.

TWO MORE MINDS.

NOTHING makes a man strong like a call upon him for help—a fact which points at a unity more delicate and close and profound than heart has yet perceived. It is but " a modern instance" how a mother, if she be but a hen, becomes bold as a tigress for her periled offspring. A stranger will fight for the stranger who puts his trust in him. The most foolish of men will search his musty brain to find wise saws for his boy. An anxious man, going to his friend to borrow, may return having lent him instead. The man who has found nothing yet in the world save food for the hard, sharp, clear intellect, will yet cast an eye around the universe to see if perchance there may not be a God somewhere for the hungering heart of his friend. The poor, but lovely, the doubting, yet living faith of Dorothy arose, stretched out its crippled wings, and began to arrange and straighten their disordered feathers. It is a fair sight, any creature, be it but a fly, dressing its wings! Dorothy's were feeble, ruffled, their pen-feathers bent and a little crushed ; but Juliet's were full of mud, paralyzed with disuse, and grievously singed in the smoldering fire of her secret. A butterfly that has burned its wings is not very unlike a caterpillar again.

"Look here, Juliet," said Dorothy : "there must be some way out of it, or there is no saving God in the universe.— Now don't begin to say there isn't, because, you see, it is your only chance. It would be a pity to make a fool of yourself by being over-wise, to lose every thing by taking it for granted there is no God. If after all there should be one, it would be the saddest thing to perish for want of Him. I won't say I am as miserable as you, for I haven't a husband to trample on my heart ; but I am miserable enough, and want dreadfully to be saved. I don't call this life worth living. Nothing is right, nothing goes well— there is no harmony in me. I don't call it life at all. I want music and light in me. I want a God to save me out of this wretchedness. I want health."

"I thought you were never ill, Dorothy," murmured Juliet listlessly.

"Is it possible you do not know what I mean ? " returned Dorothy. "Do you never feel wretched and sick in your very soul ?—disgusted with yourself, and longing to be lifted up out of yourself into a region of higher conditions altogether ? "

That kind of thing Juliet had been learning to attribute to the state of her health—had partly learned : it is hard to learn any thing false *thoroughly*, for it *can not* so be learned. It is true that it is often, perhaps it is generally, in troubled health, that such thoughts come first ; but in nature there are facts of color that the cloudy day reveals. So sure am I that many things which illness has led me to see are true, that I would endlessly rather never be well than lose sight of them. "So would any madman say of his fixed idea." I will keep my madness, then, for therein most do I desire the noble : and to desire what I desire, if it be but to desire, is better than to have all you offer us in the name of truth. Through such desire and the hope of its attainment, all greatest things have been wrought in the earth : I too have my unbelief as well as you—I can not believe that a lie on the belief of which has depended our highest development. You may say you have a higher to bring in. But that higher you have become capable of by the precedent lie. Yet you vaunt truth ! You would sink us low indeed, making out falsehood our best nourishment—at some period of our history at least. If, however, what I call true and high, you call false and low—my assertion that you have never seen that of which I so speak will not help—then is there nothing left us but to part, each go his own road, and wait the end—which according to my expectation will show the truth, according to yours, being nothing, will show nothing.

"I can not help thinking, if we could only get up there," Dorothy went on, —"I mean into a life of which I can at least dream—if I could but get my head and heart into the kingdom of Heaven, I should find that everything else would come right. I believe it is God Himself I want—nothing will do but Himself in me. Mr. Wingfold says that we find things all wrong about us, that they keep going against our will and our liking, just to drive things right inside us, or at least to drive us where we can get them put right; and that, as soon as their work is done, the waves will lie down at our feet, or if not, we shall at least walk over their crests."

"It sounds very nice, and would comfort any body that wasn't in trouble," said Juliet; "but you wouldn't care one bit for it all any more than I do, if you had pain and love like mine pulling at your heart."

"I have seen a mother make sad faces enough over the baby at her breast," said Dorothy. "Love and pain seem so strangely one in this world, the wonder is how they will ever get parted. What God must feel like, with this world hanging on to Him with all its pains and cries——!"

"It's His own fault," said Juliet bitterly. "Why did He make us—or why did He not make us good? I'm sure I don't know where was the use of making me!"

"Perhaps not much yet," replied Dorothy, "but then He hasn't made you, He hasn't done with you yet. He is making you now, and you don't like it."

"No, I don't—if you call this making. Why does He do it? He could have avoided all this trouble by leaving us alone."

"I put something like the same question once to Mr. Wingfold," said Dorothy, "and he told me it was impossible to show any one the truths of the kingdom of Heaven; he must learn them for himself. 'I can do little more,' he said, 'than give you my testimony that it seems to me all right. If God has not made you good, He has made you with the feeling that you ought to be good, and at least a half-conviction that to Him you have to go for help to become good. When you are good, then you will know why

He did not make you good at first, and will be perfectly
satisfied with the reason, because you will find it good and
just and right—so good that it was altogether beyond the
understanding of one who was not good. I don't think,' he
said, 'you will ever get a thoroughly satisfactory answer to
any question till you go to Himself for it—and then it may
take years to make you fit to receive, that is to understand
the answer.' Oh Juliet! sometimes I have felt in my heart
as if—I am afraid to say it, even to you,——"

"*I* shan't be shocked at any thing; I am long past that,"
sighed Juliet.

"It is not of you I am afraid," said Dorothy. "It is a
kind of awe of the universe I feel. But God is the universe; His is the only ear that will hear me; and He knows
my thoughts already. Juliet, I feel sometimes as if I *must*
be good for God's sake; as if I was sorry for Him, because
He has such a troublesome nursery of children, that will not
or can not understand Him, and will not do what He tells
them, and He all the time doing the very best for them He
can."

"It may be all very true, or all great nonsense, Dorothy,
dear; I don't care a bit about it. All I care for is—I don't
know what I care for—I don't care for any thing any more
—there is nothing left to care for. I love my husband with
a heart like to break—oh, how I wish it would! He hates
and despises me and I dare not wish that he wouldn't. If
he were to forgive me quite, I should yet feel that he ought
to despise me, and that would be all the same as if he did,
and there is no help. Oh, how horrid I look to him! I
can't bear it. I fancied it was all gone; but there it is, and
there it must be forever. I don't care about a God. If
there were a God, what would He be to me without my
Paul?"

"I think, Juliet, you will yet come to say, 'What would
my Paul be to me without my God?' I suspect we have no
more idea than that lonely fly on the window there, what it
would be *to have a God*."

"I don't care. I would rather go to hell with my Paul
than go to Heaven without him," moaned Juliet.

"But what if God should be the only where to find your
Paul?" said Dorothy. "What if the gulf that parts you is
just the gulf of a God not believed in—a universe which
neither of you can cross to meet the other—just because you
do not believe it is there at all?"

Juliet made no answer—Dorothy could not tell whether from feeling or from indifference. The fact was, the words conveyed no more meaning to Juliet than they will to some of my readers. Why do I write them then? Because there are some who will understand them at once, and others who will grow to understand them. Dorothy was astonished to find herself saying them. The demands of her new office of comforter gave shape to many half-formed thoughts, substance to many shadowy perceptions, something like music to not a few dim feelings moving within her; but what she said hardly seemed her own at all.

Had it not been for Wingfold's help, Dorothy might not have learned these things in this world; but had it not been for Juliet, they would have taken years more to blossom in her being, and so become her own. Her faint hope seemed now to break forth suddenly into power. Whether or not she was saying such things as were within the scope of Juliet's apprehension, was a matter of comparatively little moment. As she lay there in misery, rocking herself from side to side on the floor, she would have taken hold of nothing. But love is the first comforter, and where love and truth speak, the love will be felt where the truth is never perceived. Love indeed is the highest in all truth; and the pressure of a hand, a kiss, the caress of a child, will do more to save sometimes than the wisest argument, even rightly understood. Love alone is wisdom, love alone is power; and where love seems to fail it is where self has stepped between and dulled the potency of its rays.

Dorothy thought of another line of expostulation.

"Juliet," she said, "suppose you were to drown yourself and your husband were to repent?"

"That is the only hope left me. You see yourself I have no choice."

"You have no pity, it seems; for what then would become of him? What if he should come to himself in bitter sorrow, in wild longing for your forgiveness, but you had taken your forgiveness with you, where he had no hope of ever finding it? Do you want to punish him? to make him as miserable as yourself? to add immeasurably to the wrong you have done him, by going where no word, no message, no letter can pass, no cry can cross? No, Juliet—death can set nothing right. But if there be a God, then nothing can go wrong but He can set it right, and set it right better than it was before."

" He could not make it better than it was."

" What !—is that your ideal of love—a love that fails in the first trial ? If He could not better that, then indeed He were no God worth the name."

" Why then did He make us such—make such a world as is always going wrong ? "

" Mr. Wingfold says it is always going righter the same time it is going wrong. I grant He would have had no right to make a world that might go further wrong than He could set right at His own cost. But if at His own cost He turn its ills into goods ? its ugliness into favor ? Ah, if it should be so, Juliet ! It *may* be so. I do not know. I have not found Him yet. Help me to find Him. Let us seek Him together. If you find Him you can not lose your husband. If Love is Lord of the world, love must yet be Lord in his heart. It will wake, if not sooner, yet when the bitterness has worn itself out, as Mr. Wingfold says all evil must, because its heart is death and not life."

" I don't care a straw for life. If I could but find my husband, I would gladly die forever in his arms. It is not true that the soul longs for immortality. I don't. I long only for love—for forgiveness—for my husband."

" But would you die so long as there was the poorest chance of regaining your place in his heart ? "

" No. Give me the feeblest chance of that, and I will live. I could live forever on the mere hope of it."

" I can't give you any hope, but I have hope of it in my own heart."

Juliet rose on her elbow.

" But I am disgraced ! " she said, almost indignantly. " It would be disgrace to him to take me again ! I remember one of the officers' wives——. No, no ! he hates and despises me. Besides I could never look one of his friends in the face again. Every body will say I ran away with some one—or that he sent me away because I was wicked. You all had a prejudice against me from the very first."

" Yes, in a way," confessed Dorothy. " It always seemed as if we did not know you and could not get at you, as if you avoided us—with your heart, I mean ;—as if you had resolved we should not know you—as if you had something you were afraid we should discover."

" Ah, there it was, you see ! " cried Juliet. " And now the hidden thing is revealed ! That was it : I never could get rid of the secret that was gnawing at my life. Even when I was hardly aware of it, it was there. Oh, if I had only been ugly, then Paul would never have thought of me ! "

She threw herself down again and buried her face.

"Hide me ; hide me," she went on, lifting to Dorothy her hands clasped in an agony, while her face continued turned from her. "Let me stay here. Let me die in peace. Nobody would ever think I was here."

"That is just what has been coming and going in my mind," answered Dorothy. "It is a strange old place : you might be here for months and nobody know."

"Oh ! wouldn't you mind it ? I shouldn't live long. I couldn't, you know ! "

"I will be your very sister, if you will let me," replied Dorothy ; "only then you must do what I tell you—and begin at once by promising not to leave the house till I come back to you."

As she spoke she rose.

"But some one will come," said Juliet, half-rising, as if she would run after her.

"No one will. But if any one should—come here, I will show you a place where nobody would find you."

She helped her to rise, and led her from the room to a door in a rather dark passage. This she opened, and, striking a light, showed an ordinary closet, with pegs for hanging garments upon. The sides of it were paneled, and in one of them, not readily distinguishable, was another door. It opened into a room lighted only by a little window high up in a wall, through whose dusty, cobwebbed panes, crept a modicum of second-hand light from a stair.

"There ! " said Dorothy. " If you should hear any sound before I come back, run in here. See what a bolt there is to the door. Mind you shut both. You can close that shutter over the window too if you like—only nobody can look in at it without getting a ladder, and there isn't one about the place. I don't believe any one knows of this room but myself."

Juliet was too miserable to be frightened at the look of it—which was wretched enough. She promised not to leave the house, and Dorothy went. Many times before she returned had Juliet fled from the sounds of imagined approach, and taken refuge in the musty dusk of the room withdrawn. When at last Dorothy came, she found her in it trembling.

She came, bringing a basket with every thing needful for breakfast. She had not told her father any thing : he was too simple, she said to herself, to keep a secret with comfort ; and she would risk any thing rather than discovery while yet she did not clearly know what ought to be done. Her version of the excellent French proverb—*Dans le doute, abstiens-toi*—was, *When you are not sure, wait*—which goes a little further, inasmuch as it indicates expectation, and may imply faith. With difficulty she prevailed upon her to take some tea, and a little bread and butter, feeding her like a child, and trying to comfort her with hope. Juliet sat on the floor, leaning against the wall, the very picture of despair, white like alabaster, rather than marble—with a bluish whiteness. Her look was of one utterly lost.

"We'll let the fire out now," said Dorothy ; "for the sun is shining in warm, and there had better be no smoke. The wood is rather scarce too. I will get you some more, and here are matches : you can light it again when you please."

She then made her a bed on the floor with a quantity of wood shavings, and some shawls she had brought, and when she had lain down upon it, kneeled beside her, and covering her face with her hands, tried to pray. But it seemed as if all the misery of humanity was laid upon her, and God would not speak : not a sound would come from her throat, till she burst into tears and sobs. It struck a strange chord in the soul of the wife to hear the maiden weeping over her. But it was no private trouble, it was the great need common to all men that opened the fountain of her tears. It was hunger after the light that slays the darkness, after a comfort to confront every woe, a life to lift above death, an antidote to all wrong. It was one of the groanings of the spirit that can not be uttered in words articulate, or even formed into thoughts defined. But Juliet was filled only with the thought of herself and her husband, and the tears of her friend but bedewed the leaves of her bitterness, did not reach the dry roots of her misery.

Dorothy's spirit revived when she found herself once more alone in the park on her way home the second time. She must be of better courage, she said to herself. Struggling in the Slough of Despond, she had come upon one worse mired than she, for whose sake she must search yet more vigorously after the hidden stepping-stones—the peaks whose bases are the center of the world.

"God help me!" she said ever and anon as she went, and every time she said it, she quickened her pace and ran.

It was just breakfast-time when she reached the house. Her father was coming down the stair.

"Would you mind, father," she said as they sat, "if I were to make a room at the Old House a little comfortable?"

"I mind nothing you please to do, Dorothy," he answered. "But you must not become a recluse. In your search for God, you must not forsake your neighbor."

"If only I could find my neighbor!" she returned, with a rather sad smile. "I shall never be able even to look for him, I think, till I have found One nearer first."

"You have surely found your neighbor when you have found his wounds, and your hand is on the oil-flask," said her father, who knew her indefatigable in her ministrations.

"I don't feel it so," she answered. "When I am doing things for people, my arms seem to be miles long."

As soon as her father left the table, she got her basket again, filled it from the larder and store-room, laid a book or two on the top, and telling Lisbeth she was going to the Old House for the rest of the day, set out on her third journey thither. To her delight she found Juliet fast asleep. She sat down, rather tired, and began to reflect. Her great fear was that Juliet would fall ill, and then what was to be done? How was she to take the responsibility of nursing her? But she remembered how the Lord had said she was to take no thought for the morrow; and therewith she began to understand the word. She saw that one can not *do* any thing in to-morrow, and that all care which can not be put into the work of to-day, is taken out of it. One thing seemed clear—that, so long as it was Juliet's desire to remain concealed from her husband, she had no right to act against that desire. Whether Juliet was right or wrong, a sense of security was for the present absolutely necessary to quiet her mind. It seemed therefore, the first thing she had to do was to make that concealed room habitable for her. It was dreadful to think of her being there alone at night, but her trouble was too great to leave much room for fear—and anyhow there was no choice. So while Juliet slept, she set about cleaning it, and hard work she found it. Great also was the labor afterward, when, piece by piece, at night or in the early morning, she carried thither every thing necessary to make abode in it clean and warm and soft.

The labor of love is its own reward, but Dorothy received much more. For, in the fresh impulse and freedom born of this service, she soon found, not only that she thought better and more clearly on the points that troubled her, but that, thus spending herself, she grew more able to believe there must be One whose glory is perfect ministration. Also, her anxious concentration of thought upon the usurping thoughts of others, with its tendency to diseased action in the logical powers, was thereby checked, much to her relief. She was not finding an atom of what is called proof; but when the longing heart finds itself able to hope that the perfect is the fact, that the truth is alive, that the lovely is rooted in eternal purpose, it can go on without such proof as belongs to a lower stratum of things, and can not be had in these. When we rise into the mountain air, we require no other testimony than that of our lungs that we are in a healthful atmosphere. We do not find it necessary to submit it to a quantitative analysis; we are content that we breathe with joy, that we grow in strength, become lighter-hearted and better-tempered. Truth is a very different thing from fact; it is the loving contact of the soul with spiritual fact, vital and potent. It does its work in the soul independently of all faculty or qualification there for setting it forth or defending it. Truth in the inward parts is a power, not an opinion. It were as poor a matter as any held by those who deny it, if it had not its vitality in itself, if it depended upon any buttressing of other and lower material.

How should it be otherwise? If God be so near as the very idea of Him necessitates, what other availing proof of His existence can there be, than such *awareness* as must come of the developing relation between Him and us? The most satisfying of intellectual proofs, if such were to be had, would be of no value. God would be no nearer to us for them all. They would bring about no blossoming of the mighty fact. While He was in our very souls, there would yet lie between Him and us a gulf of misery, of no-knowledge.

Peace is for those who *do* the truth, not those who opine it. The true man troubled by intellectual doubt, is so troubled unto further health and growth. Let him be alive and hopeful, above all obedient, and he will be able to wait for the deeper content which must follow with completer insight. Men may say such a man but deceives himself, that there is nothing of the kind he pleases himself with imagining ; but this is at least worth reflecting upon—that while the man who aspires fears he may be deceiving himself, it is the man who does not aspire who asserts that he is. One day the former may be sure, and the latter may cease to deny, and begin to doubt.

CHAPTER XXXVII.

THE DOCTOR'S STUDY.

Paul Faber's condition, as he sat through the rest of that night in his study, was about as near absolute misery as a man's could well be, in this life, I imagine. The woman he had been watching through the first part of it as his essential bliss, he had left in a swoon, lying naked on the floor, and would not and did not go near her again. How could he ? Had he not been duped, sold, married to ―― ?―That way madness lay ! His pride was bitterly wounded. Would it had been mortally ! but pride seems in some natures to thrive upon wounds, as in others does love. Faber's pride grew and grew as he sat and brooded, or, rather, was brooded upon.

He, Paul Faber, who knew his own worth, his truth, his love, his devotion—he, with his grand ideas of woman and purity and unity, conscious of deserving a woman's best regards—he, whose love (to speak truly his unworded, undefined impression of himself) any woman might be proud to call hers—he to be thus deceived ! to have taken to his bosom one who had before taken another to hers, and thought it yet good enough for him ! It would not bear thinking ! Indignation and bitterest sense of wrong almost crazed him. For evermore he must be a hypocrite, going about with the knowledge of that concerning himself which he would not have known by others ! This was how the woman, whom he had brought back from death with the life of his own heart, had served him ! Years ago she had sacrificed her bloom to some sneaking wretch who flattered a

God with prayers, then enticed and bewitched and married *him!*

In all this thinking there was no thought but for himself —not one for the woman whose agony had been patent even to his wrath-blinded eyes. In what is the wretchedness of our condition more evident than in this, that the sense of wrong always makes us unjust? It is a most humbling thought. God help us. He forgot how she had avoided him, resisted him, refused to confess the love which his goodness, his importunities, his besieging love had compelled in her heart. It was true she ought either to have refused him absolutely and left him, or confessed and left the matter with him; but he ought to have remembered for another, if ever he had known it for himself, the hardness of some duties; and what duty could be more torturing to a delicate-minded woman than either of those—to leave the man she loved in passionate pain, sore-wounded with a sense of undeserved cruelty, or to give him the strength to send her from him by confessing to his face what she could not recall in the solitude of her own chamber but the agony would break out wet on her forehead! We do our brother, our sister, grievous wrong, every time that, in our selfish justice, we forget the excuse that mitigates the blame. That God never does, for it would be to disregard the truth. As He will never admit a false excuse, so will He never neglect a true one. It may be He makes excuses which the sinner dares not think of; while the most specious of false ones shrivel into ashes before Him. A man is bound to think of all just excuse for his offender, for less than the righteousness of God will not serve his turn.

I would not have my reader set Faber down as heartless. His life showed the contrary. But his pride was roused to such furious self-assertion, that his heart lay beaten down under the sweep of its cyclone. Its turn was only delayed. The heart is always there, and rage is not. The heart is a constant, even when most intermittent force. It can bide its time. Nor indeed did it now lie quite still; for the thought of that white, self-offered sacrifice, let him rave as he would against the stage-trickery of the scene, haunted him so, that once and again he had to rouse an evil will to restrain him from rushing to clasp her to his bosom.

Then there was the question: why now had she told him all—if indeed she had made a clean breast of it? Was it from love to him, or reviving honesty in herself? From neither, he said. Superstition alone was at the root of it. She had been to church, and the preaching of that honest idiotic enthusiast, Wingfold, had terrified her.—Alas! what refuge in her terror had she found with her husband?

Before morning he had made up his mind as to the course he would pursue. He would not publish his own shame, but neither would he leave the smallest doubt in her mind as to what he thought of her, or what he felt toward her. All should be utterly changed between them. He would behave to her with extreme, with marked politeness; he would pay her every attention woman could claim, but her friend, her husband, he would be no more. His thoughts of vengeance took many turns, some of them childish. He would always call her *Mrs. Faber*. Never, except they had friends, would he sit in the same room with her. To avoid scandal, he would dine with her, if he could not help being at home, but when he rose from the table, it would be to go to his study. If he happened at any time to be in the room with her when she rose to retire, he would light her candle, carry it up stairs for her, open the door, make her a polite bow, and leave her. Never once would he cross the threshold of her bedroom. She should have plenty of money; the purse of an adventuress was a greedy one, but he would do his best to fill it, nor once reproach her with extravagance—of which fault, let me remark, she had never yet shown a sign. He would refuse her nothing she asked of him—except it were in any way himself. As soon as his old aunt died, he would get her a brougham, but never would he sit in it by her side. Such, he thought, would be the vengeance of a gentleman. Thus he fumed and raved and trifled, in an agony of selfish suffering—a proud, injured man; and all the time the object of his vengeful indignation was lying insensible on the spot where she had prayed to him, her loving heart motionless within a bosom of ice.

In the morning he went to his dressing-room, had his bath, and went down to breakfast, half-desiring his wife's appearance, that he might begin his course of vindictive torture. He could not eat, and was just rising to go out, when the door opened, and the parlor-maid, who served also as Juliet's attendant, appeared.

"I can't find mis'ess nowhere, sir," she said.

Faber understood at once that she had left him, and a

terror, neither vague nor ill-founded, possessed itself of
him. He sprung from his seat, and darted up the stair to
her room. Little more than a glance was necessary to
assure him that she had gone deliberately, intending it
should be forever. The diamond ring lay on her dressing-
table, spending itself in flashing back the single ray of the
sun that seemed to have stolen between the curtains to find
it ; her wedding ring lay beside it, and the sparkle of the
diamonds stung his heart like a demoniacal laughter over
it, the more horrible that it was so silent and so lovely : it
was but three days since, in his wife's presence, he had been
justifying suicide with every argument he could bring to
bear. It was true he had insisted on a proper regard to
circumstances, and especially on giving due consideration
to the question, whether the act would hurt others more
than it would relieve the person contemplating it ; but,
after the way he had treated her, there could be no doubt
how Juliet, if she thought of it at all, was compelled to
answer it. He rushed to the stable, saddled Ruber, and
galloped wildly away. At the end of the street he remembered that he had not a single idea to guide him. She was
lying dead somewhere, but whether to turn east or west or
north or south to find her, he had not the slightest notion.
His condition was horrible. For a moment or two he was
ready to blow his brains out : that, if the orthodox were
right, was his only chance for over-taking her. What a
laughing-stock he would then be to them all ! The strangest,
wildest, maddest thoughts came and went as of themselves,
and when at last he found himself seated on Ruber in the
middle of the street, an hour seemed to have passed. It
was but a few moments, and the thought that roused him
was : could she have betaken herself to her old lodging at
Owlkirk ? It was not likely ; it was possible : he would ride
and see.

"They will say I murdered her," he said to himself as he
rode—so little did he expect ever to see her again. "I
don't care. They may prove it if they can, and hang me. I
shall make no defense. It will be but a fit end to the farce
of life."

He laughed aloud, struck his spurs in Ruber's flanks,
and rode wildly. He was desperate. He knew neither
what he felt nor what he desired. If he had found her
alive, he would, I do not doubt, have behaved to her cruelly.
His life had fallen in a heap about him ; he was ruined,

and she had done it, he said, he thought, he believed. He was not aware how much of his misery was occasioned by a shrinking dread of the judgments of people he despised. Had he known it, he would have been yet more miserable, for he would have scorned himself for it. There is so much in us that is beyond our reach !

Before arriving at Owlkirk, he made up his mind that, if she were not there, he would ride to the town of Broughill —not in the hope of any news of her, but because there dwelt the only professional friend he had in the neighbor-hood—one who sympathized with his view of things, and would not close his heart against him because he did not believe that this horrid, ugly, disjointed thing of a world had been made by a God of love. Generally, he had been in the habit of dwelling on the loveliness of its develop-ments, and the beauty of the gradual adaptation of life to circumstance ; but now it was plainer to him than ever, that, if made at all, it was made by an evil being ; "—for," he said, and said truly, "a conscious being without a heart must be an evil being." This was the righteous judgment of a man who could, by one tender, consoling word, have made the sun rise upon a glorious world of conscious womanhood, but would not say that word, and left that world lying in the tortured chaos of a slow disintegration. This conscious being with a heart, this Paul Faber, who saw that a God of love was the only God supposable, set his own pride so far above love, that his one idea was, to satisfy the justice of his outraged dignity by the torture of the sinner ! —even while all the time dimly aware of rebuke in his soul. If she should have destroyed herself, he said once and again as he rode, was it more than a just sacrifice to his wronged honor ? As such he would accept it. If she had, it was best—best for her, and best for him ! What so much did it matter ! She was very lovely !—true—but what was the quintessence of dust to him ? Where either was there any great loss ? He and she would soon be wrapped up in the primal darkness, the mother and grave of all things, to-gether !—no, not together ; not even in the dark of nothing-ness could they two any more lie together ! Hot tears forced their way into his eyes, whence they rolled down, the lava of the soul, scorching his cheeks. He struck his spurs into Ruber fiercely, and rode madly on.

At length he neared the outskirts of Broughill. He had ridden at a fearful pace across country, leaving all to his

horse, who had carried him wisely as well as bravely. But
Ruber, although he had years of good work left in him, was
not in his first strength, and was getting exhausted with his
wild morning. For, all the way, his master, apparently
unconscious of every thing else, had been immediately aware
of the slightest slackening of muscle under him, the least
faltering of the onward pace, and, in the temper of the savage, which wakes the moment the man of civilization is hard
put to it, the moment he flagged, still drove the cruel spurs
into his flanks, when the grand, unresenting creature would
rush forward at straining speed—not, I venture to think, so
much in obedience to the pain, as in obedience to the will of
his master, fresh recognized through the pain.

Close to the high road, where they were now approaching
it through the fields, a rail-fence had just been put up,
inclosing a piece of ground which the owner wished to let
for building. That the fact might be known, he was about
to erect a post with a great board announcing it. For this
post a man had dug the hole, and then gone to his dinner.
The inclosure lay between Faber and the road, in the direct
line he was taking. On went Ruber blindly—more blindly
than his master knew, for, with the prolonged running, he
had partially lost his sight, so that he was close to the fence
before he saw it. But he rose boldly, and cleared it—to
light, alas! on the other side with a foreleg in the hole.
Down he came with a terrible crash, pitched his master into
the road upon his head, and lay groaning with a broken leg.
Faber neither spoke nor moved, but lay as he fell. A poor
woman ran to his assistance, and finding she could do nothing for him, hurried to the town for help. His friend, who
was the first surgeon in the place, flew to the spot, and had
him carried to his house. It was a severe case of concussion of the brain.

Poor old Ruber was speedily helped to a world better
than this for horses, I trust.

Meantime Glaston was in commotion. The servants had
spread the frightful news that their mistress had vanished,
and their master ridden off like a madman. "But he won't
find her alive, poor lady! I don't think," was the general
close of their communication, accompanied by a would-be
wise and really sympathetic shake of the head. In this
conclusion most agreed, for there was a general impression
of something strange about her, partly occasioned by the
mysterious way in which Mrs. Puckridge had spoken con-

cerning her illness and the marvelous thing the doctor had done to save her life. People now supposed that she had gone suddenly mad, or, rather, that the latent madness so plain to read in those splendid eyes of hers had been suddenly developed, and that under its influence she had rushed away, and probably drowned herself. Nor were there wanting, among the discontented women of Glaston, some who regarded the event—vaguely to their own consciousness, I gladly admit—as *almost a judgment* upon Faber for marrying a woman of whom nobody knew any thing.

Hundreds went out to look for the body down the river. Many hurried to an old quarry, half full of water, on the road to Broughill, and peered horror-stricken over the edge, but said nothing. The boys of Glaston were mainly of a mind that the pond at the Old House was of all places the most likely to attract a suicide, for with the fascination of its horrors they were themselves acquainted. Thither therefore they sped ; and soon Glaston received its expected second shock in the tidings that a lady's bonnet had been found floating in the frightful pool : while in the wet mass the boys brought back with them, some of her acquaintance recognized with certainty a bonnet they had seen Mrs. Faber wear. There was no room left for doubt ; the body of the poor lady was lying at the bottom of the pool ! A multitude rushed at once to the spot, although they knew it was impossible to drag the pool, so deep was it, and for its depth so small. Neither would she ever come to the surface, they said, for the pikes and eels would soon leave nothing but the skeleton. So Glaston took the whole matter for ended, and began to settle down again to its own affairs, condoling greatly with the poor gentleman, such a favorite ! who, so young, and after such a brief experience of marriage, had lost, in such a sad way, a wife so handsome, so amiable, so clever. But some said a doctor ought to have known better than marry such a person, however handsome, and they hoped it would be a lesson to him. On the whole, so sorry for him was Glaston, that, if the doctor could then have gone about it invisible, he would have found he had more friends and fewer enemies than he had supposed.

For the first two or three days no one was surprised that he did not make his appearance. They thought he was upon some false trail. But when four days had elapsed and no news was heard of him, for his friend knew nothing of what had happened, had written to Mrs. Faber, and the letter lay unopened, some began to hint that he must have had a hand in his wife's disappearance, and to breathe a presentiment that he would never more be seen in Glaston. On the morning of the fifth day, however, his accident was known, and that he was lying insensible at the house of his friend, Dr. May ; whereupon, although here and there might be heard the expression of a pretty strong conviction as to the character of the visitation, the sympathy both felt and uttered was larger than before. The other medical men immediately divided his practice amongst them, to keep it together against his possible return, though few believed he would ever again look on scenes darkened by the memory of bliss so suddenly blasted.

For weeks his recovery was doubtful, during which time, even if they had dared, it would have been useless to attempt acquainting him with what all believed the certainty of his loss. But when at length he woke to a memory of the past, and began to desire information, his friend was compelled to answer his questions. He closed his lips, bowed his head on his breast, gave a great sigh, and held his peace. Every one saw that he was terribly stricken.

———————

CHAPTER XXXVIII.

THE MIND OF JULIET.

THERE was one, however, who, I must confess, was not a little relieved at the news of what had befallen Faber. For, although far from desiring his death, which indeed would have ruined some of her warmest hopes for Juliet, Dorothy greatly dreaded meeting him. She was a poor dissembler, hated even the shadow of a lie, and here was a fact, which, if truth could conceal it, must not be known. Her dread had been, that, the first time she saw Faber, it would be beyond her power to look innocent, that her knowledge would be legible in her face ; and much she hoped their first encounter might be in the presence of Helen or some other ignorant friend, behind whose innocent front she might shelter her conscious secrecy. To truth such a silence must feel like a culpable deception, and I do not think such a painful position can ever arise except from wrong some-where. Dorothy could not tell a lie. She could not try to tell one ; and if she had tried, she would have been instantly discovered through the enmity of her very being to the lie she told ; from her lips it would have been as transparent as the truth. It is no wonder therefore that she felt relieved when first she heard of the durance in which Faber was lying. But she felt equal to the withholding from Juliet of the knowledge of her husband's condition for the present. She judged that, seeing she had saved her friend's life, she had some right to think and choose for the preservation of that life.

Meantime she must beware of security, and cultivate caution ; and so successful was she, that weeks passed, and not a single doubt associated Dorothy with knowledge where others desired to know. Not even her father had a suspicion in the direction of the fact. She knew he would one day approve both of what she did, and of her silence concerning it. To tell him, thoroughly as he was to be trusted, would be to increase the risk ; and besides, she had no right to reveal a woman's secret to a man.

It was a great satisfaction, however, notwithstanding her dread of meeting him, to hear that Faber had at length returned to Glaston ; for if he had gone away, how could they have ever known what to do? For one thing, if he were beyond their knowledge, he might any day, in full con-fidence, go and marry again.

Her father not unfrequently accompanied her to the Old House, but Juliet and she had arranged such signals, and settled such understandings, that the simple man saw noth-ing, heard nothing, forefelt nothing. Now and then a little pang would quaver through Dorothy's bosom, when she caught sight of him peering down into the terrible dusk of the pool, or heard him utter some sympathetic hope for the future of poor Faber ; but she comforted herself with the thought of how glad he would be when she was able to tell him all, and how he would laugh over the story of their pre-cautions against himself.

Her chief anxiety was for Juliet's health, even more for the sake of avoiding discovery, than for its own. When the nights were warm she would sometimes take her out in the park, and every day, one time or another, would make her walk in the garden while she kept watch on the top of the steep slope. Her father would sometimes remark to a friend how Dorothy's love of solitude seemed to grow upon her ; but the remark suggested nothing, and slowly Juliet was being forgotten at Glaston.

It seemed to Dorothy strange that she did not fall ill. For the first few days she was restless and miserable as human being could be. She had but one change of mood : either she would talk feverously, or sit in the gloomiest silence, now and then varied with a fit of abandoned weeping. Every time Dorothy came from Glaston, she would overwhelm her with questions—which at first Dorothy could easily meet, for she spoke absolute fact when she said she knew nothing concerning her husband. When at length the cause of his absence was understood, she told her he was with his friend, Dr. May, at Broughill. Knowing the universal belief that she had committed suicide, nothing could seem more natural. But when, day after day, she heard the same thing for weeks, she began to fear he would never be able to resume his practice, at least at Glaston, and wept bitterly at the thought of the evil she had brought upon him who had given her life, and love to boot. For her heart was a genuine one, and dwelt far more on the wrong her too eager love had done him, than on the hardness with which he had resented it. Nay, she admired him for the fierceness of his resentment, witnessing, in her eyes, to the purity of the man whom his neighbors regarded as wicked.

After the first day, she paid even less heed to any thing of a religious kind with which Dorothy, in the strength of her own desire after a perfect stay, sought to rouse or console her. When Dorothy ventured on such ground, which grew more and more seldom, she would sit listless, heedless, with a far-away look. Sometimes when Dorothy fancied she had been listening a little, her next words would show that her thoughts had been only with her husband. When the subsiding of the deluge of her agony, allowed words to carry meaning to her, any hint at supernal consolation made her angry, and she rejected every thing Dorothy said, almost with indignation. To seem even to accept such comfort, she would have regarded as traitorous to her husband. Not the devotion of the friend who gave up to her all of her life she could call her own, sufficed to make her listen even with a poor patience. So absorbed was she in her trouble, that she had no feeling of what poor Dorothy had done for her. How can I blame her, poor lady ! If existence was not a thing to be enjoyed, as for her it certainly was not at present, how was she to be thankful for what seemed its preservation ? There was much latent love to Dorothy in her heart ; I may go further and say there was much latent love to God in her heart, only the latter was *very* latent as yet. When her heart was a little freer from grief and the agony of loss, she would love Dorothy ; but God must wait with his own patience—wait long for the child of His love to learn that her very sorrow came of His dearest affection. Who wants such affection as that ? says the unloving. No one, I answer ; but every one who comes to know it, glorifies it as the only love that ever could satisfy his being.

Dorothy, who had within her the chill of her own doubt, soon yielded to Juliet's coldness, and ceased to say any thing that could be called religious. She saw that it was not the time to speak ; she must content herself with being. Nor had it ever been any thing very definite she could say. She had seldom gone beyond the expression of her own hope, and the desire that her friend would look up. She could say that all the men she knew, from books or in life, of the most delicate honesty, the most genuine repentance, the most rigid self-denial, the loftiest aspiration, were Christian men ; but she could neither say her knowledge of history or of life was large, nor that, of the men she knew who professed to believe, the greater part were honest, or much ashamed, or rigid against themselves, or lofty toward God. She saw that her part was not instruction, but ministration, and that in obedience to Jesus in whom she hoped to believe. What matter that poor Juliet denied Him ? If God commended His love toward us, in that while we were yet sinners Christ died for us, He would be pleased with the cup of cold water given to one that was not a disciple. Dorothy dared not say she was a disciple herself ; she dared only say that right gladly would she become one, if she could. If only the lovely, the good, the tender, the pure, the grand, the adorable, were also the absolutely true !—true not in the human idea only, but in absolute fact, in divine existence ! If the story of Jesus was true, then joy to the universe, for all was well ! She waited, and hoped, and prayed and ministered.

There is a great power in quiet, for God is in it. Not seldom He seems to lay His hand on one of His children, as a mother lays hers on the restless one in the crib, to still him. Then the child sleeps, but the man begins to live up from the lower depths of his nature. So the winter comes to still the plant whose life had been rushing to blossom and fruit. When the hand of God is laid upon a man, vain moan, and struggle and complaint, it may be indignant outcry follows ; but when, outwearied at last, he yields, if it be in dull submission to the inexorable, and is still, then the God at the heart of him, the God that is there or the man could not be, begins to grow. This point Juliet had not yet reached, and her trouble went on. She saw no light, no possible outlet. Her cries, her longings, her agonies, could not reach even the ears, could never reach the heart of the man who had cast her off. He believed her dead, might go and marry another, and what would be left her then? Nothing but the death from which she now restrained herself, lest, as Dorothy had taught her, she should deny him the fruits of a softening heart and returning love. The moment she heard that he sought another, she would seek Death and assuredly find him. One letter she would write to leave behind her, and then go. He should see and understand that the woman he despised for the fault of the girl, was yet capable of the noblest act of a wife : she would die that he might live— that it might be well with her husband. Having entertained, comprehended and settled this idea in her mind, she became quieter. After this, Dorothy might have spoken without stirring up so angry an opposition. But it was quite as well she did not know it, and did not speak.

I have said that Dorothy wondered she did not fall ill. There was a hope in Juliet's mind of which she had not spoken, but upon which, though vaguely, she built further hope, and which may have had part in her physical endurance : the sight of his baby might move the heart of her husband to pardon her !

But the time, even with the preoccupation of misery, grew very dreary. She had never had any resources in herself except her music, and even if here she had had any opportunity of drawing upon that, what is music but a mockery to a breaking heart ? Was music ever born of torture, of misery ? It is only when the cloud of sorrow is sinking in the sun-rays, that the song-larks awake and ascend. A glory of some sort must fringe the skirts of any sadness, the light of the sorrowing soul itself must be shed upon it, and the cloud must be far enough removed to show the reflected light, before it will yield any of the stuff of which songs are made. And this light that gathers in song, what is it but hope behind the sorrow—hope so little recognized as such, that it is often called despair? It is reviving and not decay that sings even the saddest of songs.

Juliet had had little consciousness of her own being as an object of reflection. Joy and sorrow came and went; she had never brooded. Never until now, had she known any very deep love. Even that she bore her father had not ripened into the grand love of the woman-child. She forgot quickly; she hoped easily; she had had some courage, and naturally much activity; she faced necessity by instinct, and took almost no thought for the morrow—but this after the fashion of the birds, not after the fashion required of those who can consider the birds; it is one thing to take no thought, for want of thought, and another to take no thought, from sufficing thought, whose flower is confidence. The one way is the lovely way of God in the birds—the other, His lovelier way in his men and women. She had in her the making of a noble woman—only that is true of every woman; and it was no truer of her than of every other woman, that, without religion, she could never be, in any worthy sense, a woman at all. I know how narrow and absurd this will sound to many of my readers, but such simply do not know what religion means, and think I do not know what a woman means. Hitherto her past had always turned to a dream as it glided away from her; but now, in the pauses of her prime agony, the tide rose from the infinite sea to which her river ran, and all her past was borne back upon her, even to her far-gone childish quarrels with her silly mother, and the neglect and disobedience she had too often been guilty of toward her father. And the center of her memories was the hot coal of that one secret; around that they all burned and hissed. Now for the first time her past *was*, and she cowered and fled from it, a slave to her own history, to her own deeds, to her own concealment. Alas, like many another terror-stricken child, to whom the infinite bosom of tenderness and love stretches out arms of shelter and healing and life, she turned to the bosom of death, and imagined there a shelter of oblivious darkness! For life is a thing so deep, so high, so pure, so far above the reach of common thought, that, although shadowed out in all the harmonic glories of color, and speech, and song, and scent, and motion, and shine, yea, even of eyes and loving hands, to common minds—and the more merely intellectual, the commoner are they—it seems but a phantasm. To unchildlike minds, the region of love and worship, to which lead the climbing stairs of duty, is but a nephelocockygia ; they acknowledge the stairs, however, thank God, and if they will but climb, a hand will be held out to them. Now, to pray to a God, the very thought of whose possible existence might seem enough to turn the coal of a dead life into a diamond of eternal radiance, is with many such enough to stamp a man a fool. It will surprise me nothing in the new world to hear such men, finding they are not dead after all, begin at once to argue that they were quite right in refusing to act upon any bare possibility—forgetting that the questioning of possibilities has been the source of all scientific knowledge. They may say that to them there seemed no possibility ; upon which will come the question—whence arose their incapacity for seeing it ? In the meantime, that the same condition which constitutes the bliss of a child, should also be the essential bliss of a man, is incomprehensible to him in whom the child is dead, or so fast asleep that nothing but a trumpet of terror can awake him. That the rules of the nursery—I mean the nursery where the true mother is the present genius, not the hell at the top of a London house—that the rules of the nursery over which broods a wise mother with outspread wings of tenderness, should be the laws also of cosmic order, of a world's well-being, of national greatness, and of all personal dignity, may well be an old-wives'-fable to the man who dabbles at saving the world by science, education, hygiene and other economics. There is a knowledge that will do it, but of that he knows so little, that he will not allow it to be a knowledge at all. Into what would he save the world ? His paradise would prove a ten times more miserable condition than that out of which he thought to rescue it.

But any thing that gives objectivity to trouble, that lifts the cloud so far that, if but for a moment, it shows itself a cloud, instead of being felt an enveloping, penetrating, palsying mist—setting it where the mind can in its turn prey upon it, can play with it, paint it, may come to sing of it, is a great help toward what health may yet be possible for the troubled soul. With a woman's instinct, Dorothy borrowed from the curate a volume of acertain more attractive edition of Shakespeare than she herself possessed, and left it in Juliet's way, so arranged that it should open at the tragedy of Othello. She thought that, if she could be drawn into sympathy with suffering like, but different and apart from her own, it would take her a little out of herself, and might lighten the pressure of her load. Now Juliet had never read a play of Shakespeare in her life, and knew Othello only after the vulgar interpretation, as the type, that is, of jealousy ; but when, in a pause of the vague reverie of feeling which she called thought, a touch of ennui supervening upon suffering, she began to read the play, the condition of her own heart afforded her the insight necessary for descrying more truly the Othello of Shakespeare's mind. She wept for Desdemona's innocence and hard fate ; but she pitied more the far harder fate of Othello, and found the death of both a consolation for the trouble their troubles had stirred up in her.

The curate was in the habit of scribbling on his books, and at the end of the play, which left a large blank on the page, had written a few verses : as she sat dreaming over the tragedy, Juliet almost unconsciously took them in. They were these :

> In the hot hell o'
> Jealousy shines Othello—
> Love in despair,
> An angel in flames !
> While pure Desdemona
> Waits him alone, a
> Ghost in the air,
> White with his blames.

Becoming suddenly aware of their import, she burst out weeping afresh, but with a very different weeping—Ah, if it might be so ! Soon then had the repentant Othello, rushing after his wife, explained all, and received easiest pardon : he had but killed her. Her Paul would not even do that for her ! He did not love her enough for that. If she had but thrown herself indeed into the lake, then perhaps—who could tell !—she might now be nearer to him than she should ever be in this world.

All the time, Dorothy was much and vainly exercised as to what might become possible for the bringing of them together again. But it was not as if any misunderstanding had arisen between them : such a difficulty might any moment be removed by an explanation. The thing that divided them was the original misunderstanding, which lies, deep and black as the pit, between every soul and the soul next it, where self and not God is the final thought. The gulf is forever crossed by "bright shoots of everlasting-ness," the lightnings of involuntary affection ; but nothing less than the willed love of an infinite devotion will serve to close it ; any moment it may be lighted up from beneath, and the horrible distance between them be laid bare. Into this gulf it was that, with absolute gift of himself, the Lord, doing like his Father, cast Himself ; and by such devotion alone can His disciples become fellow-workers with Him, help to slay the evil self in the world, and rouse the holy self to like sacrifice, that the true, the eternal life of men, may arise jubilant and crowned. Then is the old man of claims and rights and disputes and fears, re-born a child whose are all things and who claims and fears nothing.

In ignorance of Faber's mood, whether he mourned over his harshness, or justified himself in resentment, Dorothy could but wait, and turned herself again to think what could be done for the consolation of her friend.

Could she, knowing her prayer might be one which God would not grant, urge her to pray ! For herself, she knew, if there was a God, what she desired must be in accordance with His will ; but if Juliet cried to him to give her back her husband, and He did not, would not the silent refusal, the deaf ear of Heaven, send back the cry in settled despair upon her spirit ? With her own fear Dorothy feared for her friend. She had not yet come to see that, in whatever trouble a man may find himself, the natural thing being to make his request known, his brother may heartily tell him to pray. Why, what can a man do but pray ? He is here —helpless ; and his Origin, the breather of his soul, his God, may be somewhere. And what else should he pray about but the thing that troubles him ? Not surely the thing that does not trouble him ? What is the trouble there for, but to make him cry ? It is the pull of God at his being. Let a man only pray. Prayer is the sound to which not merely is the ear of the Father open, but for which that ear is listening. Let him pray for the thing he thinks he needs : for what else, I repeat, can he pray ? Let a man cry for that in whose loss life is growing black : the heart of the Father is open. Only let the man know that, even for his prayer, the Father will not give him a stone. But let the man pray, and let God see to it how to answer him. If in his childishness and ignorance he should ask for a serpent, he will not give him a serpent. But it may yet be the Father will find some way of giving him his heart's desire. God only knows how rich God is in power of gift. See what He has done to make Himself able to give to His own heart's desire. The giving of His Son was as the knife with which He would divide Himself amongst His children. He knows, He only, the heart, the needs, the deep desires, the hungry eternity, of each of them all. Therefore let every man ask of God, Who giveth to all men liberally and upbraideth not—and see at least what will come of it.

But he will speak like one of the foolish if he say thus: "Let God hear me, and give me my desire, and I will trust in Him." That would be to tempt the Lord his God. If a father gives his children their will instead of his, they may well turn on him again and say: "Was it then the part of a father to give me a scorpion because, not knowing what it was, I asked for it? I besought him for a fancied joy, and lo! it is a sorrow for evermore!"

But it may be that sometimes God indeed does so, and to such a possible complaint has this reply in Himself: "I gave thee what thou wouldst, because not otherwise could I teach the stiff-necked his folly. Hadst thou been patient, I would have made the thing a joy ere I gave it thee; I would have changed the scorpion into a golden beetle, set with rubies and sapphires. Have thou patience now."

One thing is clear, that poor Juliet, like most women, and more men, would never have begun to learn any thing worth learning, if she had not been brought into genuine, downright trouble. Indeed I am not sure but some of those who seem so good as to require no trouble, are just those who have already been most severely tried.

CHAPTER XXXIX.

ANOTHER MIND.

But while the two ladies were free of all suspicion of danger, and indeed were quite safe, they were not alone in the knowledge of their secret. There was one who, for some time, had been on the track of it, and had long ago traced it with certainty to its covert: indeed he had all but seen into it from the first. But, although to his intimate friends known as a great and indeed wonderful talker, he was generally regarded as a somewhat silent man, and in truth possessed to perfection the gift of holding his tongue. Except that his outward insignificance was so great as to pass the extreme, he was not one to attract attention ; but those who knew Wingfold well, heard him speak of Mr. Polwarth, the gate-keeper, oftener than of any other ; and from what she heard him say, Dorothy had come to have a great reverence for the man, although she knew him very little.

In returning from Nestley with Juliet by her side, Helen had taken the road through Osterfield Park. When they reached Polwarth's gate, she had, as a matter of course, pulled up, that they might have a talk with the keeper. He had, on the few occasions on which he caught a passing glimpse of Miss Meredith, been struck with a something in her that to him seemed to take from her beauty—that look of strangeness, namely, which every one felt, and which I imagine to have come of the consciousness of her secret, holding her back from blending with the human wave ; and now, therefore, while the carriage stood, he glanced often at her countenance.

From long observation, much silence and gentle pondering ; from constant illness, and frequent recurrence of great suffering ; from loving acceptance of the same, and hence an overflowing sympathy with every form of humanity, even that more dimly revealed in the lower animals, and especially suffering humanity ; from deep acquaintance with the motions of his own spirit, and the fullest conviction that one man is as another ; from the entire confidence of all who knew him, and the results of his efforts to help them ; above all, from persistently dwelling in the secret place of the Most High, and thus entering into the hidden things of life from the center whence the issues of them diverged— from all these had been developed in him, through wisest use, an insight into the natures of men, a power of reading the countenance, an apprehension of what was moving in the mind, a contact, almost for the moment a junction with the goings on of their spirits, which at times revealed to him not only character, and prevailing purpose or drift of nature, but even the main points of a past moral history. Sometimes indeed he would recoil with terror from what seemed the threatened dawn in him of a mysterious power, probably latent in every soul, of reading the future of a person brought within certain points of spiritual range. What startled him, however, may have been simply an involuntary conclusion, instantaneously drawn, from the plain convergence of all the forces in and upon the individual toward a point of final deliverance or of near catastrophe : when "the mortal instruments" are steadily working for evil, the only hope of deliverance lies in catastrophe.

When Polwarth had thus an opportunity of reading Juliet's countenance, it was not wearing its usual expression : the ferment set at work in her mind by the curate's sermon had intensified the strangeness of it, even to something almost of definement ; and it so arrested him that after the ponies had darted away like birds, he stood for a whole minute in the spot and posture in which they had left him.

"I never saw Polwarth look *distrait* before," said the curate, and was about to ask Juliet whether she had not been bewitching him, when the far-away, miserable look of her checked him, and he dropped back into his seat in silence.

But Polwarth had had no sudden insight into Juliet's condition ; all he had seen was, that she was strangely troubled—and that with no single feeling ; that there was an undecided contest in her spirit ; that something was required of her which she had not yet resolved to yield. Almost the moment she vanished from his sight, it dawned upon him that she had a secret. As one knows by the signs of the heavens that the matter of a storm is in them and must break out, so Polwarth had read in Juliet's sky the inward throes of a pent convulsion.

He knew something of the doctor, for he had met him again and again where he himself was trying to serve ; but they had never had conversation together. Faber had not an idea of what was in the creature who represented to him one of Nature's failures at man-making ; while Polwarth, from what he heard and saw of the doctor, knew him better than he knew himself ; and although the moment when he could serve him had not begun to appear, looked for such a moment to come. There was so much good in the man, that his heart longed to give him something worth having. How Faber would have laughed at the notion ! But Polwarth felt confident that one day the friendly doctor would be led out of the miserable desert where he cropped thistles and sage and fancied himself a hero. And now in the drawn look of his wife's face, in the broken lights of her eye, in the absorption and the start, he thought he perceived the quarter whence unwelcome deliverance might be on its way, and resolved to keep attention awake for what might appear. In his inmost being he knew that the mission of man is to help his neighbors. But in as much as he was ready to help, he recoiled from meddling. To meddle is to destroy the holy chance. Meddlesomeness is the very opposite of helpfulness, for it consists in forcing your self into another self, instead of opening your self as a refuge to the other. They are opposite extremes, and, like all extremes, touch. It is not correct that extremes meet ; they lean back to back. To Polwarth, a human self was a shrine to be approached with reverence, even when he bore deliverance in his hand. Anywhere, everywhere, in the seventh heaven or the seventh hell, he could worship God with the outstretched arms of love, the bended knees of joyous adoration, but in helping his fellow, he not only worshiped but served God—ministered, that is, to the wants of God—doing it unto Him in the least of His. He knew that, as the Father unresting works for the weal of men, so every son, following the Master-Son, must work also. Through weakness and suffering he had learned it. But he never doubted that his work as much as his bread would be given him, never rushed out wildly snatching at something to do for God, never helped a lazy man to break stones, never preached to foxes. It was what the Father gave him to do that he cared to do, and that only. It was the man next him that he helped—the neighbor in need of the help he had. He did not trouble himself greatly about the happiness of men, but when the time and the opportunity arrived in which to aid the struggling birth of the eternal bliss, the whole strength of his being responded to the call. And now, having felt a thread vibrate, like a sacred spider he sat in the center of his web of love, and waited and watched.

In proportion as the love is pure, and only in proportion to that, can such be a pure and real calling. The least speck of self will defile it—a little more may ruin its most hopeful effort.

Two days after, he heard, from some of the boys hurrying to the pond, that Mrs. Faber was missing. He followed them, and from a spot beyond the house, looking down upon the lake, watched their proceedings. He saw them find her bonnet—a result which left him room to doubt. Almost the next moment a wavering film of blue smoke rising from the Old House caught his eye. It did not surprise him, for he knew Dorothy Drake was in the habit of going there—knew also by her face for what she went : accustomed to seek solitude himself, he knew the relations of it. Very little had passed between them. Sometimes two persons are like two drops running alongside of each other down a window-pane : one marvels how it is they can so long escape running together. Persons fit to be bosom friends will meet and part for years, and never say much beyond good-morning and good-night.

But he bethought him that he had not before known her light a fire, and the day certainly was not a cold one. Again, how was it that with the cries of the boys in her ears, searching for a sight of the body in her very garden, she had never come from the house, or even looked from a window? Then it came to his mind what a place for conceal-ment the Old House was : he knew every corner of it ; and thus he arrived at what was almost the conviction that Mrs. Faber was there. When a day or two had passed, he was satisfied that, for some reason or other, she was there for refuge. The reason must be a good one, else Dorothy would not be aiding—and it must of course have to do with her husband.

He next noted how, for some time, Dorothy never went through his gate, although he saw reason to believe she went to the Old House every day. After a while, however, she went through it every day. They always exchanged a few words as she passed, and he saw plainly enough that she carried a secret. By and by he began to see the hover of words unuttered about her mouth ; she wished to speak about something but could not quite make up her mind to it. He would sometimes meet her look with the corre-sponding look of " Well, what is it ? " but thereupon she would invariably seem to change her mind, would bid him good morning, and pass on.

CHAPTER XL.

WHEN Faber at length returned to Glaston, his friends were shocked at his appearance. Either the hand of the Lord, or the hand of crushing chance, had been heavy upon him. A pale, haggard, worn, enfeebled man, with an eye of suffering, and a look that shrunk from question, he repaired to his desolate house. In the regard of his fellow-townsmen he was as Job appeared to the eyes of his friends; and some of them, who knew no more of religion than the sound of its name, pitied him that he had not the comfort of it. All Glaston was tender to him. He walked feebly, seldom showed the ghost of a smile, and then only from kindness, never from pleasure. His face was now almost as white as that of his lost Juliet. His brother doctors behaved with brotherly truth. They had attended to all his patients, poor as well as rich, and now insisted that he should resume his labors gradually, while they fulfilled his lack. So at first he visited only his patients in the town, for he was unable to ride; and his grand old horse, Ruber, in whom he trusted, and whom he would have ventured sooner to mount than Niger, was gone! For weeks he looked like a man of fifty; and although by degrees the restorative influences of work began to tell upon him, he never recovered the look of his years. Nobody tried to comfort him. Few dared, for very reverence, speak to the man who carried in him such an awful sorrow. Who would be so heartless as counsel him to forget it? and what other counsel was there for one who refused like him? Who could have brought himself to say to him—" There is loveliness yet left, and within thy reach : take the good, etc. ; forget the nothing that has been, in the something that may yet for awhile avoid being nothing too ; comfort thy heart with a fresh love : the time will come to forget both in the everlasting tomb of the ancient darkness " ? Few men would consent to be comforted in accordance with their professed theories of life ; and more than most would Faber, at this period of his suffering, have scorned such truth for comfort. As it was, men gave him a squeeze of the hand, and women a tearful look ; but from their sympathy he derived no faintest pleasure, for he knew he deserved nothing that came from heart of tenderness. Not that he had begun to condemn himself for his hardness to the woman who, whatever her fault, yet honored him by confessing it, or to bemoan her hard fate to whom a man had not been a hiding-place from the wind, a covert from the tempest of life, a shadow-shelter from the scorching of her own sin. As he recovered from the double shock, and, his strength slowly returning, his work increased, bringing him again into the run of common life, his sense of desolation increased. As his head ached less, his heart ached the more, nor did the help he ministered to his fellows any longer return in comfort to himself. Hitherto his regard of annihilation had been as of something so distant, that its approach was relatively by degrees infinitesimal, but as the days went on, he began to derive a gray consolation from the thought that he must at length cease to exist. He would not hasten the end; he would be brave, and see the play out. Only it was all so dull! If a woman looked kindly at him, if for a moment it gave him pleasure, the next it was as an arrow in his heart. What a white splendor was vanished from his life! Where were those great liquid orbs of radiating darkness?—where was that smile with its flash of whiteness?—that form so lithe, yet so stately, so perfect in modulation?—where were those hands and feet that spoke without words, and took their own way with his heart?—those arms——? His being shook to its center. One word of tenderness and forgiveness, and all would have been his own still!—But on what terms?—Of dishonor and falsehood, he said, and grew hard again. He was sorry for Juliet, but she and not he was to blame. She had ruined his life, as well as lost her own, and his was the harder case, for he had to live on, and she had taken with her all the good the earth had for him. She had been the sole object of his worship; he had acknowledged no other divinity; she was the loveliness of all things; but she had dropped from her pedestal, and gone down in the sea that flows waveless and windless and silent around the worlds. Alas for life! But he would bear on till its winter came. The years would be as tedious as hell; but nothing that ends can be other than brief. Not willingly even yet would he fail of what work was his. The world was bad enough; he would not leave it worse than he had found it. He would work life out, that he might die in peace. Fame truly there was none for him,

but his work would not be lost.   The wretched race of men
would suffer a little the less that he had lived.   Poor comfort, if more of health but ministered to the potency of such
anguish as now burrowed in him like a mole of fire!

There had been a time when, in the young pathos of
things, he would shut his eyes that the sunset might not
wound him so sore ; now, as he rode homeward into the
fronting sunset, he felt nothing, cared for nothing, only ached
with a dull aching through body and soul.   He was still
kind to his fellows, but the glow of the kindness had vanished, and truest thanks hardly waked the slightest thrill.

He very seldom saw Wingfold now, and less than ever
was inclined toward his doctrine ; for had it not been
through him this misery had come upon him?   Had he not,
with the confidence of all the sciences, uttered the merest
dreams as eternal truths?   How could poor Juliet help
supposing he knew the things he asserted, and taking
them for facts?   The human heart was the one unreasonable thing, sighing ever after that which is not!   Sprung
from nothing, it yet desired a creator!—at least some
hearts did so : his did not ; he knew better!

There was of course no reason in this.   Was the thing
not a fact which she had confessed? was he not a worshiper of fact? did he not even dignify it with the name of
truth? and could he wish his wife had kept the miserable
fact to herself, leaving him to his fools'-paradise of ignorance?   Why then should he feel resentment against the man
whose teaching had only compelled her to confess it?—But
the thing was out of the realm of science and its logic.

Sometimes he grew fierce, and determined to face every
possible agony, endure all, and dominate his misery ; but
ever and anon it returned with its own disabling sickness,
bringing the sense of the unendurable.   Of his own motion
he saw nobody except in his practice.   He studied hard,
even to weariness and faintness, contrived strange experiments, and caught, he believed, curious peeps into the house
of life.   Upon them he founded theories as wild as they
were daring, and hob-nobbed with death and corruption.
But life is at the will of the Maker, and misery can not kill
it.   By degrees a little composure returned, and the old
keen look began to revive.   But there were wrinkles on the
forehead that had hitherto been smooth as ivory ; furrows,
the dry water-courses of sorrow, appeared on his cheeks,
and a few silvery threads glinted in his hair.   His step was

heavy, and his voice had lost its ring—the cheer was out of
it.   He no more obtruded his opinions, for, as I have said,
he shrunk from all interchange, but he held to them as firmly
as ever.   He was not to be driven from the truth by suffering ! But there was a certain strange movement in his
spirit of which he took no note—a feeling of resentment, as
if against a God that yet did not exist, for making upon
him the experiment whether he might not, by oppression, be
driven to believe in Him.

When Dorothy knew of his return, and his ways began to
show that he intended living just as before his marriage,
the time seemed come for telling Juliet of the accident and
his recovery from the effects of it.   She went into violent
hysterics, and the moment she could speak, blamed Dorothy
bitterly for not having told her before.

"It is all your lying religion ! " she said.

"Your behavior, Juliet," answered Dorothy, putting on
the matron, and speaking with authority, "shows plainly
how right I was.   You were not to be trusted, and I knew it.
Had I told you, you would have rushed to him, and been
anything but welcome.   He would not even have known
you ; and you would have been two on the doctor's hands.
You would have made every thing public, and when your
husband came to himself, would probably have been the
death of him after all."

" He may have begun to think more kindly of me by that
time," said Juliet, humbled a little.

" We must not act on *may-haves*," answered Dorothy.

" You say he looks wretched now," suggested Juliet.

" And well he may, after concussion of the brain, not to
mention what preceded it," said Dorothy.

She had come to see that Juliet required very plain
speaking.   She had so long practiced the art of deceiving
herself that she was skillful at it.   Indeed, but for the fault
she had committed, she would all her life long have been
given to petting and pitying, justifying and approving of
herself.   One can not help sometimes feeling that the only
chance for certain persons is to commit some fault sufficient
to shame them out of the self-satisfaction in which they
burrow.   A fault, if only it be great and plain enough to
exceed their powers of self-justification, may then be, of
God's mercy, not indeed an angel of light to draw them, but
verily a goblin of darkness to terrify them out of themselves.
For the powers of darkness are His servants also, though

incapable of knowing it : He who is first and last can, even of those that love the lie, make slaves of the truth. And they who will not be sons shall be slaves, let them rant and wear crowns as they please in the slaves' quarters.

" You must not expect him to get over such a shock all at once," said Dorothy. "—It may be," she continued, " that you were wrong in running away from him. I do not pretend to judge between you, but, perhaps, after the injury you had done him, you ought to have left it with him to say what you were to do next. By taking it in your own hands, you may have only added to the wrong."

" And who helped me ? " returned Juliet, in a tone of deep reproach.

" Helped you to run from him, Juliet !—Really, if you were in the habit of behaving to your husband as you do to me——! " She checked herself, and resumed calmly— " You forget the facts of the case, my dear. So far from helping you to run from him, I stopped you from running so far that neither could he find you, nor you return to him again. But now we must make the best of it by waiting. We must find out whether he wants you again, or your absence is a relief to him. If I had been a man, I should have been just as wild as he."

She had seen in Juliet some signs that self-abhorrence was wanting, and self-pity reviving, and she would connive at no unreality in her treatment of herself. She was one thing when bowed to the earth in misery and shame, and quite another if thinking herself hardly used on all sides.

It was a strange position for a young woman to be in— that of watcher over the marriage relations of two persons, to neither of whom she could be a friend otherwise than *ab extra.* Ere long she began almost to despair. Day after day she heard or saw that Faber continued sunk in himself, and how things were going there she could not tell. Was he thinking about the wife he had lost, or brooding over the wrong she had done him ? There was the question—and who was to answer it ? At the same time she was all but certain, that, things being as they were, any reconciliation that might be effected would owe itself merely to the raising, as it were of the dead, and the root of bitterness would soon trouble them afresh. If but one of them had begun the task of self-conquest, there would be hope for both. But of such a change there was in Juliet as yet no sign.

Dorothy then understood her position—it was wonderful with what clearness, but solitary necessity is a hot sun to ripen. What was she to do? To what quarter—could she to any quarter look for help? Naturally she thought first of Mr. Wingfold. But she did not feel at all sure that he would consent to receive a communication upon any other understanding than that he was to act in the matter as he might see best; and would it be right to acquaint him with the secret of another when possibly he might feel bound to reveal it? Besides, if he kept it hid, the result might be blame to him; and blame, she reasoned, although a small matter in regard to one like herself, might in respect of a man in the curate's position involve serious consequences. While she thus reflected, it came into her mind with what enthusiasm she had heard him speak of Mr. Polwarth, attributing to him the beginnings of all enlightenment he had himself ever received. Without this testimony, she would not have once thought of him. Indeed she had been more than a little doubtful of him, for she had never felt attracted to him, and from her knowledge of the unhealthy religious atmosphere of the chapel, had got unreasonably suspicious of cant. She had not had experience enough to distinguish with any certainty the speech that comes from the head and that which comes out of the fullness of the heart. A man must talk out of that which is in him; his well must give out the water of its own spring; but what seems a well may be only a cistern, and the water by no means living water. What she had once or twice heard him say, had rather repelled than drawn her; but Dorothy had faith, and Mr. Wingfold had spoken. Might she tell him? Ought she not to seek his help? Would he keep the secret? Could he help if he would? Was he indeed as wise as they said?

In the meantime, little as she thought it, Polwarth had been awaiting a communication from her; but when he found that the question whose presence was so visible in her whole bearing, neither died nor bore fruit, he began to think whether he might not help her to speak. The next time, therefore, that he opened the gate to her, he held in his hand a little bud he had just broken from a monthly rose. It was a hard little button, upon which the green leaves of its calyx clung as if choking it.

"What is the matter with this bud, do you think, Miss Drake?" he asked.

"That you have plucked it," she answered sharply, throwing a suspicious glance in his face.

"No; that can not be it," he answered with a quiet smile of intelligence. "It has been just as you see it for the last three days. I only plucked it the moment I saw you coming."

"Then the frost has caught it."

"The frost *has* caught it," he answered; "but I am not quite sure whether the cause of its death was not rather its own life than the frost."

"I don't see what you mean by that, Mr. Polwarth," said Dorothy, doubtfully, and with a feeling of discomfort.

"I admit it sounds paradoxical," returned the little man. "What I mean is, that the struggle of the life in it to unfold itself, rather than any thing else, was the cause of its death."

"But the frost was the cause of its not being able to unfold itself," said Dorothy.

"That I admit," said Polwarth; "and perhaps a weaker life in the flower would have yielded sooner. I may have carried too far an analogy I was seeking to establish between it and the human heart, in which repression is so much more dangerous than mere oppression. Many a heart has withered like my poor little bud, because it did not know its friend when it saw him."

Dorothy was frightened. He knew something! Or did he only suspect? Perhaps he was merely guessing at her religious troubles, wanting to help her. She must answer carefully.

"I have no doubt you are right, Mr. Polwarth," she said; "but there are some things it is not wise, and other things it would not be right to speak about."

"Quite true," he answered. "I did not think it wise to say any thing sooner, but now I venture to ask how the poor lady does?"

"What lady?" returned Dorothy, dreadfully startled, and turning white.

"Mrs. Faber," answered Polwarth, with the utmost calmness. "Is she not still at the Old House?"

"Is it known, then?" faltered Dorothy.

"To nobody but myself, so far as I am aware," replied the gatekeeper.

"And how long have you known it?"

"From the very day of her disappearance, I may say."

" Why didn't you let me know sooner ? " said Dorothy, feeling aggrieved, though she would have found it hard to show wherein lay the injury.

" For more reasons than one," answered Polwarth ; " but one will be enough : you did not trust me. It was well therefore to let you understand I could keep a secret. I let you know now only because I see you are troubled about her. I fear you have not got her to take any comfort, poor lady ! "

Dorothy stood silent, gazing down with big, frightened eyes at the strange creature who looked steadfastly up at her from under what seemed a huge hat—for his head was as large as that of a tall man. He seemed to be reading her very thoughts.

" I can trust you, Miss Drake," he resumed. " If I did not, I should have at once acquainted the authorities with my suspicions ; for, you will observe, you are hiding from a community a fact which it has a right to know. But I have faith enough in you to believe that you are only waiting a fit time, and have good reasons for what you do. If I can give you any help, I am at your service."

He took off his big hat, and turned away into the house.

Dorothy stood fixed for a moment or two longer, then walked slowly away, with her eyes on the ground. Before she reached the Old House, she had made up her mind to tell Polwarth as much as she could without betraying Juliet's secret, and to ask him to talk to her, for which she would contrive an opportunity.

For some time she had been growing more anxious every day. No sign of change showed in any quarter ; no way opened through the difficulties that surrounded them, while these were greatly added to by the likelihood appearing that another life was on its way into them. What was to be done ? How was she in her ignorance so to guard the hopeless wife that motherhood might do something to console her ? She had two lives upon her hands, and did indeed want counsel. The man who knew their secret already— the minor prophet, she had heard the curate call him— might at least help her to the next step she must take.

Juliet's mental condition was not at all encouraging. She was often ailing and peevish, behaving as if she owed Dorothy grudge instead of gratitude. And indeed to her- self Dorothy would remark that if nothing more came out of it than seemed likely now, Juliet would be under no very ponderous obligation to her. She found it more and more difficult to interest her in any thing. After Othello she did not read another play. Nothing pleased her but to talk about her husband. If Dorothy had seen him, Juliet had endless questions to put to her about him; and when she had answered as many of them as she could, she would put them all over again afresh. On one occasion when Dorothy could not say she believed he was, when she saw him, thinking about his wife, Juliet went into hysterics. She was growing so unmanageable that if Dorothy had not partially opened her mind to Polwarth, she must at last have been compelled to give her up. The charge was wearing her out; her strength was giving way, and her temper growing so irritable that she was ashamed of herself—and all without any good to Juliet. Twice she hinted at letting her husband know where she was, but Juliet, although, on both occasions, she had a moment before been talking as if Dorothy alone prevented her from returning to him, fell on her knees in wild distress, and entreated her to bear with her. At the smallest approach of the idea toward actuality, the recollection rushed scorching back—of how she had implored him, how she had humbled herself soul and body before him, how he had turned from her with loathing, would not put forth a hand to lift her from destruction and to restore her to peace, had left her naked on the floor, nor once returned "to ask the spotted princess how she fares"—and she shrunk with agony from any real thought of again supplicating his mercy.

Presently another difficulty began to show in the near distance: Mr. Drake, having made up his mind as to the alterations he would have effected, had begun to think there was no occasion to put off till the spring, and talked of commencing work in the house at no distant day. Dorothy therefore proposed to Juliet that, as it was impossible to conceal her there much longer, she should go to some distant part of the country, where she would contrive to follow her. But the thought of moving further from her husband, whose nearness, though she dared not seek him, seemed her only safety, was frightful to Juliet. The wasting anxiety she caused Dorothy did not occur to her. Sorrow is not selfish, but many persons are in sorrow entirely selfish. It makes them so important in their own eyes, that they seem to have a claim upon all that people can do for them.

To the extent therefore, of what she might herself have

known without Juliet's confession, Dorothy, driven to her
wits' end, resolved to open the matter to the gatekeeper ;
and accordingly, one evening on her way home, called at
the lodge, and told Polwarth where and in what condition
she had found Mrs. Faber, and what she had done with her ;
that she did not think it the part of a friend to advise her
return to her husband at present ; that she would not herself hear of returning ; that she had no comfort, and her
life was a burden to her ; and that she could not possibly
keep her concealed much longer, and did not know what
next to do.

Polwarth answered only that he must make the acquaintance of Mrs. Faber. If that could be effected, he believed
he should be able to help them out of their difficulties.
Between them, therefore, they must arrange a plan for his
meeting her.

CHAPTER XLI.

THE OLD GARDEN.

THE next morning, Juliet, walking listlessly up and down
the garden, turned the corner of a yew hedge, and came
suddenly upon a figure that might well have appeared one
of the kobolds of German legend. He was digging slowly
but steadily, crooning a strange song—so low that, until she
saw him she did not hear him.

She started back in dismay. The kobold neither raised
his head nor showed other sign than the ceasing of his song
that he was aware of her presence. Slowly and steadily he
went on with his work. He was trenching the ground deep,
still throwing the earth from the bottom to the top. Juliet,
concluding he was deaf, and the ceasing of his song acci-
dental, turned softly, and would have retreated. But Polwarth, so far from being deaf, heard better than most
people. His senses, indeed, had been sharpened by his in-
firmities—all but those of taste and smell, which were fitful,
now dull and now exquisitely keen. At the first movement breaking the stillness into which consternation had
cast her, he spoke.

" Can you guess what I am doing, Mrs. Faber ? " he said,
throwing up a spadeful and a glance together, like a man
who could spare no time from his work.

Juliet's heart got in the way, and she could not answer
him. She felt much as a ghost, wandering through a house,
might feel, if suddenly addressed by the name she had
borne in the old days, while yet she was clothed in the garments of the flesh. Could it be that this man led such a
retired life that, although living so near Glaston, and seeing so many at his gate, he had yet never heard that she
\ad passed from the ken of the living ? Or could it be that
Dorothy had betrayed her ? She stood quaking. The situation was strange. Before her was a man who did not seem
to know that what he knew concerning her was a secret
from all the world besides ! And with that she had a sudden insight into the consequence of the fact of her existence
coming to her husband's knowledge : would it not add to
his contempt and scorn to know that she was not even
dead ? Would he not at once conclude that she had been
contriving to work on his feelings, that she had been specu-
lating on his repentance, counting upon and awaiting such
a return of his old fondness, as would make him forget all
her faults, and prepare him to receive her again with delight ?—But she must answer the creature ! Ill could she
afford to offend him ! But what was she to say ? She had
utterly forgotten what he had said to her. She stood staring at him, unable to speak. It was but for a few moments,
but they were long as minutes. And as she gazed, it seemed
as if the strange being in the trench had dug his way up
from the lower parts of the earth, bringing her secret with
him, and come to ask her questions. What an earthy yet
unearthly look he had ! Almost for the moment she
believed the ancient rumors of other races than those of
mankind, that shared the earth with them, but led such
differently conditioned lives, that, in the course of ages,
only a scanty few of the unblending natures crossed each
other's path, to stand astare in mutual astonishment.

Polwarth went on digging, nor once looked up. After a
little while he resumed, in the most natural way, speaking
as if he had known her well :

" Mr. Drake and I were talking, some weeks ago, about
a certain curious little old-fashioned flower in my garden at
the back of the lodge. He asked me if I could spare him a
root of it. I told him I could spare him any thing he would

like to have, but that I would gladly give him every flower in my garden, roots and all, if he would but let me dig three yards square in his garden at the Old House, and have all that came up of itself for a year."

He paused again. Juliet neither spoke nor moved. He dug rather feebly for a gnome, with panting, asthmatic breath.

"Perhaps you are not aware, ma'am," he began again, and ceasing his labor stood up leaning on the spade, which was nearly as high as himself, "that many of the seeds which fall upon the ground do not grow, yet, strange to tell, retain the power of growth. I suspect myself, but have not had opportunity of testing the conjecture, that such fall in their pods, or shells, and that before these are sufficiently decayed to allow the sun and moisture and air to reach them, they have got covered up in the soil too deep for those same influences. They say fishes a long time bedded in ice will come to life again : I can not tell about that, but it is well enough known that if you dig deep in any old garden, such as this, ancient, perhaps forgotten flowers, will appear. The fashion has changed, they have been neglected or uprooted, but all the time their life is hid below. And the older they are, the nearer perhaps to their primary idea ! "

By this time she was far more composed, though not yet had she made up her mind what to say, or how to treat the dilemma in which she found herself.

After a brief pause therefore, he resumed again :

"I don't fancy," he said, with a low, asthmatic laugh, "that we shall have many forgotten weeds come up. They all, I suspect, keep pretty well in the sun. But just think how the fierce digging of the crisis to which the great Husbandman every now and then leads a nation, brings back to the surface its old forgotten flowers. What virtues, for instance, the Revolution brought to light as even yet in the nature of the corrupted nobility of France ! "

"What a peculiar goblin it is ! " thought Juliet, beginning to forget herself a little in watching and listening to the strange creature. She had often seen him before, but had always turned from him with a kind of sympathetic shame : of course the poor creature could not bear to be looked at ; he must know himself improper !

"I have sometimes wondered," Polwarth yet again resumed, "whether the troubles without end that some people

seem born to—I do not mean those they bring upon themselves—may not be as subsoil plows, tearing deep into the
family mold, that the seeds of the lost virtues of their race
may in them be once more brought within reach of sun and
air and dew. It would be a pleasant, hopeful thought if one
might hold it. Would it not, ma'am ? "

" It would indeed," answered Juliet with a sigh, which
rose from an undefined feeling that if some hidden virtue
would come up in her, it would be welcome. How many
people would like to be good, if only they might be good
without taking trouble about it ! They do not like goodness
well enough to hunger and thirst after it, or to sell all that
they have that they may buy it ; they will not batter at the
gate of the kingdom of Heaven; but they look with pleasure
on this or that aerial castle of righteousness, and think it
would be rather nice to live in it ! They do not know that
it is goodness all the time their very being is pining after,
and that they are starving their nature of its necessary food.
Then Polwarth's idea turned itself round in Juliet's mind,
and grew clearer, but assumed reference to weeds only, and
not flowers. She thought how that fault of hers had, like the
seed of a poison-plant, been buried for years, unknown to
one alive, and forgotten almost by herself—so diligently forgotten indeed, that it seemed to have gradually slipped
away over the horizon of her existence ; and now here it
was at the surface again in all its horror and old reality ! nor
that merely, for already it had blossomed and borne its
rightful fruit of dismay—an evil pod, filled with a sickening
juice, and swarming with gray flies.—But she must speak,
and, if possible, prevent the odd creature from going and
publishing in Glaston that he had seen Mrs. Faber, and she
was at the Old House.

" How did you know I was here ? " she asked abruptly.

" How do you know that I knew, ma'am ? " returned
Polwarth, in a tone which took from the words all appearance
of rudeness.

" You were not in the least surprised to see me," she
answered.

" A man," returned the dwarf, " who keeps his eyes open
may almost cease to be surprised at any thing. In my time
I have seen so much that is wonderful—in fact every thing
seems to me so wonderful that I hardly expect to be surprised any more."

He said this, desiring to provoke conversation. But

Juliet took the answer for an evasive one, and it strengthened her suspicion of Dorothy. She was getting tired of
her! Then there was only one thing left!—The minor
prophet had betaken himself again to his work, delving
deeper, and throwing slow spadeful after spadeful to the
surface.

"Miss Drake told you I was here!" said Juliet.

"No, indeed, Mrs. Faber. No one told me," answered
Polwarth. "I learned it for myself. I could hardly help
finding it out."

"Then—then—does every body know it?" she faltered,
her heart sinking within her at the thought.

"Indeed, ma'am, so far as I know, not a single person
is aware you are alive except Miss Drake and myself. I
have not even told my niece who lives with me, and who
can keep a secret as well as myself."

Juliet breathed a great sigh of relief.

"Will you tell me why you have kept it so secret?" she
asked.

"Because it was your secret, ma'am, not mine."

"But you were under no obligation to keep my secret."

"How do you justify such a frightful statement as that,
ma'am?"

"Why, what could it matter to you?"

"Every thing."

"I do not understand. You have no interest in me.
You could have no inducement."

"On the contrary, I had the strongest inducement : I
saw that an opportunity might come of serving you."

"But that is just the unintelligible thing to me. There
is no reason why you should wish to serve me!" said
Juliet, thinking to get at the bottom of some design.

"There you mistake, ma'am. I am under the most absolute and imperative obligation to serve you—the greatest
under which any being can find himself."

"What a ridiculous, crooked little monster!" said
Juliet to herself. But she began the same moment to think
whether she might not turn the creature's devotion to good
account. She might at all events insure his silence.

"Would you be kind enough to explain yourself?" she
said, now also interested in the continuance of the conversation.

"I would at once," replied Polwarth, "had I sufficient
ground for hoping you would understand my explanation."

"I do not know that I am particularly stupid," she returned, with a wan smile.

"I have heard to the contrary," said Polwarth. "Yet I can not help greatly doubting whether you will understand what I am now going to tell you. For I will tell you—on the chance : I have no secrets—that is, of my own.—I am one of those, Mrs. Faber," he went on after a moment's pause, but his voice neither became more solemn in tone, nor did he cease his digging, although it got slower, "who, against the *non-evidence* of their senses, believe there is a Master of men, the one Master, a right perfect Man, who demands of them, and lets them know in themselves the rectitude of the demand that they also shall be right and true men, that is, true brothers to their brothers and sisters of mankind. It is recorded too, and I believe it, that this Master said that any service rendered to one of His people was rendered to Himself. Therefore, for love of His will, even if I had no sympathy with you, Mrs. Faber, I should feel bound to help you. As you can not believe me interested in yourself, I must tell you that to betray your secret for the satisfaction of a love of gossip, would be to sin against my highest joy, against my own hope, against the heart of God, from which your being and mine draws the life of its every moment."

Juliet's heart seemed to turn sick at the thought of such a creature claiming brotherhood with her. That it gave ground for such a claim, seemed for the moment an irresistible argument against the existence of a God.

In her countenance Polwarth read at once that he had blundered, and a sad, noble, humble smile irradiated his. It had its effect on Juliet. She would be generous and forgive his presumption : she knew dwarfs were always conceited—that wise Nature had provided them with high thoughts wherewith to add the missing cubit to their stature. What repulsive things Christianity taught ! Her very flesh recoiled from the poor ape !

"I trust you are satisfied, ma'am," the kobold added, after a moment's vain expectation of a word from Juliet, "that your secret is safe with me."

"I am," answered Juliet, with a condescending motion of her stately neck, saying to herself in feeling if not in conscious thought,—"After all he is hardly human ! I may accept his devotion as I would that of a dog ! "

The moment she had thus far yielded, she began to long

to speak of her husband. Perhaps he can tell her something of him ! At least he could talk about him. She would
have been eager to look on his reflection, had it been possible, in the mind of a dog that loved him. She would turn
the conversation in a direction that might find him.

"But I do not see," she went on, "how you, Mr. Polwarth—I think that is your name—how you can, consistently with your principles,——"

"Excuse me, ma'am : I can not even, by silence, seem to
admit that you know any thing whatever of my principles."

"Oh !" she returned, with a smile of generous confession, " I was brought up to believe as you do."

"That but satisfies me that for the present you are incapable of knowing any thing of my principles."

"I do not wonder at your thinking so," she returned, with
the condescension of superior education, as she supposed,
and yet with the first motion of an unconscious respect for
the odd little monster.—He, with wheezing chest, went on
throwing up the deep, damp, fresh earth, to him smelling of
marvelous things. Ruth would have ached all over to see
him working so hard !—" Still," Juliet went on, " supposing
your judgment of me correct, that only makes it the stranger
you should imagine that in serving such a one, you are
pleasing Him you call your Master. He says whosoever denies Him before men He will deny before the angels of God."

"What my Lord says He will do, He will do, as He meant
it when He said it : what He tells me to do, I try to understand and do. Now He has told me of all things not to say
that good comes of evil. He condemned that in the Pharisees as the greatest of crimes. When, therefore, I see a man
like your husband, helping his neighbors near and far,
being kind, indeed loving, and good-hearted to all men,"—
Here a great sigh, checked and broken into many little
ones, came in a tremulous chain from the bosom of the wife
—" I am bound to say that man is not scattering his Master
abroad. He is indeed opposing Him in words : he speaks
against the Son of Man ; but that the Son of Man Himself
says shall be forgiven him. If I mistake in this, to my own
Master I stand or fall."

"How can He be his Master if he does not acknowledge
Him ?"

"Because the very tongue with which he denies Him is
yet His. I am the master of the flowers that will now grow
by my labor, though not one of them will know me—how

much more must He be the Master of the men He has called
into being, though they do not acknowledge Him! If the
story of the gospel be a true one, as with my heart and soul
and all that is in me I believe it is, then Jesus of Nazareth
is Lord and Master of Mr. Faber, and for him not to acknowledge it is to fall from the summit of his being. To deny
one's Master, is to be a slave."

"You are very polite!" said Mrs. Faber, and turned
away. She recalled her imaginary danger, however, and turning again, said, "But though I differ from you in opinion,
Mr. Polwarth, I quite recognize you as no common man, and
put you upon your honor with regard to my secret."

"Had you entrusted me with your secret, ma'am, the
phrase would have had more significance. But, obeying my
Master, I do not require to think of my own honor. Those
who do not acknowledge their Master, can not afford to forget it. But if they do not learn to obey Him, they will find
by the time they have got through what they call life, they
have left themselves little honor to boast of."

"He has guessed my real secret!" thought poor Juliet,
and turning away in confusion, without a word of farewell,
went straight into the house. But before Dorothy, who had
been on the watch at the top of the slope, came in, she had
begun to hope that the words of the forward, disagreeable,
conceited dwarf had in them nothing beyond a general
remark.

When Dorothy entered, she instantly accused her of
treachery. Dorothy, repressing her indignation, begged she
would go with her to Polwarth. But when they reached the
spot, the gnome had vanished.

He had been digging only for the sake of the flowers
buried in Juliet, and had gone home to lie down. His
bodily strength was exhausted, but will and faith and purpose never forsook the soul cramped up in that distorted
frame. When greatly suffering, he would yet suffer with his
will—not merely resigning himself to the will of God, but
desiring the suffering that God willed. When the wearied
soul could no longer keep the summit of the task, when not
strength merely, but the consciousness of faith and duty
failed him, he would cast faith and strength and duty, all his
being, into the gulf of the Father's will, and simply suffer,
no longer trying to feel any thing—waiting only until the
Life should send him light.

Dorothy turned to Juliet.

"You might have asked Mr. Polwarth, Juliet, whether I had betrayed you," she said.

"Now I think of it, he did say you had not told him. But how was I to take the word of a creature like that?"

"Juliet," said Dorothy, very angry, "I begin to doubt if you were worth taking the trouble for!"

She turned from her, and walked toward the house. Juliet rushed after her and caught her in her arms.

"Forgive me, Dorothy," she cried. "I am not in my right senses, I do believe. What *is* to be done now this—man knows it?"

"Things are no worse than they were," said Dorothy, as quickly appeased as angered. "On the contrary, I believe we have the only one to help us who is able to do it. Why, Juliet, why what am I to do with you when my father sends the carpenters and bricklayers to the house? They will be into every corner! He talks of commencing next week, and I am at my wits' end."

"Oh! don't forsake me, Dorothy, after all you have done for me," cried Juliet. "If you turn me out, there never was creature in the world so forlorn as I shall be—absolutely helpless, Dorothy!"

"I will do all I can for you, my poor Juliet; but if Mr. Polwarth do not think of some way, I don't know what will become of us. You don't know what you are guilty of in despising him. Mr. Wingfold speaks of him as far the first man in Glaston."

Certainly Mr. Wingfold, Mr. Drew, and some others of the best men in the place, did think him, of those they knew, the greatest in the kingdom of Heaven. Glaston was altogether of a different opinion. Which was the right opinion, must be left to the measuring rod that shall finally be applied to the statures of men.

The history of the kingdom of Heaven—need I say I mean a very different thing from what is called *church-history?*—is the only history that will ever be able to show itself a history—that can ever come to be thoroughly written, or to be read with a clear understanding; for it alone will prove able to explain itself, while in doing so it will explain all other attempted histories as well. Many of those who will then be found first in the eternal record, may have been of little regard in the eyes of even their religious contemporaries, may have been absolutely unknown to generations that came after, and were yet the men of life and potency, working as

light, as salt, as leaven, in the world.   When the real worth
of things is, over all, the measure of their estimation, then
is the kingdom of our God and His Christ.

CHAPTER XLII.

THE POTTERY.

It had been a very dry autumn, and the periodical rains
had been long delayed, so that the minister had been able
to do much for the houses he had bought, called the Pottery.
There had been but just rain enough to reveal the advantage of the wall he had built to compel the water to keep
the wider street.   Thoroughly dry and healthy it was impossible to make them, at least in the time ; but it is one thing
to have the water all about the place you stand on, and
another to be up to the knees in it.   Not at that point only,
however, but at every spot where the water could enter
freely, he had done what he could provisionally for the
defense of his poor colony—for alas ! how much among the
well-to-do, in town or city, are the poor like colonists only !
—and he had great hopes of the result.   Stone and brick
and cement he had used freely, and one or two of the people
about began to have a glimmering idea of the use of money
after a gospel fashion—that is, for thorough work where and
because it was needed.   The curate was full of admiration
and sympathy.   But the whole thing gave great dissatisfaction to others not a few.   For, as the currents of inundation
would be somewhat altered in direction and increased in
force by his obstructions, it became necessary for several
others also to add to the defenses of their property, and this
of course was felt to be a grievance.   Their personal incon-
veniences were like the shilling that hides the moon, and,
in the resentment they occasioned, blinded their hearts to
the seriousness of the evils from which their merely temporary annoyance was the deliverance of their neighbors.
A fancy of prescriptive right in their own comforts out-
weighed all the long and heavy sufferings of the others.
Why should not their neighbors continue miserable, when
they had been miserable all their lives hitherto ? Those who,

On the contrary, had been comfortable all their lives, and liked it so much, ought to continue comfortable—even at their expense. Why not let well alone? Or if people would be so unreasonable as to want to be comfortable too, when nobody cared a straw about them, let them make themselves comfortable without annoying those superior beings who had been comfortable all the time!—Persons who, consciously or unconsciously, reason thus, would do well to read with a little attention the parable of the rich man and Lazarus, wherein it seems recognized that a man's having been used to a thing may be just the reason, not for the continuance, but for the alteration of his condition. In the present case the person who most found himself aggrieved, was the dishonest butcher. A piece of brick wall which the minister had built in contact with the wall of his yard, would indubitably cause such a rise in the water at the descent into the area of his cellar, that, in order to its protection in a moderate flood—in a great one the cellar was always filled—the addition to its defense of two or three more rows of bricks would be required, carrying a correspondent diminution of air and light. It is one of the punishments overtaking those who wrong their neighbors, that not only do they feel more keenly than others any injury done to themselves, but they take many things for injuries that do not belong to the category. It was but a matter of a few shillings at the most, but the man who did not scruple to charge the less careful of his customers for undelivered ounces, gathering to pounds and pounds of meat, resented bitterly the necessity of the outlay. He knew, or ought to have known, that he had but to acquaint the minister with the fact, to have the thing set right at once; but the minister had found him out, and he therefore much preferred the possession of his grievance to its removal. To his friends he regretted that a minister of the gospel should be so corrupted by the mammon of unrighteousness as to use it against members of his own church: that, he said, was not the way to make friends with it. But on the pretense of a Christian spirit, he avoided showing Mr. Drake any sign of his resentment; for the face of his neighbors shames a man whose heart condemns him but shames him not. He restricted himself to grumbling, and brooded to counterplot the mischiefs of the minister. What right had he to injure him for the sake of the poor? Was it not written in the Bible: Thou shalt not favor the poor man in his cause? Was it not written also: For every

man shall bear his own burden ? That was common sense !
He did his share in supporting the poor that were church-
members, but was he to suffer for improvements on Drake's
property for the sake of a pack of roughs !   Let him be
charitable at his own cost ! etc., etc.   Self is prolific in argument.

It suited Mr. Drake well, notwithstanding his church
republican theories, against which, in the abstract, I could
ill object, seeing the whole current of Bible teaching is
toward the God-inspired ideal commonwealth—it suited a
man like Mr. Drake well, I say, to be an autocrat, and was
a most happy thing for his tenants, for certainly no other
system of government than a wise autocracy will serve in
regard to the dwellings of the poor.   And already, I repeat,
he had effected not a little.   Several new cottages had
been built, and one incorrigible old one pulled down.   But
it had dawned upon him that, however desirable it might be
on a dry hill-side, on such a foundation as this a cottage was
the worst form of human dwelling that could be built.   For
when the whole soil was in time of rain like a full sponge,
every room upon it was little better than a hollow in a cloud,
and the right thing must be to reduce contact with the soil
as much as possible.   One high house, therefore, with many
stories, and stone feet to stand upon, must be the proper
kind of building for such a situation.   He must lift the first
house from the water, and set as many more houses as convenient upon it.

He had therefore already so far prepared for the building
of such a house as should lift a good many families far above
all deluge ; that is, he had dug the foundation, and deep,
to get at the more solid ground.   In this he had been pre-
cipitate, as not unfrequently in his life ; for while he was
yet meditating whether he should not lay the foundation
altogether solid, of the unporous stone of the neighborhood,
the rains began, and there was the great hole, to stand all
the winter full of water, in the middle of the cottages !

The weather cleared again, but after a St. Martin's
summer unusually prolonged, the rain came down in terrible
earnest.   Day after day, the clouds condensed, grew water,
and poured like a squeezed sponge.   A wet November
indeed it was—wet overhead—wet underfoot—wet all
round ! and the rivers rose rapidly.

When the Lythe rose beyond a certain point, it overflowed
into a hollow, hardly a valley, and thereby a portion of it

descended almost straight to Glaston. Hence it came that
in a flood the town was invaded both by the rise of the river
from below, and by this current from above, on its way to
rejoin the main body of it, and the streets were soon turned
into canals. The currents of the slowly swelling river and
of its temporary branch then met in Pine street, and formed
not a very rapid, but a heavy run at ebb tide; for Glaston,
though at some distance from the mouth of the river, measuring by its course, was not far from the sea, which was
visible across the green flats, a silvery line on the horizon.
Landward, beyond the flats, high ground rose on all sides,
and hence it was that the floods came down so deep upon
Glaston.

On a certain Saturday it rained all the morning heavily,
but toward the afternoon cleared a little, so that many
hoped the climax had been reached, while the more experienced looked for worse. After sunset the clouds gathered
thicker than before, and the rain of the day was as nothing
to the torrent descending with a steady clash all night.
When the slow, dull morning came Glaston stood in the
middle of a brown lake, into which water was rushing from
the sky in straight, continuous lines. The prospect was dis-
composing. Some, too confident in the apparent change,
had omitted needful precautions, in most parts none were
now possible, and in many more none would have been of
use. Most cellars were full, and the water was rising on the
ground-floors. It was a very different affair from a flood in
a mountainous country, but serious enough, though without
immediate danger to life. Many a person that morning
stepped out of bed up to the knee in muddy water.

With the first of the dawn the curate stood peering from
the window of his dressing-room, through the water that
coursed down the pane, to discover the state of the country;
for the window looked inland from the skirt of the town.
All was gray mist, brown water, and sheeting rain. The
only things clear were that not a soul would be at church
that morning, and that, though he could do nothing to
divide them the bread needful for their souls, he might do
something for some of their bodies. It was a happy thing
it was Sunday, for, having laid in their stock of bread the
day before, people were not so dependent on the bakers,
half whose ovens must now be full of water. But most of
the kitchens must be flooded, he reasoned, the fire-wood
soaking, and the coal in some cellars inaccessible. The

very lucifer-matches in many houses would be as useless as the tinderbox of a shipwrecked sailor. And if the rain were to cease at once the water would yet keep rising for many hours. He turned from the window, took his bath in homœopathic preparation, and then went to wake his wife.

She was one of those blessed women who always open their eyes smiling. She owed very little of her power of sympathy to personal suffering; the perfection of her health might have made one who was too anxious for her spiritual growth even a little regretful. Her husband there-fore had seldom to think of sparing her when any thing had to be done. She could lose a night's sleep without the smallest injury, and stand fatigue better than most men; and in the requirements of the present necessity there would be mingled a large element of adventure, almost of frolic, full of delight to a vigorous organization.

"What a good time of it the angels of wind and flame must have!" said the curate to himself as he went to wake her. "What a delight to be embodied as a wind, or a flame, or a rushing sea!—Come, Helen, my help! Glaston wants you," he said softly in her ear.

She started up.

"What is it, Thomas?" she said, holding her eyes wider open than was needful, to show him she was capable.

"Nothing to frighten you, darling," he answered, "but plenty to be done. The river is out, and the people are all asleep. Most of them will have to wait for their breakfast, I fear. We shall have no prayers this morning."

"But plenty of divine service," rejoined Helen, with a smile for what her aunt called one of his whims, as she got up and seized some of her garments.

"Take time for your bath, dear," said her husband.

"There will be time for that afterward," she replied. "What shall I do first?"

"Wake the servants, and tell them to light the kitchen fire, and make all the tea and coffee they can. But tell them to make it good. We shall get more of every thing as soon as it is light. I'll go and bring the boat. I had it drawn up and moored in the ruins ready to float yesterday. I wish I hadn't put on my shirt though: I shall have to swim for it, I fear."

"I shall have one aired before you come back," said Helen.

"Aired!" returned her husband: "you had better say

watered. In five minutes neither of us will have a dry
stitch on. I'll take it off again, and be content with my
blue jersey."

He hurried out into the rain. Happily there was no
wind.

Helen waked the servants. Before they appeared she
had the fire lighted, and as many utensils as it would ac-
commodate set upon it with water. When Wingfold returned, he found her in the midst of her household, busily
preparing every kind of eatable and drinkable they could lay
hands upon.

He had brought his boat to the church yard and moored
it between two headstones : they would have their breakfast
first, for there was no saying when they might get any
lunch, and food is work. Besides, there was little to be
gained by rousing people out of their good sleep : there was
no danger yet.

"It is a great comfort," said the curate, as he drank his
coffee, "to see how Drake goes in heart and soul for his
tenants. He is pompous—a little, and something of a fine
gentleman, but what is that beside his great truth ! That
work of his is the simplest act of Christianity of a public
kind I have ever seen !"

"But is there not a great change on him since he had his
money ?" said Helen. "He seems to me so much humbler
in his carriage and simpler in his manners than before."

"It is quite true," replied her husband. "It is mortify-
ing to think," he went on after a little pause, "how many of
our clergy, from mere beggarly pride, holding their rank
superior—as better accredited servants of the Carpenter of
Nazareth, I suppose—would look down on that man as a
hedge-parson. The world they court looked down upon
themselves from a yet greater height once, and may come
to do so again. Perhaps the sooner the better, for then
they will know which to choose. Now they serve Mammon
and think they serve God."

"It is not quite so bad as that, surely !" said Helen.

"If it is not worldly pride, what is it ? I do not think
it is spiritual pride. Few get on far enough to be much in
danger of that worst of all vices. It must then be church-
pride, and that is the worst form of worldly pride, for it is
a carrying into the kingdom of Heaven of the habits and
judgments of the kingdom of Satan. I am wrong ! such
things can not be imported into the kingdom of Heaven :

they can only be imported into the Church, which is bad
enough. Helen, the churchman's pride is a thing to turn a
saint sick with disgust, so utterly is it at discord with the
lovely human harmony he imagines himself the minister of.
He is the Pharisee, it may be the good Pharisee, of the
kingdom of Heaven ; but if the proud churchman be in the
kingdom at all, it must be as one of the least in it.   I don't
believe one in ten who is guilty of this pride is aware of the
sin of it.   Only the other evening I heard a worthy canon
say, it may have been more in joke than appeared, that he
would have all dissenters burned. Now the canon would
not hang one of them—but he does look down on them
all with contempt. Such miserable paltry weaknesses and
wickednesses, for in a servant of the Kingdom the feeling
which suggests such a speech is wicked, are the moth holes
in the garments of the Church, the teredo in its piles, the
dry rot in its floors, the scaling and crumbling of its but-
tresses. They do more to ruin what such men call the
Church, even in outward respects, than any of the rude
attacks of those whom they thus despise. He who, in the
name of Christ, pushes his neighbor from him, is a schis-
matic, and that of the worst and only dangerous type ! But
we had better be going. It's of no use telling you to take
your waterproof ; you'd only be giving it to the first poor
woman we picked up."

"I may as well have the good of it till then," said Helen,
and ran to fetch it, while the curate went to bring his boat
to the house.

When he opened the door, there was no longer a spot of
earth or of sky to be seen—only water, and the gray sponge
filling the upper air, through which coursed multitudinous
perpendicular runnels of water. Clad in a pair of old trow-
sers and a jersey, he went wading, and where the ground
dipped, swimming, to the western gate of the churchyard.
In a few minutes he was at the kitchen window, holding the
boat in a long painter, for the water, although quite up to
the rectory walls, was not yet deep enough there to float
the boat with any body in it. The servants handed him out
the great cans they used at school-teas, full of hot coffee,
and baskets of bread, and he placed them in the boat, covering them with a tarpaulin. Then Helen appeared at the
door, in her waterproof, with a great fur-cloak—to throw
over him, she said, when she took the oars, for she meant to
have her share of the fun : it was so seldom there was any

going on a Sunday !—How she would have shocked her aunt, and better women than she !

"To-day," said the curate, "we shall praise God with the *mirth* of the good old hundredth psalm, and not with the *fear* of the more modern version."

As he spoke he bent to his oars, and through a narrow lane the boat soon shot into Pine-street—now a wide canal, banked with houses dreary and dead, save where, from an upper window, peeped out here and there a sleepy, dismayed countenance. In silence, except for the sounds of the oars, and the dull rush of water everywhere, they slipped along.

"This *is* fun !" said Helen, where she sat and steered.

"Very quiet fun as yet," answered the curate. "But it will get faster by and by."

As often as he saw any one at a window, he called out that tea and coffee would be wanted for many a poor creature's breakfast. But here they were all big houses, and he rowed swiftly past them, for his business lay, not where there were servants and well-stocked larders, but where there were mothers and children and old people, and little but water besides. Nor had they left Pine street by many houses before they came where help was right welcome. Down the first turning a miserable cottage stood three feet deep in the water. Out jumped the curate with the painter in his hand, and opened the door.

On the bed, over the edge of which the water was lapping, sat a sickly young woman in her night-dress, holding her baby to her bosom. She stared for a moment with big eyes, then looked down, and said nothing ; but a rose-tinge mounted from her heart to her pale cheek.

"Good morning, Martha !" said the curate cheerily. "Rather damp—ain't it ? Where's your husband ?"

"Away looking for work, sir," answered Martha, in a hopeless tone.

"Then he won't miss you. Come along. Give me the baby."

"I can't come like this, sir. I ain't got no clothes on."

"Take them with you. You can't put them on : they're all wet. Mrs. Wingfold is in the boat : she'll see to every thing you want. The door's hardly wide enough to let the boat through, or I'd pull it close up to the bed for you to get in."

She hesitated.

"Come along," he repeated. "I won't look at you. Or
wait—I'll take the baby, and come back for you. Then you
won't get so wet."

He took the baby from her arms, and turned to the
door.

"It ain't you as I mind, sir," said Martha, getting into the
water at once and following him, "—no more'n my own
people ; but all the town'll be at the windows by this
time."

"Never mind ; we'll see to you," he returned.

In half a minute more, with the help of the windowsill,
she was in the boat, the fur-cloak wrapped about her and
the baby, drinking the first cup of the hot coffee.

"We must take her home at once," said the curate.

"You said we should have fun !" said Helen, the tears
rushing into her eyes.

She had left the tiller, and, while the mother drank her
coffee, was patting the baby under the cloak. But she had
to betake herself to the tiller again, for the curate was not
rowing straight.

When they reached the rectory, the servants might all
have been grandmothers from the way they received the
woman and her child.

"Give them a warm bath together," said Helen, "as
quickly as possible.—And stay, let me out, Thomas—I must
go and get Martha some clothes. I shan't be a minute."

The next time they returned, Wingfold, looking into the
kitchen, could hardly believe the sweet face he saw by the
fire, so refined in its comforted sadness, could be that of
Martha. He thought whether the fine linen, clean and
white, may not help the righteousness even of the saints a
little.

Their next take was a boat-load of children and an old
grandmother. Most of the houses had a higher story, and
they took only those who had no refuge. Many more, however, drank of their coffee and ate of their bread. The
whole of the morning they spent thus, calling, on their passages, wherever they thought they could get help or find
accommodation. By noon a score of boats were out rendering similar assistance. The water was higher than it had
been for many years, and was still rising. Faber had laid
hands upon an old tub of a salmon-coble, and was the first
out after the curate. But there was no fun in the poor doc-

tor's boat. Once the curate's and his met in the middle of Pine street—both as full of people as they could carry. Wingfold and Helen greeted Faber frankly and kindly. He returned their greeting with solemn courtesy, rowing heavily past.

By lunch-time, Helen had her house almost full, and did not want to go again : there was so much to be done ! But her husband persuaded her to give him one hour more : the servants were doing so well ! he said. She yielded. He rowed her to the church, taking up the sexton and his boy on their way. There the crypts and vaults were full of water. Old wood-carvings and bits of ancient coffins were floating about in them. But the floor of the church was above the water : he landed Helen dry in the porch, and led her to the organ-loft. Now the organ was one of great power ; seldom indeed, large as the church was, did they venture its full force : he requested her to pull out every stop, and send the voice of the church, in full blast, into every corner of Glaston. He would come back for her in half an hour and take her home. He desired the sexton to leave all the doors open, and remember that the instrument would want every breath of wind he and his boy could raise.

He had just laid hold of his oars, when out of the porch rushed a roar of harmony that seemed to seize his boat and blow it away upon its mission like a feather—for in the delight of the music the curate never felt the arms that urged it swiftly along. After him it came pursuing, and wafted him mightily on. Over the brown waters it went rolling, a grand billow of innumerable involving and involved waves. He thought of the spirit of God that moved on the face of the primeval waters, and out of a chaos wrought a cosmos. " Would," he said to himself, " that ever from the church door went forth such a spirit of harmony and healing of peace and life ! But the church's foes are they of her own household, who with the axes and hammers of pride and exclusiveness and vulgar priestliness, break the carved work of her numberless chapels, yea, build doorless screens from floor to roof, dividing nave and choir and chancel and transepts and aisles into sections numberless, and, with the evil dust they raise, darken for ages the windows of her clerestory ! "

The curate was thinking of no party, but of individual spirit. Of the priestliness I have encountered, I can not deteɪmine whether the worse belonged to the Church of England or a certain body of Dissenters.

CHAPTER XLIII.

THE GATE-LODGE.

Mᴿ ꞴꞇᴠꞮꞇ had his horses put to, then taken away again, and an old hunter saddled. But half-way from home he came to a burst bridge, and had to return, much to the relief of his wife, who, when she had him in the house again, could enjoy the rain, she said : it was so cosey and comfortable to feel you could not go out, or any body call. I presume she therein seemed to take a bond of fate, and doubly assure the every-day dullness of her existence. Well, she was a good creature, and doubtless a corner would be found for her up above, where a little more work would probably be required of her.

Polwarth and his niece Ruth rose late, for neither had slept well. When they had breakfasted, they read together from the Bible : first the uncle read the passage he had last got light upon—he was always getting light upon passages, and then the niece the passage she had last been gladdened by ; after which they sat and chatted a long time by the kitchen fire.

"I am afraid your asthma was bad last night, uncle dear," said Ruth. "I heard your breathing every time I woke."

"It was, rather," answered the little man, "but I took my revenge, and had a good crow over it."

"I know what you mean, uncle : do let me hear the crow."

He rose, and slowly climbing the stair to his chamber, returned with a half sheet of paper in his hand, resumed his seat, and read the following lines, which he had written in pencil when the light came :

Satan, avaunt !
  Nay, take thine hour ;
Thou canst not daunt,
  Thou hast no power ;

Be welcome to thy nest,
Though it be in my breast.

Burrow amain ;
  Dig like a mole ;
Fill every vein
  With half-burned coal ;
Puff the keen dust about,
And all to choke me out.

Fill music's ways
  With creaking cries,
That no loud praise
  May climb the skies ;
And on my laboring chest
Lay mountains of unrest.

My slumber steep
  In dreams of haste,
That only sleep,
  No rest I taste—
With stiflings, rimes of rote,
And fingers on the throat.

Satan, thy might
  I do defy ;
Live core of night,
  I patient lie :
A wind comes up the gray
Will blow thee clean away.

Christ's angel, Death,
  All radiant white,
With one cold breath
  Will scare thee quite,
And give my lungs an air
As fresh as answered prayer.

So, Satan, do
  Thy worst with me,
Until the True
  Shall set me free,
And end what He began,
By making me a man.

"It is not much of poetry, Ruth!" he said, raising his
eyes from the paper ; "—no song of thrush or blackbird !
I am ashamed that I called it a cock-crow—for that is one
of the finest things in the world—a clarion defiance to
darkness and sin—far too good a name for my poor jingle
—except, indeed, you call it a Cochin-china-cock-crow—
from out a very wheezy chest !"

"'My strength is made perfect in weakness,'" said Ruth

solemnly, heedless of the depreciation. To her the verses were as full of meaning as if she had made them herself.

"I think I like the older reading better—that is, without the *My*," said Polwarth : "'Strength is made perfect in weakness.' Somehow—I can not explain the feeling—to hear a grand aphorism, spoken in widest application, as a fact of more than humanity, of all creation, from the mouth of the human God, the living Wisdom, seems to bring me close to the very heart of the universe. Strength—strength itself—all over—is made perfect in weakness ;—a law of being, you see, Ruth ! not a law of Christian growth only, but a law of growth, even all the growth leading up to the Christian, which growth is the highest kind of creation. The Master's own strength was thus perfected, and so must be that of His brothers and sisters. Ah, what a strength must be his !—how patient in endurance—how gentle in exercise—how mighty in devotion—how fine in its issues, perfected by such suffering ! Ah, my child, you suffer sorely sometimes—I know it well ! but shall we not let patience have her perfect work, that we may—one day, Ruth, one day, my child—be perfect and entire, wanting nothing ?"

Led by the climax of his tone, Ruth slipped from her stool on her knees. Polwarth kneeled beside her, and said :

"O Father of life, we praise Thee that one day Thou wilt take Thy poor crooked creatures, and give them bodies like Christ's, perfect as His, and full of Thy light. Help us to grow faster—as fast as Thou canst help us to grow. Help us to keep our eyes on the opening of Thy hand, that we may know the manna when it comes. O Lord, we rejoice that we are Thy making, though Thy handiwork is not very clear in our outer man as yet. We bless Thee that we feel Thy hand making us. What if it be in pain ! Evermore we hear the voice of the potter above the hum and grind of his wheel. Father, Thou only knowest how we love Thee. Fashion the clay to Thy beautiful will. To the eyes of men we are vessels of dishonor, but we know Thou dost not despise us, for Thou hast made us, and Thou dwellest with us. Thou hast made us love Thee, and hope in Thee, and in Thy love we will be brave and endure. All in good time, O Lord. Amen."

While they thus prayed, kneeling on the stone floor of the little kitchen, dark under the universal canopy of cloud, the rain went on clashing and murmuring all around, rush-

ing from the eaves, and exploding with sharp hisses in the
fire, and in the mingled noise they had neither heard a low
tap, several times repeated, nor the soft opening of the
door that followed. When they rose from their knees, it
was therefore with astonishment they saw a woman standing
motionless in the doorway, without cloak or bonnet, her
dank garments clinging to her form and dripping with rain.

When Juliet woke that morning, she cared little that the
sky was dull and the earth dark. A selfish sorrow, a selfish
love even, makes us stupid, and Juliet had been growing
more and more stupid. Many people, it seems to me,
through sorrow endured perforce and without a gracious
submission, slowly sink in the scale of existence. Such are
some of those middle-aged women, who might be the very
strength of social well-being, but have no aspiration, and
hope only downward—after rich husbands for their daughters, it may be—a new bonnet or an old coronet—the devil
knows what.

Bad as the weather had been the day before, Dorothy had
yet contrived to visit her, and see that she was provided
with every necessary ; and Juliet never doubted she would
come that day also. She thought of Dorothy's ministrations as we so often do of God's—as of things that come of
themselves for which there is no occasion to be thankful.

When she had finished the other little house-work required
for her comfort, a labor in which she found some little res-
pite from the gnawings of memory and the blankness of
anticipation, she ended by making up a good fire, though
without a thought of Dorothy's being wet when she arrived,
and sitting down by the window, stared out at the pools,
spreading wider and wider on the gravel walks beneath her.
She sat till she grew chilly, then rose and dropped into an
easy chair by the fire, and fell fast asleep.

She slept a long time, and woke in a terror, seeming to
have waked herself with a cry. The fire was out, and the
hearth cold. She shivered and drew her shawl about her.
Then suddenly she remembered the frightful dream she had
had.

She dreamed that she had just fled from her husband and
gained the park, when, the moment she entered it, something seized her from behind, and bore her swiftly, as in the
arms of a man—only she seemed to hear the rush of wings
behind her—the way she had been going. She struggled in
terror, but in vain ; the power bore her swiftly on, and she

knew whither. Her very being recoiled from the horrible
depth of the motionless pool, in which, as she now seemed
to know, lived one of the loathsome creatures of the semi-
chaotic era of the world, which had survived its kind as well
as its coevals, and was ages older than the human race. The
pool appeared—but not as she had known it, for it boiled
and heaved, bubbled and rose. From its lowest depths it
was moved to meet and receive her ! Coil upon coil it
lifted itself into the air, towering like a waterspout, then
stretched out a long, writhing, shivering neck to take her
from the invisible arms that bore her to her doom. The
neck shot out a head, and the head shot out the tongue of
a water-snake. She shrieked and woke, bathed in terror.

With the memory of the dream not a little of its horror
returned ; she rose to shake it off, and went to the window.
What did she see there ? The fearsome pool had entered
the garden, had come half-way to the house, and was plainly
rising every moment. More or less the pool had haunted
her ever since she came ; she had seldom dared go nearer
it than half-way down the garden. But for the dulling
influence of her misery, it would have been an unendurable
horror to her, now it was coming to fetch her as she had
seen it in her warning dream ! Her brain reeled ; for a
moment she gazed paralyzed with horror, then turned from
the window, and, with almost the conviction that the fiend
of her vision was pursuing her, fled from the house, and
across the park, through the sheets of rain, to the gate-lodge,
nor stopped until, all unaware of having once thought of
him in her terror, she stood at the door of Polwarth's
cottage.

Ruth was darting toward her with outstretched hands,
when her uncle stopped her.

"Ruth, my child," he said, "run and light a fire in the
parlor. I will welcome our visitor."

She turned instantly, and left the room. Then Polwarth
went up to Juliet, who stood trembling, unable to utter
a word, and said, with perfect old-fashioned courtesy, "You
are heartily welcome, ma'am. I sent Ruth away that I
might first assure you that you are as safe with her as with me.
Sit here a moment, ma'am. You are so wet, I dare not
place you nearer to the fire.—Ruth !"

She came instantly.

"Ruth," he repeated, "this lady is Mrs. Faber. She is
còme to visit us for a while. Nobody must know of it.—

You need not be at all uneasy, Mrs. Faber. Not a soul will come near us to-day. But I will lock the door, to secure time, if any one should.—You will get Mrs. Faber's room ready at once, Ruth. I will come and help you. But a spoonful of brandy in hot water first, please.—Let me move your chair a little, ma'am—out of the draught."

Juliet in silence did every thing she was told, received the prescribed antidote from Ruth, and was left alone in the kitchen.

But the moment she was freed from one dread, she was seized by another ; suspicion took the place of terror ; and as soon as she heard the toiling of the goblins up the creaking staircase, she crept to the foot of it after them, and with no more compunction than a princess in a fairy-tale, set herself to listen. It was not difficult, for the little inclosed staircase carried every word to the bottom of it.

" I *thought* she wasn't dead ! " she heard Ruth exclaim joyfully ; and the words and tone set her wondering.

" I saw you did not seem greatly astonished at the sight of her ; but what made you think such an unlikely thing ? " rejoined her uncle.

" I saw you did not believe she was dead. That was enough for me."

" You are a witch, Ruth ! I never said a word one way or the other."

" Which showed that you were thinking, and made me think. You had something in your mind which you did not choose to tell me yet."

" Ah, child ! " rejoined her uncle, in a solemn tone, " how difficult it is to hide any thing ! I don't think God wants any thing hidden. The light is His region, His kingdom, His palace-home. It can only be evil, outside or in, that makes us turn from the fullest light of the universe. Truly one must be born again to enter into the kingdom ! "

Juliet heard every word, heard and was bewildered. The place in which she had sought refuge was plainly little better than a kobold-cave, yet merely from listening to the talk of the kobolds without half understanding it, she had begun already to feel a sense of safety stealing over her, such as she had never been for an instant aware of in the Old House, even with Dorothy beside her.

They went on talking, and she went on listening. They were so much her inferiors there could be no impropriety in doing so !

"The poor lady," she heard the man-goblin say, "has had some difference with her husband ; but whether she wants to hide from him or from the whole world or from both, she only can tell. Our business is to take care of her, and do for her what God may lay to our hand. What she desires to hide, is sacred to us. We have no secrets of our own, Ruth, and have the more room for those of other people who are unhappy enough to have any. Let God reveal what He pleases : there are many who have no right to know what they most desire to know. She needs nursing, poor thing ! We will pray to God for her."

"But how shall we make her comfortable in such a poor little house ?" returned Ruth. "It is the dearest place in the world to me—but how will she feel in it ? "

"We will keep her warm and clean," answered her uncle, " and that is all an angel would require."

"An angel !—yes," answered Ruth : "for angels don't eat ; or, at least, if they do, for I doubt if you will grant that they don't, I am certain that they are not so hard to please as some people down here. The poor, dear lady is delicate—you know she has always been—and I am not much of a cook."

"You are a very good cook, my dear. Perhaps you do not know a great many dishes, but you are a dainty cook of those you do know. Few people can have more need than we to be careful what they eat,—we have got such a pair of troublesome cranky little bodies ; and if you can suit them, I feel sure you will be able to suit any invalid that is not fastidious by nature rather than necessity."

"I will do my best," said Ruth cheerily, comforted by her uncle's confidence. "The worst is that, for her own sake, I must not get a girl to help me."

"The lady will help you with her own room," said Polwarth. "I have a shrewd notion that it is only the *fine* ladies, those that are so little of ladies that they make so much of being ladies, who mind doing things with their own hands. Now you must go and make her some tea, while she gets in bed. She is sure to like tea best."

Juliet retreated noiselessly, and when the woman-gnome entered the kitchen, there sat the disconsolate lady where she had left her, still like the outcast princess of a fairy-tale : she had walked in at the door, and they had immediately begun to arrange for her stay, and the strangest thing to Juliet was that she hardly felt it strange. It was only as if she had come a day sooner than she was expected —which indeed was very much the case, for Polwarth had been looking forward to the possibility, and latterly to the likelihood of her becoming their guest.

" Your room is ready now," said Ruth, approaching her timidly, and looking up at her with her woman's childlike face on the body of a child.   " Will you come ? "

Juliet rose and followed her to the garret-room with the dormer window, in which Ruth slept.

" Will you please get into bed as fast as you can," she said, " and when you knock on the floor I will come and take away your clothes and get them dried.   Please to wrap this new blanket round you, lest the cold sheets should give you a chill.   They are well aired, though.   I will bring you a hot bottle, and some tea.   Dinner will be ready soon."

So saying she left the chamber softly.   The creak of the door as she closed it, and the white curtains of the bed and window, reminded Juliet of a certain room she once occupied at the house of an old nurse, where she had been happier than ever since in all her life, until her brief bliss with Faber : she burst into tears, and weeping undressed and got into bed.   There the dryness and the warmth and the sense of safety soothed her speedily ; and with the comfort crept in the happy thought that here she lay on the very edge of the high road to Glaston, and that nothing could be more probable than that she would soon see her husband ride past.   With that one hope she could sit at a window watching for centuries !   " O Paul ! Paul ! my Paul ! " she moaned.   " If I could but be made clean again for you ! I would willingly be burned at the stake, if the fire would only make me clean, for the chance of seeing you again in the other world ! "   But as the comfort into her brain, so the peace of her new surroundings stole into her heart. The fancy grew upon her that she was in a fairy-tale, in which she must take every thing as it came, for she could not alter the text.   Fear vanished ; neither staring eyes nor creeping pool could find her in the guardianship of the benevolent goblins.   She fell fast asleep ; and the large, clear, gray eyes of the little woman gnome came and looked at her as she slept, and their gaze did not rouse her. Softly she went, and came again ; but, although dinner was then ready, Ruth knew better than to wake her.   She knew that sleep is the chief nourisher in life's feast, and would not withdraw the sacred dish.   Her uncle said sleep was God's

contrivance for giving man the help he could not get into
him while he was awake. So the loving gnomes had their
dinner together, putting aside the best portions of it against
the waking of the beautiful lady lying fast asleep above.

CHAPTER XLIV.

THE CORNER OF THE BUTCHER'S SHOP.

ALL that same Sunday morning, the minister and Dorothy had of course plenty of work to their hand, for their
more immediate neighbors were all of the poor. Their own
house, although situated on the very bank of the river, was
in no worse plight than most of the houses in the town, for
it stood upon an artificial elevation ; and before long, while
it had its lower parts full of water like the rest, its upper
rooms were filled with people from the lanes around. But
Mr. Drake's heart was in the Pottery, for he was anxious as
to the sufficiency of his measures. Many of the neighbors,
driven from their homes, had betaken themselves to his
inclosure, and when he went, he found the salmon-fishers
still carrying families thither. He set out at once to get
what bread he could from the baker's, a quantity of meat
from the butcher, cheese, coffee, and tins of biscuits and
preserved meat from the grocers : all within his bounds were
either his own people or his guests, and he must do what he
could to feed them. For the first time he felt rich, and
heartily glad and grateful that he was. He could please
God, his neighbor, and himself all at once, getting no end
of good out of the slave of which the unrighteous make a
god.

He took Dorothy with him, for he would have felt helpless on such an expedition without her judgment ; and, as
Lisbeth's hands were more than full, they agreed it was
better to take Amanda. Dorothy was far from comfortable
at having to leave Juliet alone all day, but the possibility of
her being compelled to omit her customary visit had been
contemplated between them, and she could not fail to
understand it on this the first occasion. Anyhow, better
could not be, for the duty at home was far the more press-

ing. That day she showed an energy which astonished
even her father. Nor did she fail of her reward. She
received insights into humanity which grew to real knowledge. I was going to say that, next to an insight into the
heart of God, an insight into the heart of a human being is
the most precious of things ; but when I think of it—what
is the latter but the former ? I will say this at least, that
no one reads the human heart well, to whom the reading
reveals nothing of the heart of the Father. The wire-gauze
of sobering trouble over the flaming flower of humanity,
enabled Dorothy to see right down into its fire-heart, and
distinguish there the loveliest hues and shades. Where the
struggle for own life is in abeyance, and the struggle for
other life active, there the heart that God thought out and
means to perfect, the pure love-heart of His humans,
reveals itself truly, and is gracious to behold. For then the
will of the individual sides divinely with his divine impulse,
and his heart is unified in good. When the will of the man
sides perfectly with the holy impulses in him, then all is
well ; for then his mind is one with the mind of his Maker ;
God and man are one.

Amanda shrieked with delight when she was carried to
the boat, and went on shrieking as she floated over flower-
beds and box-borders, caught now and then in bushes and
overhanging branches. But the great fierce current, ridg-
ing the middle of the brown lake as it followed the tide out
to the ocean, frightened her a little. The features of the
flat country were all but obliterated ; trees only and houses
and corn-stacks stood out of the water, while in the direction of the sea where were only meadows, all indication of
land had vanished ; one wide, brown level was everywhere,
with a great rushing serpent of water in the middle of it.
Amanda clapped her little hands in ecstasy. Never was
there such a child for exuberance of joy ! her aunt thought.
Or, if there were others as glad, where were any who let
the light of their gladness so shine before men, invading,
conquering them as she did with the rush of her joy !
Dorothy held fast to the skirt of her frock, fearing every
instant the explosive creature would jump overboard in
elemental sympathy. But, poled carefully along by Mr.
Drake, they reached in safety a certain old shed, and getting in at the door of the loft where a cow-keeper stored his
hay and straw, through that descended into the heart of
the Pottery, which its owner was delighted to find—not

indeed dry under foot with such a rain falling, but free from lateral invasion.

His satisfaction, however, was of short duration. Dorothy went into one of the nearer dwellings, and he was crossing an open space with Amanda, to get help from a certain cottage in unloading the boat and distributing its cargo, when he caught sight of a bubbling pool in the middle of it. Alas! it was from a drain, whose covering had burst with the pressure from within. He shouted for help. Out hurried men, women and children on all sides. For a few moments he was entirely occupied in giving orders, and let Amanda's hand go : everybody knew her, and there seemed no worse mischief within reach for her than dabbling in the pools, to which she was still devoted.

Two or three spades were soon plying busily, to make the breach a little wider, while men ran to bring clay and stones from one of the condemned cottages. Suddenly arose a great cry, and the crowd scattered in all directions. The wall of defense at the corner of the butcher's shop had given away, and a torrent was galloping across the Pottery, straight for the spot where the water was rising from the drain. Amanda, gazing in wonder at the flight of the people about her, stood right in its course, but took no heed of it, or never saw it coming. It caught her, swept her away, and tumbled with her, foaming and roaring, into the deep foundation of which I have spoken. Her father had just missed her, and was looking a little anxiously round, when a shriek of horror and fear burst from the people, and they rushed to the hole. Without a word spoken he knew Amanda was in it. He darted through them, scattering men and women in all directions, but pulling off his coat as he ran.

Though getting old, he was far from feeble, and had been a strong swimmer in his youth. But he plunged heedlessly, and the torrent, still falling some little height, caught him, and carried him almost to the bottom. When he came to the top, he looked in vain for any sign of the child. The crowd stood breathless on the brink. No one had seen her, though all eyes were staring into the tumult. He dived, swam about beneath, groping in the frightful opacity, but still in vain. Then down through the water came a shout, and he shot to the surface—to see only something white vanish. But the recoil of the torrent from below caught her, and just as he was diving again, brought her up almost within arm's-length of him. He darted to her, clasped her, and gained the brink. He could not have got out, though the cavity was now brimful, but ready hands had him in safety in a moment. Fifty arms were stretched to take the child, but not even to Dorothy would he yield her. Ready to fall at every step, he blundered through the water, which now spread over the whole place, and followed by Dorothy in mute agony, was making for the shed behind which lay his boat, when one of the salmon fishers, who had brought his coble in at the gap, crossed them, and took them up. Mr. Drake dropped into the bottom of the boat, with the child pressed to his bosom. He could not speak.

"To Doctor Faber's! For the child's life!" said Dorothy, and the fisher rowed like a madman.

Faber had just come in. He undressed the child with his own hands, rubbed her dry, and did every thing to initi-ate respiration. For a long time all seemed useless, but he persisted beyond the utmost verge of hope. Mr. Drake and Dorothy stood in mute dismay. Neither was quite a *child* of God yet, and in the old man a rebellious spirit murmured: it was hard that he should have evil for good! that his endeavors for his people should be the loss of his child!

Faber was on the point of ceasing his efforts in utter despair, when he thought he felt a slight motion of the diaphragm, and renewed them eagerly. She began to breathe. Suddenly she opened her eyes, looked at him for a moment, then with a smile closed them again. To the watchers heaven itself seemed to open in that smile. But Faber dropped the tiny form, started a pace backward from the bed, and stood staring aghast. The next moment he threw the blankets over the child, turned away, and almost staggered from the room. In his surgery he poured himself out a glass of brandy, swallowed it neat, sat down and held his head in his hands. An instant after, he was by the child's side again, feeling her pulse, and rubbing her limbs under the blankets.

The minister's hands had turned blue, and he had begun to shiver, but a smile of sweetest delight was on his face.

"God bless me!" cried the doctor, "you've got no coat on! and you are drenched! I never saw any thing but the child!"

"He plunged into the horrible hole after her," said

Dorothy. "How wicked of me to forget him for any child under the sun! He got her out all by himself, Mr. Faber! —Come home, father dear.—I will come back and see to Amanda as soon as I have got him to bed."

"Yes, Dorothy; let us go," said the minister, and put his hand on her shoulder. His teeth chattered and his hand shook.

The doctor rang the bell violently.

"Neither of you shall leave this house to-night.—Take a hot bath to the spare bedroom, and remove the sheets," he said to the housekeeper, who had answered the summons. "My dear sir," he went on, turning again to the minister, "you must get into the blankets at once. How careless of me! The child's life will be dear at the cost of yours."

"You have brought back the soul of the child to me, Mr. Faber," said the minister, trembling, "and I can never thank you enough."

"There won't be much to thank me for, if you have to go instead.—Miss Drake, while I give your father his bath, you must go with Mrs. Roberts, and put on dry clothes. Then you will be able to nurse him."

As soon as Dorothy, whose garments Juliet had been wearing so long, was dressed in some of hers, she went to her father's room. He was already in bed, but it was long before they could get him warm. Then he grew burning hot, and all night was talking in troubled dreams. Once Dorothy heard him say, as if he had been talking to God face to face: "O my God, if I had but once seen Thee, I do not think I could ever have mistrusted Thee. But I could never be quite sure."

The morning brought lucidity. How many dawns a morning brings! His first words were "How goes it with the child?" Having heard that she had had a good night, and was almost well, he turned over, and fell fast asleep. Then Dorothy, who had been by his bed all night, resumed her own garments, and went to the door.

CHAPTER XLV.

THE rain had ceased, and the flood was greatly diminished. It was possible, she judged, to reach the Old House, and after a hasty breakfast, she set out, leaving her father to Mrs. Roberts's care. The flood left her no choice but go by the high road to Polwarth's gate, and then she had often to wade through mud and water. The moment she saw the gatekeeper, she knew somehow by his face that Juliet was in the lodge. When she entered, she saw that already her new circumstances were working upon her for peace. The spiritual atmosphere, so entirely human, the sense that she was not and would not be alone, the strange talk which they held openly before her, the food they coaxed her to eat, the whole surrounding of thoughts and things as they should be, was operating far more potently than could be measured by her understanding of their effects, or even consciousness of their influences. She still looked down upon the dwarfs, condescended to them, had a vague feeling that she honored them by accepting their ministration—for which, one day, she would requite them handsomely. Not the less had she all the time a feeling that she was in the society of ministering spirits of God, good and safe and true. From the Old House to the cottage was from the Inferno to the Purgatorio, across whose borders faint wafts from Paradise now and then strayed wandering. Without knowing it, she had begun already to love the queer little woman, with the wretched body, the fine head, and gentle, suffering face ; while the indescribable awe, into which her aversion to the kobold, with his pigeon-chest, his wheezing breath, his great head, and his big, still face, which to such eyes as the curate's seemed to be looking into both worlds at once, had passed over, bore no unimportant part in that portion of her discipline here commenced. One of the loftiest spirits of the middle earth, it was long before she had quite ceased to regard him as a power of the nether world, partly human, and at once something less and something more. Yet even already she was beginning to feel at home with them ! True, the world in

which they really lived was above her spiritual vision, as
beyond her intellectual comprehension, yet not the less was
the air around them the essential air of homeness ; for the
truths in which their spirits lived and breathed, were the same
which lie at the root of every feeling of home-safety in the
world, which make the bliss of the child in his mother's bed,
the bliss of young beasts in their nests, of birds under their
mother's wing.   The love which inclosed her was far too
great for her—as the heaven of the mother's face is beyond
the understanding of the new-born child over whom she
bends ; but that mother's face is nevertheless the child's joy
and peace.   She did not yet recognize it as love, saw only
the ministration ; but it was what she sorely needed : she
said the sort of thing suited her, and at once began to fall
in with it.   What it cost her entertainers, with organization
as delicate as uncouth, in the mere matter of bodily labor,
she had not an idea—imagined indeed that she gave them
no trouble at all, because, having overheard the conversation
between them upon her arrival, she did herself a part of
the work required for her comfort in her own room.   She
never saw the poor quarters to which Ruth for her sake had
banished herself—never perceived the fact that there was
nothing good enough wherewith to repay them except
worshipful gratitude, love, admiration, and submission—
feelings she could not even have imagined possible in regard
to such inferiors.

And now Dorothy had not a little to say to Juliet about
her husband.   In telling what had taken place, however, she
had to hear many more questions than she was able to
answer.

"Does he really believe me dead, Dorothy?" was one of
them.

"I do not believe there is one person in Glaston who
knows what he thinks," answered Dorothy.   "I have not
heard of his once opening his mouth on the subject.   He is
just as silent now as he used to be ready to talk."

"My poor Paul!" murmured Juliet, and hid her face
and wept.

Indeed not a soul in Glaston or elsewhere knew a single
thought he had.   Certain mysterious advertisements in the
county paper were imagined by some to be his and to refer
to his wife.   Some, as the body had never been seen, did
begin to doubt whether she was dead.   Some, on the other
hand, hinted that her husband had himself made away with

her—for, they argued, what could be easier to a doctor, and why, else, did he make no search for the body? To Dorothy this supposed fact seemed to indicate a belief that she was not dead—perhaps a hope that she would sooner betray herself if he manifested no anxiety to find her. But she said nothing of this to Juliet.

Her news of him was the more acceptable to the famished heart of the wife, that, from his great kindness to them all, and especially from the perseverance which had restored to them their little Amanda, Dorothy's heart had so warmed toward him, that she could not help speaking of him in a tone far more agreeable to Juliet than hitherto she had been able to use. His pale, worn look, and the tokens of trouble throughout his demeanor, all more evident upon nearer approach, had also wrought upon her; and she so described his care, anxiety, and tenderness over Amanda, that Juliet became jealous of the child, as she would have been of any dog she saw him caress. When all was told, and she was weary of asking questions to which there were no answers, she fell back in her chair with a sigh : alas, she was no nearer to him for the hearing of her ears! While she lived she was open to his scorn, and deserved it the more that she had *seemed* to die ! She must die ; for then at last a little love would revive in his heart, ere he died too and followed her nowhither. Only first she must leave him his child to plead for her :—she used sometimes to catch herself praying that the infant might be like her.

" Look at my jacket ! " said Dorothy. It was one of Juliet's, and she hoped to make her smile.

" Did Paul see you with my clothes on ? " she said angrily.

Dorothy started with the pang of hurt that shot through her. But the compassionate smile on the face of Polwarth, who had just entered, and had heard the last article of the conversation, at once set her right. For not only was he capable of immediate sympathy with emotion, but of reveal-ing at once that he understood its cause. Ruth, who had come into the room behind him, second only to her uncle in the insight of love, followed his look by asking Dorothy if she might go to the Old House, as soon as the weather per-mitted, to fetch some clothes for Mrs. Faber, who had brought nothing with her but what she wore ; whereupon Dorothy, partly for leisure to fight her temper, said she would go herself, and went. But when she returned, she gave the bag to Ruth at the door, and went away without

seeing Juliet again.   She was getting tired of her selfishness,
she said to herself.   Dorothy was not herself yet perfect in
love—which beareth all things, believeth all things, hopeth
all things, endureth all things.

Faber too had been up all night—by the bedside of the
little Amanda.   She scarcely needed such close attendance,
for she slept soundly, and was hardly at all feverish.   Four
or five times in the course of the night, he turned down the
bed-clothes to examine her body, as if he feared some injury not hitherto apparent.   Of such there was no sign.

In his youth he had occupied himself much with comparative anatomy and physiology.   His predilection for
these studies had greatly sharpened his observation, and he
noted many things that escaped the eyes of better than ordinary observers.   Amongst other kinds of things to which he
kept his eyes open, he was very quick at noting instances of
the strange persistency with which Nature perpetuates
minute peculiarities, carrying them on from generation to
generation.   Occupied with Amanda, a certain imperfection
in one of the curves of the outer ear attracted his attention.
It is as rare to see a perfect ear as to see a perfect form, and
the varieties of unfinished curves are many ; but this imperfection was very peculiar.   At the same time it was so slight,
that not even the eye of a lover, none save that of a man of
science, alive to minutest indications, would probably have
seen it.   The sight of it startled Faber not a little ; it was
the second instance of the peculiarity that had come to his
knowledge.   It gave him a new idea to go upon, and when
the child suddenly opened her eyes, he saw another face
looking at him out of hers.   The idea then haunted him ;
and whether it was that it assimilated facts to itself, or that
the signs were present, further search afforded what was to
him confirmation of the initiatory suspicion.

Notwithstanding the state of feebleness in which he found
Mr. Drake the next morning, he pressed him with question
upon question, amounting to a thorough cross-examination
concerning Amanda's history, undeterred by the fact that,
whether itself merely bored, or its nature annoyed him, his
patient plainly disrelished his catechising.   It was a subject
which, as his love to the child increased, had grown less and
less agreeable to Mr. Drake : she was to him so entirely his
own that he had not the least desire to find out any thing
about her, to learn a single fact or hear a single conjecture
to remind him that she was not in every sense as well as the

best, his own daughter.   He was therefore not a little annoyed at the persistency of the doctor's questioning, but, being a courteous man, and under endless obligation to him for the very child's sake as well as his own, he combated disinclination, and with success, acquainting the doctor with every point he knew concerning Amanda.   Then first the doctor grew capable of giving his attention to the minister himself ; whose son if he had been, he could hardly have shown him greater devotion.   A whole week passed before he would allow him to go home.   Dorothy waited upon him, and Amanda ran about the house.   The doctor and she had been friends from the first, and now, when he was at home, there was never any doubt where Amanda was to be found.

The same day on which the Drakes left him, Faber started by the night-train for London, and was absent three days.

Amanda was now perfectly well, but Mr. Drake continued poorly.   Dorothy was anxious to get him away from the river-side, and proposed putting the workmen into the Old House at once.   To this he readily consented, but would not listen to her suggestion that in the meantime he should go to some watering-place.   He would be quite well in a day or two, and there was no rest for him, he said, until the work so sadly bungled was properly done.   He did not believe his plans were defective, and could not help doubting whether they had been faithfully carried out.   But the builder, a man of honest repute, protested also that he could not account for the yielding of the wall, except he had had the mishap to build over some deep drain, or old well, which was not likely, so close to the river.   He offered to put it up again at his own expense, when perhaps they might discover the cause of the catastrophe.

Sundry opinions and more than one rumor were current among the neighbors.   At last they were mostly divided into two parties, the one professing the conviction that the butcher, who was known to have some grudge at the minister, had, under the testudo-shelter of his slaughter-house, undermined the wall ; the other indignantly asserting that the absurdity had no foundation except in the evil thoughts of churchmen toward dissenters, being in fact a wicked slander.   When the suggestion reached the minister's ears, he, knowing the butcher, and believing the builder, was inclined to institute investigations ; but as such a course was not likely to lead the butcher to repentance, he resolved instead to consult with him how his premises might be included in the defense. The butcher chuckled with conscious success, and for some months always chuckled when sharpening his knife ; but by and by the coals of fire began to scorch, and went on scorching—the more that Mr. Drake very soon became his landlord, and voluntarily gave him several advantages. But he gave strict orders that there should be no dealings with him. It was one thing, he said, to be good to the sinner, and another to pass by his fault without confession, treating it like a mere personal affair which might be forgotten. Before the butcher died, there was not a man who knew him who did not believe he had undermined the wall. He left a will assigning all his property to trustees, for the building of a new chapel, but when his affairs came to be looked into, there was hardly enough to pay his debts.

The minister was now subject to a sort of ague, to which he paid far too little heed. When Dorothy was not immediately looking after him, he would slip out in any weather to see how things were going on in the Pottery. It was no wonder, therefore, that his health did not improve. But he could not be induced to regard his condition as at all serious.

CHAPTER XLVI.

THE MINISTER'S STUDY.

HELEN was in the way of now and then writing music to any song that specially took her fancy—not with foolish hankering after publication, but for the pleasure of brooding in melody upon the words, and singing them to her husband. One day he brought her a few stanzas, by an unknown poet, which, he said, seemed to have in them a slightly new element. They pleased her more than him, and began at once to sing themselves. No sooner was her husband out of the room than she sat down to her piano with them. Before the evening, she had written to them an air with a simple accompaniment. When she now sung the verses to him, he told her, to her immense delight, that he understood and liked them far better. The next morning, having carried out one or two little suggestions he had made, she was singing them by herself in the drawing-room, when Faber, to whom she had sent because one of her servants was ill, entered. He made a sign begging her to continue, and she finished the song.

" Will you let me see the words," he said.

She handed them to him. He read them, laid down the manuscript, and, requesting to be taken to his patient, turned to the door. Perhaps he thought she had laid a music-snare for him.

The verses were these :

A YEAR SONG.

Sighing above,
  Rustling below,
Through the woods
  The winds go.
Beneath, dead crowds ;
  Above, life bare ;
And the besom winds
  Sweep the air.
Heart, leave thy woe ;
Let the dead things go.

Through the brown leaves
  Gold stars push ;
A mist of green
  Veils the bush.
Here a twitter,
  There a croak !
They are coming—
  The spring-folk !
Heart, be not dumb ;
Let the live things come.

Through the beach
  The winds go,
With a long speech,
  Loud and slow.
The grass is fine,
  And soft to lie in ;
The sun doth shine
  The blue sky in.
Heart, be alive ;
Let the new things thrive.

Round again !
  Here now—
A rimy fruit
  On a bare bough !

> There the winter
> And the snow ;
> And a sighing ever
> To fall and go !
> *Heart, thy hour shall be ;*
> *Thy dead will comfort thee.*

Faber was still folded in the atmosphere of the song when, from the curate's door, he arrived at the minister's, resolved to make that morning a certain disclosure—one he would gladly have avoided, but felt bound in honor to make. The minister grew pale as he listened, but held his peace. Not until the point came at which he found himself personally concerned, did he utter a syllable.

I will in my own words give the substance of the doctor's communication, stating the facts a little more fairly to him than his pride would allow him to put them in his narrative.

Paul Faber was a student of St. Bartholomew's, and during some time held there the office of assistant house-surgeon. Soon after his appointment, he being then three and twenty, a young woman was taken into one of the wards, in whom he gradually grew much interested. Her complaint caused her much suffering, but was more tedious than dangerous.

Attracted by her sweet looks, but more by her patience, and the gratitude with which she received the attention shown her, he began to talk to her a little, especially during a slight operation that had to be not unfrequently performed. Then he came to giving her books to read, and was often charmed with the truth and simplicity of the remarks she would make. She had been earning her living as a clerk, had no friends in London, and therefore no place to betake herself to in her illness but the hospital. The day she left it, in the simplicity of her heart, and with much timidity, she gave him a chain she had made for him of her hair. On the ground of supplementary attention, partly desirable, partly a pretext, but unassociated with any evil intent, he visited her after in her lodging. The joy of her face, the light of her eyes when he appeared, was enchanting to him. She pleased every gentle element of his nature ; her worship flattered him, her confidence bewitched him. His feelings toward her were such that he never doubted he was her friend. He did her no end of kindness ; taught her much ; gave her good advice as to her behavior, and the dangers she was in ; would have protected her from every enemy, real and imaginary, while all the time, undesignedly, he was depriving her of the very nerve of self-defense. He still gave her books—and good books —Carlyle even, and Tennyson ; read poetry with her, and taught her to read aloud ; went to her chapel with her sometimes of a Sunday evening —for he was then, so he said, and so he imagined, a thorough believer in revelation. He took her to the theater, to pictures, to concerts, taking every care of her health, her manners, her principles. But one enemy he forgot to guard her against : how is a man to protect even the woman he loves from the hidden god of his idolatry—his own grand contemptible self ?

It is needless to set the foot of narration upon every step of the slow-descending stair. With all his tender feelings and generous love of his kind, Paul Faber had not yet learned the simplest lesson of humanity—that he who would not be a murderer, must be his brother's keeper—still more his sister's, protecting every woman first of all from himself —from every untruth in him, chiefly from every unhallowed approach of his lower nature, from every thing that calls itself love and is but its black shadow, i ts demon ever murmuring *I love*, that it may devour. The priceless reward of such honesty is the power to love better ; but let no man insult his nature by imagining himself noble for so carrying himself. As soon let him think himself noble that he is no swindler. Doubtless Faber said to himself as well as to her, and said it yet oftener when the recoil of his selfishness struck upon the door of his conscience and roused Don Worm, that he would be true to her forever. But what did he mean by the words ? Did he know ? Had they any sense of which he would not have been ashamed even before the girl herself ? Would such truth as he contemplated make of him her hiding-place from the wind, her covert from the tempest ? He never even thought whether to marry her or not, never vowed even in his heart not to marry another. All he could have said was, that at the time he had no intention of marrying another, and that he had the intention of keeping her for himself indefinitely, which may be all the notion some people have of *eternally*. But things went well with them, and they seemed to themselves, notwithstanding the tears shed by one of them in secret, only the better for the relation between them.

At length a child was born. The heart of a woman is indeed infinite, but time, her presence, her thoughts, her hands are finite : she could not *seem* so much a lover as before, because she must be a mother now : God only can think of two things at once. In his enduring selfishness, Faber felt the child come between them, and reproached her neglect, as he called it. She answered him gently and reasonably ; but now his bonds began to weary him. She saw it, and in the misery of the waste vision opening before her eyes, her temper, till now sweet as devoted, began to change. And yet, while she loved her child the more passionately that she loved her forebodingly, almost with the love of a woman already forsaken, she was nearly mad sometimes with her own heart, that she could not give herself so utterly as before to her idol.

It took but one interview after he had confessed it to himself, to reveal the fact to her that she had grown a burden to him. He came a little seldomer, and by degrees which seemed to her terribly rapid, more and more seldom. He had never recognized duty in his relation to her. I do not mean that he had not done the effects of duty toward her ; love had as yet prevented the necessity of appeal to the stern daughter of God. But what love with which our humanity is acquainted can keep healthy without calling in the aid of Duty ? Perfect Love is the mother of all duties and all virtues, and needs not be admonished of her children ; but not until Love is perfected, may she, casting out Fear, forget also Duty. And hence are the conditions of such a relation altogether incongruous. For the moment the man, not yet debased, admits a thought of duty, he is aware that far more is demanded of him than, even for the sake of purest right, he has either the courage or the conscience to yield. But even now Faber had not the most distant intention of forsaking her; only why should he let her burden him, and make his life miserable ? There were other pleasures besides the company of the most childishly devoted of women : why should he not take them ? Why should he give all his leisure to one who gave more than the half of it to her baby ?

He had money of his own, and, never extravagant upon himself, was more liberal to the poor girl than ever she desired. But there was nothing mercenary in her. She was far more incapable of turpitude than he, for she was of a higher nature, and loved much where he loved only a little. She was nobler, sweetly prouder than he. She had sacrificed all to him for love—could accept nothing from him without the love which alone is the soul of any gift, alone makes it rich. She would not, could not see him unhappy. In her fine generosity, struggling to be strong, she said to herself, that, after all, she would leave him richer than she was before—richer than he was now. He would not want the child he had given her; she would, and she could, live for her, upon the memory of two years of such love as, comforting herself in sad womanly pride, she flattered herself woman had seldom enjoyed. She would not throw the past from her because the weather of time had changed; she would not mar every fair memory with the inky sponge of her present loss. She would turn her back upon her sun ere he set quite, and carry with her into the darkness the last gorgeous glow of his departure. While she had his child, should she never see him again, there remained a bond between them—a bond that could never be broken. He and she met in that child's life—her being was the eternal fact of their unity.

Both she and he had to learn that there was yet a closer bond between them, necessary indeed to the fact that a child *could* be born of them, namely, that they two had issued from the one perfect Heart of love. And every heart of perplexed man, although, too much for itself, it can not conceive how the thing should be, has to learn that there, in that heart whence it came, lies for it restoration, consolation, content. Herein, O God, lies a task for Thy perfection, for the might of Thy imagination—which needs but Thy will (and Thy suffering?) to be creation!

One evening when he paid her a visit after the absence of a week, he found her charmingly dressed, and merry, but in a strange fashion which he could not understand. The baby, she said, was down stairs with the landlady, and she free for her Paul. She read to him, she sang to him, she bewitched him afresh with the graces he had helped to develop in her. He said to himself when he left her that surely never was there a more gracious creature—and she was utterly his own! It was the last flicker of the dying light—the gorgeous sunset she had resolved to carry with her in her memory forever. When he sought her again the next evening, he found her landlady in tears. She had vanished, taking with her nothing but her child, and her child's garments. The gown she had worn the night before hung in her bedroom—every thing but what she must then be wearing was left behind. The woman wept, spoke of her with genuine affection, and said she had paid every thing. To his questioning she answered that they had gone away in a cab : she had called it, but knew neither the man nor his number. Persuading himself she had but gone to see some friend, he settled himself in her rooms to await her return, but a week rightly served to consume his hope. The iron entered into his soul, and for a time tortured him. He wept—but consoled himself that he wept, for it proved to himself that he was not heartless. He comforted himself further in the thought that she knew where to find him and that when trouble came upon her, she would remember how good he had been to her, and what a return she had made for it. Because he would not give up every thing to her, liberty and all, she had left him ! And in revenge, having so long neglected him for the child, she had for the last once roused in her every power of enchantment, had brought her every charm into play, that she might lastingly bewitch him with the old spell, and the undying memory of their first bliss—then left him to his lonely misery ! She had done what she could for the ruin of a man of education, a man of family, a man on the way to distinction !—a man of genius, he said even, but he was such only as every man is : he was a man of latent genius.

But verily, though our sympathy goes all with a woman like her, such a man, howeuer little he deserves, and however much he would scorn it, is far more an object of pity. She has her love, has not been false thereto, and one day will through suffering find the path to the door of rest. When she left him, her soul was endlessly richer than his. The music, of which he said she knew nothing, in her soul moved a deep wave, while it blew but a sparkling ripple on his ; the poetry they read together echoed in a far profounder depth of her being, and I do not believe she came to loathe it as he did ; and when she read of Him who reasoned that the sins of a certain woman must have been forgiven her, else how could she love so much, she may well have been able, from the depth of such another loving heart, to believe utterly in Him—while we know that her poor, shrunken lover came to think it manly, honest, reasonable, meritorious to deny Him.

Weeks, months, years passed, but she never sought him ; and he so far forgot her by ceasing to think of her, that at length, when a chance bubble did rise from the drowned memory, it broke instantly and vanished. As to the child, he had almost forgotten whether *it* was a boy or a girl.

But since, in his new desolation, he discovered her, beyond a doubt, in the little Amanda, old memories had been crowding back upon his heart, and he had begun to perceive how Amanda's mother must have felt when she saw his love decaying visibly before her, and to suspect that it was in the self-immolation of love that she had left him. His own character had been hitherto so uniformly pervaded with a refined selfishness as to afford no standpoint of a different soil, whence by contrast to recognize the true nature of the rest ; but now it began to reveal itself to his conscious judgment. And at last it struck him that twice he had been left—by women whom he loved—at least by women who loved him. Two women had trusted him utterly, and he had failed them both ! Next followed the thought stinging him to the heart, that the former was the purer of the two ; that the one on whom he had looked down because of her lack of education, and her familiarity with humble things and simple forms of life, knew nothing of what men count evil, while she in whom he had worshiped refinement, intellect, culture, beauty, song—she who, in love-teachableness had received his doctrine against all the prejudices of her education, was——what she had confessed herself !

But, against all reason and logic, the result of this comparison was, that Juliet returned fresh to his imagination in all the first witchery of her loveliness ; and presently he found himself for the first time making excuses for her ; if she had deceived him she had deceived him from love ; whatever her past, she had been true to him, and was, from the moment she loved him, incapable of wrong.—He had cast her from him, and she had sought refuge in the arms of the only rival he ever would have had to fear—the bare-ribbed Death !

Naturally followed the reflection—what was he to demand purity of any woman ?—Had he not accepted—yes, tempted, enticed from the woman who preceded her, the sacrifice of one of the wings of her soul on the altar of his selfishness ! then driven her from him, thus maimed and helpless, to the mercy of the rude blasts of the world ! She, not he ever, had been the noble one, the bountiful giver, the victim of shameless ingratitude. Flattering himself that misery would drive her back to him, he had not made a single effort to find her, or mourned that he could never make up to her

for the wrongs he had done her.   He had not even hoped
for a future in which he might humble himself before her !
What room was there here to talk of honor ! If she had not
sunk to the streets it was through her own virtue, and none
of his care ! And now she was dead ! and his child, but for
the charity of a despised superstition, would have been
left an outcast in the London streets, to wither into the
old-faced weakling of a London workhouse !

CHAPTER XLVII.

THE BLOWING OF THE WIND.

SMALLER and smaller Faber felt as he pursued his plain,
courageous confession of wrong to the man whose life was
even now in peril for the sake of his neglected child.
When he concluded with the expression of his conviction
that Amanda was his daughter, then first the old minister
spoke.   His love had made him guess what was coming,
and he was on his guard.

"May I ask what is your object in making this statement
to me, Mr. Faber ?" he said coldly.

"I am conscious of none but to confess the truth, and
perform any duty that may be mine in consequence of the
discovery," said the doctor.

"Do you wish this truth published to the people of Glaston ?" inquired the minister, in the same icy tone.

"I have no such desire : but I am of course prepared to
confess Amanda my child, and to make you what amends
may be possible for the trouble and expense she has occasioned you."

"Trouble !   Expense !" cried the minister fiercely.
"Do you mean in your cold-blooded heart, that, because
you, who have no claim to the child but that of self-indulgence—because you believe her yours, I who have for years
carried her in my bosom, am going to give her up to a man,
who, all these years, has made not one effort to discover his
missing child ?   In the sight of God, which of us is her
father ?   But I forget ; that is a question you can not
understand.   Whether or not you are her father, I do not

care a straw. You have not *proved* it ; and I tell you that, until the court of chancery orders me to deliver up my darling to you, to be taught there is no living Father of men—and that by the fittest of all men to enforce the lie—not until then will I yield a hair of her head to you. God grant, if you were her father, her mother had more part in her than you !—A thousand times rather I would we had both perished in the roaring mud, than that I should have to give her up to you."

He struck his fist on the table, rose, and turned from him. Faber also rose, quietly, silent and pale. He stood a moment, waiting. Mr. Drake turned. Faber made him an obeisance, and left the room.

The minister was too hard upon him. He would not have been so hard but for his atheism ; he would not have been so hard if he could have seen into his soul. But Faber felt he deserved it. Ere he reached home, however, he had begun to think it rather hard that, when a man confessed a wrong, and desired to make what reparation he could, he should have the very candor of his confession thus thrown in his teeth. Verily, even toward the righteous among men, candor is a perilous duty.

He entered the surgery. There he had been making some experiments with peroxide of manganese, a solution of which stood in a bottle on the table. A ray of brilliant sunlight was upon it, casting its shadow on a piece of white paper, a glorious red. It caught his eyes. He could never tell what it had to do with the current of his thoughts, but neither could he afterward get rid of the feeling that it had had some influence upon it. For as he looked at it, scarcely knowing he did, and thinking still how hard the minister had been upon him, suddenly he found himself in the minister's place, and before him Juliet making her sad confession : how had he met that confession ? The whole scene returned, and for the first time struck him right on the heart, and then first he began to be in reality humbled in his own eyes. What if, after all, he was but a poor creature ? What if, instead of having any thing to be proud of, he was in reality one who, before any jury of men or women called to judge him, must hide his head in shame ?

The thought once allowed to enter and remain long enough to be questioned, never more went far from him. For a time he walked in the midst of a dull cloud, first of dread, then of dismay—a cloud from which came thunders, and lightnings, and rain. It passed, and a doubtful dawn rose dim and scared upon his consciousness, a dawn in which the sun did not appear, and on which followed a gray, solemn day. A humbler regard of himself had taken the place of confidence and satisfaction. An undefined hunger, far from understood by himself, but having vaguely for its object clearance and atonement and personal purity even, had begun to grow, and move within him. The thought stung him with keen self-contempt, yet think he must and did, that a woman might be spotted not a little, and yet be good enough for him in the eyes of retributive justice. He saw plainly that his treatment of his wife, knowing what he did of himself, was a far worse shame than any fault of which a girl, such as Juliet was at the time, could have been guilty. And with that, for all that he believed it utterly in vain, his longing after the love he had lost, grew and grew, ever passing over into sickening despair, and then springing afresh ; he longed for Juliet as she had prayed to him— as the only power that could make him clean ; it seemed somehow as if she could even help him in his repentance for the wrong done to Amanda's mother. The pride of the Pharisee was gone, the dignity of the husband had vanished, and his soul longed after the love that covers a multitude of sins, as the air in which alone his spirit could breathe and live and find room. I set it down briefly : the change passed upon him by many degrees, with countless alternations of mood and feeling, and without the smallest conscious change of opinion.

The rest of the day after receiving Faber's communication, poor Mr. Drake roamed about like one on the verge of insanity, struggling to retain lawful dominion over his thoughts. At times he was lost in apprehensive melancholy, at times roused to such fierce anger that he had to restrain himself from audible malediction. The following day Dorothy would have sent for Faber, for he had a worse attack of the fever than ever before, but he declared that the man should never again cross his threshold. Dorothy concluded there had been a fresh outbreak between them of the old volcano. He grew worse and worse, and did not object to her sending for Dr. Mather ; but he did not do him much good. He was in a very critical state, and Dorothy was miserable about him. The fever was persistent, and the cough which he had had ever since the day that brought his illness, grew worse. His friends would gladly have prevailed upon him to seek a warmer climate, but he would not hear of it.

Upon one occasion, Dorothy, encouraged by the presence of Dr. Mather, was entreating him afresh to go somewhere from home for a while.

"No, no : what would become of my money?" he answered, with a smile which Dorothy understood. The doctor imagined it the speech of a man whom previous poverty and suddenly supervening wealth had made penurious.

"Oh !" he remarked reassuringly, "you need not spend a penny more abroad than you do at home. The difference in the living would, in some places, quite make up for the expense of the journey."

The minister looked bewildered for a moment, then seemed to find himself, smiled again, and replied—

"You do not quite understand me : I have a great deal of money to spend, and it ought to be spent here in England where it was made—God knows how."

"You may get help to spend it in England, without throwing your life away with it," said the doctor, who could not help thinking of his own large family.

"Yes, I dare say I might—from many---but it was given *me* to spend—in destroying injustice, in doing to men as others ought to have done to them. My preaching was such a poor affair that it is taken from me, and a lower calling given me—to spend money. If I do not well with that, then indeed I am a lost man. If I be not faithful in that which is another's, who will give me that which is my own ? If I can not further the coming of Christ, I can at least make a road or two, exalt a valley or two, to prepare His way before Him."

Thereupon it was the doctor's turn to smile. All that was to him as if spoken in a language unknown, except that he recognized the religious tone in it. "The man is true to his profession," he said to himself, "—as he ought to be of course ; but catch me spending *my* money that way, if I had but a hold of it !"

His father died soon after, and he got a hold of the money he called *his*, whereupon he parted with his practice, and by idleness and self-indulgence, knowing all the time what he was about, brought on an infirmity which no skill could cure, and is now a grumbling invalid, at one or another of the German spas. I mention it partly because many preferred this man to Faber on the ground that he went to church every Sunday, and always shook his head at the other's atheism.

Faber wrote a kind, respectful letter, somewhat injured in tone, to the minister, saying he was much concerned to hear that he was not so well, and expressing his apprehension that he himself had been in some measure the cause of his relapse. He begged leave to assure him that he perfectly recognized the absolute superiority of Mr. Drake's claim to the child. He had never dreamed of asserting any right in her, except so much as was implied in the acknowledgment of his duty to restore the expense which his wrong and neglect had caused her true father ; beyond that he well knew he could make no return save in gratitude ; but if he might, for the very partial easing of his conscience, be permitted to supply the means of the child's education, he was ready to sign an agreement that all else connected with it should be left entirely to Mr. Drake. He begged to be allowed to see her sometimes, for, long ere a suspicion had crossed his mind that she was his, the child was already dear to him. He was certain that her mother would have much preferred Mr. Drake's influence to his own, and for her sake also, he would be careful to disturb nothing. But he hoped Mr. Drake would remember that, however unworthy, he was still her father.

The minister was touched by the letter, moved also in the hope that an arrow from the quiver of truth had found in the doctor a vulnerable spot. He answered that he should be welcome to see the child when he would ; and that she should go to him when he pleased. He must promise, however, as the honest man every body knew him to be, not to teach her there was no God, or lead her to despise the instructions she received at home.

The word *honest* was to Faber like a blow. He had come to the painful conclusion that he was neither honest man nor gentleman. Doubtless he would have knocked any one down who told him so, but then who had the right to take with him the liberties of a conscience ? Pure love only, I suspect, can do that without wrong. He would not try less to be honest in the time to come, but he had never been, and could no more ever feel honest. It did not matter much. What was there worth any effort ? All was flat and miserable—a hideous long life ! What did it matter what he was, so long as he hurt nobody any more ! He was tired of it all.

It added greatly to his despondency that he found he
could no longer trust his temper. That the cause might be
purely physical was no consolation to him. He had been
accustomed to depend on his imperturbability, and now he
could scarcely recall the feeling of the mental condition.
He did not suspect how much the change was owing to his
new-gained insight into his character, and the haunting
dissatisfaction it caused.

To the minister he replied that he had been learning a
good deal of late, and among other things that the casting
away of superstition did not necessarily do much for the
development of the moral nature ; in consequence of which
discovery, he did not feel bound as before to propagate the
negative portions of his creed. If its denials were true, he
no longer believed them powerful for good ; and merely as
facts he did not see that a man was required to disseminate
them. Even here, however, his opinion must go for little,
seeing he had ceased to care much for any thing, true or
false. Life was no longer of any value to him, except indeed he could be of service to Amanda. Mr. Drake might
be assured she was the last person on whom he would wish
to bring to bear any of the opinions so objectionable in his
eyes. He would make him the most comprehensive promise to that effect. Would Mr. Drake allow him to say one
thing more ?—He was heartily ashamed of his past history ;
and if there was one thing to make him wish there were a
God—of which he saw no chance—it was that he might beg
of Him the power to make up for the wrongs he had done,
even if it should require an eternity of atonement. Until
he could hope for that, he must sincerely hold that his was
the better belief, as well as the likelier—namely, that the
wronger and the wronged went into darkness, friendly with
oblivion, joy and sorrow alike forgotten, there to bid adieu
both to reproach and self-contempt. For himself he had no
desire after prolonged existence. Why should he desire to
live a day, not to say forever—worth nothing to himself, or
to any one ? If there were a God, he would rather entreat
Him, and that he would do humbly enough, to unmake him
again. Certainly, if there were a God, He had not done
over well by His creatures, making them so ignorant and
feeble that they could not fail to fall. Would Mr. Drake
have made his Amanda so ?

When Wingfold read the letter of which I have thus
given the substance—it was not until a long time after,

in Polwarth's room—he folded it softly together and
said :

"When he wrote that letter, Paul Faber was already becoming not merely a man to love, but a man to revere."
After a pause he added, "But what a world it would be,
filled with contented men, all capable of doing the things
for which they would despise themselves."

It was some time before the minister was able to answer
the letter except by sending Amanda at once to the doctor
with a message of kind regards and thanks. But his inability to reply was quite as much from the letter's giving
him so much to think of first, as from his weakness and
fever. For he saw that to preach, as it was commonly understood, the doctrine of the forgiveness of sins to such a
man, would be useless : he would rather believe in a God
who would punish them, than in One who would pass them
by. To be told he was forgiven, would but rouse in him
contemptuous indignation. "What is that to me?" he
would return. "I remain what I am." Then grew up in
the mind of the minister the following plant of thought :
"Things divine can only be shadowed in the human ; what
is in man must be understood of God with the divine difference—not only of degree, but of kind, involved in the fact
that He makes me, I can make nothing, and if I could,
should yet be no less a creature of Him the Creator ; therefore, as the heavens are higher than the earth, so His
thoughts are higher than our thoughts, and what we call His
forgiveness may be, must be something altogether trans-
cending the conception of man—overwhelming to such
need as even that of Paul Faber, whose soul has begun to
hunger after righteousness, and whose hunger must be a
hunger that will not easily be satisfied." For a poor nature
will for a time be satisfied with a middling God ; but as the
nature grows richer, the ideal of the God desired grows
greater. The true man can be satisfied only with a God of
magnificence, never with a God such as in his childhood and
youth had been presented to Faber as the God of the Bible.
That God only whom Christ reveals to the humble seeker,
can ever satisfy human soul.

Then it came into the minister's mind, thinking over
Faber's religion toward his fellows, and his lack toward God,
how when the young man asked Jesus what commandments
he must keep up that he might inherit eternal life, Jesus
did not say a word concerning those of the first table—not

a word, that is, about his duty toward God ; He spoke only
of his duty toward man.   Then it struck him that our Lord
gave him no sketch or summary or part of a religious system—only told him what he asked, the practical steps by
which he might begin to climb toward eternal life.   One
thing he lacked—namely, God Himself, but as to how God
would meet him, Jesus says nothing, but Himself meets him
on those steps with the offer of God.   He treats the duties
of the second table as a stair to the first—a stair which,
probably by its crumbling away in failure beneath his feet
as he ascended, would lift him to such a vision and such a
horror of final frustration, as would make him stretch forth
his hands, like the sinking Peter, to the living God, the life
eternal which he blindly sought, without whose closest
presence he could never do the simplest duty aright, even
of those he had been doing from his youth up.   His measure of success, and his sense of utter failure, would together
lift him *toward* the One Good.

Thus, looking out upon truth from the cave of his
brother's need, and seeing the direction in which the
shadow of his atheism fell, the minister learned in what direction the clouded light lay, and turning his gaze thither-
ward, learned much.   It is only the aged who have dropped
thinking that become stupid.   Such can learn no more,
until first their young nurse Death has taken off their clothes,
and put the old babies to bed.   Of such was not Walter
Drake.   Certain of his formerly petted doctrines he now
threw away as worse than rubbish ; others he dropped with
indifference ; of some it was as if the angels picked his pockets without his knowing it, or ever missing them ; and still
he found, whatever so-called doctrine he parted with, that
the one glowing truth which had lain at the heart of it, buried, mired, obscured, not only remained with him, but shone
out fresh, restored to itself by the loss of the clay-lump of
worldly figures and phrases, in which the human intellect
had inclosed it.   His faith was elevated, and so confirmed.

CHAPTER XLVIII.

THE BORDER-LAND.

MR. DREW, the draper, was, of all his friends, the one who most frequently visited his old pastor. He had been the first, although a deacon of the church, in part to forsake his ministry, and join the worship of, as he honestly believed, a less scriptural community, because in the abbey church he heard better news of God and His Kingdom : to him rightly the gospel was every thing, and this church or that, save for its sake, less than nothing and vanity. It had hurt Mr. Drake not a little at first, but he found Drew in consequence only the more warmly his personal friend, and since learning to know Wingfold, had heartily justified his defection ; and now that he was laid up, he missed something any day that passed without a visit from the draper. One evening Drew found him very poorly, though neither the doctor nor Dorothy could prevail upon him to go to bed. He could not rest, but kept walking about, his eye feverish, his pulse fluttering. He welcomed his friend even more warmly than usual, and made him sit by the fire, while he paced the room, turning and turning, like a caged animal that fain would be king of infinite space.

"I am sorry to see you so uncomfortable," said Mr. Drew.

"On the contrary, I feel uncommonly well," replied the pastor. "I always measure my health by my power of thinking ; and to-night my thoughts are like birds—or like bees rather, that keep flying in delight from one lovely blossom to another. Only the fear keeps intruding that an hour may be at hand, when my soul will be dark, and it will seem as if the Lord had forsaken me."

"But does not *our daily bread* mean our spiritual as well as our bodily bread ? " said the draper. "Is it not just as wrong in respect of the one as of the other to distrust God for to-morrow when you have enough for to-day ? Is He a God of times and seasons, of this and that, or is He the All in all ? "

"You are right, old friend," said the minister, and ceasing his walk, he sat down by the fire opposite him. "I am faithless still.—O Father in Heaven, give us this day our daily bread.—I suspect, Drew, that I have had as yet no more than the shadow of an idea how immediately I—we live upon the Father.—I will tell you something. I had been thinking what it would be if God were now to try me with heavenly poverty, as for a short time he tried me with earthly poverty—that is, if he were to stint me of life itself—not give me enough of Himself to live upon—enough to make existence feel a good. The fancy grew to a fear, laid hold upon me, and made me miserable. Suppose, for instance, I said to myself, I were no more to have any larger visitation of thoughts and hopes and aspirations than old Mrs. Bloxam, who sits from morning to night with the same stocking on her needles, and absolutely the same expression, of as near nothing as may be upon human countenance, nor changes whoever speaks to her ! ”

" She says the Lord is with her," suggested the draper.

" Well ! ” rejoined the minister, in a slow, cogitative tone.

" And plainly life is to her worth having," added the draper. " Clearly she has as much of life as is necessary to her present stage."

" You are right. I have been saying just the same things to myself ; and, I trust, when the Lord comes, He will not find me without faith. But just suppose life *were* to grow altogether uninteresting ! Suppose certain moods —such as you, with all your good spirits and blessed temper, must surely sometimes have experienced—suppose they were to become fixed, and life to seem utterly dull, God nowhere, and your own dreary self, and nothing but that self, everywhere ! ”

" Let me read you a chapter of St. John," said the draper.

" Presently I will. But I am not in the right mood just this moment. Let me tell you first how I came by my present mood. Don't mistake me : I am not possessed by the idea—I am only trying to understand its nature, and set a trap fit to catch it, if it should creep into my inner premises, and from an idea swell to a seeming fact.—Well, I had a strange kind of a vision last night—no, not a vision—yes, a kind of vision—anyhow a very strange experience. I don't know whether the draught the doctor gave me—I wish I had poor Faber back—this fellow is fitter to doctor oxen and mules than men !—I don't know whether the draught had any thing to do with it—I thought I tasted something sleepy in it—anyhow, thought is thought, and truth is truth, whatever drug, no less than whatever joy or sorrow, may

have been midwife to it.   The first I remember of the mental experience, whatever it may have to be called, is, that I
was coming awake—returning to myself after some period
wherein consciousness had been quiescent.   Of place, or
time, or circumstance, I knew nothing.   I was only growing
aware of being.   I speculated upon nothing.   I did not even
say to myself, 'I was dead, and now I am coming alive.'   I
only felt.   And I had but one feeling—and that feeling was
love—the outgoing of a longing heart toward—I could not
tell what ;—toward—I can not describe the feeling—toward
the only existence there was, and that was every thing ;—
toward pure being, not as an abstraction, but as the one
actual fact, whence the world, men, and me—a something I
knew only by being myself an existence.   It was more me
than myself ; yet it was not me, or I could not have loved
it.   I never thought me myself by myself ; my very existence was the consciousness of this absolute existence in and
through and around me : it made my heart burn, and the
burning of my heart was my life—and the burning was the
presence of the Absolute.   If you can imagine a growing
fruit, all blind and deaf, yet loving the tree it could neither
look upon nor hear, knowing it only through the unbroken
arrival of its life therefrom—that is something like what I
felt.   I suspect the *form* of the feeling was supplied by a
shadowy memory of the time before I was born, while yet
my life grew upon the life of my mother.

"By degrees came a change.   What seemed the fire in
me, burned and burned until it began to grow light ; in
which light I began to remember things I had read and
known about Jesus Christ and His Father and my Father.
And with those memories the love grew and grew, till I
could hardly bear the glory of God and His Christ, it made
me love so intensely.   Then the light seemed to begin to
pass out beyond me somehow, and therewith I remembered
the words of the Lord, 'Let your light so shine before men,'
only I was not letting it shine, for while I loved like that, I
could no more keep it from shining than I could the sun.
The next thing was, that I began to think of one I had
loved, then of another and another and another—then of
all together whom ever I had loved, one after another, then
all together.   And the light that went out from me was as
a nimbus infolding every one in the speechlessness of my
love.   But lo ! then, the light staid not there, but, leaving
them not, went on beyond them, reaching and infolding

every one of those also, whom, after the manner of men, I had on earth merely known and not loved. And therewith I knew that, for all the rest of the creation of God, I needed but the hearing of the ears or the seeing of the eyes to love each and every one, in his and her degree ; whereupon such a perfection of bliss awoke in me, that it seemed as if the fire of the divine sacrifice had at length seized upon my soul, and I was dying of absolute glory—which is love and love only. I had all things, yea the All. I was full and unutterably, immeasurably content. Yet still the light went flowing out and out from me, and love was life and life was light and light was love. On and on it flowed, until at last it grew eyes to me, and I could see. Lo ! before me was the multitude of the brothers and sisters whom I loved—individually—a many, many—not a mass ;—I loved every individual with that special, peculiar kind of love which alone belonged to that one, and to that one alone. The sight dazzled the eyes which love itself had opened. I said to myself, ' Ah, how radiant, how lovely, how divine they are ! and they are mine, every one—the many, for I love them !'

"Then suddenly came a whisper—not to my ear—I heard it far away, but whether in some distant cave of thought, away beyond the flaming walls of the universe, or in some forgotten dungeon-corner of my own heart, I could not tell. ' O man,' it said, ' what a being, what a life is thine ! See all these souls, these fires of life, regarding and loving thee ! It is in the glory of thy love their faces shine. Their hearts receive it, and send it back in joy. Seest thou not all their eyes fixed upon thine ? Seest thou not the light come and go upon their faces, as the pulses of thy heart flow and ebb ? See, now they flash, and now they fade ! Blessed art thou, O man, as none else in the universe of God is blessed !'

"It was, or seemed, only a voice. But therewith, horrible to tell, the glow of another fire arose in me—an orange and red fire, and it went out from me, and withered all the faces, and the next moment there was darkness—all was black as night. But my being was still awake—only if then there was bliss, now was there the absolute blackness of darkness, the positive negation of bliss, the recoil of self to devour itself, and forever. The consciousness of being was intense, but in all the universe was there nothing to enter that being, and make it other than an absolute loneliness.

It was, and forever, a loveless, careless, hopeless monotony of self-knowing—a hell with but one demon, and no fire to make it cry : my self was the hell, my known self the demon of it—a hell of which I could not find the walls, cold and dark and empty, and I longed for a flame that I might know there was a God.   Somehow I only remembered God as a word, however ; I knew nothing of my whence or whither.   One time there might have been a God, but there was none now : if there ever was one, He must be dead. Certainly there was no God to love—for if there was a God, how could the creature whose very essence was to him an evil, love the Creator of him ?   I had the word *love*, and I could reason about it in my mind, but I could not call up the memory of what the feeling of it was like.   The blackness grew and grew.   I hated life fiercely.   I hated the very possibility of a God who had created me a blot, a blackness.   With that I felt blackness begin to go out from me, as the light had gone before—not that I remembered the light ; I had forgotten all about it, and remembered it only after I awoke.   Then came the words of the Lord to me : ' If therefore the light that is in thee be darkness, how great is that darkness ! '   And I knew what was coming : oh, horror ! in a moment more I should see the faces of those I had once loved, dark with the blackness that went out from my very existence ; then I should hate them, and my being would then be a hell to which the hell I now was would be a heaven !   There was just grace enough left in me for the hideousness of the terror to wake me.   I was cold as if I had been dipped in a well.   But oh, how I thanked God that I was what I am, and might yet hope after what I may be ! "

The minister's face was pale as the horse that grew gray when Death mounted him ; and his eyes shone with a feverous brilliancy.   The draper breathed a deep breath, and rubbed his white forehead.   The minister rose and began again to pace the room.   Drew would have taken his departure, but feared leaving him in such a state.   He bethought himself of something that might help to calm him, and took out his pocket-book.   The minister's dream had moved him deeply, but he restrained himself all he could from manifesting his emotion.

"Your vision," he said, " reminds me of some verses of Mr. Wingfold's, of which Mrs. Wingfold very kindly let me take a copy.   I have them here in my pocket-book ; may I read them to you ? "

The minister gave rather a listless consent, but that was enough for Mr. Drew's object, and he read the following poem.

SHALL THE DEAD PRAISE THEE?

I can not praise Thee. By his instrument
  The organ-master sits, nor moves a hand ;
For see the organ pipes o'erthrown and bent,
  Twisted and broke, like corn-stalks tempest-fanned !

I well could praise Thee for a flower, a dove ;
  But not for life that is not life in me ;
Not for a being that is less than love—
  A barren shoal half-lifted from a sea,

And for the land whence no wind bloweth ships,
  And all my living dead ones thither blown—
Rather I'd kiss no more their precious lips,
  Than carry them a heart so poor and prone.

Yet I do bless Thee Thou art what Thou art,
  That Thou dost know Thyself what Thou dost know—
A perfect, simple, tender, rhythmic heart,
  Beating Thy blood to all in bounteous flow.

And I can bless Thee too for every smart,
  For every disappointment, ache, and fear ;
For every hook Thou fixest in my heart,
  For every burning cord that draws me near.

But prayer these wake, not song. Thyself I crave.
  Come Thou, or all Thy gifts away I fling.
Thou silent, I am but an empty grave ;
  Think to me, Father, and I am a king.

Then, like the wind-stirred bones, my pipes shall quake,
  The air burst, as from burning house the blaze ;
And swift contending harmonies shall shake
  Thy windows with a storm of jubilant praise.

Thee praised, I haste me humble to my own—
  Then love not shame shall bow me at their feet,
Then first and only to my stature grown,
  Fulfilled of love, a servant all-complete.

At first the minister seemed scarcely to listen, as he sat with closed eyes and knitted brows, but gradually the wrinkles disappeared like ripples, an expression of repose

supervened, and when the draper lifted his eyes at the close
of his reading, there was a smile of quiet satisfaction on the
now aged-looking countenance.   As he did not open his
eyes, Drew crept softly from the room, saying to Dorothy
as he left the house, that she *must* get him to bed as soon as
possible.   She went to him, and now found no difficulty in
persuading him.   But something, she could not tell what,
in his appearance, alarmed her, and she sent for the doctor.
He was not at home, and had expected to be out all night.
She sat by his bedside for hours, but at last, as he was
quietly asleep, ventured to lay herself on a couch in the
room.   There she too fell fast asleep, and slept till morning,
undisturbed.

When she went to his bedside, she found him breathing
softly, and thought him still asleep.   But he opened his
eyes, looked at her for a moment fixedly, and then said :

" Dorothy, child of my heart ! things may be very different from what we have been taught, or what we may of
ourselves desire ; but every difference will be the step of
an ascending stair—each nearer and nearer to the divine
perfection which alone can satisfy the children of a God,
alone supply the poorest of their cravings."

She stooped and kissed his hand, then hastened to get
him some food.

When she returned, he was gone up the stair of her future,
leaving behind him, like a last message that all was well, the
loveliest smile frozen upon a face of peace.   The past had
laid hold upon his body ; he was free in the Eternal.   Dorothy was left standing at the top of the stair of the present.

CHAPTER XLIX.

EMPTY HOUSES.

THE desolation that seized on Dorothy seemed at first
overwhelming.   There was no refuge for her.   The child's
tears, questions, and outbreaks of merriment were but a
trouble to her.   Even Wingfold and Helen could do little
for her.   Sorrow was her sole companion, her sole *comfort*
for a time against the dreariness of life.   Then came some-

thing better. As her father's form receded from her, his spirit drew nigh. I mean no phantom out of Hades—no consciousness of local presence : such things may be—I think *sometimes* they are ; but I would rather know my friend better through his death, than only be aware of his presence about me ; that will one day follow—how much the more precious that the absence will have doubled its revelations, its nearness ! To Dorothy her father's character, especially as developed in his later struggles after righteousness—the root-righteousness of God, opened itself up day by day. She saw him combating his faults, dejected by his failures, encouraged by his successes ; and he grew to her the dearer for his faults, as she perceived more plainly how little he had sided, how hard he had fought with them. The very imperfections he repudiated gathered him honor in the eyes of her love, sowed seeds of perennial tenderness in her heart. She saw how, in those last days, he had been overcoming the world with accelerated victory, and growing more and more of the real father that no man can be until he has attained to the sonship. The marvel is that our children are so tender and so trusting to the slow developing father in us. The truth and faith which the great Father has put in the heart of the child, makes him the nursing father of the fatherhood in his father ; and thus in part it is, that the children of men will come at last to know the great Father. The family, with all its powers for the development of society, is a family because it is born and rooted in, and grows out of the very bosom of God. Gabriel told Zacharias that his son John, to make ready a people prepared for the Lord, should turn the hearts of the fathers to the children.

Few griefs can be so paralyzing as, for a time, that of a true daughter upon the departure, which at first she feels as the loss, of a true parent ; but through the rifts of such heartbreaks the light of love shines clearer, and where love is, there is eternity : one day He who is the Householder of the universe, will begin to bring out of its treasury all the good old things, as well as the better new ones. How true must be the bliss up to which the intense realities of such sorrows are needful to force the way for the faithless heart and feeble will ! Lord, like Thy people of old, we need yet the background of the thunder-cloud against which to behold Thee ; but one day the only darkness around Thy dwelling will be the too much of Thy brightness. For Thou art the perfection which every heart sighs toward, no mind can attain unto. If Thou wast One whom created mind could embrace, Thou wouldst be too small for those whom Thou hast made in Thine own image, the infinite creatures that seek their God, a Being to love and know infinitely. For the created to know perfectly would be to be damned forever in the nutshell of the finite. He who is His own cause, alone can understand perfectly and remain infinite, for that which is known and that which knows are in Him the same infinitude.

Faber came to see Dorothy—solemn, sad, kind. He made no attempt at condolence, did not speak a word of comfort ; but he talked of the old man, revealing for him a deep respect ; and her heart was touched, and turned itself toward him. Some change, she thought, must have passed upon him. Her father had told her nothing of his relation to Amanda. It would have to be done some day, but he shrunk from it. She could not help suspecting there was more between Faber and him than she had at first imagined ; but there was in her a healthy contentment with ignorance, and she asked no questions. Neither did Faber make any attempt to find out whether she knew what had passed ; even about Amanda and any possible change in her future he was listless. He had never been a man of plans, and had no room for any now under the rubbish of a collapsed life. His days were gloomy and his nights troubled. He dreamed constantly either of Amanda's mother, or of Juliet —sometimes of both together, and of endless perplexity between them. Sometimes he woke weeping. He did ˙not now despise his tears, for they flowed neither from suffering nor self-pity, but from love and sorrow and repentance. A question of the possibility of his wife's being yet alive would occasionally occur to him, but he always cast the thought from him as a folly in which he dared not indulge lest it should grow upon him and unman him altogether. Better she were dead than suffering what his cruelty might have driven her to : he had weakened her self-respect by insult, and then driven her out helpless.

People said he took the loss of his wife coolly ; but the fact was that, in every quiet way, he had been doing all man could do to obtain what information concerning her there might possibly be to be had. Naturally he would have his proceedings as little as possible in the public mouth ; and to employ the police or the newspapers in such a quest was too horrible. But he had made inquiries in all directions. He had put a question or two to Polwarth, but at that time he *knew* nothing of her, and did not feel bound to disclose his suspicions. Not knowing to what it might not expose her, he would not betray the refuge of a woman with a woman. Faber learned what every body had learned, and for a time was haunted by the horrible expectation of further news from the lake. Every knock at the door made him start and turn pale. But the body had not floated, and would not now.

We have seen that, in the light thrown upon her fault from the revived memory of his own, a reaction had set in : the tide of it grew fiercer as it ran. He had deposed her idol—the God who she believed could pardon, and the bare belief in whom certainly could comfort her ; he had taken the place with her of that imaginary, yet, for some, necessary being ; but when, in the agony of repentant shame, she looked to him for the pardon he alone could give her, he had turned from her with loathing, contempt, and insult ! He was the one in the whole earth, who, by saying to her *Let it be forgotten*, could have lifted her into life and hope ! She had trusted in him, and he, an idol indeed, had crumbled in the clinging arms of her faith ! Had she not confessed to him what else he would never have known, humbling herself in a very ecstasy of repentance ? Was it not an honor to any husband to have been so trusted by his wife ? And had he not from very scorn refused to strike her ! Was she not a woman still ? a being before whom a man, when he can no longer worship, must weep ? Could *any* fault, ten times worse than she had committed, make her that she was no woman ? that he, merely as a man, owed her nothing ? Her fault was grievous ; it stung him to the soul : what then was it not to her ? Not now for his own shame merely, or the most, did he lament it, but for the pity of it, that the lovely creature should not be clean, had not deserved his adoration ; that she was not the ideal woman ; that a glory had vanished from the earth ; that she he had loved was not in herself worthy. What then must be her sadness ! And this was his—the man's—response to her agony, this his balm for her woe, his chivalry, his manhood—to dash her from him, and do his potent part to fix forever upon her the stain which he bemoaned ! Stained ? Why then did he not open his arms wide and take her, poor sad stain and all, to the bosom of a love which, by the very agony of its own grief

and its pity over hers, would have burned her clean? What
did it matter for him? What was he? What was his honor?
Had he had any, what fitter use for honor than to sacrifice
it for the redemption of a wife? That would be to honor
honor. But he had none. There was not a stone on the
face of the earth that would consent to be thrown at her by
him!

Ah men! men! gentlemen! was there ever such a poor
sneaking scarecrow of an idol as that gaping straw-stuffed
inanity you worship, and call *honor*? It is not Honor; it
is but *your* honor. It is neither gold, nor silver, nor honest
copper, but a vile, worthless pinchbeck. It may be, however,
for I have not the honor to belong to any of your clubs,
that you no longer insult the word by using it at all. It
may be you have deposed it, and enthroned another word
of less significance to you still. But what the recognized
slang of the day may be is nothing—therefore unnecessary
to what I have to say—which is, that the man is a wretched
ape who will utter a word about a woman's virtue, when in
himself, soul and body, there is not a clean spot; when his
body nothing but the furnace of the grave, his soul nothing
but the eternal fire can purify. For him is many a harlot
far too good: she is yet capable of devotion; she would,
like her sisters of old, recognize the Holy if she saw Him,
while he would pass by his Maker with a rude stare, or the
dullness of the brute which he has so assiduously cultivated
in him.

By degrees Faber grew thoroughly disgusted with himself, then heartily ashamed. Were it possible for me to
give every finest shade and gradation of the change he
underwent, there would be still an unrepresented mystery
which I had not compassed. But were my analysis correct
as fact itself, and my showing of it as exact as words could
make it, never a man on whom some such change had not at
least begun to pass, would find in it any revelation. He
ceased altogether to vaunt his denials, not that now he had
discarded them, but simply because he no longer delighted
in them. They were not interesting to him any more. He
grew yet paler and thinner. He ate little and slept ill—and
the waking hours of the night were hours of torture. He
was out of health, and he knew it, but that did not comfort
him. It was wrong and its misery that had made him ill,
not illness that had made him miserable. Was he a weakling, a fool not to let the past be the past? " Things with-

out all remedy should be without regard : what's done is done." But not every strong man who has buried his murdered in his own garden, and set up no stone over them, can forget where they lie. It needs something that is not strength to be capable of that. The dead alone can bury their dead so ; and there is a bemoaning that may help to raise the dead. But sometimes such dead come alive un-bemoaned. Oblivion is not a tomb strong enough to keep them down. The time may come when a man will find his past but a cenotaph, and its dead all walking and making his present night hideous. And when such dead walk so, it is a poor chance they do not turn out vampires.

When she had buried her dead out of her sight, Dorothy sought solitude and the things unseen more than ever. The Wingfolds were like swallows about her, never folding their wings of ministry, but not haunting her with bodily visitation. She never refused to see them, but they under-stood : the hour was not yet when their presence would be a comfort to her. The only comfort the heart can take must come—not from, but through itself. Day after day she would go into the park, avoiding the lodge, and there brood on the memories of her father and his late words. And ere long she began to feel nearer to him than she had ever felt while he was with her. For, where the outward sign has been understood, the withdrawing of it will bring the inward fact yet nearer. When our Lord said the spirit of Himself would come to them after He was gone, He but promised the working of one of the laws of His Father's kingdom : it was about to operate in loftiest grade.

Most people find the first of a bereavement more tolerable than what follows. They find in its fever a support. When the wound in the earth is closed, and the wave of life has again rushed over it, when things have returned to their wonted, now desiccated show, then the very Sahara of deso-lation opens around them, and for a time existence seems almost insupportable. With Dorothy it was different. Alive in herself, she was hungering and thirsting after life, therefore death could not have dominion over her.

To her surprise she found also—she could not tell how the illumination had come—she wondered even how it should ever have been absent—that, since her father's death, many of her difficulties had vanished. Some of them, remember-ing there had been such, she could hardly recall sufficiently to recognize them. She had been lifted into a region above

that wherein moved the questions which had then disturbed
her peace.   From a point of clear vision, she saw the things
themselves so different, that those questions were no longer
relevant.   The things themselves misconceived, naturally
no satisfaction can be got from meditation upon them, or
from answers sought to the questions they suggest.   If it be
objected that she had no better ground for believing than
before, I answer that, if a man should be drawing life from
the heart of God, it could matter little though he were
unable to give a satisfactory account of the mode of its
derivation.   That the man lives is enough.   That another
denies the existence of any such life save in the man's self-
fooled imagination, is nothing to the man who lives it.   His
business is not to raise the dead, but to live—not to convince
the blind that there is such a faculty as sight, but to make
good use of his eyes.   He may not have an answer to any
one objection raised by the adopted children of Science—
their adopted mother raises none—to that which he believes ;
but there is no more need that that should trouble him,
than that a child should doubt his bliss at his mother's
breast, because he can not give the chemical composition of
the milk he draws : that in the thing which is the root of the
bliss, is rather beyond chemistry.   Is a man not blessed in his
honesty, being unable to reason of the first grounds of
property ? If there be truth, that truth must be itself—must
exercise its own blessing nature upon the soul which receives
it in loyal understanding—that is, in obedience.   A man may
accept no end of things as facts which are not facts, and his
mistakes will not hurt him.   He may be unable to receive
many facts as facts, and neither they nor his refusal of
them will hurt him.   He may not a whit the less be
living in and by the truth.   He may be quite unable to
answer the doubts of another, but if, in the progress of his
life, those doubts should present themselves to his own soul,
then will he be able to meet them : he is in the region where
all true answers are gathered.   He may be unable to receive
this or that embodiment or form of truth, not having yet grown
to its level ; but it is no matter so long as when he sees a
truth he does it : to see and not do would at once place him
in eternal danger.   Hence a man of ordinary intellect and
little imagination, may yet be so radiant in nobility as, to the
true poet-heart, to be right worshipful.   There is in the man
who does the truth the radiance of life essential, eternal—a
glory infinitely beyond any that can belong to the intellect,

beyond any that can ever come within its scope to be judged, proven, or denied by it. Through experiences doubtful even to the soul in which they pass, the life may yet be flowing in. To know God is to be in the secret place of all knowledge ; and to trust Him changes the atmosphere surrounding mystery and seeming contradiction, from one of pain and fear to one of hope : the unknown may be some lovely truth in store for us, which yet we are not good enough to apprehend. A man may dream all night that he is awake, and when he does wake, be none the less sure that he is awake in that he thought so all the night when he was not ; but he will find himself no more able to prove it than he would have been then, only able to talk better about it. The differing consciousnesses of the two conditions can not be *produced* in evidence, or embodied in forms of the understanding. But my main point is this, that not to be intellectually certain of a truth, does not prevent the heart that loves and obeys that truth from getting its truth-good, from drawing life from its holy *factness*, present in the love of it.

As yet Dorothy had no plans, except to carry out those of her father, and, mainly for Juliet's sake, to remove to the old house as soon as ever the work there was completed. But the repairs and alterations were of some extent, and took months. Nor was she desirous of shortening Juliet's sojourn with the Polwarths : the longer that lasted with safety, the better for Juliet, and herself too, she thought.

On Christmas eve, the curate gave his wife a little poem. Helen showed it to Dorothy, and Dorothy to Juliet. By this time she had had some genuine teaching—far more than she recognized as such, and the spiritual song was not altogether without influence upon her. Here it is :

THAT HOLY THING.

They all were looking for a king
   To slay their foes, and lift them high :
Thou cam'st a little baby thing
   That made a woman cry.

O Son of Man, to right my lot
   Naught but Thy presence can avail ;
Yet on the road Thy wheels are not,
   Nor on the sea Thy sail.

My how or when Thou wilt not heed,
   But come down Thine own secret stair,
That Thou mayst answer all my need,
   Yea, every by-gone prayer.

CHAPTER L.

THE spring was bursting in bud and leaf before the work-men were out of the Old House. The very next day, Dorothy commenced her removal. Every stick of the old furniture she carried with her ; every book of her father's she placed on the shelves of the library he had designed. But she took care not to seem neglectful of Juliet, never failing to carry her the report of her husband as often as she saw him. It was to Juliet like an odor from Paradise making her weep, when Dorothy said that he looked sad— "so different from his old self!"

One day Dorothy ventured, hardly to hint, but to ap-proach a hint of mediation. Juliet rose indignant : no one, were he an angel from Heaven, should interfere between her husband and her! If they could not come together without that, there should be a mediator, but not such as Dorothy meant!

"No, Dorothy!" she resumed, after a rather prolonged silence ; "the very word *mediation* would imply a gulf be-tween us that could not be passed. But I have one petition to make to you, Dorothy. You *will* be with me in my trouble—won't you ?"

"Certainly, Juliet—please God, I will."

"Then promise me, if I can't get through—if I am going to die, that you will bring him to me. I *must* see my Paul once again before the darkness."

"Wouldn't that be rather unkind—rather selfish ?" re-turned Dorothy.

She had been growing more and more pitiful of Paul.

Juliet burst into tears, called Dorothy cruel, said she meant to kill her. How was she to face it but in the hope of death ? and how was she to face death but in the hope of seeing Paul once again for the last time ? She was certain she was going to die ; she knew it ! and if Dorothy would not promise, she was not going to wait for such a death !

"But there will be a doctor," said Dorothy, "and how am I——"

Juliet interrupted her—not with tears but words of indignation : Did Dorothy dare imagine she would allow any man but her Paul to come near her ? Did she ? Could she ? What did she think of her ? But of course she was prejudiced against her ! It was too cruel !

The moment she could get in a word, Dorothy begged her to say what she wished.

" You do not imagine, Juliet," she said, " that I could take such a responsibility on myself ! "

" I have thought it all over," answered Juliet. " There are women properly qualified, and you must find one. When she says I am dying,—when she gets frightened, you will send for my husband ? Promise me."

" Juliet, I will," answered Dorothy, and Juliet was satisfied.

But notwithstanding her behavior's continuing so much the same, a change, undivined by herself as well as unsuspected by her friend, had begun to pass upon Juliet. Every change must begin further back than the observation of man can reach—in regions, probably, of which we have no knowledge. To the eyes of his own wife, a man may seem in the gall of bitterness and the bond of iniquity, when " larger, other eyes than ours " may be watching with delight the germ of righteousness swell within the inclosing husk of evil. Sooner might the man of science detect the first moment of actinic impact, and the simultaneously following change in the hitherto slumbering acorn, than the watcher of humanity make himself aware of the first movement of repentance. The influences now for some time operative upon her, were the more powerful that she neither suspected nor could avoid them. She had a vague notion that she was kind to her host and hostess ; that she was patronizing them ; that her friend Dorothy, with whom she would afterwards arrange the matter, filled their hands for her use ; that, in fact, they derived benefit from her presence ; —and surely they did, although not as she supposed. The only benefits they reaped were invaluable ones—such as spring from love and righteousness and neighborhood. She little thought how she interfered with the simple pleasures and comforts of the two ; how many a visit of friends, whose talk was a holy revelry of thought and utterance, Polwarth warded, to avoid the least danger of her discovery ; how often fear for her shook the delicate frame of Ruth ; how often her host left some book unbought, that he might procure instead some thing to tempt her to eat ; how often her

hostess turned faint in cooking for her.   The crooked creatures pitied, as well they might, the lovely lady ; they believed that Christ was in her ; that the deepest in her was
the nature He had made—His own, and not that which she
had gathered to herself—and thought her own.   For the
sake of the Christ hidden in her, her own deepest, best,
purest self ; that she might be lifted from the dust-heap of
the life she had for herself ruined, into the clear air of a pure
will and the Divine Presence, they counted their best labor
most fitly spent.   It is the human we love in each other—
and the human is the Christ.   What we do not love is the
devilish—no more the human than the morrow's wormy mass
was the manna of God.   To be for the Christ in a man, is
the highest love you can give him ; for in the unfolding
alone of that Christ can the individuality, the genuine
peculiarity of the man, the man himself, be perfected—the
flower of his nature be developed, in its own distinct loveliness, beauty, splendor, and brought to its idea.

The main channel through which the influences of the
gnomes reached the princess, was their absolute simplicity.
They spoke and acted what was in them.   Through this
open utterance, their daily, common righteousness revealed
itself—their gentleness, their love of all things living, their
care of each other, their acceptance as the will of God concerning them of whatever came, their general satisfaction
with things as they were—though it must in regard to some
of them have been in the hope that they would soon pass
away, for one of the things Juliet least could fail to observe
was their suffering patience.   They always spoke as if they
felt where their words were going—as if they were hearing
them arrive—as if the mind they addressed were a bright
silver table on which they must not set down even the cup
of the water of life roughly : it must make no scratch, no
jar, no sound beyond a faint sweet salutation.   Pain had
taught them not sensitiveness but delicacy.   A hundred are
sensitive for one that is delicate.   Sensitiveness is a miserable, a cheap thing in itself, but invaluable if it be used for
the nurture of delicacy.   They refused to receive offense,
their care was to give none.   The burning spot in the center of that distorted spine, which ought to have lifted Ruth
up to a lovely woman, but had failed and sunk, and ever
after ached bitterly as if with defeat, had made her pitiful
over the pains of humanity : she could bear it, for there
was something in her deeper than pain ; but alas for those

who were not thus upheld ! Her agony drove her to pray for the whole human race, exposed to like passion with her. The asthmatic choking which so often made Polwarth's nights a long misery, taught him sympathy with all prisoners and captives, chiefly with those bound in the bonds of an evil conscience : to such he held himself specially devoted. They thought little of bearing pain : to know they had caused it would have been torture. Each, graciously uncomplaining, was tender over the ailing of the other.

Juliet had not been long with them before she found the garments she had in her fancy made for them, did not fit them, and she had to devise. afresh. They were not gnomes, kobolds, goblins, or dwarfs, but a prince and princess of sweet nobility, who had loved each other in beauty and strength, and knew that they were each crushed in the shell of a cruel and mendacious enchantment. How they served each other ! The uncle would just as readily help the niece with her saucepans, as the niece would help the uncle to find a passage in Shakespeare or a stanza in George Herbert. And to hear them talk !

For some time Juliet did not understand them, and did not try. She had not an idea what they were talking about. Then she began to imagine they must be weak in the brain —a thing not unlikely with such spines as theirs—and had silly secrets with each other, like children, which they enjoyed talking about chiefly because none could understand but themselves. Then she came to fancy it was herself and her affairs they were talking about, deliberating upon—in some mental if not lingual gibberish of their own. By and by it began to disclose itself to her, that the wretched creatures, to mask their misery from themselves, were actually playing at the kingdom of Heaven, speaking and judging and concluding of things of this world by quite other laws, other scales, other weights and measures than those in use in it. Every thing was turned topsy-turvy in this their game of make-believe. Their religion was their chief end and interest, and their work their play, as lightly followed as diligently. What she counted their fancies, they seemed to count their business ; their fancies ran over upon their labor, and made every day look and feel like a harvest-home, or the eve of a long-desired journey, for which every preparation but the last and lightest was over. Things in which she saw no significance made them look very grave, and what she would have counted of some importance to such as they, drew a mere smile from them. She saw all with bewildered eyes, much as his neighbors looked upon the strange carriage of Lazarus, as represented by Robert Browning in the wonderful letter of the Arab physician. But after she had begun to take note of their sufferings, and come to mark their calm, their peace, their lighted eyes, their ready smiles, the patience of their very moans, she began to doubt whether somehow they might not be touched to finer issues than she. It was not, however, until after having, with no little reluctance and recoil, ministered to them upon an occasion in which both were disabled for some hours, that she began to *feel* they had a hold upon something unseen, the firmness of which hold made it hard to believe it closed upon an unreality. If there was nothing there, then these dwarfs, in the exercise of their foolish, diseased, distorted fancies, came nearer to the act of creation than any grandest of poets ; for these their inventions did more than rectify for them the wrongs of their existence, not only making of their chaos a habitable cosmos, but of themselves heroic dwellers in the same. Within the charmed circle of this their well-being, their unceasing ministrations to her wants, their thoughtfulness about her likings and dislikings, their sweetness of address, and wistful watching to discover the desire they might satisfy or the solace they could bring, seemed every moment enticing her. They soothed the aching of her wounds, mollified with ointment the stinging rents in her wronged humanity.

At first, when she found they had no set prayers in the house, she concluded that, for all the talk of the old gnome in the garden, they were not very religious. But by and by she began to discover that no one could tell when they might not be praying. At the most unexpected times she would hear her host's voice somewhere uttering tones of glad beseeching, of out-poured adoration. One day, when she had a bad headache, the little man came into her room, and, without a word to her, kneeled by her bedside, and said, " Father, who through Thy Son knowest pain, and Who dost even now in Thyself feel the pain of this Thy child, help her to endure until Thou shalt say it is enough, and send it from her. Let it not overmaster her patience ; let it not be too much for her. What good it shall work in her, Thou, Lord, needest not that we should instruct Thee." Therewith he rose, and left the room,

For some weeks after, she was jealous of latent design to bring their religion to bear upon her ; but perceiving not a single direct approach, not the most covert hint of attack, she became gradually convinced that they had no such intent. Polwarth was an absolute serpent of holy wisdom, and knew that upon certain conditions of the human being the only powerful influences of religion are the all but insensible ones. A man's religion, he said, ought never to be held too near his neighbor. It was like violets : hidden in the banks, they fill the air with their scent ; but if a bunch of them is held to the nose, they stop away their own sweetness.

Not unfrequently she heard one of them reading to the other, and by and by, came to join them occasionally. Sometimes it would be a passage of the New Testament, sometimes of Shakespeare, or of this or that old English book, of which, in her so-called education, Juliet had never even heard, but of which the gatekeeper knew every landmark. He would often stop the reading to talk, explaining and illustrating what the writer meant, in a way that filled Juliet with wonder. " Strange ! " she would say to herself ; " I never thought of that ! " She did not suspect that it would have been strange indeed if she had thought of it.

In her soul began to spring a respect for her host and hostess, such as she had never felt toward God or man. When, despite of many revulsions it was a little established, it naturally went beyond them in the direction of that which they revered. The momentary hush that preceded the name of our Lord, and the smile that so often came with it ; the halo, as it were, which in their feeling surrounded Him ; the confidence of closest understanding, the radiant humility with which they approached His idea ; the way in which they brought the commonest question side by side with the ideal of Him in their minds, considering the one in the light of the other, and answering it thereby ; the way in which they took all He said and did on the fundamental understanding that His relation to God was perfect, but His relation to men as yet an imperfect, endeavoring relation, because of their distance from His Father ; these, with many another outcome of their genuine belief, began at length to make her feel, not merely as if there had been, but as if there really were such a person as Jesus Christ. The idea of Him ruled potent in the lives of the two, filling heart and brain and hands and feet : how could she help a certain awe before it, such as she had never felt !

Suddenly one day the suspicion awoke in her mind, that the reason why they asked her no questions, put out no feelers after discovery concerning her, must be that Dorothy had told them every thing : if it was, never again would she utter word good or bad to one whose very kindness, she said to herself, was betrayal ! The first moment therefore she saw Polwarth alone, unable to be still an instant with her doubt unsolved, she asked him, " with sick assay," but point-blank, whether he knew why she was in hiding from her husband.

" I do not know, ma'am," he answered.

" Miss Drake told you nothing ? " pursued Juliet.

" Nothing more than I knew already : that she could not deny when I put it to her."

" But how did you know any thing ? " she almost cried out, in a sudden rush of terror as to what the public knowledge of her might after all be.

" If you will remember, ma'am," Polwarth replied, " I told you, the first time I had the pleasure of speaking to you, that it was by observing and reasoning upon what I observed, that I knew you were alive and at the Old House. But it may be some satisfaction to you to see how the thing took shape in my mind."

Thereupon he set the whole process plainly before her.

Fresh wonder, mingled with no little fear, laid hold upon Juliet. She felt not merely as if he could look into her, but as if he had only to look into himself to discover all her secrets.

" I should not have imagined you a person to trouble himself to that extent with other people's affairs," she said, turning away.

" So far as my service can reach, the things of others are also mine," replied Polwarth, very gently.

" But you could not have had the smallest idea of serving me when you made all those observations concerning me."

" I had long desired to serve your husband, ma'am. Never from curiosity would I have asked a single question about you or your affairs. But what came to me I was at liberty to understand if I could, and use for lawful ends if I might."

Juliet was silent. She dared hardly think, lest the gnome should see her very thoughts in their own darkness. Yet she yielded to one more urgent question that kept pushing

to get out.   She tried to say the words without thinking of
the thing, lest he should thereby learn it.

"I suppose then you have your own theory as to my
reasons for seeking shelter with Miss Drake for a while?"
she said—and the moment she said it, felt as if some demon
had betrayed her, and used her organs to utter the words.

"If I have, ma'am," answered Polwarth, "it is for myself
alone.   I know the sacredness of married life too well to
speculate irreverently on its affairs.   I believe that many an
awful crisis of human history is there passed—such, I presume, as God only sees and understands.   The more carefully such are kept from the common eye and the common
judgment, the better, I think."

If Juliet left him with yet a little added fear, it was also
with growing confidence, and some comfort, which the feeble
presence of an infant humility served to enlarge.

Polwarth had not given much thought to the question of
the cause of their separation.   That was not of his business.
What he could not well avoid seeing was, that it could
hardly have taken place since their marriage.   He had at
once, as a matter of course, concluded that it lay with the
husband, but from what he had since learned of Juliet's
character, he knew she had not the strength either of moral
opinion or of will to separate, for any reason past and gone,
from the husband she loved so passionately ; and there he
stopped, refusing to think further.   For he found himself on
the verge of thinking what, in his boundless respect for
women, he shrank with deepest repugnance from entertain-
ing even as a transient flash of conjecture.

One trifle I will here mention, as admitting laterally a
single ray of light upon Polwarth's character.   Juliet had
come to feel some desire to be useful in the house beyond
her own room, and descrying not only dust, but what she
judged disorder in her *landlord's* little library—for such she
chose to consider him—which, to her astonishment in such
a mere cottage, consisted of many more books than her
husband's, and ten times as many readable ones, she offered
to dust and rearrange them properly : Polwarth instantly
accepted her offer, with thanks—which were solely for the
kindness of the intent, he could not possibly be grateful for
the intended result—and left his books at her mercy.   I do
not know another man who, loving his books like Polwarth,
would have done so.   Every book had its own place.   He
could—I speak advisedly—have laid his hand on any book

of at least three hundred of them, in the dark. While he used them with perfect freedom, and cared comparatively little about their covers, he handled them with a delicacy that looked almost like respect. He had seen ladies handle books, he said, laughing, to Wingfold, in a fashion that would have made him afraid to trust them with a child. It was a year after Juliet left the house before he got them by degrees muddled into order again ; for it was only as he used them that he would alter their places, putting each, when he had done with it for the moment, as near where it had been before as he could ; thus, in time, out of a neat chaos, restoring a useful work-a-day world.

Dorothy's thoughts were in the meantime much occupied for Juliet. Now that she was so sadly free, she could do more for her. She must occupy her old quarters as soon as possible after the workmen had finished. She thought at first of giving out that a friend in poor health was coming to visit her, but she soon saw that would either involve lying or lead to suspicion, and perhaps discovery, and resolved to keep her presence in the house concealed from the outer world as before. But what was she to do with respect to Lisbeth ? Could she trust her with the secret ? She certainly could not trust Amanda. She would ask Helen to take the latter for a while, and do her best to secure the silence of the former.

She so represented the matter to Lisbeth as to rouse her heart in regard to it even more than her wonder. But her injunctions to secrecy were so earnest, that the old woman was offended. She was no slip of a girl, she said, who did not know how to hold her tongue. She had had secrets to keep before now, she said ; and in proof of her perfect trustworthiness, was proceeding to tell some of them, when she read her folly in Dorothy's fixed regard, and ceased.

"Lisbeth," said her mistress, "you have been a friend for sixteen years, and I love you ; but if I find that you have given the smallest hint even that there is a secret in the house, I solemnly vow you shall not be another night in it yourself, and I shall ever after think of you as a wretched creature who periled the life of a poor, unhappy lady rather than take the trouble to rule her own tongue."

Lisbeth trembled, and did hold her tongue, in spite of the temptation to feel herself for just one instant the most important person in Glaston.

As the time went on, Juliet became more fretful, and more

confiding. She was never cross with Ruth—why, she could not have told ; and when she had been cross to Dorothy, she was sorry for it. She never said she was sorry, but she tried to make up for it. Her husband had not taught her the virtue, both for relief and purification, that lies in the *acknowledgment* of wrong. To take up blame that is our own, is to wither the very root of it.

Juliet was pleased at the near prospect of the change, for she had naturally dreaded being ill in the limited accommodation of the lodge. She formally thanked the two crushed and rumpled little angels, begged them to visit her often, and proceeded to make her very small preparations with a fitful cheerfulness. Something might come of the change, she flattered herself. She had always indulged a vague fancy that Dorothy was devising help for her ; and it was in part the disappointment of nothing having yet justified the expectation, that had spoiled her behavior to her. But for a long time Dorothy had been talking of Paul in a different tone, and that very morning had spoken of him even with some admiration : it might be a prelude to something ! Most likely Dorothy knew more than she chose to say ! She dared ask no question for the dread of finding herself mistaken. She preferred the ignorance that left room for hope. But she did not like all Dorothy said in his praise ; for her tone, if not her words, seemed to imply some kind of change in him. He might have his faults, she said to herself, like other men, but she had not yet discovered them ; and any change would, in her eyes, be for the worse. Would she ever see her own old Paul again ?

One day as Faber was riding at a good round trot along one of the back streets of Glaston, approaching his own house, he saw Amanda, who still took every opportunity of darting out at an open door, running to him with outstretched arms, right in the face of Niger, just as if she expected the horse to stop and take her up. Unable to trust him so well as his dear old Ruber, he dismounted, and taking her in his arms, led Niger to his stable. He learned from her that she was staying with the Wingfolds, and took her home, after which his visits to the rectory were frequent.

The Wingfolds could not fail to remark the tenderness with which he regarded the child. Indeed it soon became clear that it was for her sake he came to them. The change that had begun in him, the loss of his self-regard following on the loss of Juliet, had left a great gap in his conscious being : into that gap had instantly begun to shoot the all-clothing greenery of natural affection. His devotion to her did not at first cause them any wonderment. Every body loved the little Amanda, they saw in him only another of the child's conquests, and rejoiced in the good the love might do him. Even when they saw him looking fixedly at her with eyes over clear, they set it down to the frustrated affection of the lonely, wifeless, childless man. But by degrees they did come to wonder a little : his love seemed to grow almost a passion. Strange thoughts began to move in their minds, looking from the one to the other of this love and the late tragedy.

"I wish," said the curate one morning, as they sat at breakfast, "if only for Faber's sake, that something definite was known about poor Juliet. There are rumors in the town, roving like poisonous fogs. Some profess to believe he has murdered her, getting rid of her body utterly, then spreading the report that she had run away. Others say she is mad, and he has her in the house, but stupefied with drugs to keep her quiet. Drew told me he had even heard it darkly hinted that he was making experiments upon her, to discover the nature of life. It is dreadful to think what a man is exposed to from evil imaginations groping after theory. I dare hardly think what might happen should these fancies get rooted among the people. Many of them are capable of brutality. For my part, I don't believe the poor woman is dead yet."

Helen replied she did not believe that, in her sound mind, Juliet would have had the resolution to kill herself ; but who could tell what state of mind she was in at the time ? There was always something mysterious about her—something that seemed to want explanation.

Between them it was concluded that, the next time Faber came, Wingfold should be plain with him. He therefore told him that if he could cast any light on his wife's disappearance, it was most desirable he should do so ; for reports were abroad greatly to his disadvantage. Faber answered, with a sickly smile of something like contempt, that they had had a quarrel the night before, for which he was to blame ; that he had left her, and the next morning she was gone, leaving every thing, even to her wedding-ring, behind her, except the clothes she wore ; that he had done all he could to find her, but had been utterly foiled. More he could not say.

The next afternoon, he sought an interview with the curate in his study, and told him every thing he had told Mr. Drake. The story seemed to explain a good deal more than it did, leaving the curate with the conviction that the disclosure of this former relation had caused the quarrel between him and his wife, and more doubtful than ever as to Juliet's having committed suicide.

CHAPTER LI.

THE NEW OLD HOUSE.

It was a lovely moon-lighted midnight when they set out, the four of them, to walk from the gate across the park to the Old House. Like shadows they flitted over the green sward, all silent as shadows. Scarcely a word was spoken as they went, and the stray syllable now and then, was uttered softly as in the presence of the dead. Suddenly but gently opened in Juliet's mind a sense of the wonder of life. The moon, having labored through a heap of cloud into a lake of blue, seemed to watch her with curious interest as she toiled over the level sward. The air now and then made a soundless sigh about her head, like a waft of wings invisible. The heavenly distances seemed to have come down and closed her softly in. All at once, as if waked from an eternity of unconsciousness, she found herself, by no will of her own, with no power to say nay, present to herself—a target for sorrow to shoot at, a tree for the joy-birds to light upon and depart—a woman, scorned of the man she loved, bearing within her another life, which by no will of its own, and with no power to say nay, must soon become aware of its own joys and sorrows, and have no cause to bless her for her share in its being. Was there no one to answer for it? Surely there must be a heart-life somewhere in the universe, to whose will the un-self-willed life could refer for the justification of its existence, for its motive, for the idea of it that should make it seem right to itself—to whom it could cry to have its divergence from that idea rectified ! Was she not now, she thought, upon her silent way to her own death-bed, walking, walking, the phantom of herself, in her own funeral ? What if, when the bitterness of death was past, and her child was waking in this world, she should be waking in another, to a new life, inevitable as the former—another, yet the same ? We know not whence we came—why may we not be going whither we know not ? We did not know we were coming here, why may we not be going there without knowing it—this much more open-eyed, more aware that we know we do not know ? That terrible morning, she had come this way, rushing swiftly to her death : she was caught and dragged back from Hades, to be thereafter—now, driven slowly toward it, like an ox to the slaughter ! She could not avoid her doom—she *must* encounter that which lay before her. That she shrunk from it with fainting terror was nothing ; on she must go ! What an iron net, what a combination of all chains and manacles and fetters and iron-masks and cages and prisons was this existence—at least to a woman, on whom was laid the burden of the generations to follow ! In the lore of centuries was there no spell whereby to be rid of it ? no dark saying that taught how to make sure death should be death, and not a fresh waking ? That the future is unknown, assures only danger ! New circumstances have seldom to the old heart proved better than the new piece of cloth to the old garment.

Thus meditated Juliet. She was beginning to learn that, until we get to the heart of life, its outsides will be forever fretting us ; that among the mere garments of life, we can never be at home. She was hard to teach, but God's circumstance had found her.

When they came near the brow of the hollow, Dorothy ran on before, to see that all was safe. Lisbeth was of course the only one in the house. The descent was to Juliet like the going down to the gates of Death.

Polwarth, who had been walking behind with Ruth, stepped to her side the moment Dorothy left her. Looking up in her face, with the moonlight full upon his large features, he said,

"I have been feeling all the way, ma'am, as if Another was walking beside us—the same who said, 'I am with you always even to the end of the world.' He could not have meant that only for the few that were so soon to follow Him home ; He must have meant it for those also who should believe by their word. Becoming disciples, all promises the Master made to His disciples are theirs."

"It matters little for poor me," answered Juliet with a sigh. "You know I do not believe in Him."

"But I believe in Him," answered Polwarth, "and Ruth believes in Him, and so does Miss Drake; and if He be with us, he can not be far from you."

With that he stepped back to Ruth's side, and said no more.

Dorothy opened the door quickly, the moment their feet were on the steps; they entered quickly, and she closed it behind them at once, fearful of some eye in the night. How different was the house from that which Juliet had left! The hall was lighted with a soft lamp, showing dull, warm colors on walls and floor. The dining-room door stood open; a wood-fire was roaring on the hearth, and candles were burning on a snowy table spread for a meal. Dorothy had a chamber-candle in her hand. She showed the Polwarths into the dining-room, then turning to Juliet, said,

"I will take you to your room, dear."

"I have prepared your old quarters for you," she said, as they went up the stair.

With the words there rushed upon Juliet such a memory of mingled dreariness and terror, that she could not reply.

"You know it will be safest," added Dorothy, and as she spoke, set the candle on a table at the top of the stair.

They went along the passage, and she opened the door of the closet. All was dark.

She opened the door in the closet, and Juliet started back with amazement. It was the loveliest room! and—like a marvel in a fairy-tale—the great round moon was shining gloriously, first through the upper branches of a large yew, and then through an oriel window, filled with lozenges of soft greenish glass, through which fell a lovely picture on the floor in light and shadow and something that was neither or both. Juliet turned in delight, threw her arms round Dorothy, and kissed her.

"I thought I was going into a dungeon," she said, "and it is a room for a princess!"

"I sometimes almost believe, Juliet," returned Dorothy, "that God will give us a great surprise one day."

Juliet was tired, and did not want to hear about God. If Dorothy had done all this, she thought, for the sake of reading her a good lesson, it spoiled it all. She did not understand the love that gives beyond the gift, that mantles over the cup and spills the wine into the spaces of eternal hope. The room was so delicious that she begged to be excused from going down to supper. Dorothy suggested it would not be gracious to her friends. Much as she respected, and indeed loved them, Juliet resented the word *friends*, but yielded.

The little two would themselves rather have gone home —it was so late—but staid, fearing to disappoint Dorothy. If they did run a risk by doing so, it was for a good reason —therefore of no great consequence.

" How your good father will delight to watch you here sometimes, Miss Drake," said Polwarth, " if those who are gone are permitted to see, walking themselves unseen."

Juliet shuddered. Dorothy's father not two months gone, and the dreadful little man to talk to her like that !

" Do you then think," said Dorothy, " that the dead only seem to have gone from us?" and her eyes looked like store-houses of holy questions.

" I know so little," he answered, " that I dare hardly say I *think* any thing. But if, as our Lord implies, there be no such thing as that which the change appears to us—nothing like that we are thinking of when we call it *death*—may it not be that, obstinate as is the appearance of separation, there is, notwithstanding, none of it ?—I don't care, mind : His will *is*, and that is every thing. But there can be no harm, where I do not know His will, in venturing a *may be*. I am sure He likes His little ones to tell their fancies in the dimmits about the nursery fire. Our souls yearning after light of any sort must be a pleasure to him to watch.—But on the other hand, to resume the subject, it may be that, as it is good for us to miss them in the body that we may the better find them in the spirit, so it may be good for them also to miss our bodies that they may find our spirits."

" But," suggested Ruth, " they had that kind of discipline while yet on earth, in the death of those who went before them ; and so another sort might be better for them now. Might it not be more of a discipline for them to see, in those left behind, how they themselves, from lack of faith, went groping about in the dark, while crowds all about them knew perfectly what they could not bring themselves to believe ?"

" It might, Ruth, it might ; nor do I think any thing to the contrary. Or it might be given to some and not to others, just as it was good for them. It may be that some can see some, or can see them sometimes, and watch their ways in partial glimpses of revelation. Who knows who may be about the house when all its mortals are dead for the night, and the last of the fires are burning unheeded! There are so many hours of both day and night—in most houses—in which those in and those out of the body need never cross each others' paths! And there are tales, legends, reports, many mere fiction doubtless, but some possibly of a different character, which represent this and that doer of evil as compelled, either by the law of his or her own troubled being, or by some law external thereto, ever, or at fixed intervals, to haunt the moldering scenes of their past, and ever dream horribly afresh the deeds done in the body. These, however, tend to no proof of what we have been speaking about, for such ʻ extravagant and erring spirit ' does not haunt the living from love, but the dead from suffering. In this life, however, few of us come really near to each other in the genuine simplicity of love, and that may be the reason why the credible stories of love meeting love across the strange difference are so few. It is a wonderful touch, I always think, in the play of Hamlet, that, while the prince gazes on the spirit of his father, not-ing every expression and gesture—even his dress, as he passes through his late wife's chamber, Gertrude, less un-faithful as widow than as wife, not only sees nothing, but by no sigh or hint, no sense in the air, no beat of her own heart, no creep even of her own flesh, divines his presence —is not only certain that she sees nothing, but that she sees all there is. She is the dead, not her husband. To the dead all are dead. The eternal life makes manifest both life and death."

" Please, Mr. Polwarth," said Juliet, " remember it is the middle of the night. No doubt it is just the suitable time, but I would rather not make one in an orgy of horrors. We have all to be alone presently."

She hated to hear about death, and the grandest of words, Eternal Life, which to most means nothing but prolonged existence, meant to her just death. If she had stolen a magic spell for avoiding it, she could not have shrunk more from any reference to the one thing commonest and most inevitable. Often as she tried to imagine the reflection of her own death in the mind of her Paul, the mere mention of the ugly thing seemed to her ill-mannered, almost in-decent.

" The Lord is awake all night," said Polwarth, rising, " and therefore the night is holy as the day.—Ruth, we should be rather frightened to walk home under that awful sky, if we thought the Lord was not with us."

" The night is fine enough," said Juliet.

" Yes," said Ruth, replying to her uncle, not to Juliet; " but even if He were asleep—you remember how He slept once, and yet reproached His disciples with their fear and doubt."

" I do ; but in the little faith with which He reproached them, He referred, not to Himself, but to His Father. Whether He slept or waked it was all one : the Son may sleep, for the Father never sleeps."

They stood beside each other, taking their leave : what little objects they were, opposite the two graceful ladies, who also stood beside each other, pleasant to look upon. Sorrow and suffering, lack and weakness, though plain to see upon them both, had not yet greatly dimmed their beauty. The faces of the dwarfs, on the other hand, were marked and lined with suffering ; but the suffering was dominated by peace and strength. There was no sorrow there, little lack, no weakness or fear, and a great hope. They never spent any time in pitying themselves ; the trouble that alone ever clouded their sky, was the suffering of others. Even for this they had comfort—their constant ready help consoled both the sufferer and themselves.

" Will you come and see me, if you die first, uncle ? " said Ruth, as they walked home together in the moonlight. " You will think how lonely I am without you."

" If it be within the law of things, if I be at liberty, and the thing seem good for you, my Ruth, you may be sure I will come to you. But of one thing I am pretty certain, that such visions do not appear when people are looking for them. You must not go staring into the dark trying to see me. Do your work, pray your prayers, and be sure I love you : if I am to come, I will come. It may be in the hot noon or in the dark night : it may be with no sight and no sound, yet a knowledge of presence; or I may be watching you, helping you perhaps and you never know it until I come to fetch you at the last,—if I may. You have been daughter and sister, and mother to me, my Ruth. You have been my one in the world. God, I think sometimes, has planted about you and me, my child, a cactus-hedge of ugliness, that we might be so near and so lonely as to learn love as few have learned it in this world—love without fear, or doubt, or pain, or anxiety—with constant satisfaction in presence, and calm content in absence. Of the last, however, I can not boast much, seeing we have not been parted a day for—how many years is it, Ruth?—Ah, Ruth! a bliss beyond speech is waiting us in the presence of the Master, where, seeing Him as He is, we shall grow like Him and be no more either dwarfed or sickly. But you will have the same face, Ruth, else I should be forever missing something."

"But you do not think we shall be perfect all at once?"

"No, not all at once ; I can not believe that : God takes time to what He does—the doing of it is itself good. It would be a sight for heavenly eyes to see you, like a bent and broken and withered lily, straightening and lengthening your stalk, and flushing into beauty.—But fancy what it will be to see at length to the very heart of the person you love, and love Him perfectly—and that *you* can love *Him!* Every love will then be a separate heaven, and all the heavens will blend in one perfect heaven—the love of God—the All in all."

They were walking like children, hand in hand : Ruth pressed that of her uncle, for she could not answer in words.

Even to Dorothy their talk would have been vague, vague from the intervening mist of her own atmosphere. To them it was vague only from the wide stretch of its horizon, the distance of its zenith. There is all difference between the vagueness belonging to an imperfect sight, and the vagueness belonging to the distance of the outlook. But to walk on up the hill of duty, is the only way out of the one into the other. I think some only know they are laboring, hardly know they are climbing, till they find themselves near the top.

CHAPTER LII.

THE LEVEL OF THE LYTHE.

DOROTHY's faith in Polwarth had in the meantime largely increased. She had not only come to trust him thoroughly, but gained much strength from the confidence. As soon as she had taken Juliet her breakfast the next morning, she went to meet him in the park, for so they had arranged the night before.

She had before acquainted him with the promise Juliet had exacted from her, that she would call her husband the moment she seemed in danger—a possibility which Juliet regarded as a certainty ; and had begged him to think how they could contrive to have Faber within call. He had now a plan to propose with this object in view, but began, apparently, at a distance from it.

"You know, Miss Drake," he said, "that I am well acquainted with every yard of this ground. Had your honored father asked me whether the Old House was desirable for a residence, I should have expressed considerable doubt. But there is one thing which would greatly improve it—would indeed, I hope, entirely remove my objection to it. Many years ago I noted the state of the stone steps leading up to the door : they were much and diversely out of the level ; and the cause was evident with the first great rain : the lake filled the whole garden—to the top of the second step. Now this, if it take place only once a year, must of course cause damp in the house. But I think there is more than that will account for. I have been in the cellars repeatedly, both before and since your father bought it ; and always found them too damp. The cause of it, I think, is, that the foundations are as low as the ordinary level of the water in the pond, and the ground at that depth is of large gravel : it seems to me that the water gets through to the house. I should propose, therefore, that from the bank of the Lythe a tunnel be commenced, rising at a gentle incline until it pierces the basin of the lake. The ground is your own to the river, I believe ?"

"It is," answered Dorothy. "But I should be sorry to empty the lake altogether."

"My scheme," returned Polwarth, "includes a strong sluice, by which you could keep the water at what height you pleased, and at any moment send it into the river. The only danger would be of cutting through the springs ; and I fancy they are less likely to be on the side next the river where the ground is softer, else they would probably have found their way directly into it, instead of first hollowing out the pond."

"Would it be a difficult thing to do ?" asked Dorothy.

"I think not," answered Polwarth. "But with your permission I will get a friend of mine, an engineer, to look into it."

"I leave it in your hands," said Dorothy.—"Do you think we will find any thing at the bottom?"

"Who can tell? But we do not know how near the bottom the tunnel may bring us; there may be fathoms of mud below the level of the river-bed.—One thing, thank God, we shall not find there!"

The same week all was arranged with the engineer. By a certain day his men were to be at work on the tunnel.

For some time now, things had been going on much the same with all in whom my narrative is interested. There come lulls in every process, whether of growth or of tempest, whether of creation or destruction, and those lulls, coming as they do in the midst of force, are precious in their influence—because they are only lulls, and the forces are still at work. All the time the volcano is quiet, something is going on below. From the first moment of exhaustion, the next outbreak is preparing. To be faint is to begin to gather, as well as to cease to expend.

Faber had been growing better. He sat more erect on his horse; his eye was keener, his voice more kindly, though hardly less sad, and his step was firm. His love to the child, and her delight in his attentions, were slowly leading him back to life. Every day, if but for a moment, he contrived to see her, and the Wingfolds took care to remove every obstacle from the way of their meeting. Little they thought why Dorothy let them keep the child so long. As little did Dorothy know that what she yielded for the sake of the wife, they desired for the sake of the husband.

At length one morning came a break: Faber received a note from the gate-keeper, informing him that Miss Drake was having the pond at the foot of her garden emptied into the Lythe by means of a tunnel, the construction of which was already completed. They were now boring for a small charge of gunpowder expected to liberate the water. The process of emptying would probably be rapid, and he had taken the liberty of informing Mr. Faber, thinking he might choose to be present. No one but the persons employed would be allowed to enter the grounds.

This news gave him a greater shock than he could have believed possible. He thought he had "supped full of horrors!" At once he arranged with his assistant for being absent the whole day; and rode out, followed by his groom. At the gate Polwarth joined him, and walked beside him to the Old House, where his groom, he said, could put up the horses.   That done, he accompanied him to the mouth of the tunnel, and there left him.

Faber sat down on the stump of a felled tree, threw a big cloak, which he had brought across the pommel of his saddle, over his knees, and covered his face with his hands.   Before him the river ran swiftly toward the level country, making a noise of watery haste ; also the wind was in the woods, with the noises of branches and leaves, but the only sounds he heard were the blows of the hammer on the boring-chisel, coming dull, and as if from afar, out of the depths of the earth.   What a strange, awful significance they had to the heart of Faber !   But the end was delayed hour after hour, and there he still sat, now and then at a louder noise than usual lifting up a white face, and staring toward the mouth of the tunnel.   At the explosion the water would probably rush in a torrent from the pit, and in half an hour, perhaps, the pond would be empty.   But Polwarth had taken good care there should be no explosion that day.   Ever again came the blow of iron upon iron, and the boring had begun afresh.

Into her lovely chamber Dorothy had carried to Juliet the glad tidings that her husband was within a few hundred yards of the house, and that she might trust Mr. Polwarth to keep him there until all danger was over.

Juliet now manifested far more courage than she had given reason to expect.   It seemed as if her husband's nearness gave her strength to do without his presence.

At length the child, a lovely boy, lay asleep in Dorothy's arms.   The lovelier mother also slept.   Polwarth was on his way to stop the work, and let the doctor know that its completion must be postponed for a few days, when he heard the voice of Lisbeth behind him, calling as she ran.   He turned and met her, then turned again and ran, as fast as his little legs could carry him, to the doctor.

"Mr. Faber," he cried, "there is a lady up there at the house, a friend of Miss Drake's, taken suddenly ill.   You are wanted as quickly as possible."

Faber answered not a word, but went with hasty strides up the bank, and ran to the house.   Polwarth followed as fast as he could, panting and wheezing.   Lisbeth received the doctor at the door.

"Tell my man to saddle *my* horse, and be at the back door immediately," he said to her.

Polwarth followed him up the stair to the landing, where

Dorothy received Faber, and led him to Juliet's room. The dwarf seated himself on the top of the stair, almost within sight of the door.

CHAPTER LIII.

MY LADY'S CHAMBER.

WHEN Faber entered, a dim, rosy light from drawn window-curtains filled the air ; he could see little more than his way to the bed. Dorothy was in terror lest the discovery he must presently make, should unnerve the husband for what might be required of the doctor. But Juliet kept her face turned aside, and a word from the nurse let him know at once what was necessary. He turned to Dorothy, and said,

"I must send my man home to fetch me something ; " then to the nurse, and said, "Go on as you are doing ; " then once more to Dorothy, saying, "Come with me, Miss Drake : I want writing things."

He led the way from the room, and Dorothy followed. But scarcely were they in the passage, when the little man rose and met them. Faber would have pushed past him, annoyed, but Polwarth held out a little phial to him.

"Perhaps that is what you want, sir," he said.

The doctor caught it hastily, almost angrily, from his hand, looked at it, uncorked it, and put it to his nose.

"Thank you," he said, "this is just what I wanted," and returned instantly to the chamber.

The little man resumed his patient seat on the side, breathing heavily. Ten minutes of utter silence followed. Then Dorothy passed him with a note in her hand, and hurried down the stair. The next instant Polwarth heard the sound of Niger's hoofs tearing up the slope behind the house.

"I have got some more medicines here, Miss Drake," he said, when she reappeared on the stair.

As he spoke he brought out phial after phial, as if his pockets widened out below into the mysterious recesses of the earth to which as a gnome he belonged. Dorothy, however, told him it was not a medicine the doctor wanted now, but something else, she did not know what. Her face was dreadfully white, but as calm as an ice field. She went back into the room, and Polwarth sat down again.

Not more than twenty minutes had passed when he heard again the soft thunder of Niger's hoofs upon the sward; and in a minute more up came Lisbeth, carrying a little morocco case, which she left at the door of the room.

Then an hour passed, during which he heard nothing. He sat motionless, and his troubled lungs grew quiet.

Suddenly he heard Dorothy's step behind him, and rose.

"You had better come down stairs with me," she said, in a voice he scarcely knew, and her face looked almost as if she had herself passed through a terrible illness.

"How is the poor lady?" he asked.

"The immediate danger is over, the doctor says, but he seems in great doubt. He has sent me away. Come with me: I want you to have a glass of wine."

"Has he recognized her?"

"I do not know. I haven't seen any sign of it yet. But the room is dark.—We can talk better below."

"I am in want of nothing, my dear lady," said Polwarth. "I should much prefer staying here—if you will permit me. There is no knowing when I might be of service. I am far from unused to sick chambers."

"Do as you please, Mr. Polwarth," said Dorothy, and going down the stair, went into the garden.

Once more Polwarth resumed his seat.

There came the noise of a heavy fall, which shook him where he sat. He started up, went to the door of the chamber, listened a moment, heard a hurried step and the sweeping of garments, and making no more scruple, opened it and looked in.

All was silent, and the room was so dark he could see nothing. Presently, however, he descried, in the middle of the floor, a prostrate figure that could only be the doctor, for plainly it was the nurse on her knees by him. He glanced toward the bed. There all was still.

"She is gone!" he thought with himself; "and the poor fellow has discovered who she was!"

He went in.

"Have you no brandy?" he said to the nurse.

"On that table," she answered.

"Lay his head down, and fetch it."

Notwithstanding his appearance, the nurse obeyed : she knew the doctor required brandy, but had lost her presence of mind.

Polwarth took his hand. The pulse had vanished—and no wonder ! Once more, utterly careless of himself, had the healer drained his own life-spring to supply that of his patient—knowing as little now what that patient was to him as he knew then what she was going to be. A thrill had indeed shot to his heart at the touch of her hand, scarcely alive as it was, when first he felt her pulse ; what he saw of her averted face through the folded shadows of pillows and curtains both of window and bed, woke wild suggestions ; as he bared her arm, he almost gave a cry : it was fortunate that there was not light enough to show the scar of his own lancet ; but, always at any critical moment self-possessed to coldness, he schooled himself now with sternest severity. He insisted to himself that he was in mortal danger of being fooled by his imagination—that a certain indelible imprint on his brain had begun to phosphoresce. If he did not banish the fancies crowding to overwhelm him, his patient's life, and probably his own reason as well, would be the penalty. Therefore, with will obstinately strained, he kept his eyes turned from the face of the woman, drawn to it as they were even by the terror of what his fancy might there show him, and held to his duty in spite of growing agony. His brain, he said to himself, was so fearfully excited, that he must not trust his senses : they would reflect from within, instead of transmitting from without. And victoriously did he rule, until, all the life he had in gift being exhausted, his brain, deserted by his heart, gave way, and when he turned from the bed, all but unconscious, he could only stagger a pace or two, and fell like one dead.

Polwarth got some brandy into his mouth with a teaspoon. In about a minute, his heart began to beat.

"I must open another vein," he murmured as if in a dream.

When he had swallowed a third teaspoonful, he lifted his eyelids in a dreary kind of way, saw Polwarth, and remembered that he had something to attend to—a patient at the moment on his hands, probably—he could not tell.

"Tut ! give me a wine-glass of the stuff," he said.

Polwarth obeyed. The moment he swallowed it, he rose, rubbing his forehead as if trying to remember, and mechani-

cally turned toward the bed.   The nurse, afraid he might
not yet know what he was about, stepped between, saying
softly,

"She is asleep, sir, and breathing quietly."

"Thank God !" he whispered with a sigh, and turning
to a couch, laid himself gently upon it.

The nurse looked at Polwarth, as much as to say : "Who
is to take the command now ?"

"I shall be outside, nurse : call me if I can be useful to
you," he replied to the glance, and withdrew to his watch
on the top of the stair.

After about a quarter of an hour, the nurse came out.

"Do you want me ?" said Polwarth, rising hastily.

"No, sir," she answered.   "The doctor says all immediate danger is over, and he requires nobody with him.   I am
going to look after my baby.   And please, sir, nobody is to
go in, for he says she must not be disturbed.   The slightest
noise might spoil every thing : she must sleep now all she
can."

"Very well," said Polwarth, and sat down again.

The day went on ; the sun went down ; the shadows
deepened ; and not a sound came from the room.   Again
and again Dorothy came and peeped up the stair, but seeing
the little man at his post, like Zacchæus up the sycamore,
was satisfied, and withdrew.   But at length Polwarth
bethought him that Ruth would be anxious, and rose
reluctantly.   The same instant the door opened, and Faber
appeared.   He looked very pale and worn, almost haggard.

"Would you call Miss Drake ?" he said.

Polwarth went, and following Dorothy up the stair again,
heard what Faber said.

"She is sleeping beautifully, but I dare not leave her.   I
must sit up with her to-night.   Send my man to tell my
assistant that I shall not be home.   Could you let me have
something to eat, and you take my place ?   And there is
Polwarth ! *he* has earned his dinner, if any one has.   I do
believe we owe the poor lady's life to him."

Dorothy ran to give the message and her own orders.
Polwarth begged she would tell the groom to say to Ruth
as he passed that all was well ; and when the meal was
ready, joined Faber.

It was speedily over, for the doctor seemed anxious to be
again with his patient.   Then Dorothy went to Polwarth.
Both were full of the same question : had Faber recognized

his wife or not ? Neither had come to a certain conclusion. Dorothy thought he had, but that he was too hard and proud to show it ; Polwarth thought he had not, but had been powerfully reminded of her. He had been talking strangely, he said, during their dinner, and had drunk a good deal of wine in a hurried way.

Polwarth's conclusion was correct : it was with an excitement almost insane, and a pleasure the more sorrowful that he was aware of its transientness, a pleasure now mingling, now alternating with utter despair, that Faber returned to sit in the darkened chamber, watching the woman who with such sweet torture reminded him of her whom he had lost. What a strange, unfathomable thing is the pleasure given us by a likeness ! It is one of the mysteries of our humanity. Now she had seemed more, now less like his Juliet; but all the time he could see her at best only very partially. Ever since his fall, his sight had been weak, especially in twilight, and even when, once or twice, he stood over her as she slept, and strained his eyes to their utmost, he could not tell what he saw. For, in the hope that, by the time it did come, its way would have been prepared by a host of foregone thoughts, Dorothy had schemed to delay as much as she could the discovery which she trusted in her heart must come at last; and had therefore contrived, not by drawn curtains merely, but by closed Venetian shutters as well, to darken the room greatly. And now he had no light but a small lamp, with a shade.

He had taken a book with him, but it was little he read that night. At almost regular intervals he rose to see how his patient fared. She was still floating in the twilight shallows of death, whether softly drifting on the ebb-tide of sleep, out into the open sea, or, on its flow, again up the river of life, he could not yet tell. Once the nurse entered the room to see if any thing were wanted. Faber lifted his head, and motioned her angrily away, making no ghost of a sound. The night wore on, and still she slept. In his sleepless and bloodless brain strangest thoughts and feelings went and came. The scents of old roses, the stings of old sins, awoke and vanished, like the pulsing of fire-flies. But even now he was the watcher of his own moods ; and when among the rest the thought would come : "What if this *should* be my own Juliet ! Do not time and place agree with the possibility ? " and for a moment life seemed as if it would burst into the very madness of delight, ever and again his common sense drove him to conclude that his imagination was fooling him. He dared not yield to the intoxicating idea. If he did, he would be like a man drinking poison, well knowing that every sip, in itself a delight, brought him a step nearer to agony and death ! When she should wake, and he let the light fall upon her face, he knew—so he said to himself—he *knew* the likeness would vanish in an appalling unlikeness, a mockery, a scoff of the whole night and its lovely dream—in a face which, if beautiful as that of an angel, not being Juliet's would be to him ugly, unnatural, a discord with the music of his memory. Still the night was checkered with moments of silvery bliss, in the indulgence of the mere, the known fancy of what it would be if it *were* she, vanishing ever in the reviving rebuke, that he must nerve himself for the loss of that which the morning must dispel. Yet, like one in a dream, who knows it is but a dream, and scarce dares breathe lest he should break the mirrored ecstasy, he would not carry the lamp to the bedside: no act of his should disperse the airy flicker of the lovely doubt, not a movement, not a nearer glance, until stern necessity should command.

History knows well the tendency of things to repeat themselves. Similar circumstances falling together must incline to the production of similar consequent events.

Toward morning Juliet awoke from her long sleep, but she had the vessel of her brain too empty of the life of this world to recognize barely that which was presented to her bodily vision. Over the march of two worlds, that of her imagination, and that of fact, her soul hovered fluttering, and blended the presentment of the two in the power of its unity.

The only thing she saw was the face of her husband, sadly lighted by the dimmed lamp. It was some distance away, near the middle of the room: it seemed to her miles away, yet near enough to be addressed. It was a more beautiful face now than ever before—than even then when first she took it for the face of the Son of Man—more beautiful, and more like Him, for it was more humane. Thin and pale with suffering, it was nowise feeble, but the former self-sufficiency had vanished, and a still sorrow had taken its place.

He sat sunk in dim thought. A sound came that shook him as with an ague fit. Even then he mastered his emotion, and sat still as a stone. Or was it delight unmastered, and awe indefinable, that paralyzed him? He dared not move lest he should break the spell. Were it fact, or were it but yet further phantom play on his senses, it should unfold itself; not with a sigh would he jar the unfolding, but, ear only, listen to the end. In the utter stillness of the room, of the sleeping house, of the dark, embracing night, he lay in famished wait for every word.

"O Jesus," said the voice, as of one struggling with weariness, or one who speaks her thoughts in a dream, imagining she reads from a book, a gentle, tired voice —— "O Jesus! after all, Thou art there! They told me Thou wast dead, and gone nowhere! They said there never was such a One! And there Thou art! O Jesus, what *am* I to do? Art Thou going to do any thing with me?—I wish I were a leper, or any thing that Thou wouldst make clean! But how couldst Thou, for I never quite believed in Thee, and never loved Thee before? And there was my Paul! oh, how I loved my Paul! and *he* wouldn't do it. I begged and begged him, for he was my husband when I was alive— I begged him to take me and make me clean, but he wouldn't: he was too pure to pardon me. He let me lie in the dirt! It was all right of him, but surely, Lord, Thou couldst afford to pity a poor girl that hardly knew what she was doing. My heart is very sore, and my whole body is ashamed, and I feel so stupid! Do help me if Thou canst. I denied Thee, I know; but then I cared for nothing but my husband; and the denial of a silly girl could not hurt Thee, if indeed Thou art Lord of all worlds!—I know Thou wilt forgive me for that. But, O Christ, please, if Thou canst any way do it, make me fit for Paul. Tell him to beat me and forgive me.—O my Saviour, do not look at me so, or I shall forget Paul himself, and die weeping for joy. Oh, my Lord! Oh, my Paul!"

For Paul had gently risen from his chair, and come one step nearer—where he stood looking on her with such a smile as seldom has been upon human face—a smile of unutterable sorrow, love, repentance, hope. She gazed, speechless now, her spirit drinking in the vision of that smile. It was like mountain air, like water, like wine, like eternal life! It was forgiveness and peace from the Lord of all. And had her brain been as clear as her heart, could she have taken it for less? If the sinner forgave her, what did the Perfect?

Paul dared not go nearer—partly from dread of the con-

sequences of increased emotion. Her lips began to move
again, and her voice to murmur, but he could distinguish
only a word here and there. Slowly the eyelids fell over
the great dark eyes, the words dissolved into syllables, the
sounds ceased to be words at all, and vanished : her soul
had slipped away into some silent dream.

Then at length he approached on tiptoe. For a few
moments he stood and gazed on the sleeping countenance—
then dropped on his knees, and cried,

" God, if Thou be anywhere, I thank Thee."

Reader, who knowest better, do not mock him. Gently
excuse him. His brain was excited ; there was a commotion in the particles of human cauliflower ; a rush of
chemical changes and interchanges was going on ; the
tide was setting for the vasty deep of marvel, which was
nowhere but within itself. And then he was in love with
his wife, therefore open to deceptions without end, for is
not all love a longing after what never was and never can
be ?

He was beaten. But scorn him not for yielding. Think
how he was beaten. Could he help it that the life in him
proved too much for the death with which he had sided ?
Was it poltroonery to desert the cause of ruin for that
of growth ? of essential slavery for ordered freedom ?
of disintegration for vital and enlarging unity ? He
had "said to corruption, Thou art my father : to the
worm, Thou art my mother, and my sister ; " but a Mightier
than he, the Life that lighteth every man that cometh into
the world, had said, " O thou enemy, destruction shall have
a perpetual end ; " and he could not stand against the life
by which he stood. When it comes to this, what can a man
do ? Remember he was a created being—or, if you will not
allow that, then something greatly less. If not "loved into
being " by a perfect Will, in his own image of life and law,
he had but a mother whom he never could see, because she
could never behold either herself or him : he was the offspring of the dead, and must be pardoned if he gave a foolish cry after a parent worth having.

Wait, thou who countest such a cry a weak submission,
until, having refused to take thine hour with thee, thine hour
overtakes thee : then see if thou wilt stand out. Another's
battle is easy. God only knows with what earthquakes and
thunders, that hour, on its way to find thee, may level the
mountains and valleys between. If thou wouldst be per-

fect in the greatness of thy way, thou must learn to live in
the fire of thy own divine nature turned against thy conscious self : learn to smile content in that, and thou wilt
out-satan Satan in the putridity of essential meanness, yea,
self-satisfied in very virtue of thy shame, thou wilt count it
the throned apotheosis of inbred honor.   But seeming is not
being—least of all self-seeming.   Dishonor will yet be dishonor, if all the fools in creation should be in love with it,
and call it glory.

In an hour, Juliet woke again, vaguely remembering a
heavenly dream, whose odorous air yet lingered, and made
her happy, she knew not why.   Then what a task would
have been Faber's !   For he must not go near her.   The
balance of her life trembled on a knife-edge, and a touch
might incline it toward death.   A sob might determine the
doubt.

But as soon as he saw sign that her sleep was beginning
to break, he all but extinguished the light, then having felt
her pulse, listened to her breathing, and satisfied himself
generally of her condition, crept from the room, and calling
the nurse, told her to take his place.   He would be either
in the next room, he said, or within call in the park.

He threw himself on the bed, but could not rest : rose
and had a bath ; listened at Juliet's door, and hearing no
sound, went to the stable.   Niger greeted him with a neigh
of pleasure.   He made haste to saddle him, his hands
trembling so that he could hardly get the straps into the
girth buckles.

"That's Niger !" said Juliet, hearing his whinny.   "Is
he come ?"

"Who, ma'am ?" asked the nurse, a stranger to Glaston,
of course.

"The doctor—is he come ?"

"He's but just gone, ma'am.   He's been sitting by you
all night—would let no one else come near you.   Rather
peculiar, in my opinion !"

A soft flush, all the blood she could show, tinged her
cheek.   It was Hope's own color—the reflection of a red
rose from a white.

CHAPTER LIV.

FABER sprung upon Niger's back, and galloped wildly through the park. His soul was like a southern sea under a summer tornado. The slow dawn was gathering under a smoky cloud with an edge of cold yellow ; a thin wind was abroad ; rain had fallen in the night, and the grass was wet and cool to Niger's hoofs ; the earth sent up a savor, which like a soft warp was crossed by a woof of sweet odors from leaf-buds and wild flowers, and spangled here and there with a silver thread of bird song—for but few of the beast-angels were awake yet. Through the fine consorting mass of silence and odor, went the soft thunder ot Niger's gallop over the turf. His master's joy had overflowed into him : the creatures are not all stupid that can not speak ; some of them are *with us* more than we think. According to the grand old tale, God made his covenant with all the beasts that came out of the ark as well as with Noah ; for them also he set his bow of hope in the cloud of fear ; they are God's creatures, God bless them ! and if not exactly human, are, I think, something more than *humanish.* Niger gave his soul with his legs to his master's mood that morning. He was used to hard gallops with him across country, but this was different ; this was plainly a frolic, the first he had had since he came into his service ; and a frolic it should be !

A deeper, loftier, lovelier morning was dawning in Faber's world unseen. One dread burden was lifted from his being ; his fierce pride, his unmanly cruelty, his spotless selfishness, had not hunted a woman soul quite into the moldy jaws of the grave ; she was given back to him, to tend, and heal, and love as he had never yet dreamed of loving ! Endless was the dawn that was breaking in him ; unutterably sweet the joy. Life was now to be lived—not endured. How he would nurse the lily he had bruised and broken ! From her own remorse he would shield her. He would be to her a summer land—a refuge from the wind, a covert from the tempest. He would be to her like that Saviour for whom, in her wandering fancy, she had taken him : never more in vaguest thought would he turn from her. If, in any evil mood, a thought unkind should dare glance back at her past, he would clasp her the closer to his heart, the more to be shielded that the shield itself was so poor. Once he laughed aloud as he rode, to find himself actually wondering whether the story of the resurrection *could* be true ; for what had the restoration of his Juliet in common with the out-worn superstition ? In any overwhelming joy, he concluded, the heart leans to lovely marvel.

But there is as much of the reasonable as of to us the marvelous in that which alone has ever made credible proffer toward the filling of the gulf whence issue all the groans of humanity. Let Him be tested by the only test that can, on the supposition of His asserted nature, be applied to Him—that of obedience to the words He has spoken—words that commend themselves to every honest nature. Proof of other sort, if it could be granted, would, leaving our natures where they were, only sink us in condemnation.

Why should I pursue the story further ? and if not here, where better should I stop ? The true story has no end—no end. But endlessly dreary would the story be, were there no Life living by its own will, no perfect Will, one with an almighty heart, no Love in whom we live and move and have our being. Offer me an eternity in all things else after my own imagination, but without a perfect Father, and I say, no ; let me die, even as the unbelieving would have it. Not believing in the Father of Jesus, they are *right* in not desiring to live. Heartily do I justify them therein. For all this talk and disputation about immortality, wherein is regarded only the continuance of consciousness beyond what we call death, it is to me, with whatever splendor of intellectual coruscation it be accompanied, but little better than a foolish babble, the crackling of thorns under a pot. Apart from Himself, God forbid there should be any immortality. If it could be proved apart from Him, then apart from Him it could be, and would be infinite damnation. It is an impossibility, and were but an unmitigated evil. And if it be impossible without Him, it can not be believed without Him : if it could be proved without Him, the belief so gained would be an evil. Only with the knowledge of the Father of Christ, did the endlessness of being become a doctrine of bliss to men. If He be the first life, the Author of his own, to speak after the language of men, and the origin and source of all other life, it can be only by knowing Him that we can know whether we shall live or die. Nay more, far more !—the knowledge of Him by such innermost contact as is possible only between creator and created, and possible only when the created has aspired to be one with the will of the creator, such knowledge and such alone is life to the created ; it is the very life, that alone for the sake of which God created us. If we are one with God in heart, in righteousness, in desire, no death can touch us, for we are life, and the garment of immortality, the endless length of days which is but the mere shadow of the eternal, follows as a simple necessity : He is not the God of the dead, or of the dying, but of the essentially alive. Without this inmost knowledge of Him, this oneness with Him, we have no life in us, for *it is life*, and that for the sake of which all this outward show of things, and our troubled condition in the midst of them, exists. All that is mighty, grand, harmonious, therefore in its own nature true, is. If not, then dearly I thank the grim Death, that I shall die and not live. Thus undeceived, my only terror would be that the unbelievers might be but half right, and there might be a life, so-called, beyond the grave without a God.

My brother man, is the idea of a God too good or too foolish for thy belief ? or is it that thou art not great enough or humble enough to hold it ? In either case, I will believe it for thee and for me. Only be not stiff-necked when the truth begins to draw thee : thou wilt find it hard if she has to go behind and drive thee—hard to kick against the divine goads, which, be thou ever so mulish, will be too much for thee at last. Yea, the time will come when thou wilt goad thyself toward the divine. But hear me this once more : the God, the Jesus, in whom I believe, are not the God, the Jesus, in whom you fancy I believe : you know them not ; your idea of them is not mine. If you knew them you would believe in them, for to know them is to believe in them. Say not, " Let Him teach me, then," except you mean it in submissive desire ; for He has been teaching you all this time : if you have been doing His teaching, you are on the way to learn more ; if you hear and do not heed, where is the wonder that the things I tell you sound in your ears as the muttering of a dotard ? They convey to you nothing, it may be : but that which makes of them words—words—words, lies in you, not in me. Yours is the killing power. They would bring you life, but the death in him that knoweth and doeth not is strong ; in your air they drop and die, winged things no more.

For days Faber took measures not to be seen by Juliet. But he was constantly about the place, and when she woke from a sleep, they had often to tell her that he had been by her side all the time she slept. At night he was either in her room or in the next chamber. Dorothy used to say to her that if she wanted her husband, she had only to go to sleep. She was greatly tempted to pretend, but would not.

At length Faber requested Dorothy to tell Juliet that the doctor said she might send for her husband when she pleased. Much as he longed to hear her voice, he would not come without her permission.

He was by her side the next moment. But for minutes not a word was spoken ; a speechless embrace was all.

It does not concern me to relate how by degrees they came to a close understanding. Where love is, everything is easy, or, if not easy, yet to be accomplished. Of course Faber made his return confession in full. I will not say that Juliet had not her respondent pangs of retrospective jealousy. Love, although an angel, has much to learn yet, and the demon Jealousy may be one of the school masters of her coming perfection : God only knows. There must be a divine way of casting out the demon ; else how would it be hereafter ?

Unconfessed to each other, their falls would forever have been between to part them ; confessed, they drew them together in sorrow and humility and mutual consoling.

The little Amanda could not tell whether Juliet's house or Dorothy's was her home : when at the one, she always talked of the other as *home*. She called her father *papa*, and Juliet *mamma ;* Dorothy had been *auntie* from the first. She always wrote her name, *Amanda Duck Faber*. From all this the gossips of Glaston explained every thing satisfactorily : Juliet had left her husband on discovering that he had a child of whose existence he had never told her ; but learning that the mother was dead, yielded at length, and was reconciled. That was the nearest they ever came to the facts, and it was not needful they should ever know more. The talkers of the world are not on the jury of the court of the universe. There are many, doubtless, who need the shame of a public exposure to make them recognize their own doing for what it is ; but of such Juliet had not been. Her husband knew her fault—that was enough : he knew also his own immeasurably worse than hers, but when they folded each other to the heart, they left their faults outside—as God does, when He casts our sins behind His back, in utter uncreation.

I will say nothing definite as to the condition of mind at which Faber had arrived when last Wingfold and he had a talk together. He was growing, and that is all we can require of any man. He would not say he was a believer in the supernal, but he believed more than he said, and he never talked against belief. Also he went as often as he could to church, which, little as it means in general, did not mean little when the man was Paul Faber, and where the minister was Thomas Wingfold.

It is time for the end. Here it is—in a little poem, which, on her next birthday, the curate gave Dorothy :

> O wind of God, that blowest in the mind,
>   Blow, blow and wake the gentle spring in me ;
> Blow, swifter blow, a strong, warm summer wind,
>   Till all the flowers with eyes come out to see ;
>   Blow till the fruit hangs red on every tree,
> And our high-soaring song-larks meet thy dove—
> High the imperfect soars, descends the perfect Love.

> Blow not the less though winter cometh then ;
>   Blow, wind of God, blow hither changes keen ;
> Let the spring creep into the ground again,
>   The flowers close all their eyes, not to be seen :
>   All lives in thee that ever once hath been :
> Blow, fill my upper air with icy storms ;
> Breathe cold, O wind of God, and kill my canker-worms

Johannesen
Printing & Publishing
❧ Treasures ☙
Old & New

P.O. box 24   707-986-7465
Whitethorn, CA   Phone or Fax
95589 U.S.A.   707-986-1656

Titles for 1992
by the same Author
uniform with this Edition

Series 1
What's Mine's Mine
Sir Gibbie
Donal Grant
Castle Warlock
A Rough Shaking
There and Back

Series 2
At The Back of the North Wind
Paul Faber, Surgeon
The Vicar's Daughter
Guild Court, A London Story
Home Again and
The Elect Lady

Crown 8vo, cloth,
some with Frontispieces, some with Illustrations.
Printed on acid-free, recycled paper.
Request these fine volumes from your bookseller
or
Contact Johannesen.

GEORGE MACDONALD (1824-1905)

– Of special interest to young people –
Dealings with the Fairies. 1867
At the Back of the North Wind. 1871
Ranald Bannerman's Boyhood. 1871
The Princess and the Goblin. 1872
Gutta Percha Willie : the Working Genius. 1873
The Wise Woman, A Parable. 1875
The Princess and Curdie. 1883
Cross Purposes, and the Shadows. 1886
A Rough Shaking. A Tale. 1890
The Light Princess. 1890

– Fiction –
Phantastes : A Faerie Romance for Men and Women. 1858
David Elginbrod. 1863
Adela Cathcart. 1864
The Portent. A Story of the Inner Vision of the
      Highlanders commonly called the Second Sight.
      1864
Alec Forbes of Howglen. 1865
Annals of a Quiet Neighbourhood. 1867
Guild Court : A London Story. 1868
Robert Falconer. 1868
The Seaboard Parish. 1868
The Vicar's Daughter. 1872
Wilfrid Cumbermede. 1872
Malcolm. 1875
Thomas Wingfold,Curate. 1876
St George and St Michael. 1876
The Marquis of Lossie. 1877
Sir Gibbie. 1879
Paul Faber, Surgeon. 1879
Mary Marston. 1881
Castle Warlock. A Homely Romance. 1882
Weighed and Wanting. 1882

Bibliography Cont.

The Gifts of the Christ Child and Other Tales.
    2 vols. 1882 [Later pbd as Stephen Archer
    and Other Tales, n.d.]
Donal Grant. 1883
What's Mine's Mine. 1886
Home Again. A Tale. 1887
The Elect Lady. 1888
There and Back. 1891
The Flight of the Shadow. 1891
Heather and Snow. 1893
Lilith. A Romance. 1895
Salted with Fire. A Tale. 1897.

                    – Other Writings –
Within and Without. A Poem. 1855
Poems. 1857
The Disciple and Other Poems. 1867
Unspoken Sermons. 3 sers. 1867–89.
The Miracles of Our Lord. 1870.
England's Antiphon. 1874
Exotics. 1876. [Verse.]
A Book of Strife, in the Form of the Diary of
    an Old Soul. 1880;1909;1913.
Orts. 1882;1893 (enlarged, as A Dish of Orts).
A Threefold Cord. Poems by Three Friends.
    1883 (priv. ptd). [Edited by MacDonald.]
The Tragedie of Hamlet. 1885.
A Cabinet of Gems, cut and polished by Sir
    Philip Sidney, now for their More Radiance
    presented without their Setting by George
    MacDonald. 1891.
The Hope of the Gospel. 1892
The Poetical Works of George MacDonald.
    2 vols. 1893
Rampolli: 1897. [Poems.]